Love's Providence

A Novel

Jennifer H. Westall

Jennifer H. Westall
www.jenniferhwestall.com

Publisher's Note: This is a work of fiction. Names, characters, places, and incidents are a product of the author's imagination. Locales and public names are sometimes used for atmospheric purposes. Any resemblance to actual people, living or dead, or to businesses, companies, events, institutions, or locales is completely coincidental.

Book Layout ©2014 BookDesignTemplates.com

Love's Providence/ Jennifer H. Westall. – 2nd ed.
ISBN 978-0-9908759-2-5

To Wendy, my first and most loyal fan.

Acknowledgements

I'd like to thank my family for all their support—David, the chief fluff-cutter, and my sweet boys who continuously remind me to quit daydreaming and get them something to eat.

I will always owe my friends who read through countless re-writes a debt I can never repay. Thank you, Wendy, for being so enthusiastic from the beginning and always encouraging me to continue. To my sweet friend Shari, without whom I might never have made it through the last year, thank you from the bottom of my heart.

Of course I have to thank all my former Midway students for putting up with me for so long, for making me smile almost every day, and for being blessings in ways they'll never know. To the Four Awesome Chics: your enthusiasm and craziness got us through some pretty difficult days of problem solving, and I will always remember you guys when I need a good laugh.

To all the rest of you who were so encouraging and support-ive, my parents, Eve, Christy, Dana, Alicia, and William, thank you so much.

And of course, most of all, I thank you for reading, and I hope you'll enjoy this little bit of my heart.

Chapter One

March 18

Birmingham, Alabama

Months had gone by. *Months.* And with each passing day, Lily Brennon could only watch as the boy she'd loved most of her life sank further and further into depression. It was like watching him fade from color to black and white.

She'd tried everything she could think of—yelling, pushing, encouragement, silence—nothing had helped. How did you even begin to comfort someone whose nightmares had crossed over into reality?

Standing in his living room doorway, she watched Jackson drop the phone into his lap and listened to his deep sigh of resignation. She wanted to give up as well. Especially if that phone call had been what she thought it was.

"Who was that?" she asked.

He pushed the bag of ice off his knee, and it landed beside the recliner with a crunch on the hardwood floor. He pulled the top strap of his knee brace back in place, tightening it while he gritted his teeth.

"Clayton."

Her heart sank. She'd hoped for the best, but she'd known for some time now that Randall Clayton couldn't be trusted.

"What did he say?"

"I knew this would happen. Knew it as soon as my knee popped."

She waited for more, but he dropped his head back and closed his eyes. The uneasiness in her gut bloomed, but she pushed it back. She had to stay positive.

"So what did he say?"

"It's over. Nobody wants me now. Not even the team in Germany."

"But there has to be a team somewhere."

"No, Lily!" He opened his eyes and glared at her. "Didn't you hear me? I was a long-shot at best to begin with. Now look at me." He gestured toward his leg as though he'd like to rip it off his body. "I can't be ready to try out by June."

"What about next year? Guys come back from injuries all the time."

He shook his head. "Just because Coach pulled some strings and got me in once doesn't mean he can do it again."

"You can't just give up. Don't lose your faith now. You'll see. God is still working all things for your good. He knows the plans he has for you-"

"Stop quoting scripture. I'm so sick of that. It's the last thing I need right now. God isn't helping me. He's just pummeling me like it's funny to watch me suffer."

She knelt in front of him and laid her hand over his, struck by the warmth of his skin—the rest of him had gone so cold. He jerked it away like her hope might be contagious.

"Look," she said, "I know this has been hard, and I'm so sorry you're going through this. I just want to help. I'm sure things will get better."

"You're so naïve. It's not going to get better." He rubbed the back of his neck and stared at the ceiling.

For a fleeting moment she thought of slapping him. That's what she would have done a few months ago, but what good would it do now? Nothing had worked. Besides, he was supposed to be the strong one, the one who listened and offered a silver lining to every problem. She was the fighter, the scrappy one he'd had to hold back more than a few times. This reversal of roles was like trying to steady the human gyro ride at the fair, and she was failing miserably.

She barely even recognized him anymore. There was nothing left of the boy who'd once taught her how to sink a free throw, or how to bait a fishing hook in exactly the right spot so she wouldn't kill the cricket. She ached to reach out for him, to feel him hold her again and whisper in her ear, to see him smile. He was the one who'd saved her, so many times in so many ways. How could she be so useless now when he needed her?

She glanced around, taking in the disheveled living room. How often had they laughed at the mismatched furniture—the neon orange futon that nearly sunk to the floor when they sat on it, the oversized wicker chair he'd found beside the dumpster on campus? Even the recliner Matthew had brought with him when he'd moved in had several tears patched with duct tape. She'd given Jackson such a hard time for renting a dump, but she'd admired his reasons. Matthew was so much better off since moving in with him. Another person he'd saved.

She had to think of something, some way to bring back the Jackson she'd always loved. After everything he'd done for her, she couldn't just give up on him.

"Come on," she said. "Your dad wouldn't want you to quit."

The corner of his eye twitched, but remained fixed on the black television screen behind her.

"He's dead. He doesn't want anything."

"I know he wouldn't want to see you throw away your future."

"What future? Did you miss the part earlier about no D-League tryouts, no overseas ball? Those were my only chances at getting to the NBA."

"But there's so much more to your life than basketball. You'll have your degree soon, and you can still get a great job. And we'll be together. I thought you wanted those things."

He leaned his head back and dug his fingers into the arm rests.

"I don't know what I want right now, okay? Just stop hovering over me all the time. I just want to be left alone."

She pushed herself up and shoved back another instinct to fight. A break was a good idea. She might say something she'd regret.

"Fine. I just wanted to help. But obviously I can't say or do anything right." She turned and slung her backpack up from the floor. "I have to be at practice soon anyway, and at some point I have to study for midterms."

She waited for him to respond, hoping for any sign of the connection they'd once shared. She sighed and threw up her hands.

"Just call me tomorrow when you get up."

"No, Lily. That's not what I meant." His gaze fell as he fumbled with the phone in his lap. "I mean, I really want to be left alone. I can't do this anymore."

"What?" Her heart tripped and raced forward.

"I just need to figure some things out, get my bearings again."

"What do you mean? Are you breaking up with me?"

Nothing. Not a nod, a denial, nothing.

Her stomach rolled as her heart thudded against her chest. Things were bad, yes. But breaking up? She hadn't even considered it as a possibility. They hadn't spent more than a couple of days apart in over twelve years.

She registered the metal warming between her fingers as she rubbed her necklace—*the* necklace. She dropped it and focused on controlling her fear. He couldn't mean breaking up. He was just upset. But he hadn't said a word yet. He just stared at the floor.

"Jackson?"

"Look, forget about me, okay?"

The knots in her stomach jerked and twisted even more. She had to get out of there before she lost it. Crossing the small living room in a few deliberate strides, she gripped the doorknob and forced it to turn. She glanced back at him slumped in the recliner and pulled her emotions back into check.

"I thought you loved me," she said.

He sighed and finally looked at her, but still he said nothing.

"Do you still...love me?" she asked.

More empty silence. She shivered as though a cold wind had swept through the room, and she hugged her chest.

"Jackson?"

"I don't know, okay? I don't know anything right now."

It was as good as a punch to the gut.

"I see."

It took every ounce of her strength not to slam the door when she left. As she walked down the sidewalk in a daze, she wondered if all of it had really happened. It couldn't have. Surely he'd get past this and they would be okay. Was she really supposed to forget him? How did you forget a part of yourself?

March 19

Brunswick, Georgia

Alex Walker lay in his bed refusing to open his eyes. He'd tried so hard not to fall asleep, willing himself to be prepared for when she woke up, but exhaustion had taken over sometime before dawn. And another chance to make things right had passed him by.

He didn't need to look across the bed to know—he could feel her absence all around him. Still, some small hopeful part of his brain sent his hand wandering across the cool sheet, searching.

Nothing.

He opened his eyes and pushed himself up to the side of the bed, pausing to listen to the silence. Her shirt and slacks were no longer strewn across the floor, and she'd even made her side of the bed. He dropped his head into his hands and swore.

How could he have let this happen again? The empty beer bottles beside the bed were enough of an answer. But he still should have known better. Her promises never withstood the light of day.

He forced himself to get up and walk through the house, verifying that every last drop of her was gone. He was beginning to think that maybe he'd dreamed the whole thing, but the lipstick-smeared wine glass in the kitchen sink slapped him with a good dose of reality.

He leaned over and gripped the side of the sink, channeling his frustration into his knuckles as they turned from pink to white.

Never again. Adrian was never going to do this to him again.

Chapter Two

June 30

St. Simons Island, Georgia

Waves tumbled over the rocks outside her window and scattered the murky images of Lily's dream. She tried to cling to them, to coax them to return. But a shrill screech severed the connection for good. She cracked her eyelids open and made out a mocking bird on the porch rail.

"Shut up." She closed her eyes, but her dream had already slipped out of focus. And just like that, Jackson was gone again, leaving the dull ache in her chest that never waned completely.

The bird outside her window shrieked again. It was worse than an alarm clock. At least that had a snooze button. She rolled over and checked the clock on the nightstand. Not even eight. She'd have to kill the bird.

She caught the smell of pancakes, and her mood lifted a bit. Her dad was making breakfast. Maybe she could spend some time with him before everyone else got up.

She rolled out of bed and took a quick glance in the mirror over the dresser. It wasn't a pretty picture, but morning really wasn't her thing anyway. Half of her hair had fallen out of its ponytail, and her bloodshot eyes ached for sleep. If it had been someone else, she'd swear they had a bad hangover.

She slid her feet into her slippers and headed across the beach house. The floorboards creaked, and a light dusting of sand covered the floor, but the furniture was clean and comfortable, and the rhythm of the ocean on the rocks below had finally soothed her to sleep in the early morning hours.

She could hear her dad humming his favorite hymn as she reached the kitchen. She stopped in the doorway and watched as he poured batter onto the griddle. His large frame filled most of the tiny kitchen, much like the one where they'd lived when she was little. The details of that house had faded long ago, but she remembered the pale yellow walls, the clock shaped like a hen, the small round table near the window.

On cold winter mornings, she'd sneak up on her dad before the sun rose, climb in his lap and listen to his voice echo deep in his chest as he read his Bible. Then they'd make pancakes for her mom, completely wrecking the kitchen in the process. She couldn't really remember whether her mom had cared for the pancakes or the mess, but Lily had loved those mornings with her dad. She wished she could do that now, just climb in his lap and pour out her fears as he hugged them away. But that was a long time ago, and a lot more had changed besides the kitchen.

"I thought you might be up a little early this morning." He glanced at her sideways then flipped a pancake over.

"How did you know?" she asked.

He put down the spatula and leaned back against the counter, folding his arms over his chest.

"I can still tell when something's bothering you. You haven't been yourself since you got home from school. I thought you might perk up on the way down here, that maybe you'd be excited to go somewhere new this year. But maybe I was wrong."

"I'm sorry." She couldn't hold his gaze. "I am glad to be here. It's just..."

He paused before scooping several pancakes onto a plate. Then he poured more batter onto the griddle. "You know, you can talk to me, Lily. Maybe I can help."

He studied her like she was one of the many floor plans that littered his office, ready to find and solve any problem. She almost believed he could. But the words just wouldn't come, and he finally let out a sigh.

"You hungry?" he asked.

She shook her head, and he frowned. She knew what he was thinking. She could almost recite the lecture brewing in his mind. *Lily, you're getting too thin...* But thankfully, he thought better of it and turned back to the pancakes.

She reached for a wooden chair at the breakfast table just inside the doorway. It scraped the tiled floor as she dragged it across, and she cringed. The last thing she wanted was to wake anyone else. She sat down and pulled her knees up to her chin.

"Not sleeping again?" He scooped the last batch of pancakes onto a plate.

"Not really."

He sat down across from her, eying her with the unspoken lecture still dying to get out. He closed his tattered Bible and set it aside, making room for his plate. Then he bowed his head and mouthed a silent prayer. When he finished, he stabbed at a pancake with a little too much force, and it slipped off the end of his fork.

"Did something happen?" he asked.

She chewed on her fingernail and fidgeted with the lonely plastic sunflower in the vase on the table. He finally got a bite in his mouth.

"I saw him," she said.

He furrowed his brow for only a moment before his face softened. The pity in his eyes almost undid her, and she had to look away. Outside the kitchen window, she watched the drooping Spanish moss waving in the breeze, whispering encouragement, telling her to go on. He dropped his fork and leaned back in his chair.

"Where did you see him?"

"At a bookstore in Birmingham a couple of days before we left. I was looking for some reading to bring with me and he just appeared out of nowhere."

"What did you do?"

"Nothing. I couldn't think of anything to say."

"How about hello?"

He cracked a grin, but she sighed and looked away.

"It doesn't matter anyway. He didn't even see me. He was standing in the aisle holding a book, and I just turned and walked away before he looked up."

She hugged her knees tighter. He pushed his plate aside and leaned forward, lacing his fingers on the table.

"I thought things were getting better."

"I thought so too."

"Lily, you've got to find a way to put Jackson behind you. I know it's hard. I know he meant a lot to you, but it's been three months."

"I know how long it's been." She darted a glance at him. "I know I have to move on. I just can't seem to figure that part out. I thought I was doing okay, but then wham, I'm right back where I was three months ago."

"It's always tough when you have a setback," he said. "Sometimes moving on with your life is painful, but you have to do it for your own good."

It figured he'd say that. Lord knows she wouldn't want to do anything for someone else's good. Moving on had been easy for him. He'd gotten a brand new family, complete with a beautiful wife and a perfect daughter to replace her.

"Good morning!"

As if on cue, her step-sister Kara bounded into the kitchen, blond waves bouncing in time with her steps. Either she had slept all night and maintained her perfect hair and make-up, or she'd gotten up at the crack of dawn. Both options were appalling. She flashed a bright smile, but it faded when she stopped in front of the breakfast sitting on the counter. She wrinkled her nose and pressed her lips into a pout as she turned toward them.

"I thought you were making bacon and eggs this morning."

Her dad pushed away from the table and carried his plate over to the sink.

"I changed my mind. We'll have that tomorrow."

She crossed her arms and sighed, raising her eyes up to his.

"Oh, don't look at me like that," he continued. "That quit working by the time you were out of pigtails."

She shrugged. "Had to try."

She placed a pancake on her plate and took the seat he'd vacated as she chirped hello. Lily offered a grunt in her general direction, hoping she would exit as quickly as she'd appeared.

"I see you're as cheerful as ever," Kara said.

"I'd hate to disappoint."

Kara raised a perfectly sculpted eyebrow as she took her first bite. She continued to stare at Lily until she was done chewing.

"So? What are we talking about? You two looked deep in conversation."

"Nothing."

"Lily's a little blue," her dad said, leaning back against the counter as he sipped his coffee.

Kara covered her mouth and laughed. "That's the understatement of the year. She's practically a Smurf."

"Hey now-" he scolded.

"Forget it," Lily said.

Kara swallowed and shook her head. "Oh please. Like I need three guesses to figure out what—or should I say who?—you were talking about." She leaned forward and pointed her fork at Lily. "Let me give you a little piece of advice. Jackson is old news, and frankly, you're starting to move from sympathetic to *pa*-thetic. If you ask me, it's way past time to move on and get your line back in the water."

"Excuse me? What are you talking about?"

"You know. The whole other-fish-in-the-sea thing." Lily just stared, and Kara finally rolled her eyes. "Oh come on. You're the one who's all into fishing. I was just trying to speak in terms you'd understand."

"Maybe you should try speaking in terms *you* understand."

"Maybe you should try getting over yourself for five minutes. We're vacationing on a beautiful island for a whole week. Please don't tell me you're going to ruin it for everyone by moping around here the entire time pining over Jackson."

"Kara-" her dad warned.

Lily pushed herself up and leaned onto the table.

"Well, I hardly expect you to understand. You're just a kid. Who have you ever been in love with?"

Kara's eyes widened. "I am not a kid. And if anyone's been acting like one, it's you."

"My goodness! What is going on in here?"

Lily heard her stepmother's voice from behind her, and straightened.

"Nothing," she said.

"Kara?"

Lily didn't have to look to know that Diane was practically pinning Kara to the wall with her eyes. Kara swallowed and glanced at her dad.

"It's nothing Mom, really. I was just trying to help."

She sat back down and concentrated on her food. Lily stepped away from the table as Diane glided over to the counter and gave her dad a peck on the cheek. Like Kara, she too had every strand of blond hair in place, and her turquoise blouse and white capris were freshly pressed.

"Anything I should know about, Stephen?"

He shook his head and handed her a cup of coffee. "Nah, just some sisterly advice gone awry."

Diane observed Lily with cool eyes over the top of her mug as she took a sip. She tapped her porcelain nails on the cup several times before speaking.

"Everything okay with you, Lily? You seem flustered."

"Yes, ma'am. I'm fine."

"You sure?"

Lily nodded and took a step toward the door. "I think I'll just get my run out of the way early today."

"Well, don't rush off because of us. Stay and eat breakfast." Diane smiled, but Lily could never tell whether or not it was genuine.

Her dad frowned and wrapped his hand around Diane's waist, stabbing Lily with unexpected resentment.

"I thought you might relax some while we're here, Lily. Don't push yourself right now."

She shook her head, still surprised when he just didn't get it. Hadn't he been an athlete too?

"Look, I'm not about to let some little freshman come in and steal my position. I have to push myself."

"At least eat something," he said.

She sighed and reached for a pancake, shoving half of it in her mouth. The rest she tossed onto a plate on the counter.

"Gotta go," she said after a big swallow.

She headed back across the living room as her dad called out one more time.

"Don't forget your-"

"I know, Dad! I'm not twelve anymore. Besides, bees don't fly around on the beach."

Lily went back to her room, kicked her slippers across the floor, and dug through her suitcase until she found her running clothes and shoes. She should have known breakfast with her dad wouldn't help. Maybe she shouldn't have even come on vacation with them at all. No matter what she did to make things right, no matter how pleasant her conversations with Diane or Kara might be, she was always the odd-shaped piece that didn't quite fit in the puzzle.

She plopped onto the bed and dropped her clothes to the floor. She'd never truly realized how much she'd depended on Jackson and his family. Without him, she really was alone.

"You okay?" Kara asked from the doorway.

Lily glanced up and went back to putting on her shoes.

"Yeah. I'm good."

Kara stepped into the room and toyed with the chain hanging from the ceiling fan.

"I'm sorry if I upset you."

"Don't worry about it. We're fine." Lily dropped her foot on-to the floor with a thud. "I do have to get going, though. I don't want to have a heat stroke out there."

"Mind if I come along?"

"What about Rachel?"

"Still sleeping."

She'd prefer to sweat her problems out alone, but she had to admit having Kara along would help push her. The runt had ac-tually done well at the State track meet just a month earlier.

"Sure," she said. "But if you outrun me again, I'll have to beat you senseless."

Kara grinned. "You'll have to catch me first."

Later that evening, Lily stood on the playground and squeezed the sand between her toes as a warm, moist breeze swirled strands of hair around her face. The village shops by the pier had been teeming with tourists all afternoon, but most of them had closed down hours ago. The sounds of traffic and screaming kids had faded into a gentle lapping of the ocean against the nearby rocks.

Her feet ached from walking around for the past several hours, and her head was beginning to throb as well. To make matters worse, her dad had insisted that she keep an eye on Kara and her cousin Rachel, which meant an evening full of aimlessly wandering through tourist shops and listening to shallow comparisons of one guy after another. At this point, she wanted nothing more than to go back to the beach house, put her feet up, and relax with a good book.

A few yards away, Kara and Rachel competed to see who could swing the highest. As much as they insisted on being treated like adults, it was amazing how childish they could be. She rolled her eyes and sighed, glancing down at her watch. Nearly time to go.

"Y'all about ready?" she called.

Rachel jumped out of her swing first, followed by Kara who narrowly missed landing on her rear. Rachel doubled over with laughter, and Lily couldn't help but laugh too. Kara flushed bright red as she glanced around to see if anyone else had seen her stumble.

"Nice," Lily said.

Kara ignored her and straightened her clothes. Rachel slid her feet into her sandals and tugged her shorts back into place, though they still left little to the imagination. She smoothed her dark hair and picked her purse up off the ground. Then suddenly she squealed like a mouse and waved Kara toward her.

"Look, those cops over there are cute!"

Lily followed her gaze to the massive live oaks that provided a canopy over a picnic area of the park. It was empty now except

for two officers talking quietly at a picnic table in the lamp
light, their bikes resting in a rack nearby. From several yards
away they appeared similar—broad shoulders, dark hair, well-
built. Nothing spectacular.

"You're hopeless," Lily said. "They're way too old for you to
even think about."

Rachel shrugged. "So? Cute is just cute. Age doesn't factor."

Lily looked at them again. Maybe Rachel was right, but she
wasn't interested in another lame discussion about guys like
they were a tasty dessert item.

"They're all right, I guess. Not really my type."

Kara snorted. "Oh please. I think you have to date more than
one person to have a type."

Rachel laughed and looked away from Lily's glare.

"Well, you are the expert," Lily said. "How many boyfriends
have you had?"

Kara took a few steps closer and jutted her chin at Lily. "I
know a lot more than you think. I know that hanging out with
one guy since you were nine years old doesn't make you an expert. You wouldn't even know what to do if a great guy was interested in you."

"Sure I would. I'd say thanks but no thanks."

"Oh my word, Lil. Seriously. There's something wrong with
you."

"I don't care what you think about me. I don't want to date
right now."

Rachel's mouth fell open. "Really?"

"Look, I just want to enjoy my vacation. You know, relax a
little, read a good book, take a walk on the beach. I don't need
drama."

Kara shook her head. "I'm not talking about a serious relationship here. Look around. There are cute guys everywhere. Loosen up and have some fun."

"I don't need a guy around to have fun."

Kara winked at Rachel. "Well, if you're going to be hanging around us, you better get used to cute guys being around. In fact, I think we should start right now." She nodded toward the tree where the cops were still seated. Rachel's face lit up.

"Oh no," Lily said. "We're going back to the house. It's nearly midnight."

But they sped away before she could stop them, so she threw her hands in the air and followed. This was going to be humiliating. As she approached the officers, the girls sang hello in unison. She could just imagine what these two gentlemen must be thinking. Leaning back on their elbows in identical poses, both of the officers grinned at the girls.

Then she caught a glance from the one on the left, and his eyes traveled down her legs. A sliver of a smirk played at the corner of his lips. Maybe gentleman wasn't the right word. Kara rattled off introductions, oblivious to the amusement on their faces.

"I'm Kara. This is my sister, Lily, and our cousin, Rachel."

Lily offered a polite nod. There had to be a way to exit gracefully, but she couldn't think of one. Kara and Rachel dropped onto the bench of a picnic table opposite the officers, looking entirely too eager. They were practically panting.

"I'm Steve," the one on the right said. "It's nice to meet you, ladies." His smile lit up his whole face, and his eyes had a warm puppy-like expression. Lily relaxed a little. At least one of them was friendly anyway.

"You can just call him Poindexter." The other officer's eyes sparked with mischief, and Steve slapped him across the chest.

"I know you don't want me to tell them what they can call you, *Rambo.*"

"Rambo?" Rachel asked, tilting her head.

He waved his hand to dismiss the question. "Forget it. It's not that funny anyway."

On closer inspection, the nickname seemed fitting given his dark waves and bulging muscles. He probably did think he was some sort of action hero. She could practically see him admiring his biceps in a mirror.

"So what *is* your name, Rambo?" Lily asked.

Their eyes met, and his lips tipped into a smirk.

"Walker. Alex Walker."

Yep, definitely an action hero.

"So what are you supposed to be?" she asked. "Double-oh-six-and-a-half?" The retort slipped out before Lily could catch it.

Steve snickered and looked away from Alex's murderous glance.

"Well, you can just call me Daddy." He cocked an eyebrow at her, an obvious challenge, but his grin never changed.

Lily held his gaze, irritated by the way her stomach flipped. Must have been something she'd eaten.

Rachel finally broke the awkward silence. "So, um, is it usually this quiet around here?"

Steve shook his head. "Nah, it'll pick up tomorrow, trust me. This place'll be crawling with people and screaming kids."

"And plenty of little boys for you girls to play with, I'm sure," Alex added.

Rachel's chest sprang out as she huffed. "We are not little girls, and we are not interested in little boys."

"How old do you think we are anyway?" Kara asked.

Lily couldn't wait for this response. Alex had wandered into dangerous waters, but he seemed oblivious. He put his fingers to his chin and assessed them.

"Hmm, let me see."

Steve waved off the challenge. "I can't ever tell." He sent a knowing grin at Lily, and she couldn't help but smile back. At least he had some sense.

"Well," Alex said, looking first at Kara, then at Rachel. "With all the make-up, you look about twenty-one. So I'd have to say you two are about thirteen, maybe fourteen."

Kara's mouth dropped open and Rachel gasped. Lily could barely control her laughter.

"What?" Rachel exclaimed. "I am fifteen, almost sixteen!"

"And *I* am already sixteen!" Kara folded her arms across her chest.

"Whoa! Don't get your panties in a wad." Alex threw up his hands in surrender. "I was just giving you a hard time."

As the girls continued to sulk, he winked at Lily. Something about him sent a shiver down her arms.

"And how about you?" he asked.

She hesitated. She shouldn't let him bait her into comments she might regret. Arrogant or not, he was an officer of the law, a position she had always been taught to respect.

Rachel finally spoke for her. "She actually *is* twenty-one."

Kara lifted a brow, a puzzled look that seemed to ask if she was okay. Lily decided to ignore it and Alex as well.

She turned and looked out over the ocean, wishing she could enjoy it alone. The ocean and sky had melted into one large black expanse, but she could hear the waves tumble into the rocks not far away.

"So, how long have you been police officers?" Kara asked.

"Seven years for me," Steve answered.

"You're kidding. You don't seem that old."

Steve laughed. "I went into the police academy right out of high school. Been doing this since I was eighteen."

Lily glanced at Kara and caught the slight nod toward Steve. She knew she was being rude, but what did Kara expect? Flirting with a stranger wasn't going to fill the hole in her chest. Still, she supposed she should at least be polite.

"That's pretty young to become a cop," Lily said. "You didn't think about going to college?"

"Nah." He grinned like the thought was absurd. "I never wanted to do anything but be a cop. Dad's a cop. Mom's a cop. Just seemed natural."

He smiled at her again, and the warmth of it reached out to her. It wasn't much, but it made her smile. Maybe getting to know Steve wasn't the worst idea in the world.

Alex caught the flush in Lily's cheeks as she smiled at Steve, and he took a quick glance at his partner. Steve was the nicest guy he'd ever met. Too nice. And he wasn't about to let some snobby chick get the wrong idea about him. Besides, no matter how nice he was, even Steve could be tempted by a hot girl, and he had to admit this one was a looker. Her legs had caught his attention first—long, athletic—but it was her eyes that he kept coming back to. They were cool and aloof, wandering over everything in the park, except him. He could tell from the moment she walked over that she'd rather be anywhere else. Until now.

He'd have to nip the flirting before she mistook Steve's goofy grin for something more than friendly conversation.

"So that makes you about, what, twenty-five?" Lily asked.

"Yep, I'm getting old." Steve's chest shook with his chuckle.

"Thankfully you finally found a good woman to take care of you in your waning years." Alex darted his eyes over to Lily as he spoke, satisfied with the subtle fall of her smile.

Steve's face lit up with his crooked grin, unaware of the hope he'd just crushed.

"Yeah, I got a good one alright."

"How long is it to the wedding?" Alex threw that one in for good measure.

Steve looked up at the stars as if he expected the answer to be spelled out as a connect-the-dots puzzle.

"I guess about six weeks or so." He looked back down at the girls and grinned. "I don't have much to do with the planning. I'm just supposed to show up on time."

The younger two dove into questions about the wedding, though Steve never seemed to give good enough answers. Lily hung back, of course, her eyes drifting down the beach. She crossed her arms over her chest and shifted her weight back and forth like she couldn't wait to get out of there. The lights of the ice cream parlor across the parking lot went dark, and she looked down at her watch with visible relief.

"We should probably get going."

The blond glanced at her watch as well. "We still have a little time left. What's the big hurry?"

"You two are supposed to be back by midnight." Lily pointed a look directly at the brunette with all the make-up. "Your parents would kill me if I let you stay out late, and you know it."

"A few minutes isn't going to hurt anything," she whined.

He watched Lily squirm. She looked like a kid in desperate need of a bathroom break. Too good to hang out with public servants probably.

"Yeah, Lily," he said. "What's the hurry? Don't you like us?"

"Uh, well..." she stammered. "It's not that. I just don't want them to get in trouble."

"Let me guess," he said. "You do everything you're told and you've never disappointed anyone." She opened her mouth to respond, but he cut her off. "You've never missed a single curfew in your life, have you?"

"What's it to you?"

"Well, that must be an exciting life."

She swung her weight to the other hip and shot bullets of contempt from her eyes.

"Just because I take my responsibilities seriously doesn't mean I can't have a good time."

"Oh, I'm sure you're the life of the party."

Little Miss Perfect was making this way too easy. She turned and jerked her head at the other two.

"Let's go."

They stood up and flashed adorable smiles. Then they sang their goodbye as bubbly as they had their hello. The brunette flipped her hair and winked, and he stifled a laugh. That girl was going to be trouble in another year or two.

Lily, on the other hand, was already trouble. He could feel it. Something about her still lingered after she'd disappeared, like the aftertaste of an expensive wine. It reminded him of why he hated the stuff.

Chapter Three

July 1

Birmingham, Alabama

Jackson climbed out of the rusty Oldsmobile handed down from his mom and pushed the door closed. The squeak in the hinges was getting louder every day, and this time it was accompanied by a loud pop. That door had to be close to falling off, and no amount of oil seemed to relieve it. Just another item on the long list of repairs he needed but couldn't afford. Sooner or later he was going to have to find a job that paid real money.

He pushed his hair off his brow and gently stretched his knee as he glanced around. It was sore and a little swollen from therapy, but at least he wasn't hobbling around on crutches anymore.

The sun was high, and heating up the morning rain on the asphalt, making a steam that hovered just above the street. He stepped onto the sidewalk and started up the small hill of his front yard, his knee aching with the effort. When he reached the top, he noticed Mr. Baker a few houses down making his way from his mailbox to his front door. The curve to his back looked even worse than it had just a week ago, and he shuffled along the walkway with his mail in hand.

Jackson thought of his session with Dr. Kipling earlier that morning—another useless hour of his life wasted with someone who had no idea how to help him. He'd promised his mom he would go, had promised to try to talk to someone, even if he didn't believe for a fraction of a second in that psychological mumbo jumbo. But this morning Dr. Kipling had told him to reach outside of himself and look for ways to help someone else. It had made sense at the time, but now it just seemed like more useless talk.

He flexed his knee again and debated with himself another minute. Maybe she was right. Maybe helping someone else would take his mind off his own loss.

Mr. Baker was only a few paces away from his front steps when Jackson finally decided it was worth a shot, but he realized he'd have to hurry to catch the old man before he was gone. He jogged a few steps, but his knee groaned as his left foot hit the ground. He tried to push through it, jogging a few more steps, but Mr. Baker was already half-way up the stairs, and Jackson still had another neighbor's yard to cross to reach him.

Suddenly his foot landed awkwardly in a small hole, and his knee lurched forward. He stumbled but caught his balance, narrowly avoiding a headlong fall into a row of shrubs as his knee sent stabbing reminders of why he shouldn't be jogging in the first place. He gripped it tight, trying to rub out the pain. A couple of houses over, Mr. Baker opened his screen door and shuffled inside.

It figured. Try and do something nice, and he was still as useless now as he'd been months ago. It was a dumb idea anyway. How do you help someone else when you can't even help yourself?

He turned and headed back across his yard, bending and stretching his leg out every few strides. He glanced down at his watch and realized he only had twenty minutes to get ready for work. He was better off anyway. Helping the old guy would have just made him late.

He pushed open the front door and scanned the living room and kitchen briefly for Matthew, but the house appeared to be empty. He headed into his bedroom and slipped his socks and shoes off. Then he took a quick shower, hoping to wash away the murky heaviness that still clung to his chest. As the water rushed over his skin, he took a deep breath and let the tension run out of him as well.

He should have tried harder to cooperate this morning. Dr. Kipling had been kind and patient with him, and he really did want to get on with his life, but it seemed impossible. Even when he did try, fate was set against him. It would be so much easier to crawl under a rock and hide.

He stepped out of the shower and wrapped the towel around his waist, catching his reflection in the mirror. At least the hours in the gym were paying off. He could make out the beginnings of his atrophied six pack. Maybe if he worked hard enough to get his outside back to normal, his insides would follow suit.

He returned to his bedroom and began searching for his uniform in all the usual places—behind the beanbag in the corner, shoved into the wicker chest at the end of his bed, and finally draped over the desk chair. His shirt was buried beneath the clothes he'd worn the day before, but his khakis were nowhere to be found. Maybe it was time to start organizing his room like an actual adult, maybe even buy a dresser.

He shuffled some clothes off his desk and noticed the small book sitting precariously on the corner. He picked it up and read the title again: *A Grief Observed,* by C. S. Lewis. Dr. Kipling had recommended it several times over the past few weeks, but he'd only picked it up a couple of days ago. He'd read the first page, but it touched way too close to home right now, and he'd meant to put it back. But something had stopped him. For a moment he'd thought he heard a familiar voice, so he'd held onto the book and glanced around.

And then he'd seen her.

Lily had walked out the door of the book store, and his entire body had turned warm and liquid. Had she seen him? He still wondered.

The front door slamming shut brought him out of his thoughts, and a few seconds later Matthew stuck his head around the open bedroom door. His black hair glistened with sweat, and a pink glow was fading out of his freckled cheeks. Jackson assumed he'd been playing basketball down at the Y, but he didn't ask, and Matthew knew better than to mention it.

"You heading off to work soon?" Matthew asked.

"If I can find my pants." Jackson turned again and pushed the covers around on his bed.

"Can I get a ride?"

"Sure. Hey, do you have any clean khakis I can borrow?"

"Are you kidding? Even if I did, they would look like Clamdiggers on you."

Jackson chuckled. "True, I guess."

He tossed the book he was holding back onto the desk and returned to the bathroom. As he tunneled through the dirty clothes hamper, he heard Matthew call from his room.

"So how did your session go with the beautiful Dr. Kipling?"

Jackson found the pants, examined them, and then brought them to his nose. Close enough. He slipped the pants on and stepped back into his bedroom to find Matthew seated on the bed. He was holding the C. S. Lewis book open.

Jackson shrugged. "It was fine. Just a bunch of psycho babble about looking for ways to help others instead of focusing on myself."

"What's this? Another stellar recommendation from the doc?"

"Yep." Jackson slipped on his shirt and tucked it in. "You know, if you want to ride with me to work, you better get ready. I'm leaving in ten minutes."

"Oh, well then I have plenty of time." Matthew grinned and tossed the book aside. He started to open his mouth but appeared to think better of it. He stood and walked through the door before turning around. Jackson searched for his boots under his bed, and when he stood up, Matthew was staring at him.

"What? I know you're dying to say something. Just spit it out."

Matthew leaned against the doorjamb with his arms over his chest.

"You seem more like your old self these days."

"What is that supposed to mean?"

"It's just good, I guess. You working out, and getting a job at the restaurant. I even saw you smile at that group of girls the other night. You know, the bachelorette party? They were flirting with you something fierce."

"They were a little drunk."

"Doesn't matter man. Every girl that comes into that place wants to be seated in your section. You gotta be killing the tips."

"Nah. I have gotten a few accidental encounters with my rear end though."

Matthew laughed and shook his head. "Well, anyway. It's good to see, that's all. You thought about asking anybody out?"

"Nope."

Jackson pushed past him and continued into the kitchen. It was too much to hope for Matthew to just take the hint and go get ready for work. As he opened the fridge and ducked down to peer inside, he heard the scrape of a chair on hardwood.

"It's just not healthy," Matthew said. "You might as well join a monastery or something."

"I'm not catholic."

"Come on, man. Go out with me and Ashley sometime. She has some cute friends."

"Why are you so interested in my love life?" Jackson pulled two sodas out of the refrigerator and passed one to Matthew. Then he took the seat across from him and popped the top of his.

"I just want to see you happy, man. That's all."

"Quit worrying about me so much. I'm fine. And dating is the last thing on my mind right now."

"See, that's how I know you're still not okay. You're wasting away the best years of your life. You could have almost any girl you wanted, and you barely even notice. That's just not right."

Jackson took a long gulp of his soda and looked out the window. How could he expect Matthew to understand? He'd probably have agreed with him a year ago, but not anymore.

"I'm just not ready."

"Is it because of Lily?"

Jackson sighed and leaned back in his chair as Matthew put his palms up in the air.

"Hey, man. I know we agreed the subject was off limits, but that was months ago. Maybe you should just call her or-"

"I don't want to talk about her."

"Look, you and Lily were there for me when mom died. I don't know where I'd be if you hadn't offered me a place to live. Probably some cardboard box in Nashville. You, Aunt Mary, Lily—all of you—made me realize how important it is to have people you love around in hard times. I just want to help."

Jackson looked down at his watch and then back up at Matthew.

"Four minutes."

He pushed away from the table and walked out the front door to his car.

St Simons Island, Georgia

Lily propped her elbows on the top rail of the pier and rested her chin in her hands. Next to her, Kara and Rachel sat dangling their legs over its edge while they watched a shrimp boat sail past with porpoises leaping behind it. Just beyond the massive bridge over the waterway a few miles west, the sun had burst into an array of pinks and oranges as it left the evening sky. The scene seemed almost surreal, and for a moment she breathed in a deep calm.

"This is beautiful," she said. "I could just toss up a hammock and go to sleep right here."

"Hmm, me too," Kara said.

Rachel leaned over the rail in front of her and glanced down at the dark water swirling around the pilings.

"Wow, I'd hate to fall in here. The water looks pretty rough."

Lily snorted, "Well, then genius, don't lean so far over the railing."

Rachel stuck her tongue out and pulled herself up. "You guys ready to head over to the putt-putt course?"

As they strolled toward the shore, Rachel yelped and grabbed Kara's arm. She pointed toward the end of the pier.

"Hey! Those are the cops we were talking to last night! Let's go say hi!"

Lily noticed the police car and the officers beside it, but before she could voice her objection, the two of them took off running.

"Great," she mumbled to herself as she continued across the pier. "Now they're going to think we're flaky tourists stalking them."

She considered keeping her distance. She could still easily keep an eye on them from the chairs beneath the live oak near the pier. That would be better than listening to that arrogant one poke fun at her.

As she passed the patrol car a couple of yards away, she caught a glance of all of them laughing. It sent a stab of regret through her. Maybe Kara was right about her. Maybe she didn't know how to have fun anymore.

Kara's eyes met hers. She jerked her head toward the others and mouthed the words, "Come on."

Well, she had to start somewhere. Maybe she wasn't the life of the party, but she'd never move on moping around by herself. So she walked over and joined Kara and Rachel, though she was determined to avoid conversation with the action hero wanna-be.

Rachel and Kara stood in front of Steve and Alex who leaned against the car with their arms crossed like it was the official pose of the evening. Rachel giggled as she flipped her hair, and Lily rolled her eyes. She forced a smile as she noticed Alex giving her a once over. One track mind.

"Hello again," he said.

Lily nodded, but she tried to focus her attention on the kids playing at the park rather than the tiny wrinkles around his eyes when he smiled at her, or the flutters in her stomach. It was exactly the reaction he'd want her to have, and she was determined not to give him the satisfaction, whether he was aware of it or not. But when she glanced back at him, he was still smiling at her, as if he already knew her secret.

She cleared her throat and turned her attention toward Steve as he answered Kara's questions about his fiancée.

"Actually, we met almost two years ago. Right after Alex and I became partners. She had such a warm smile."

His mouth widened into a huge grin pricking Lily unexpectedly. It was nice—and painful—to remember what love looked like.

"How did you meet her?" she asked.

"Alex introduced us. Chloe's his sister, and she cooked dinner for us one night."

"Wait a minute. You're marrying Alex's sister?" She couldn't help but laugh.

"What's so funny about that?" Alex asked.

"Nothing I guess. But it explains why a guy as nice as Steve would be hanging around with the likes of you."

"Ouch!" Steve laughed and elbowed Alex in the rib.

Alex smiled, but his voice iced over. "I guess I'm some horrible excuse for a human being?"

"I'm sorry...I didn't mean-"

"Hey, don't worry about it. Must be nice to be perfect."

She narrowed her eyes at him, and the moment of guilt was gone. She reminded herself of her promise to avoid him. So she retreated into her own mind again, blocking out much of their conversation. So much for moving on.

She was about to slip away when a car behind her honked its horn causing her to jump. She stepped out of the way as a green Pontiac rounded the end of the parking lot, pulled through the space between the patrol car and the opposite curb, and headed up the next row. Lily turned and leaned against the police car, not noticing until it was too late that she was standing beside Alex. His arm brushed hers, sending the hairs to attention.

She glanced at him, unable to keep herself from noticing the way the sleeves of his uniform hugged his shoulders and biceps. He reached for the sleeve closest to her and tugged it, loosening it a bit. She cleared her throat and looked away, searching for anything else to concentrate on, but she could still feel his eyes on her, and she wondered why he was trying so hard to make her squirm.

"So where are you from again?" he asked.

She forced herself to look at him, and his grin sent a warm flush up her neck and cheeks.

"Alabama." She tried to say it as lightly as possible.

"Yeah, I caught that part. Where in Alabama?"

"Uh, well that gets a little confusing sometimes."

"Well, what can you expect from an education in Alabama?"

Lily froze, the rest of her answer still hanging in her mouth. Had he really just said that? Of course he had, and whatever gymnastics her stomach had been doing disappeared.

"Oh come on," he said. "Lighten up a little. I was just kidding. Really, what's so confusing about where you live in Alabama?"

She fought back the urge to take a jab at him in return.

"Well, as I was about to say, my parents divorced when I was little and they live in different cities. My mom lives in Birmingham and my dad in Cedar Creek, about an hour away. I've lived with both of them—mom during the school year, dad during the summer—so both places feel like home. But right now I'm living with my aunt in Birmingham while I work at volleyball camps for the summer."

"Why not just live with your mom?"

"Uh, that's kind of a long story. And very boring."

"In other words, it's none of my business."

"Pretty much," she shrugged. "Sorry, no offense."

Alex glanced over at Kara and nodded. "So Kara is..."

"...my step-sister."

"I see. That explains why you two look so different."

"Yeah, she really favors my stepmom."

"Man, your stepmom must be hot."

"What?" she sputtered.

He smiled again and nudged her with his elbow.

"Dad remarried well, huh?"

She stepped away and shook her head, refusing to be baited. She was about to insist they leave when the green Pontiac rounded the cars on the next row down, clipping the tail of the car on the end. Metal screeched against metal as the Pontiac took the curve. It never even paused as it slid into a parking space beside the playground.

Steve pushed away from the patrol car and eyed the Pontiac. "Guess we should check that out."

Alex didn't move. "Let's see what happens. Maybe they'll call the police and dispatch will send someone over." He glanced at Lily sideways. "Fender benders suck."

It seemed like a good chance to walk away. Lily reached out and tapped Kara's arm.

"Let's go."

The door on the Pontiac swung open and smashed into a black sedan next to it. A lady stumbled out of the driver's side, a tiny thing with bushy hair and a miniskirt that barely covered her rear. She let out a string of curses and slammed the door, rocking the car. She bent over, examined the sedan and swayed a couple of steps sideways.

Steve nodded in her direction. "Come on, bro. Let's get this over with."

Alex pushed away from the patrol car and followed, calling information out to someone on the other end of his radio. Lily pulled Kara toward her.

"Come on. Let's get out of here."

"Hang on a sec."

They watched as Steve and Alex walked up to the bushy-haired lady, who had stumbled her way around to the passenger side of the car. Steve addressed her first.

"Ma'am? Everything all right over here?"

She shoved her hair away from her face and reached for the car door.

"What? Yeah, yeah. Everything's fine."

"Ma'am, can you step away from the vehicle for me?"

"Excuse me?"

Steve shot a glance at Alex, who moved behind her as Steve stepped in front of the car.

"Listen, ma'am. I just want to ask you a few questions. Could you please step away from the vehicle so we can talk?"

She shook her head and pulled the door open. "Can't. I'm busy."

She ducked inside the car and fumbled with something in the back seat. Alex moved closer and put his hand on the trunk.

"Excuse me, but you're going to need to step away from the vehicle, or we're going to have to place you under arrest."

Lily could hear the lady mouthing off, but wasn't sure what she said. It must have been bad because suddenly Alex grabbed for her arms, and Steve darted toward them, but the car door prevented him from helping. The lady shoved away from the open door and spun around with a baby in her arms.

"Leave me alone!" she screamed. "I didn't do anything!"

Alex and Steve sprung back, both with their hands up trying to reassure her. Lily's heart raced watching the infant's limbs flail as the woman turned from Alex to Steve.

"Ma'am, please," Steve said. "Just let us have the baby. We only want to talk. You bumped another car. We just need some information."

"I didn't hit no other car!" Her voice screeched and sent a shock up Lily's spine.

Steve reached toward her, but the lady backed away. Alex took several quick strides and grabbed her arm, shaking the baby once again. This time it wailed. Lily's heart thundered in her chest. What if she dropped the baby?

Alex pulled away, but Lily could tell he was about to go after her again. She found her feet carrying her forward before she realized it, and she called out to the lady just as Alex gripped her arm again.

"Wait!" Lily shouted. "Please, the baby's going to get hurt!"

The lady pulled away and stared wildly at Lily.

"I didn't do nothing!"

"I know. But please, just let me hold the baby while you talk to the officers."

"What do you think you're doing?" Alex growled. "Stay out of this."

But she stepped a little closer and tried to smile at the woman. The baby continued to cry and squirm in her arms, but she seemed to barely notice. Her upper body swayed back and forth like it might tip over at any moment and her eyes darted between Lily and Alex.

"I just want to help," Lily said.

Steve continued talking into his radio, and Alex inched closer to the woman.

"Hand the baby to me, and everything will be fine."

The woman backed toward the open door. "No!" She pulled the baby tighter to her chest, muffling it's screams.

Lily and Alex darted toward her at the same time. Alex grabbed one arm as Lily reached for the baby. The woman shrieked, squeezing the infant tighter.

"Get back, Lily!" Alex pried the woman's fingers back.

"I've got him!" Lily said. She felt the woman's grip loosen just enough for her to slip the baby away.

Alex had the woman on her face in barely a second. As he pulled her arms back, she struggled against him and tried to turn over. He pressed his knee into her back.

"Ma'am, I'm placing you under arrest for operating a vehicle under the influence, disorderly conduct, and endangering a child."

Lily stepped away and watched the scene in dismay as she tried to comfort the crying baby. She cradled him in her arms, gently rocking him back and forth.

"Shhh, it's okay."

Alex and Steve pulled the woman up to her feet after they'd placed handcuffs on her. Her right cheek was scratched from the pavement, and her skirt was twisted and smudged. They guided her across the parking lot to the patrol car. She struggled the entire way, turning and looking at Lily.

"Give me my baby! You can't take him!"

Steve opened the back door and pushed the woman down into the back seat. She kicked and screamed more obscenities, so he closed the door and spoke into his radio again. Alex met her as she crossed the parking lot, still cradling the baby. It had finally calmed down and was sucking on a corner of its sleeve.

"What were you trying to do? Get me fired?" Alex said.

"I was trying to help."

"You could have gotten yourself hurt, or the baby! Not to mention the fact that you have no legal authority to forcibly remove a child from its mother."

She hadn't thought of it that way.

"I'm held liable for anything you do," he continued. "So next time you're told to stay out of something, try listening."

He grabbed the baby out of her arms and pressed him to his chest. The baby screamed again.

"At least I calmed him down," she said.

Alex shifted the baby into the crook of his arm. Lily watched in horror as his head rolled backward and Alex scooped a hand underneath it.

"Do you even know what you're doing?" she asked.

He pressed his eyebrows together and turned toward the Pontiac.

"Thanks for your help. I got it from here."

As he walked away, Lily turned back toward Kara and Rachel who stood next to the patrol car gaping at her, a crowd of onlookers beginning to form behind them.

Kara shook her head. "That was crazy."

"Tell me about it," Lily said and glanced over her shoulder. "What a jerk."

Alex walked over to the open door of the Pontiac and sat down on the passenger side seat. He shifted the baby in his arms and cradled its head in his elbow. He tried not to look down at it, to focus on what he needed to do next. It was screaming, and his chest constricted with each wail. He took a deep breath and tried to force down the ache rising within him.

He dug under the seat and found a blanket and pacifier. Within seconds the baby had settled into a rhythmic sucking. He looked down and ran his thumb over the baby's cheek, allowing himself the briefest moment to imagine a different life.

Chapter Four

Lily pulled herself up to a sitting position on her towel and dusted the sand from her arms and legs. The afternoon sun had set her skin on fire, and she contemplated a dip in the ocean. But the tide had receded so far it didn't seem worth the effort.

She glanced down the beach, letting her gaze drift to the four wheelers sitting near the rocks about fifty yards away. They'd moved further down in the past half hour, which was fine with her. The way Alex rode around the beach—chest puffed out, sleeves rolled up, arms all flexed—it was so arrogant it made her want to knock him right off when they went by. He hadn't even acknowledged her existence. No apology, no polite nod of the head.

Nothing.

"Hey, Lily!"

She turned around, and Kara jogged toward her from the volleyball court near the dunes where she and Rachel had been lounging with a group of college students. Lily had noticed a few of them batting around volleyballs, which initially piqued her interest. But pick-up games weren't her style. She wanted real competition. As Kara approached, Lily shook her head.

"Uh-uh. No way."

"What?" Kara stopped and threw her hands up.

"I'm not playing."

"Why not? Come on."

"You know why." She looked past Kara to the group gathering around the court. Most were setting up chairs or spreading out towels, but a couple of guys were still hitting a ball back and forth.

"Just one game? For me?" Kara put on her most angelic face.

"Look, I'm not really in the mood."

Kara moaned and dropped her hands. "You are so irritating. Get a grip already. You love volleyball, and these guys want to play."

Lily looked again at the guys. Their technique wasn't half bad.

"Who are they anyway? They're a little old for you and Rachel."

"Whatever. Do you want to play or not?"

The tall one slammed the ball at his partner who passed it high into the air. Maybe it wouldn't be a complete waste of time.

"All right."

Kara clapped her hands and jogged back toward the group. "She said yes!"

The tall one caught the ball, and walked to the edge of the court as Lily approached. He had a shock of red hair standing on his head, and his smile had the tiniest hint of a smirk as he reached out for her hand.

"Hey, I'm Dan. Thanks for playing."

"Sure." Her cheeks warmed as he held her hand for a fraction too long.

"Joe," the short one said, offering a polite wave. He was stocky, and his scrunched up features reminded her of a pug.

"How do you want to do this?" she said.

Dan tossed the ball at his friend. "Well, how about you and Joe versus me and Kara? Seem fair?"

Lily examined Joe more closely. Maybe this hadn't been such a good idea after all. He barely came to her shoulder.

"Ah, I don't know."

Kara stepped closer and narrowed her eyes. "It'll be fine. Just play." She turned back to Dan with a bright smile. "Come on. Let's get started!"

She pulled Dan toward the closest side of the court and shot one more pointed look at Lily over her shoulder. Lily forced a smile and cleared her throat.

"All right then."

"You want to warm up first?" Joe asked.

"Sure." She pulled her right arm across her chest and then over her head to stretch out her shoulder. He handed her the ball, and she hit it against the net a couple of times before tossing it back to him.

"You can serve first. I'll block."

Through the net she watched Dan bend down and say something in Kara's ear. Kara giggled and swatted him. Lily rolled her eyes.

"You two ready?"

They continued laughing as they separated and split the court. Dan winked at Kara before looking at Lily.

"Yeah, we're ready. Serve it up, Joe!"

Lily put her hands up to block and watched Dan pass the first serve into the air. Kara stepped under it and passed it high and close to the net. As Dan leapt into the air, Lily stepped sideways and jumped, pushing her hands above the net. Dan's hit flew past her, and when she hit the ground she turned to find the ball. Joe was sprawled across the sand with the ball rolling away from him. Several of the guys seated near the court yelled insults and laughed at him.

"Great," she said under her breath.

Joe pushed himself up from the sand with a sheepish shrug. "My bad," he said.

He jogged over to the ball, scooped it up, and rolled it under the net to Dan waiting on the opposite end line.

"One zip!" Dan called out.

Joe trotted back onto the court as Lily backed away from the net. She bent her knees and watched Dan toss the ball. His serve was hard, but she was waiting on it, and passed it perfectly up to Joe. He pushed the ball up in front of her. She took several long strides and jumped as high as she could, hitting the ball with all her force. It streaked toward the back corner of the court, hitting just inside the line behind Dan.

Energy surged through her as the crowd reacted. There was a definite "Whoa!" along with a few other choice words. Joe gave her a high five.

"Nice!"

Dan's eyes widened as Kara retrieved the ball. "Good shot. You play?"

"A little." She couldn't help but smile. Something about vol- leyball—the power, the intensity of blasting a ball across the court—it sharpened all the fuzzy edges of her emotions. It was exactly what she needed right now.

Kara tossed her the ball, and she jogged to the end line to serve. Across from her, Dan crouched with a grin on his face. She smiled back and sent a deep floating ball toward him. He passed it to Kara, and after she set it up, he drove a hit toward the sharp angle near Lily.

She had to dive forward to keep the ball off the sand. She pushed up from the ground and launched her body into the air, swinging for the corner again. This time, Dan had to throw his hands up at the last minute to keep the ball from plastering his face. It sailed out of bounds.

Kara straightened and put her hands on her hips. "Come on, Lil. Quit showing off."

Dan let out a laugh, but the edge in it made it clear he wasn't amused.

"Don't worry about it, Honey. I can take it."

Joe retrieved the ball, and Lily aimed for Dan again. This time, he made a perfect pass, and after Kara's set, he hit hard shot right back at her. Lily barely had time to throw up her hands to protect her face, and the ball flew into the dunes.

She stared for a moment at the look of satisfaction on Dan's face. He made no attempt to hide his smirk now. She jogged af- ter the ball and threw it to Kara, then took her place again off the net to await her serve. Kara sent the ball right down the middle of the court, so Lily stepped in to make the pass.

"Push it up!" She inched toward the net.

Joe set it high and close to the net, too close. Lily took two steps, jumped and reached with both hands to grab the ball. She sensed Dan jumping opposite of her and tightened every muscle in her shoulders and abs. He hit the ball into her hands so hard it stung like fire. But it rebounded straight down onto his side of the court. Dan's face turned as red as his hair, and his friends in the dunes went nuts.

"You just got stuffed by a girl!" someone yelled.

Lily grinned, but Dan didn't even attempt to hide the fury in his eyes. Kara knocked the sand off the ball and tossed it under the net.

"That's okay; we'll get the next one," she said.

Dan whipped his head toward Kara. "Maybe you could help out a little."

Kara's mouth dropped open. "Excuse me?"

Dan backed away from the net as Lily picked up the ball and tossed it to Joe. She envisioned her next shot at Dan. She'd like to see him eat some sand.

Alex sat on his four-wheeler and watched Lily block Dan Johnson's hit, wishing he could hear the ribbing he was getting from the guys around him. He deserved it too. He'd had words with Dan more times than he cared to count, especially after the way he'd treated Chloe in high school.

Alex grinned as he remembered the stunned look on Dan's face the one time they had exchanged blows. Eight years hadn't erased the sweetness of the memory of his twisted bleeding nose. The fifty sprints after football practice had totally been worth it.

Beside him, Steve downed another large bottle of water and let out a sigh as he doused his hair in the remainder.

"Man, I know you've got a wedding to pay for, but couldn't you get overtime somewhere with air conditioning?" Alex pulled out his own bottle of water and took a long swig.

Steve grinned and gave Alex a hard slap on the back.

"You're the best, man." Then he laughed again. "Hey, that's funny. You actually are the best man."

"Yeah, you should go on tour with that one."

Alex wet his own neck and hair then shoved the bottle into the cup holder between his knees and glanced down the beach. The sun had reached its peak for the day, and the heat was freaking unbearable. He'd give anything for a quick dip into the ocean.

His phone vibrated, and he unclipped it from his belt. Another text. What was that now, five since that morning? She was losing it. Too bad. He had drawn a line he refused to cross, so he deleted the text without even opening it.

Loud cheering caught his attention, and he looked toward the volleyball court. Lily's partner reached out for her hand and pulled her up from the sand. She dusted off her arms and legs as he retrieved the ball.

On the other side of the court, Dan turned to Kara and pumped his fist into the air. He caught the ball from the other guy, handed it to Kara, and slapped her rear as she trotted toward the back of the court to serve.

"Maybe we should go keep an eye on Dan and the gang." Alex gripped the handlebars tighter. "It's getting a little intense over there."

"Yeah, if you say so. But I don't think Dan's the one you want to keep an eye on."

"No idea what you're talking about." He turned back to the game and watched Lily hit another hard shot into the corner. Dan dove for the ball, but it went sailing off his arm. Lily raised her hands to the sky and gave her partner a high five. Dan jumped up and dusted himself off, yelling at Kara to go get the ball. Even from this distance, Alex could see Lily's whole body tense.

"I thought you'd sworn off women from now on." Steve climbed onto his four-wheeler and released the brake.

Alex shrugged. "Nah, not women. Just being tied down." He watched Lily walk to the end line with the ball and couldn't help but admire the way her body moved, like a cat slinking after its prey.

"It doesn't matter, though. She's not my type."

"What?" Steve choked as he laughed. "She's breathing, and she's pretty. That's definitely your type."

"No way." Alex shook his head. "That girl is wound up tighter than a chastity belt on a preacher's daughter. She might even *be* a preacher's daughter."

Steve reached for the key between his knees, turning a knowing glance at him.

"Whatever you say, brother. Besides, it's probably for the best after the year you've had."

Alex didn't need a reminder. But he wasn't about to delve into a discussion about Adrian.

"Look, don't worry about me. I got no intentions of jumping into that fire."

Steve cranked his four-wheeler, and Alex followed him past the baking women on the sand. As they neared the volleyball court, Alex watched Lily toss the ball into the air and send a jump serve over the net. Dan passed the ball, and after Kara passed it back to him, he crushed it toward Lily. She ducked, and the ball flew past her head toward the dunes.

Alex and Steve stopped their vehicles a few feet away from the crowd that had gathered around to watch. When Alex turned off the motor, he heard Dan swearing at the top of his lungs.

"That ball was in," he yelled. "It touched the line!"

"No way!" Lily yelled back. "I was standing right here!"

Dan continued to protest, but several observers agreed with Lily, so he finally gave in. She retrieved the ball and jogged back to the end line on her side.

"Game point," she called out.

She tossed the ball up and took a couple of steps before leaping into the air. Then she sent the hardest shot Alex had seen yet over the net toward Dan, and it just clipped the sideline. Lily threw her arms up, her face lit with excitement. Most of the crowd echoed the celebration, but then Dan's voice rose over everyone else's.

"That was out!"

"What? You're crazy!" she yelled. "It hit the line! Everyone saw it!"

She ducked under the net and went over to the spot where the ball had hit. Then she bent over and looked at the sand, pointing at the impression the ball had made.

"See, it hit the line."

"No it didn't." Dan stepped toward her and kicked sand over the impression, partially covering it. "There's nothing there. That was from another play."

Kara reached for his arm. "Come on. Don't worry about it."

Dan shook her off and pointed toward the other side of the court, his eyes blazing at Lily.

"Get back over there and finish the game."

"We're done. The ball was in. Game over. You lose." She placed her hands on her hips and thrust her chin forward.

Dan took a couple of aggressive strides toward Lily, and Alex jumped off his four-wheeler with Steve right behind him. He pushed through a few people around the court as Lily shifted her weight forward like a mountain lion ready to spring. Dan pushed a finger toward her and let out a slew of obscenities, but she held her ground. Alex stepped between the two of them and placed his hand on Dan's heaving chest.

"Is there a problem here?" Alex said.

Dan scowled, but he stepped back. He pointed a finger at Lily.

"She's cheating!"

Alex stretched his arms and corralled Dan back a bit more. He had to admit it was nice seeing the jerk put in his place.

"Looked to me like you were the one trying to cheat." He could barely keep a straight face. "I suggest you take your beating like a man, gather up your beer and all your stuff, and find some other spot on the beach to occupy—somewhere I don't have to look at you the rest of the day."

Dan shoved a finger at his chest. "You think that uniform makes you better than me?"

"No, but it does let me throw you in jail."

Dan shot another glare over his shoulder, and then he stormed over to the dunes to get his things. Before he turned to go, he gave Alex one more sneer.

"Tell Chloe I said hi."

Alex pushed down a flare of anger, refusing to let it ignite. He wasn't worth it. Instead, he turned around to find Lily. He wasn't sure what he expected to see on her face—gratitude at the very least—but she was stomping across the court glowering at him like he'd been the one insulting her.

She stopped just in front of him and crossed her arms over her chest as she shifted her weight to one hip. Golden strands of hair whipped around her face in the breeze, and her eyes blazed a violet blue. The sight of her was something else, and his heart took a sudden jump.

"Why did you do that?" she demanded.

"Do what?"

"I can handle myself just fine. I didn't need you to rescue me."

He stared at her, his mouth nearly dropping open. Was she serious? And where was Steve? He glanced around and saw him standing on the other side of the court with Kara and Rachel, the three of them trying not to look like they were watching.

"I was just doing my job," Alex said, turning back to her.

"That's a load of crap." She took another step forward and pushed her finger into his chest. "You've been a complete jerk every time I've talked to you, and now all of a sudden you're trying to play knight in shining armor? I don't need you to-"

"Look, Miss High and Mighty, you haven't exactly been warm and fuzzy yourself. I know you think the world revolves around you, but believe it or not, I am a *real* police officer, with an *actu-al* duty to maintain some semblance of peace out here."

"I know-"

"Let me finish. Now I've known Dan since we were kids, and he was about to lose the small amount of control he had left. And as much as you probably need to have your butt kicked, I'm not about to let it happen while I'm on duty. Get it?"

She stepped back and took a deep breath, giving him a chance to catch his. She pushed some strands of hair out of her face, and if he didn't know better he would have sworn he saw regret in her eyes. She glanced over at Kara and Steve then back at him. Then she turned and walked away without a word.

An afternoon shower had cooled things off a bit, but the air quickly turned sticky as the sun fell toward the horizon. Ice cream had seemed like a great idea, but now Lily was beginning to regret the suggestion.

Rachel and Kara stood side by side looking into the glass-top freezer full of ice cream as if they were facing a choice between tan, blonde, and gorgeous, or tall, dark and handsome instead of vanilla bean or rocky road. It was pathetic. Lily was about to walk out and leave them in their anguish when they finally reached a decision.

"I'll have the rocky road," Kara said to the petite blonde behind the counter.

"And I'll have the vanilla bean," Rachel said. "We'll just swap half-way through."

Eww, Lily thought.

The blonde was visibly relieved for a final decision. She quickly filled the orders, probably afraid they'd change their minds. Then she handed the cones over the counter and extend-ed a hand to Lily for payment.

"Sorry," Lily mouthed as she handed over the money. She rolled her eyes and the blonde grinned.

They headed toward the exit, set on finally playing the putt-putt game they'd been putting off. But when Lily pushed open the door, she nearly fell out onto the sidewalk as someone pulled on it from the other side. As she fought to keep her balance, a solid pair of arms reached out to steady her.

"Whoa!" He set her upright. "Sorry, Lily."

She jerked her head up and found Steve still grasping her el-bow. He smiled and released it as he stepped back.

"No, Steve, don't worry about it."

Her stomach fluttered, and she wondered where Alex was. She hadn't yet seen one of them without the other nearby, but maybe God had listened to her prayer that she'd never see Alex again. He'd been so right about her, and the thought of apolo-gizing made her ill.

"Hey Steve," Rachel said from behind her. "Where's Alex?"

Lily's stomach flipped again, as if the mention of his name might make him magically appear.

"He's right behind me," he said. "Just chaining up the bikes."

She felt the urge to flee, and she started to stammer out an excuse when Alex rounded the corner. His smile immediately faded. Fantastic timing, she thought.

"What's going on?" He smiled at Kara and Rachel.

"I nearly flung Lily out onto the street," Steve said. "But we recovered nicely."

Alex looked at her again and she noted the change in his eyes from the previous nights. No longer dancing with laughter and mischief, they were reserved, almost polite.

"Well, good thing no one was hurt." He gave Steve a pat on the shoulder. "You ready to grab a bite?"

"Sure."

She stepped aside to let them pass, her brain screaming at her to walk away. But some reflex she had no control over suddenly sent her hand toward Alex's arm.

"Wait."

He looked at her like she was a firecracker he wanted to keep at arm's length.

"Can I talk to you for just a second?" she asked.

She expected him to say no, to tell her she was crazy, and he had nothing to say to her, but he stepped away from the door with her.

"Sure." He turned to Steve and gestured toward the door. "Just grab me a slice of pizza."

Steve agreed and headed inside, and Lily sent a silent message to Kara with her eyes. This time, miraculously, Kara seemed to understand, and she grabbed Rachel's arm and headed toward the pier. Finally alone with him, Lily's thoughts scattered with the breeze. Why had she stopped him again?

"I uh, I just wanted to say-" she started, but the way he studied her, his hazel eyes gazing into hers, made her skin shiver. "What you said today on the beach, you know-"

"Look," he said. "I shouldn't have said that stuff the way I did."

"No, I'm not saying that. What I'm trying to say is that you were right. I have been rude to you, and I wanted to apologize. I shouldn't have interfered last night, and I should have been grateful for your help this afternoon. I'm sorry."

He stared at her without a word, and she readied herself for another jab or smart remark, but he said nothing.

"Well," she said. "I should go. I hope you'll accept my apology and that you won't think I'm rude if I try to exit gracefully."

She crossed the street and parking lot as quickly as possible without looking desperate to get away. Her chest thundered with every heartbeat, and her skin was damp with sweat. What was wrong with her?

She found a cement park bench near the playground and slid onto the top, resting her elbows on her knees. Looking out over the ocean, she focused on the gentle waves sliding along in front of her as the light from the fading sun twinkled on top. Several deep breaths slowed her heart and her breathing, and she wiped her palms on her shorts. Then she closed her eyes and dropped her head into her hands.

She'd done the right thing—said she was sorry and meant it, too. So why was she so tangled up inside? It's not like she'd ever see him again.

She picked up her head and opened her eyes, but her heart thundered again. Alex was standing in front of her, his arms over his chest and head cocked to the side. He grinned at her, and before she could say anything, he reached for her hand and touched it to his lips.

Warmth spread through her hand and up her arm like liquid heat. When he looked at her again, a new spark of mischief flickered in his eyes, and she smiled.

"What was that for?" she asked.

"I know that apology back there must've killed you."

"You have no idea."

"Well, you know, you were right too. I have been a jerk. I uh, I'd try to explain if I could, but what can I say? I probably am a jerk."

"Is that your version of an apology?"

"I guess," he said. "Pretty lame, huh?"

"Yeah, actually."

He glanced around and laughed for another moment. Then he let out a deep breath and clapped his hands together.

"So, you think we could start over?"

She paused for only a second. "Absolutely."

"Hi, I'm Alex Walker." He stuck out his hand, and she shook it.

"Lily Brennon. Nice to meet you."

Chapter Five

Saint Simons Island, Georgia

Alex held Lily's hand in his and contemplated leaving the conversation right there—no insults, no yelling—just her smile. But God, what a smile. It wasn't just her mouth, though that in itself was enough to make him want a taste. Something about her pulled at him. Maybe it was her eyes, her tiny dimples, or the glow he was surprised he hadn't noticed before. But then again, had she really smiled at him before?

He dropped her hand and glanced around, sure his thoughts were on a billboard behind him. What was he supposed to say now? Starting over was a nice idea, but in reality, they were way past introductions. Besides, a familiar wrenching of his gut told him now was the time to back away, before the seed of that smile dug roots inside of him.

"I uh, I should probably get going." He gestured toward the ice cream parlor where Steve was waiting.

"Oh, sure. No problem. I'm sure you're busy."

She smiled at him again, a tiny radicle that glided into his chest and began to grow, and somewhere in his mind he knew it was already too late.

"Well, listen," he said, exhaling the last of his resistance. "I actually have about a half hour or so to grab some dinner. There's a great little deli down the block. You want to walk with me?" Dinner couldn't hurt anything.

"Uh, I don't know. We're getting along pretty well right now. Do we really want to chance it?"

"Well, I tell you what. If it looks like we might start killing each other, we'll just agree to go our separate ways. How's that?"

She glanced toward Kara and Rachel as they strolled along the pier.

"Come on," he said. "I promise I won't bite. Not tonight anyway."

"Alright, alright. Quit begging." She laughed and pushed away from the table.

She whistled at Kara and pointed toward the village; then she headed across the parking lot with him.

"Let me just tell Steve," he said.

They stopped outside the ice cream parlor where Steve was seated on a bench finishing the last few bites of his pizza. He held out a slice, but Alex shook his head and pulled a few bills out of his wallet.

"Thanks, but I think I'm going to head down to the deli for a sandwich. Want anything?"

Steve glanced over Alex's shoulder toward Lily and raised his brow. He took the bills and pushed them in his back pocket.

"Nah, take your time. If we get a call, you'll hear it."

He ignored the question in Steve's eyes and turned back to Lily. They picked their way down the block, weaving through various sidewalk displays of corny island t-shirts, various beach accessories, and the poor tourists unaware they could get the same things at the drug store on the mainland for half the price. He struggled to think of anything to talk about. Maybe he really was a jerk if the only time he felt comfortable talking to her was when he was poking fun at her or arguing with her.

"So that was a pretty intense game earlier today. You're pretty good. How long you been playing?"

She shrugged. "Seems like forever. I started playing in seventh grade just to have something to do before basketball season."

"Basketball too? Wow."

"Yeah, when I was a kid all I could do was dream about playing basketball in the Olympics, but...I don't know, volleyball just clicked for me. I fell in love with it."

"What happened to basketball?"

"I got so focused on getting a volleyball scholarship I quit playing everything else after my sophomore year."

"Did you get it? The scholarship?"

"Yeah, I did. I couldn't believe it. I was so scared it wouldn't happen for me, you know?" She pushed a strand of hair behind her ear and sighed. "Now, I can't believe it's about to be over. I can't imagine what life will be like when I can't play anymore."

"I know what you mean. I still remember my last high school football game like it just happened. I even dream I'm still playing sometimes."

She nodded and laughed. "My mom says she can hear me playing in my sleep sometimes, calling out plays and yelling at the ref."

She smiled at him and pushed her hands into her pockets as she tilted her head toward him.

"So do you like being a cop?"

"So far it's been pretty cool. Not sure I want to do it forever, but for now I like it. Well, most of it anyway. I could do without all the paperwork...and the stupid questions."

"Like what?"

"Let me see. At least once a night someone will ask what lake that is."

She laughed and pointed over her shoulder. "Seriously?"

"Yes! It's so annoying. I finally started making up names just to entertain myself. I told some lady the other day it was Lake Erie, and she believed me."

"That's so mean!"

He shrugged and laughed. "I got to get my kicks somehow. It's not like I'm chasing down criminals or busting down doors every day."

When they reached the deli at the end of the street, he pulled open the glass door and waited to let her inside first. Then he stepped up to the counter.

"You want anything?"

She looked over the desserts beneath the counter and shook her head. He ordered a roast beef sandwich and some fries; then he slid his money to the man behind the cash register who looked like he'd seen the bottom of a beer mug too many times in his life. The cashier pushed the money back across the counter.

"Keep it. We appreciate what you guys do around here."

"Keep it as a tip then."

Alex pushed the bills back. The man shook his head, but when Alex insisted further, he finally took the money and thanked him.

"Why did you do that?" Lily asked as they stepped back outside the deli and took a seat at a small table in the shade of a skinny tree sprouting through the sidewalk.

"Do what?"

"Why not just take the sandwich and be grateful for the man's appreciation?"

"I've just seen a couple of guys take advantage of stuff like that. You know, eating at certain places just so they can get it free. I do appreciate the store owners around here wanting to help us out, but it just doesn't feel right for me to take it when I know I can pay for it."

Lily rested her chin in her hand and studied him from across the table. It was unnerving. He preferred to be the one asking the questions. Her mouth tipped into a grin.

"This is a side of you I wasn't expecting. I'm not quite sure what to make of you, Alex Walker."

"Trust me, the feeling is mutual." He shoved his sandwich in his mouth and ignored the apprehension gnawing at him. She was just a tourist, nothing more.

"Tell me more about yourself." She leaned forward a little more onto her hand and grinned.

He chewed slowly and debated on how much he should disclose. "What do you want to know?"

"Anything, I guess."

He took a swig of soda and wiped his mouth with the napkin. Stalling helped.

"Not much to tell. I'm really a pretty boring guy. Besides, I'd rather hear about you."

She stifled a laugh. "You? Boring? I doubt that."

"Oh, you'd be surprised."

"Come on." She leaned back in her chair and crossed her arms. "What's your family like? I mean, I know you have an older sister that's engaged to Steve, but that's about it."

He sat forward and picked over his fries. Just a tourist, he reminded himself.

"Well, my family isn't that close. My parents divorced when I was little. Mom remarried when I was seven or eight. I don't even remember much about it."

He took another bite.

"Do you have any other brothers or sisters?" she asked.

"Nope. Just me and Chloe."

"Do you get along well?"

"She's a pain in the neck in her own way, but I guess we get along as well as any other siblings."

"What about your mom?"

"What about her?"

She laughed and threw her hands in the air. "Are you always this forthcoming? I mean, I feel like I can't get you to shut up."

"Sorry." He shrugged and forced a smile. "There's not that much to tell. And I guess I'm not use to talking about my family much."

He took another bite of the sandwich and dusted off his hands. She sat back in her chair and watched him finish eating. He wondered if he'd put her off, but he wasn't quite sure what to say. It had been some time since a woman had been interested in him for anything more than just a good time for the evening. He wasn't ready to spill his guts.

His phone vibrated on his belt again, and he flipped it open just under the table to take a quick peek.

Let's talk. Call me.

It had been one strange text after another all day, and he wasn't interested in crazy right now. She'd just have to wait. He tucked the phone back in its place, and smiled back at Lily.

When he was finished, they stood and weaved their way back through the tables and chairs to the exit. He tossed his trash and finished the last of his soda.

Time to change the subject.

Lily watched Alex out of the corner of her eye as they made their way back down the street toward the pier. His mood had shifted since she'd asked about his family, and it made her curious about how he had grown up. She hadn't even asked about his father. But seeing it made him uncomfortable, she decided to let it go. It was really none of her business anyway.

"All right, now it's your turn." Alex clapped his hands and rubbed them together. "Let's see how you like being interrogated."

"I wasn't interrogating you! Sheesh. A girl can't ask a few questions?"

He chuckled and shook his head. "Please, all you were missing was the dark room and a tiny light shining in my face."

They laughed and dodged a group of teenagers heading in the opposite direction. She brushed his arm with hers, and her fingers tingled as she wondered what it would feel like to hold his hand.

"Well, you can ask me anything." She pointed at her chest and raised her voice. "I have nothing to hide."

"Oh, I'll bet you do. Everyone does."

"Even you?"

"Even me."

She looked for a sign of humor in his face, but suddenly he seemed serious. Had she said something wrong? But before she could dwell on it, he glanced at her and grinned. Maybe he was just kidding. He elbowed her gently, and again her skin reacted.

"So what are you studying in school?" he asked.

"Math. I want to teach and coach volleyball."

"Ugh! I hate math. I think I failed Algebra twice." He wrinkled his nose like he'd gotten a whiff of something rotten.

"Maybe you just didn't have the right teacher."

"Maybe. She was pretty hot. It was very distracting."

She slapped his arm and laughed. "Just when I think you're capable of grown-up conversation!"

"What? I'm serious. She was very good-looking. I think she wound up marrying a guy a couple of years behind me in school."

Lily rolled her eyes and laughed to herself. As much as it had annoyed her to begin with, his light-hearted attitude was a nice break from the melancholy she'd been stuck in for so long. She couldn't remember the last time she'd genuinely felt happy.

Alex let out a low whistle. "Wow. You're smart, athletic, beautiful." He looked down at her sideways and winked, sending a hot blush up her neck and cheeks. "Is there anything the great Lily Brennon can't do? Surely you have an Achilles heel."

She smiled and pushed down the butterflies that had taken flight with his wink. He was good. Too good. There was no way he was sincerely interested in her. Right? She rubbed her necklace between her fingers.

"I don't know about all that. I definitely have more than a few weak spots." She looked at his smile and the tiny wrinkles around his eyes. She might have to add a few more to the list.

"I doubt that. I saw you in action today, remember? There aren't too many people around that would stand up to Dan Johnson, and you didn't back down an inch." He chuckled and ribbed her again. "You didn't even back down from me."

"I apologized for that."

"Hey, I'm not criticizing you. I think it's awesome. In fact, it'll probably make you a good teacher, being able to control situations. You might even be a good cop."

"Hardly. I should have listened to you the other night. I could have made a bad situation a lot worse with that mom and baby."

"True. But your instincts were right to protect the baby."

"What happened to him anyway?"

Alex didn't answer at first. His smile faded, and he glanced down at the sidewalk for a while.

"I'm not sure what'll happen to the kid. The mom went to jail for DUI and resisting. Probably had some warrants on her too. They usually do."

She waited for his smile to return, for the joke she was sure would follow. But his face stayed sober as he looked around the crowded street. She wanted to ask what he was thinking about, but something about his eyes, almost a painful longing in them, told her to keep silent.

They crossed the small intersection, and Lily tried not to keep looking at him, knowing it would make her look desperate. So she concentrated on the sun dress in the window as she passed. Suddenly, Alex grabbed her wrist and yanked her forward into his chest.

"Watch it," he said. He looked over her head and nodded at someone she couldn't see. "Excuse us."

She glanced behind her and caught the raised eyebrows and harrumph of a lady walking past them with her Chihuahua poking his head out of her purse. Lily's heart raced, and she tried to offer an apology. She turned back to Alex, his hand still gripping her wrist as they stood in the middle of the sidewalk. His eyes held hers, sending waves of adrenaline through her. Was he about to kiss her? Her mouth went dry with fear. This was wrong.

"Th-Thank you," she managed to breathe.

"Sure."

He didn't move, and she was sure her stomach was going to leap right out of her body. Hadn't she sworn he wouldn't have this effect on her? He finally released her arm, and they finished their stroll in silence.

She wasn't sure how it had happened, but something had changed during their walk—something wonderful and confusing. Some part of her wanted to scream "Who cares!" at the top of her lungs, to grab onto the butterflies in her stomach and see where they might take her. But it was crazy to think that way, even if he did feel the same. There were only three days of vacation left—just enough time to make a fool out of herself.

When they reached the ice cream parlor, they found Steve talking with Kara and Rachel. Lily deflected knowing grins from the girls, and focused instead on a sailboat outlined in twinkling lights sailing past the pier. She hadn't even realized the sun had gone down. She took a deep breath to settle her nerves, careful to keep her eyes away from Alex.

Once her butterflies finally settled, she glanced back over at him. He smiled and winked, sending her stomach flipping again. Just then, a dispatcher's voice crackled over their radios, and both Alex and Steve angled their ears toward their shoulders as they listened. Steve glanced up the street toward the main intersection.

"We gotta run," he said.

He went to work on the chain around his bike, and Alex looked over at Lily.

"Sorry," Alex said. "We need to hurry. There's a fight up the street." He knelt down by Steve and unlocked his bike. "Are you sticking around for a while?" She nodded her head as he straddled the bike. "Good. I'll catch up with you later."

"You know, Lauren, if I didn't know any better I might think you locked your keys in your car on purpose."

Alex shoved the slim jim down the driver's side window and popped the lock of the silver Honda. He slid it out and tossed it over the car to Steve, who walked over to the patrol car waiting down the block.

"I'm sure I don't know what you mean." Lauren's mouth tipped in a sly grin, and she cut her eyes at him.

She pulled open the door and leaned across the seat to reach for the keys in the ignition. The breeze caught her skirt and lifted it gently, revealing a set of familiar tan legs. He grinned to himself then looked away. Across the street, a group of teenage boys lounged over the hood of an old Crown Vic in the parking lot of the gas station. The bass shuddered, but he couldn't hear any of the music.

Lauren stood and slid her keys into her purse, smiling as she batted her lashes. He let his eyes take her in for a moment, knowing that was what she wanted. It was what she always wanted. Her silk white shirt dipped low on her chest, leaving little to his imagination—not that he needed it.

He still remembered the first time he'd seen her at the gym, showing more skin than skill. She'd never made any secret about her intentions toward him. That was exactly why it seemed strange she would pull a stunt to get his attention.

He'd seen her get out of the car earlier from across the street. She'd stopped about halfway across the parking lot, glanced around, and then returned to her car. She'd leaned into the car and put the keys back in the ignition. He'd wondered at the time what she was up to, but now it made sense. Pathetic. The last thing he needed was another woman trying to manipulate him.

"Well, I hope you have a wonderful evening," he said.

Her smile dropped to a pout. "So can I expect to ever hear from you again? I thought we had a good time together."

"We did. And of course you'll hear from me. Any time you want to chat just give me a call." He grinned at her and leaned closer. "You really don't have to lock your keys in the car if you want to talk. Just come by and say hi."

Her face flushed pink. "How desperate do you think I am?"

She slammed her car door and stomped away, but the sharp flower smell of her perfume lingered. He hadn't meant to tick her off. Maybe he should apologize. He considered it for only a moment. It could wait till next time.

"Still charming the ladies I see," Steve said. Alex hadn't noticed him come up beside him.

"You know me."

"Yes, I do."

Alex checked his watch. Thank God his shift was almost over. He'd had his fill of one mundane call out after another. Even the fight had proven to be nothing, just some old dude who'd had too much to drink stumbling around and yelling at people. He needed a good foot chase—a fleeing drug dealer he could tackle.

"Speaking of ladies," Steve said, bringing him back to the present. Steve nodded toward something down the street, and Alex followed his gaze. Lily, Kara, and Rachel crossed the street at the next intersection and continued toward the pier.

"Mmm hmm." Alex concentrated on the notepad in his hand, jotting down Lauren's information for the report he'd have to fill out later.

"What's up with that, anyway?"

"What do you mean?"

"You know what I mean." Steve elbowed him. "How was your little walk earlier?"

"Nice." Alex finished the note and pushed his pad into his back pocket. "She's nice."

"Nice, huh?" Steve raised an eyebrow. "Did you tell her anything?"

"No, I just walked up here to the deli, got a sandwich, and walked back in complete silence."

Steve shook his head. "You know what I mean."

"I've known her for what, five seconds? And why do you care what I've told her?"

Steve shrugged. "She just seems like a nice girl. All three of them are actually. I just think you should be careful."

"You've been hanging around Chloe too much." Alex headed across the street toward the teenage boys. "Come on, let's go tell these guys to keep it down." It wasn't much, but maybe it would change the subject.

By the time Lily, Kara, and Rachel stepped off the pier, most of the shops had closed down, and the only signs of life came from the bars and restaurants scattered along the main drag. Country music floated over the nearly deserted parking lot between the pier and Brogen's Bar, and off to her right, Lily noticed Alex and Steve hanging their bikes on the rack of a patrol car.

Her pulse jumped. Going unnoticed was a long shot, but maybe it would be best. Maybe her first impression of Alex had been off, but she wasn't ready to handle her growing attraction to him either.

But the guys had already seen them and waved, and Kara and Rachel headed toward them. Lily paused, but followed close behind. It couldn't hurt just to say hello.

As they approached, Alex caught her eye and grinned, sending a smile over her own face she couldn't control. His hair was damp with sweat, and a few curls dropped across his forehead. His black t-shirt clung to his chest, like he'd just gone for a dip in the ocean. She wondered what he looked like without the shirt.

"Hi," she breathed, her cheeks warming.

"Hey! And what have you lovely ladies been up to this evening?" he asked.

Rachel smiled and tossed her hair over her shoulder. "Just walking around."

"Defending yourselves from all the guys, no doubt," he said. "Find any you liked?"

"Maybe a couple that were worthy of our attention." Rachel's lips curled into a seductive smirk.

Alex and Steve glanced at each other and grinned.

"Whew, girl!" Steve said. "You are too young!"

Lily rolled her eyes as Rachel grinned. She was almost too much to take. But both Steve and Alex seemed to take it in good humor, and as they began to move into familiar conversation, she had to admit her enjoyment of this little group they were forming.

Kara and Rachel spoke easily with the guys, despite their nearly ten-year age difference. And Lily, who'd been annoyed and distrustful of Alex at first, now found his stories amusing. But after only a few minutes of conversation, she realized it was time to go. She turned toward Kara and tapped her watch.

"We're going to have to get going soon."

The girls' smiles dropped into identical pouts, but Lily raised a hand to stop them before they could protest.

"Sorry guys. You know the rules."

Alex shook with laughter, but stopped when Lily glared at him.

"What's so funny?" she asked.

"I've just never met someone so hell-bent on sticking to the rules all the time. Don't you ever just relax?"

"Don't start with me again."

"I'm not starting anything. You do what you need to do. I just can't figure you out, that's all."

"Lily," Kara said. "A few minutes isn't going to hurt anything. Dad won't care."

"That's not the point," she said. She was beginning to grow tired of being the babysitter for these two.

"Hey, look," Alex said, tossing his water bottle into the trash. "We get off at midnight. Why don't I give y'all a ride back to your place?"

"Oh! That would be great!" Kara squealed.

"Can you do that?" Lily asked.

"Sure, it's not a problem." He waved a hand to dismiss her concern. "I'll just radio my supervisor and tell him I'm escorting some drunk girls back to their residence."

"What?" Lily said.

"Kidding! Lighten up!"

She wasn't sure the ride home was a great idea, but Rachel and Kara were already begging with their best puppy-dog eyes. So she relented, and they walked with Alex and Steve to the patrol car parked near the pier. After a few minutes, the supervisor radioed them to call it a night. Alex informed him of his escort for the girls, and then they piled into the cruiser and waved goodbye to Steve.

The ride should have taken less than two minutes, but Rachel and Kara begged for more, so he drove past their house a couple of miles. He glanced around, and then briefly turned on the blue lights, much to the delight of Rachel and Kara, who were bombarding him with questions about the patrol car. If not for the Plexiglas separating them, Lily might have reached into the backseat to slap them into silence.

When they finally pulled up to the house, Rachel and Kara thanked him for the ride and jumped out of the car as if they suddenly realized it was on fire. They practically sprinted to the front door, giggling the entire way.

"Well, that was odd," Lily commented.

"Hmm." He nodded in agreement.

Unsure of what to do next, she reached for the door handle. "Thanks for the lift."

He covered her hand with his, stilling her momentum toward the door.

"Do you have to run off so soon?" he asked.

Her skin tingled beneath his touch. She pulled her hand away from the door as her stomach made the flutter that was becoming too common around him.

"I guess not."

He glanced around, and she followed his gaze. The street was empty except for a cat meandering along the edge of the light from a street lamp.

"You want to get out of the car?" he asked. "It's a beautiful night."

"Sure."

He climbed out and circled around to Lily's side just as she closed her door. She leaned against the side, and he stopped in front of her. He was so close she couldn't think of anything but the heat coming off him, so she pushed herself up onto the hood hoping a little more space would settle her nerves.

"Is this your first trip to Saint Simons?" he asked.

"Yeah." She looked up at the live oaks stretching their fingers out toward each other forming a canopy over the small street. "It's so beautiful and peaceful here. I'd love to stay longer."

"Well, it's getting over-crowded, but it's still a great place. I used to live in a house down the coast a bit when I was a kid."

"Really? I would've loved growing up on an island."

"Nah, it's not that great. You think you'd spend all your free time on the beach, but you'd just go about your business and forget it was even there."

"I guess," she sighed. "We all do that in our own way. We take the most beautiful things we have for granted when they're always around."

"It'd be hard to take you for granted."

He winked, and her face warmed. How could she let such an obvious line make her feel good? She must be getting desperate.

"Do you have any big plans with your family for tomorrow?" he asked.

She tried to think for a moment, but her mind was a blank. What was tomorrow? Then suddenly it came to her.

"Oh my goodness! Tomorrow is the Fourth!"

"Yeah, it's a pretty big deal around here. The fireworks off the pier are usually huge."

"That's right. I heard about that."

Alex grinned and shifted his weight like he was nervous. She knew he was waiting for an answer, but maybe she could make him squirm for a change.

"So?" he asked, leaning forward.

"What?"

He threw his head back and laughed. "You're not going to make this easy on me, are you?"

"I really don't know what you're talking about." She enjoyed watching him fumble. It was a stark contrast to the arrogant teasing she'd endured the previous nights.

He stepped closer, his scent filling her head—a combination of sweet and salt.

"Alright then," he said, leaning even closer and lowering his voice. "I'll spell it out for you. I have to be over here tomorrow by two, and I know things will be a bit crazy, but..."

He trailed off, and she nearly laughed at the sight of the great Alex Walker flustered. It was actually a relief to know he was as normal as she was. She sighed and glanced away.

"But what?"

"*But*...it would be nice to see you again, maybe talk with you some more."

"Really? I kind of got the feeling you didn't like me too much."

"Well, you were a pain in the neck at first, but things seem to have taken a turn for the better."

"*I* was a pain in the neck?" She gave him a playful shove. "You've got to be kidding. You definitely took the first place ribbon on that one."

"Oh really? Then what are you doing with me now?"

She studied his face, searching for answers to her own questions. Maybe she was just setting herself up to feel stupid.

"I don't know." It wasn't much of an answer, but at least it was honest.

He reached toward her face and pushed a blowing strand of hair behind her ear. It tickled her skin and sent a shiver of goose bumps down her arm. His hand grazed her cheek.

"Do you have any idea how beautiful you are?"

Heat raced up her neck and face. As she fought to keep her body steady, an uncontrollable grin spread across her face. She looked from his lips to his eyes and back to his lips again. She wondered what they would taste like.

As he inched closer, his eyes never leaving hers, panic surged through her and pricked her conscience once more, but she pushed it back. What harm was in a little kiss?

Just as his lips were about to touch hers, his breath tickled her skin and his finger traced the outline of her jaw, sending a wonderful chill down her neck and arms. She closed her eyes and, when his lips finally met hers, she soaked up every sensation surging through her.

Her heart thundered against her chest as he pressed his lips deep into hers, his fingers finding the nape of her neck. Everything else in the world faded, and she sank completely into the kiss, letting the waves of heat rush through her.

When he finally pulled away, he grinned down at her.

"So will I see you tomorrow?"

"Definitely."

Chapter Six

St. Simons Island, Georgia

"So once we finally get her wrestled to the ground and basically hog-tied, we realize that during all this, her miniskirt has worked its way up around her waist, and she isn't wearing anything underneath."

"No!" Lily gasped. "Oh my word. How embarrassing!"

"Yeah it was." Alex laughed and shook his head. "I just wonder how many people drove by and saw two police officers wrestling around with a half-naked woman."

They laughed together for a minute before a loud blast in the sky startled her. She stepped out from under the pavilion where she and Alex had finally found a few minutes alone and saw the fading blue and red sparks falling from the sky. She'd been looking forward to the fireworks all day, but now she was disappointed. It seemed like everyone and everything had conspired to keep her from spending any length of time with Alex all day. Every time they'd seen each other they'd barely gotten out introductions before he was called away.

"Come on." He took her hand and guided her to a low-hanging limb of a large tree near the park. "Think you can manage?"

She smiled at the two kids already sitting on the limb.

"I think so."

Another blast lit up the sky over the pier, and they both turned to watch the cascading lights.

"I have to get behind the police line now, but I'll find you when it's over, okay?" He tugged a strand of her hair and winked.

She nodded then watched him disappear among the crowd of people and lawn chairs lining the walkway leading to the pier. Beside the kids, she sat mesmerized for the next thirty minutes, occasionally searching for Alex's face among the police officers around the edge of the crowd. Toward the end, she finally spotted him several yards from the pier, talking and laughing with Steve, and even from the distance his smile made her grin.

But it faded when she saw him turn to a slender blonde woman approaching him from the crowd who had apparently called his name. He hugged her with a familiarity that sent a lead ball into her stomach. Maybe she was overreacting. Maybe it was just his sister. But the batting eyelashes and flirting smile suggested otherwise. Then the woman reached out and touched his arm as she laughed, sending a fire of embarrassment through Lily's cheeks.

What was wrong with her? Why would it matter who he flirted with? So he kissed her last night. Big deal. What right did she have to be jealous? But the sight of him smiling that way at another woman, no matter how insignificant it should be, made her want to crawl back to the beach house. How could she be so naïve as to think someone like Alex would think she was special? He could have any girl he wanted.

He smiled and talked with the woman a little longer before she hugged him again and walked away. His eyes scanned the crowd around Lily, but she slid off the limb and made her way toward the nearest bathroom.

Inside, she locked herself in a stall and leaned against the door. What was she thinking? Hadn't she been hurt enough lately? This was exactly why she'd wanted to avoid Alex to begin with. What was obviously meaningless to him meant more to her than it should, and that was a perfect recipe for heartache. She should have listened to her conscience and walked away last night when she had the chance. But she wouldn't make that mistake again.

Lily stepped out of the bathroom once she was sure the fireworks were over and there had been plenty of time for the crowd to disperse. Her throat was raw from fighting back tears, so she headed across the parking lot to the ice cream parlor for a drink.

As she rounded the last row of cars, she spotted police bikes leaned against a bench a few yards away. She turned to go, but just as she did, Alex and Steve came out of the shop with drinks in hand. Alex's face lit up when he saw her.

"Hey, where'd you go? I looked all over for you."

"Sorry." She took a step back and tried to avoid making eye contact. "I uh, had to go to the bathroom, and then I started looking for Kara and Rachel."

He put his arm over her shoulder, and her pulse quickened. He guided her toward the nearby bench.

"I have a few minutes. You want to sit down?"

She slid out from under his arm and put some distance between them.

"I can't right now. I have to meet Rachel and Kara in front of the stage for the concert."

"I thought you were just looking for them."

"I was...I am."

He wrinkled his brow. "Is something wrong?"

She looked at him then, and the genuine concern in his eyes almost made her forget. Almost.

"No, I just told them I'd meet them soon, and they weren't there. I guess I just got worried."

"Let me help you find them."

The warmth in his expression seemed so real, her resolve weakened. Maybe she'd misread the whole thing, and besides, it was silly to get so worked up over a girl that had simply smiled at him and given him a hug. The more she thought about it, the more stupid she felt for letting it bother her.

He reached for her hand, and the touch of his skin warmed her whole body. She pulled herself back together and fell into step beside him as they crossed the parking lot toward the stage, stealing glances at him as they walked.

When they reached the park where a makeshift stage had been set up overlooking the beach, Kara and Rachel waved from the opposite side.

He smiled at her. "See, there they are. Safe and sound."

"Thanks."

"Sure nothing's bothering you?"

She returned the smile, finally feeling normal again. Well, at least as normal as she'd ever felt around Alex.

"Dispatch to one ninety-six." His radio crackled, and he tilted his head toward his shoulder.

"One ninety-six, go ahead."

The dispatcher spouted off numbers and directions she couldn't comprehend, something she'd grown used to as the day had worn on.

Alex let out a long sigh. "Ten four." He looked down at her and took her hand. "I'm so sorry to do this to you again."

"You know, I'm beginning to think you might be trying to avoid me."

"Absolutely not." He stepped closer and leaned toward her ear, his breath sending goose bumps down her arm. "Do you have any idea how incredible you look right now? Or how badly I've wanted to kiss you all day?"

She dropped her eyes from his, and a blush crept up her neck and face. She hated the thrill that spread through her. How could she let herself enjoy this so much knowing it would end? She had to get a grip.

"Enjoy your concert, okay?" He kissed the top of her head. "I'll find you when it's over."

As soon as the concert ended, Lily swept her gaze over the park. Alex hadn't made it back yet. He must have gotten another call. Figured.

"I guess we should start walking back now," she said.

Kara and Rachel nodded as they slumped in their chairs. They pulled themselves up and started across the park to take the back way around the lighthouse. As they neared the swimming pool, Lily heard a sharp whistle, and she turned just as Alex called her name from the other side of the stage. She waved to him and told Rachel and Kara to go ahead. Then she hurried through the dwindling crowd trying not to look too eager.

When she reached the other side of the park where she'd seen Alex, he was nowhere in sight, so she looked in every direction for him. She had seen him. She was sure of that. He had called her name. But after a few moments of turning in circles, she thought she must have imagined it. Or maybe he had been called away again. That would be the perfect ending to a perfect day.

She headed toward the park feeling foolish and disappointed. Wrapped up in her thoughts as she passed a store, she screamed when a hand reached out and pulled her into the dark alley separating the store from the bar next door. Panic surged through her as a thick hand covered her mouth.

"Sheesh!" Alex said. "Lily, it's me."

Her heart beat wildly against her chest, and when he removed his hand, an angry heat raced through her. She shoved him back, but the space between the walls wasn't much bigger than the two of them, and he merely reached a hand back to steady his balance.

"Alex! You scared the crap out of me!"

"Sorry. I wasn't trying to." His grin said otherwise.

"Who does that to someone unless you're trying to scare them?"

"I'm sorry-"

She slapped away his effort to take her hand. "I cannot believe you just did that!"

She took a deep breath to settle her nerves. He just kept grinning at her like he was amused.

"I just wanted to get you alone for a few minutes, that's all. Calm down."

"Well, I don't see why it was necessary to scare me half to death." She huffed and pushed her hair away from her face. "You could have just asked."

"Now, what would be the fun in that?"

His eyes gleamed with mischief and she couldn't help a small grin. "Well, now that you have me here, what are you going to do with me?"

"Mmm. A little of this." He touched his lips to hers and then lifted them again. "Maybe a little of that." Then he pressed them harder, pushing her mouth open.

Her stomach dropped as he pulled her waist into his. Her hands wandered over his chest, feeling his muscles tighten beneath them. He pushed back her hair and slid his lips to her neck, his breath tickling her skin.

" *You* are going to be trouble," he mumbled into her ear.

He touched his forehead to hers and kissed her once more before pulling back to look at her.

"Well, not for long." She fumbled with her necklace. "We're leaving the day after tomorrow."

"That's exactly what I'm talking about. I can't find the girl of my dreams and then have her leave me a few days later. That's just no good."

Her face grew warm as she looked up at him, ashamed by the hope and desire welling up inside of her.

"I'm hardly the girl of your dreams. Besides, I'm sure there are plenty of girls ready and willing to fulfill your dreams who live right here." She'd already seen evidence of that.

"Yeah, can't argue there." She hit his arm, and he pretended to be hurt. "Hey, I can't help it if women find me irresistible!"

"Oh really?"

He grinned and leaned closer. "I got you, didn't I?"

"Yeah. You're *going* to get it if you keep talking like that."

"Man, I love it when you're feisty."

She shoved him away, but he grabbed her arms and used their momentum to turn her around and press her against the opposite wall. He kissed her again and again, and she felt like she was cracking open.

She was so lost in the moment, she was startled when she opened her eyes and noticed a woman at the end of the alley staring at them. The woman's mouth drew up into a tight line, and she disappeared around the corner.

"Could you get in trouble?"

"What, for making out in the alley while I'm on duty? Yes, but it might be worth it."

He sighed and ran a finger along her neck, and his mood suddenly sobered. He wrinkled his brow and lifted the gold charm.

"Do you wear this all the time?" With one hand beside her head for support, he leaned down and scrunched his face as he tried to read the inscription on the back.

"What does it say?" he asked.

She instinctively grabbed the charm, her mind racing around the explanation, but unable to quite hold onto it.

"Oh, this?" She tried to sound nonchalant. "It was just a gift."

"Just a gift, huh?" He eyed her carefully. "You play with it when you get nervous."

She stared at him, still unable to think of anything to say. She hadn't even thought of Jackson today, and that realization was both strange and wonderful.

"It's got to be special," Alex continued. "You've worn it every day, and from the looks of it I'd guess you've been wearing it for a long time."

"I guess," she shrugged.

He furrowed his brow. "Is this another area of your life that's none of my business?"

"It was just a gift." Why was this so hard?

"From who?"

"My best friend." It was the only true thing that came to her mind that seemed uncomplicated.

"Oh."

He seemed satisfied for a moment, but then he raised an eyebrow, and she knew she'd have to do better than that.

"Your best friend, huh? What, for a birthday or something?"

She took a deep breath and resigned herself to answer.

"It was when we were kids. I'd moved into the neighborhood a few months earlier, and I was always so shy." She rubbed the charm between her fingers. "I hadn't made any friends, except for Jackson, who lived a couple houses down. He was a year older, but he was the only kid around who was really nice to me. Anyway, it was getting close to Christmas, and all the classes had parties the last day of school. My class had drawn names for presents, but somehow I didn't have one."

"Wow," Alex said. "How old were you?"

"Nine."

"That's pretty sad."

"Yeah, I cried all the way home. But when I got there, Jackson was waiting for me like usual because we always rode our bikes down to the creek. But I was so upset, I didn't want to go."

She smiled to herself as she remembered the uncomfortable way Jackson had looked at her that day, especially when she'd threatened to run away again.

"So he ran back home and wrapped up one of his mother's necklaces and brought it over to me and wished me Merry Christmas."

"Well, that was nice of him."

She laughed, remembering the awkward smile on Jackson's face that day.

"All he wanted was for me to stop crying so I'd go fishing with him. But it cheered me up."

"He must be a good friend if you're still wearing the necklace."

"I hope so."

"More than a friend?"

"Does it really matter?"

He shrugged. "Just curious." He stepped back, studying her closely. "Come on, spill it. I know you must have at least dated the guy."

Her nerves tangled inside of her. She hadn't thought about how she might explain her feelings about Jackson, and she wondered why it even mattered. It's not like she and Alex were dating. Then the crackle of the radio granted her a short reprieve. He tilted his head and listened as the dispatcher gave him instructions. Then he looked back at Lily.

"I gotta run, but I want to hear more about this best friend. Can I see you again tomorrow?"

"Sure."

"I'm off duty, but I'm working security outside of Brogen's tomorrow night. Will you come by and see me?"

"Of course."

He brushed his lips with hers again and started out of the alley. Then he turned back as if he'd remembered something.

"Oh yeah. Will you bring your address and phone number tomorrow night?"

"You don't have to do that." She fiddled with her fingers and tried to avoid looking directly into his eyes.

"Do what?"

"Get my phone number and pretend like you're going to call me."

"What? Why would I do that?"

"I don't know. You tell me."

He walked back to her and took her hands. "Hey, I know we've only known each other a few days, but I've really enjoyed it. I just want to get to know you better and to be able to stay in touch with you, okay?"

She dropped her eyes, afraid her hope would be written all over her face.

"Come on, Lily. I'm not really the bad guy you seem to think I am."

"I don't think you're a bad guy. I just don't want you to feel obligated to do something you don't want to do."

He smiled and leaned closer, taking her chin in his fingers. "I never do anything I don't want to do, I promise." He kissed her again and turned to go. "Bring it tomorrow night, okay?"

She stood in the shadows for a few minutes after he left, her body not yet fully recovered from the onslaught of adrenaline.

The whole encounter had left her skin throbbing in time with her heart. She took a deep breath and steadied her nerves; then she slipped out of the alley.

As she walked along the dark streets of the island, she thought back on their conversation, wondering if he would really stay in touch. What if he wanted more? It seemed so silly to get her hopes up. They lived over six hours apart, and she would be so busy with school and volleyball, how would they ever see each other? It would be impossible. She was just setting herself up for more heartache.

She rubbed the necklace once more, repeating the inscription on the back from *First Philippians.*

"I thank my God every time I remember you."

It hadn't been there the day Jackson first gave it to her—only the praying hands on the front. But as a gift for her graduation, he'd had the inscription placed on the back with a promise between them to always pray for each other. And just as she had nearly every night for the past twelve years, she prayed for Jackson, for his safety and his peace of mind, and she wondered if he still kept his promise.

Birmingham, Alabama

"So how was your session with Dr. Kipling the other day?"

Jackson continued chewing his potatoes and concentrated on the yellow and white checkered table cloth, pretending not to notice the attempted nonchalance in his mother's question. Why couldn't they just have a simple meal together without her probing the depths of his misery?

As usual, she'd tried to be subtle for about a minute, and then quickly turned to a more direct approach when she didn't get what she wanted out of him. But tonight he was determined to get through one meal without a discussion of his *progress.*

"It was fine," he said between bites. He could feel her eyes on him, like she was picking over his wounds deciding which one to open.

"Have you read any of the book she recommended?"

"Mm hmm." He refused to look up from his plate, knowing she was staring at him from across the table with those soft brown eyes that still invited him to confess everything. How many times had they sat over this very table in this tiny kitchen talking and laughing into the early hours of the morning? He hated denying her the closeness they'd once shared, but the only way he knew to maintain balance was to push away the good along with the bad.

"Well, how is it?" she asked.

"How's what?"

She sighed and pushed herself up from the table, carrying her plate of half-eaten meatloaf over to the sink. He could hear her frustration in her strokes as she scraped the food into the disposal. She dropped the plate into the sink with a loud clank and turned around.

"You can't keep pushing your feelings down, Jackson. You're going to erupt one day."

He glanced up at her as she leaned back against the sink and crossed her arms over her chest. She was still as slender and graceful as he remembered from his childhood, though the weight she'd lost recently made her seem frail. She frowned at him, and the lines that used to frame her warm smile now accented the deep sorrow in her eyes.

"Mom, do we have to talk about this every time I come over?"

"We don't talk. I talk. You just sit there and give half answers to appease me."

"Why can't we just have dinner? Why can't we talk about work, or what we did today, or the state of the economy? Anything except what Dr. Kipling said, or how I *feel*."

He picked over the remains of his food, his stomach churning. Every time. Every freaking time he came here for dinner, he ended up puking by the time he got back to his place, and it was because she insisted on poking and prodding him to death.

She returned to the chair across from him and laid her hand over his, stroking it with her thumb. Her hand was cool and soft, the same gentle touch that had soothed his scraped knees and twisted ankles, and for a moment it was enough to make his nausea subside.

"I'm just trying to make sense of all this," she said. "We've been through so much lately. I know it must feel like God's abandoned you."

"No." He jerked his eyes up to hers. "Not abandoned. He's beaten me to a pulp. I'm just waiting for the next blow, and I have no idea why he's doing this to me."

She squeezed his hand as her eyes filled with tears.

"Oh Honey, no. He may have allowed some difficult things to happen, for reasons we don't understand, but he's holding us as we go through it. And he's working in you to bring you closer to him."

"I don't feel like I'm being held, Mom. I feel like I'm trying to swim across a river that keeps getting wider with every stroke I take."

He felt the dam he'd spent months shoring up start to give, but the flood of anger and fear behind it threatened to overwhelm him. It hurt too much, and he pulled his hand out from under hers. Picking his plate up, he walked over to the sink and washed it off, focusing on breathing.

"Jackson, please talk to me."

"I can't do this right now." He turned and faced her, hardening himself once again. "We can talk about anything else you want. Just not this."

"Alright then."

"Thank you." He leaned back against the sink and let out a breath of relief.

"So are you dating anyone?"

He could swear she smirked at him like she had won some battle he'd been unaware they were fighting.

"Well, I guess I walked right into that, didn't I?"

She grinned, and for the first time that evening, he shared her smile.

"Well, are you?"

"No, and don't start getting all nosy about anything Matthew's said. He's full of it. And don't think I haven't noticed the little conspiracy going on between you two."

She raised an eyebrow and tapped her fingers on the table.

"What about Lily?"

"And there we have it. The circle of off-limit topics is now complete."

"Oh, Jackson. Don't be sarcastic."

"Sorry. I know I said we could talk about anything, but if you're going to try to talk me into calling her, we can just skip over that and move to the next topic."

"I just don't understand. She's practically been a part-"

"A part of the family for as long as you can remember," he finished, exasperated by the constant reminder of the intricate weaving of Lily's life with his own. "I know. I've been here too."

"Then why? You two were inseparable for so long. Why suddenly cut her out of your life? Especially now."

He looked down at the floor, unable to bear the concern in her eyes.

"Look, Mom. I can't explain it. I just can't be with Lily. The past is over. It was nice, and we might have had a great life together, but it's just not possible anymore."

"Why?"

"Just because." He leaned over and placed his hands on the chair across from her, determined to stop her questions. "Lily is everything about my past that was perfect and good. God has yanked away one thing after another. First Dad, then basketball, then my future. Sooner or later, he's going to take her too. I mean, life isn't forever, you know?"

"Jackson-"

"No! I can't. I can't lose her like you lost Dad."

Tears welled up in her eyes, and she scrunched her eyebrows like she was about to scold him. A sob escaped instead, and she pushed away from the table, bolting from the room.

Jackson dropped his head and swore under his breath. He'd let his frustrations get the best of him again. She was only trying to help him, he knew that. But why couldn't she back off and let him deal with it his own way? He let out a long deep breath and pushed his hands through his hair. He'd have to go apologize.

He walked through the living room and down the hallway toward her bedroom, but he stopped when he heard a sniffle from the room on his left. He stepped into the open doorway and leaned against the frame, sucking in a breath at the sight.

His dad's office was exactly as it had been the day he died, from the papers on his desk still needing signatures, to the newspaper he'd read that morning still open to the sports section. His green UAB basketball jacket—the one Jackson had given him on signing day nearly five years earlier—hung over the back of his desk chair.

His mom sat there poring over a picture album spread out in her lap, wiping tears from her eyes with a tissue. As he watched her and looked around, a tide of frustration and anger rose up in him that propelled him into the room.

"Mom, you have got to stop this."

She startled and looked up at him.

"Stop what?"

"This!" He gestured at the walls. "This shrine you have going in here. Dad's gone! You have to let him go and move on with your life. Stop sitting in here waiting for him to walk through the door."

Even as he heard the words coming out of his mouth, he knew they were meant for himself as well. They both had to face reality.

"I can't." She laid the album across the desk and leaned forward, her voice barely above a whisper. "I can't just pack him away and put him on a shelf."

Jackson walked over and knelt in front of her, grasping her hands.

"You've got to let him go."

"Like you? The way you let go of everything? You think you have this all figured out, don't you? That if you push away everyone and everything, you can push away the pain. Well, I don't want to do that."

"That's not what I'm doing."

"Yes you are! Look at what you've done to Lily."

He stood and turned his back on her, afraid she'd know how right she was if she saw his face.

"I'm not talking about Lily."

"You might as well be. At least I lived my life with your father. I didn't bury my head in the sand to avoid any chance of pain. It may hurt now, but at least I got to spend over twenty five years loving him."

"And was it worth all this?"

She walked around and looked up at him, poking her tiny finger into his chest like a needle.

"Without a single doubt."

"How can you say that after all the pain you've been through these past few months?"

Her face softened, and he saw the tiniest hint of peace in her eyes.

"Look, it's not the memories of the good times with your dad that grieve me. It's all the time I missed with him, the time I wasted chasing after things that didn't matter. It's the silly fights, and the big ones. I wasted a lot of time with him being selfish. That's what haunts me when I can't go to sleep."

He pulled her into him, and she wrapped her arms around his waist, stroking his back like she had when he was little.

"I don't know what you want me to do," he said.

She pulled her head back and looked up at him. "Don't let her go. She's still here. You and Lily already have more memories than most people get in a lifetime. Don't throw it away because you're scared, or you lose her anyway."

He hugged her again, and the tension that had been tying him in knots began to seep out. Maybe she was right. Maybe there was still hope for him and Lily.

It wouldn't be easy. She had every right to be angry with him, and she was the most stubborn person he'd ever known. But in the end, she was his. Always had been. Nothing could change that.

Chapter Seven

Alex knew the moment he stepped through the front door that dinner with Chloe and Steve was a bad idea, but Steve had been so hopeful, and it was hard to turn him down when he simply wanted peace. But Alex knew better.

After polite greetings and small talk, they'd sat down at the cramped kitchen table in Chloe's apartment. It took less than ten minutes for her to deliver a shot across his bow.

"Any takers on the house yet?" she asked.

He chewed slowly, wondering if he should exit now and spare himself the argument. Maybe she was just making conversation, and he was overreacting, but his instincts were rarely wrong.

"Not yet," he answered.

She pushed her thick auburn curls behind her shoulder before taking a bite, and then looked over at him with wide innocent eyes.

"Not even one?"

She dabbed the corner of her mouth with her napkin, folded it precisely, and then laid it beneath the rim of her plate.

"It's been on the market for less than a month," he said.

"Still, maybe it's a sign."

Here we go, he thought. He glanced over at Steve who was engrossed in his plate of food. The poor guy had no idea what he was getting into. Frankly, he wasn't sure what Steve even saw in her.

"Maybe it just means I need to give it time."

"Why rush into this? You could hold onto it for a little longer."

"No, I can't. But that's none of your business."

He shoved another bite into his mouth and wished Chloe would do the same. She arched an eyebrow and lifted her glass to her lips. When she put the drink down, she folded her arms over the table, and he let go of any hope that she would leave him alone.

"I don't understand why you're so set on selling the house," she said. "You're rushing into decisions that you should take time to think through."

"Stop lecturing me about things you know nothing about."

"I know enough to see you're just making things worse. If you just give it some time, let things settle down-"

"Shut up, Chloe."

"Excuse me?" Her jaw dropped.

"You heard me. Now drop it. I'm sick of talking about this." He dropped his fork onto the table and pushed his chair back. "Thanks for dinner."

As he headed into the living room, both Chloe and Steve followed him voicing their objections. It didn't matter. He'd lost his appetite as well as any desire to make peace with Chloe.

"Don't leave like this," Steve said.

Alex grabbed his keys off the coffee table and headed for the door. He threw it open to leave, when Chloe finally spoke.

"She's here, Alex."

He spun around. "What?"

"She's in town. She just wants to talk."

He pointed his finger at her, trying to maintain control.

"Stay out of this, Chloe."

Then he slammed the door behind him.

St. Simons Island

It had been a stupid, stupid idea. As a general rule, Lily hardly ever wore heels because of her height, but also because they were just plain awkward. As athletic as she was, they had always been her downfall, literally. So what had possessed her to allow Kara and Rachel to dress her up in a skirt and heels for a long walk to the village to meet Alex?

As if the shoes weren't bad enough, she had let them convince her to wear one of Kara's skirts—one that she had spent the past five minutes tugging on as she walked the darkened streets. Sure, Kara could have pulled off the look with no problem, but combined with the slinky cami, Lily was sure she looked like a hooker, and had told the girls as much when they had finally let her look in a mirror.

"Oooh, maybe he'll handcuff you," Rachel had purred.

In the end, she'd left the house amid praises and with her confidence intact, but as she rounded the corner down the street from Brogen's, it plummeted to shaky at best. She'd almost twisted her ankle twice getting this far, and the last block suddenly looked like a mile. She thought about turning around, but then she saw Alex at the end of a long line of people corralled between ropes, and he waved to her.

She waved back and picked her way down the crowded sidewalk. She thought the crowd would have thinned out since the holiday was over, but if the music and dancing people at the bar were any indication, the party had just begun.

She stepped out of the crowd and into the parking lot where she got her first full view of Alex in his uniform as he checked identifications, and she nearly gasped out loud. The tan fitted pants and button-down shirt hugged every muscle, and somehow he looked even taller than before.

Dear God, what was she getting into?

As she walked closer, she heard the high-pitched screech of someone who was obviously very angry, and when she reached the end of the line, she caught sight of a young girl yelling at Alex. She was tall and thin, and when she threw her arms into the air to protest, she looked like a skinny tree flailing in a high wind.

"No! I am not leaving until you give me my license. How am I supposed to drive home without a license?"

"That's not my problem," Alex answered. He clenched his jaw, spread his feet and crossed his arms over his chest. "Maybe you should call a cab."

"You can't just take my license! I'll call and file a complaint!"

"Well, if you have a pen and paper handy I'll give you the number and the name of my supervisor if you like."

He smiled politely, which made Lily giggle. The girl practically had steam coming off her skin. The crowd behind her began to mumble, so she finally stalked away, but not before sending one last obscenity over her shoulder. When Lily finally stepped beside him, he shook his head and pressed his eyebrows together.

"I can't stand drunks," he muttered.

"Well, looks like you're having a good time," she said, hoping for a smile.

But he had a strange expression on his face when he finally turned to look at her, and she had no idea if he was even happy to see her. He let his gaze wander over her, and she was suddenly aware of every inch of her exposed skin. He grinned, but something about it was off. It wasn't a pleasant grin. He let out a low whistle. Then he chuckled and shook his head.

"What?" she asked.

"Nothing really, I just wasn't expecting..." He gestured a hand toward her. "...this, I guess."

"What do you mean?"

"Well, considering the fact that you're leaving tomorrow, doesn't it seem a little cruel to show up here looking so..."

He trailed off again, and Lily's cheeks flushed.

"So what?" she asked.

He reached for the next license and passed several people through before turning back to her with the same sarcastic grin.

"I think you know already."

"I have no idea what you're talking about. You're not making any sense."

Now this was the Alex she had met that first night. Obnoxious and cold. He chuckled at her.

"Oh please. You know you look gorgeous. And here I thought you were so conservative. Really, Miss Brennon. I'm shocked."

"I think you've gotten the wrong impression here." And maybe he hadn't been the only one.

He shook his head. "I think I got exactly the one you were shooting for."

There was no missing the edge to his voice, and she wondered if maybe she should just leave. He was obviously in a bad mood. Maybe something had happened. After all, she still barely knew him.

"Are you all right?" she asked.

"Sure. Why do you ask?"

"You seem aggravated. Did I do something wrong here?"

"No, really. I'm fine. I had a bit of a rough day." He sighed and pushed his hand through his hair. "I'm sorry if I was out of line."

She rubbed his arm and felt his muscles tense beneath her touch.

"You want to talk about it?"

"Not really. No big deal."

He checked another license then smiled at her, this time giving her a wink. The aggravation seemed to disappear, and finally she felt her stomach relax.

"So," he continued. "Did you bring your phone number?"

She nodded and reached for the folded paper in her pocket. As she watched him read it, she waited for his reaction to the small note she had written at the bottom of the page.

If you ever come across this note one day and wonder, who the heck is Lily Brennon, please just throw this away.

"What is this supposed to mean?" He gave her a curious glance.

"I just thought, you know, if you don't get around to calling."

He sighed as his shoulders fell, and he looked away. It had been a joke, sort of. She'd expected a laugh, but he seemed more defeated than anything. Then he reached into his back pocket and pulled out his wallet, fishing a business card out of it.

"Here." He pushed it toward her. She looked over the name and contact information as he continued. "You can call me anytime at this number. We have an answering service, so just leave a message and the number where you are or your cell, and I'll call you back as soon as I have a break." He placed her note inside his wallet and returned it to his pocket.

"Alex Walker, patrolman." She read the card and grinned at him. She loved the sound of his name.

"Well, hopefully it will say detective soon." He reached for another license. "I've about had my fill of doing this sh-"

She noted the word on his lips, and that he'd stopped himself before uttering the curse. It struck her as odd and exhilarating at the same time. Maybe she was having a positive effect on him after all.

"So how late do you have to work tonight?" she asked.

"I have to stay here until closing to make sure everyone leaves, so at least two, maybe later."

"Would you want to come by our house after you get off for a few minutes?"

"I don't know if I can. I have to work beach patrol tomorrow morning, so I have to be at the station by eight, and I'm going to be getting home really late as it is."

"Oh, well, you wouldn't have to stay or anything. It would just be nice to say goodbye."

"I'll try," he said as he turned back to another group of people pushing toward him. "But I can't promise anything."

As he continued to screen the customers, Lily fought to pick her stomach up from the ground. How stupid could she be? And what was with his mood swings? Feeling a sudden urge to scurry away, she mumbled something about meeting Rachel and Kara then walked back toward the house.

Lily glanced down at her watch for the tenth time in the past half hour, sighing with disgust at her lack of self-respect. After all her ranting to Kara and Rachel about how she would not be caught dead waiting for Alex, here she sat on the front porch waiting for Alex. At least Kara and Rachel were trying to distract her with card games—unsuccessfully, of course—but at least they were trying.

"Do you want to keep playing?" Kara asked. The sympathy in her face only made Lily feel more foolish.

"It's well after two," Lily said. "I don't think he's coming. Let's just go to bed."

She helped collect all the cards and told the girls goodnight as they closed the front door. She looked down the road for another moment. A gentle breeze wafted through the screen surrounding the porch, and around the corner she could hear the waves rolling in the distance.

He wasn't coming. But maybe that was best. When she was thinking clearly, she knew her attraction to him was crazy. She had enjoyed spending time with him and how he'd made her skin tingle with excitement, but it had to end sometime. Besides, this experience had helped her move forward, to forget all the pain of the past few months, and for that she was grateful.

She walked over to the porch window and climbed through to her bed beneath the frame. Then she took one last glance toward the street. Alex would not be coming by to see her, but she knew she'd sleep well. And whether or not he ever called her, she wouldn't regret allowing herself to feel alive again. She smiled and closed her eyes, the sounds of the ocean singing her to sleep.

Then a short whistle startled her awake. At least, she thought she heard a whistle. Had she even fallen asleep yet? She glanced down at her watch. Almost three. Again the same whistle came from the front of the house, and this time there was no mistaking it. She sat up and leaned out the window for a better view.

A light flashed across the yard, and when she looked closer, she could see the moonlight reflecting off a motorcycle parked on the side of the road. As her eyes adjusted to the dark, she could make out Alex's figure standing beside it, and her heart fluttered awake.

She climbed out of the window onto the front porch and tiptoed out of the screen door. The dew was already forming a cool layer over the grass, but she barely noticed the dampness on her bare feet. Before she'd gotten all the way down the driveway, Alex closed the distance between them and wrapped his arms around her, lifting her off the ground. Then before she could speak, he closed his mouth over hers, warming her all over.

"Hi," he breathed.

He pushed the hair back from her face then kissed her again. She grinned and pushed his shoulder.

"You're late. I'd already given up on you."

"I'm really sorry. I had to take the patrol car all the way back to the mainland and get my bike."

"Well, I guess I can forgive you this time. You're just lucky you made it before I was dead asleep."

He stepped back and gave her a once-over. "Yes, I am."

She laughed and shook her head. "How long do you have?"

"As long as you want."

"How about a walk on the beach?"

He glanced around at the deserted street. "Sure. Let me go change out of my uniform. I'll be right back."

She stood in the driveway as he walked over to his bike and grabbed a small bag off the back. She inhaled a long slow breath and pushed it out, trying to steady her racing heart. He took off his shirt, and she couldn't help admiring the lines of his shoulders and chest as his muscles flexed. Then he unbuttoned his pants, and she whipped her head around just before he pushed them down. She covered her mouth and tried not to laugh. Her butterflies and shock mingled together. Was he really stripping down in the middle of the street? She shook her head and laughed to herself. Nothing about Alex Walker should surprise her at this point.

In the quiet of the early morning, she thought about how different the week had turned out from what she had expected. She'd turned into the swooning girl she'd sworn she would avoid at all cost, but maybe it was worth it just to feel the blood racing through her again.

When she heard his footsteps coming toward her, she turned back around as he reached for her hand. He had put on a pair of black jeans, but had left his shirt off, and she couldn't help a nervous laugh.

"Well, don't I feel completely over-dressed." She gestured to her flannel pajama pants and well-worn Bama tank top.

"I don't know what you're talking about. You look perfectly trashy."

They crossed the yard then headed down the wooden staircase and across a bridge leading to the beach. As they stepped out onto the hard-packed sand, the wind whipped through her hair, dislodging a good bit of it from her ponytail. She reached up and tried to adjust it, realizing she must look like a total mess. But Alex didn't seem to notice, and they walked quietly toward the east for several minutes before either of them spoke.

"Hey," she began. "Thanks for coming to say goodbye to me. It really means a lot. I know you have to go back to work in a few hours. You're going to be exhausted!"

"Yeah, but it'll definitely be worth it. Besides, I'm not here to say goodbye."

She turned her head in confusion, and they stopped walking. He traced the outline of her jaw before he gave her lips a gentle kiss.

"What do you mean?" she asked.

"I came to spend time with you. And maybe to convince you that I'm not as evil as you think I am."

"Well, you do give off a strong bad-boy kind of aura, but *evil* is taking things a bit too far."

He grinned and slid his hand behind her neck. "God, you are so gorgeous. You must have to beat the guys away with a stick."

"Not really. I've always been so involved in sports and keeping my grades up that I haven't been very available. Besides, I dated Jackson for a long time."

"Ah." He stepped back a little. "The infamous Jackson. So what's his story?"

"Does it really matter?" She picked up a shattered seashell and tossed it back into the water.

"You know, it probably wouldn't matter if it didn't seem like such a difficult subject for you. It makes me curious, that's all."

"Why? Are you jealous?"

"Me?" He laughed. "Jealous? Never. I just love a good investigation."

"So now I'm under investigation. Shouldn't you be reading me my rights?"

"Only if I arrest you. You're still free to go at this point."

She smiled and picked up another shell fragment, turning it over in her hands.

"Well, the short version is that Jackson and I were best friends when we were kids. We started dating at the end of my junior year in high school, and we stopped dating this past spring."

"What happened?"

She let out a deep breath and tossed the shell. "His dad died last fall while they were playing basketball in the driveway. Just had a massive heart attack right there in front of him."

"Wow," Alex mumbled.

"Jackson did everything he could, but by the time the paramedics got there he was already gone." She could still see Jackson's ashen face as she'd rounded the corner in the hospital. "He blamed himself."

Alex nodded and shoved his hands in his pockets. His gaze drifted out toward the ocean.

"Must have been tough."

"It gets worse. He played basketball for UAB, another college in Birmingham, and he was even getting some attention from scouts for the NBA's developmental league. But a month after his dad died, he blew out his knee in a game."

"Ouch."

"All the scouts disappeared, along with his scholarship to finish his degree."

"Man. The guy couldn't buy a break. I almost feel bad for him."

"He tried to stay positive at first, but one blow after another just beat him down. He just couldn't recover. And neither did we."

"Seems like it still bothers you," he said.

"I guess I'm still just figuring things out. I'm not clinging to some desperate hope that we'll work things out, but it still feels strange. There are days when something happens, good or bad, and I get half-way through dialing his number before I remember." She sighed and tried another smile. "I just want to quit having moments like that. I'm ready to start enjoying myself again."

She reached out and ran her hand up and down his arm.

"Are you enjoying yourself now?" he asked.

"Definitely."

He leaned down and kissed her, pulling her tight against him. The warmth of his skin soothed the nerves that had sprung to life at the mention of Jackson. Alex turned her under his arm, and they continued walking down the beach.

"Why do you still wear his necklace?"

She shrugged and grasped the charm in her fingers. "I know it may not make sense, but the necklace is a promise we made to always pray for each other, and taking it off just doesn't feel right yet. He still needs my prayers." She looked up at him, unable to read his expression. "It's all very confusing."

"Well, I'm sure losing his dad and everything was tough, but he's a moron if he let you go. You don't just abandon the people you care about when something bad happens. You stick it out."

They continued down the beach a little farther before turning back around. An uncomfortable silence had joined them, and Lily wished she hadn't said so much about Jackson. But at least she didn't have to hide anything now. Besides, she would be returning to reality soon. She doubted she'd ever see Alex again.

"So when can I see you again?" he asked, as if he could read her mind.

She shrugged and tried to ignore the flutter in her chest.

"I don't know. I have a few camps to finish up this summer, and then pre-season will start at the beginning of August. Once the season gets going, I'll have tournaments and games almost every weekend, practice every day, not to mention studying."

"Whoa," he said. "So I guess that's a not-any-time-soon."

"Sorry."

"Don't be. It must be great to get to do all those things. I wish I'd gone to college instead of joining the Marines right out of high school."

"Why did you?"

"I thought about trying to play football somewhere, but the thought of sitting through more school just made me crazy. I wanted to get out and do something, you know? See the world."

She reached up for his hand that rested on her shoulder and leaned into him.

"Well I guess that's one way to do it. Military life seems like it would be tough though."

"Nah, I liked the travel. Loved being on my own, having my own money."

"So why did you get out?"

"I didn't want to spend my life being a grub. I realized that without a degree, I'd always be that guy being bossed around. So I started taking classes. I knew I didn't want to be a Marine forever, so I checked out the criminal justice classes and really liked them."

She stopped walking and faced him. "Wait, so you're going to college right now?"

"I should have an Associate's degree by next spring. Hopefully a Bachelor's a couple of years after that." He grinned and arched an eyebrow. "Don't act so shocked. I may not be a genius, but I do all right for myself."

"No, of course. I just didn't realize you were in school." She grinned up at him. "Well, well. There's more to you than meets the eye. Of course, what meets the eye is pretty good too."

She couldn't believe she'd said that out loud. He gave her a curious grin before pulling her into a deep kiss, loosening her hair from its ponytail and letting it fall into his hands.

She slid her hands up his chest, the heat of his skin a stark contrast to the cool breeze. He slipped his hands down her waist and under her shirt, searching for more.

"Wait." She pulled away and grabbed his hands.

"Is something wrong?"

"I just, um. It's just getting a little intense."

He stepped forward and placed his hands casually around her back.

"And this is a bad thing?"

His smile reached out to her, tempted her resolve, but she looked away and took a deep breath.

"Let's just say that I'm not *overly* experienced in this area, and I prefer to take things slow."

He leaned in and nuzzled her nose. "I can definitely do slow, if that's what you want."

His voice was like silk over her skin, and when he kissed her again her body almost declared mutiny. But once again, she stepped away from him.

"Alex, wait. You're not hearing me."

He sighed and ran his hand through his hair. "Okay, I'm listening. What do you need to tell me?"

"I just want to take things slow, physically I mean. I'm not use to getting so...so..."

"Heated up?" He grinned, and she couldn't help but grin also.

She cleared her throat. "Well, yes. I guess."

"Come on. You dated Jackson for, what, four or five years? And you two never, um, heated things up?"

"I knew Jackson very well by the time we started dating. And I knew we felt the same about taking things slowly, and stopping before we went too far. I barely know you at all."

"You're a virgin."

She wasn't sure if he was making a statement or asking a question.

"Well, yeah, I am. And I plan on keeping it that way until I get married." She paused for a moment before asking a question she already knew the answer to. "I take it you're not?"

"No. Is that a problem?"

"I don't know why it would be. Does it bother you that I am a virgin?"

"Nah." He waved a hand at her. "That's pretty cool actually."

"Look, let's just slow down a little, okay?"

"Of course. I understand."

They began walking again, and Alex wrapped an arm around her shoulders.

"You know, though," he mumbled into her ear. "We only have a couple of hours left at best, so if you're going to get to know me well enough to trust me, we better get started."

She laughed and slapped him across the chest. "You really have a one-track mind, don't you?"

"Oh, hush. You know you want me."

They continued down the beach a bit, walking in quiet warmth, arms wrapped around each other. Then he sat down in the sand and pulled her in front of him where she could lean back on his chest. She laid her head on his shoulder and listened to the rolling waves accompanying the seagulls.

"Why are you waiting until you get married?" he asked, breaking the music.

She hesitated, strangely nervous about sharing her faith. What if it put him off? The night had been so perfect, and she didn't want to dampen it.

"I'm a Christian," she said finally. "And my faith is a huge part of who I am. It's what gives me direction, and peace. And I believe God meant for a husband and wife to be so close that they become one. I don't want to share that with anyone but the man who's going to be with me for the rest of my life."

She waited for him to respond, expecting a joke, but he sat silently behind her and stroked her arm with his fingers.

"You're awfully quiet." She turned to look up at him.

He kissed her forehead and looked into her eyes, his as dark at the night sky. Then he squeezed her tighter and laughed.

"I was just thinking about how passionate you are about your beliefs."

"And that made you laugh?"

"No. But I was thinking. I'm going to have to marry you soon because I don't know how long I can keep my hands off you."

She grinned and another flush of warmth spread through her body.

"Well, Alex Walker, is that a proposal?"

"Maybe." He pulled her face toward his. "I think I'm going to miss you."

A wave of sadness suddenly washed over her. Maybe there would be some way to see him again.

"I can't believe I have to leave in just a couple of hours. I feel like I just got here."

He cradled her head and pressed his forehead to hers. "You could move down here and live with me. Who needs college anyway?"

"You could move to Birmingham. There are plenty of jobs for police officers."

Reality was coming hard and fast, and she didn't want him to see her cry. The faint light of daybreak eased into the eastern sky, and she couldn't put off the inevitable. So she stood and offered a hand to help him up.

"Come on. You're going to be exhausted in a couple of hours."

When they reached his motorcycle, he wrapped her into a long hug, and tears threatened to breach her control. He threw one leg over the bike and straddled the seat.

"You have my number," he said. "Seriously, give me a call sometime when you're not too busy."

"Okay."

She stared down at the pavement, afraid to look him in the eye. He reached out for her chin and lifted it until their eyes met.

"I do hope I get to see you again."

Then he kissed her one last time, stroking her cheek with his finger. He pulled his helmet over his head and took off the kick-stand, and then he reached out his hand toward her. She took it and smiled.

Don't go. The thought screamed in her head.

"Goodbye, Lily. I really had a great time."

"Me too," was all she could manage, and then she watched him crank the bike and drive away.

A flood of emotions overran her as she walked back to the window and climbed into her bed. All she could think about was wanting a few more hours with him. When she hit the bed, she pulled the pillow over her face and finally let her tears flow.

Chapter Eight

Lily sat cross-legged on the bed and stared at her phone lying in front of her. Surely if he wanted to talk he would have called by now—at the very least sent her a text message. But maybe he'd already forgotten about her. Maybe he was waiting for her to make the first call. What would she even say?

How about hello?

Her dad's words echoed in her head. It seemed so simple. Just say hello, and conversation should follow. But her stomach was in the middle of a gymnastics routine and wasn't interested in slowing down. How was she going to stay calm enough to manage a conversation?

It would be so much easier to just send him a text. Plan it carefully; be sure to say the right things. But he hadn't given her his cell number, just his work phone. At the time she hadn't thought much of it, but maybe he hadn't really wanted her to call him after all.

"This is so juvenile," she mumbled.

She glanced around the room she had taken over at her aunt's house looking for a momentary distraction. Her clothes spilled out of half-packed duffle bags in the corner. She could finish unpacking, but what was the point? She'd just repack to go to her dad's soon.

Her favorite books were piled high on the bedside table, but none of them appealed to her at the moment. Her volleyball rested at the foot of the bed, reminding her she needed to finish her ball-handling drills for the day. That could wait.

This is ridiculous, she thought. What was he going to do, anyway? Refuse to talk to her? At least if she called him she'd know for sure, and she could move on and forget about it. She picked up the phone and glanced at the business card Alex had given her. Then she punched the first few numbers and paused. Dialing a phone number should not be so difficult.

"Okay, Brennon. You're acting like a girl. Pull it together."

She tapped the last few numbers with more force than necessary, just to prove a point, but she still let out a sigh of relief when she got a recording. She could leave him a message and let him decide whether to call her back. Tapping in his extension, she took a deep breath and let it all the way out.

"Hi, Alex. It's Lily. Just calling to say hello. So, um, hello." A nervous giggle slipped out. "Give me a call if you want. I'm at my aunt's house. Or you can call my cell. Bye."

She hung up and slid further under her covers. That was brilliant. Who wouldn't want to return that phone call? She reached over to the lamp on her nightstand and twisted it off.

"You are a freaking moron," she muttered.

July 10

Birmingham, Alabama

"Okay, bring it in!" Lily blew her whistle and twenty exhausted teenage girls jogged to the center of the gym. She relished that their ponytails had lost their bounce since the morning and that the chatter had died down considerably once breathing became the main focus of their mouths.

"Good job this morning, ladies. You're doing much better with your footwork today. Come back after lunch ready to play. We'll be dividing you into teams and starting the tournament this afternoon."

She stuck her hand into the middle of the group and the girls followed her lead.

"Defense on three."

The gym echoed with the word, and the girls shuffled away into their corners of the gym. Lily jogged to a table off to the side and grabbed her keys and bottle of water. As she pushed open the gym door, sunlight flooded her vision and sent her into a fit of sneezing. Never failed.

She paused long enough for the sneezing to pass then jogged across the parking lot and pushed through the small wooded area that separated the church from her aunt's driveway. It had been a stroke of unbelievable luck that most of the volleyball camps she'd be working were taking place at the church next door to Rebecca's house. She had decided to stay there so she could avoid running into Jackson, but the pool in the backyard was definitely an added bonus.

She took the back porch steps in a single bound and looked longingly at the sparkling water. A swim would be the perfect cure to the blistering heat. Maybe she could do a pool workout this evening in place of running.

She pushed open the sliding glass door and stepped into the kitchen, welcoming the blast of air conditioning as she headed for her phone lying on the island. Grabbing the bread off the nearby pantry shelf, she pulled out a couple of slices as she checked for missed calls and tried not to get her hopes up. No numbers from Georgia. But one number sucked the breath out of her just the same.

"Jackson?"

She checked the number again, but there was no mistake. Jackson had called, but he hadn't left a message. After over three months of silence, he had the nerve to just call her out of the blue. What could he possibly want?

Before she could over-analyze it, she dialed the number, determined to demand that he leave her alone. It was only fair after all. That was exactly what he'd wanted, and she'd definitely done her part.

"Hello?"

The shock of his voice stilled her racing thoughts. It was the familiarity more than anything else. Even after such a long time, his voice was like a pair of cozy slippers. Funny how something could be so soothing and so painful at the same time.

"Um, hey. It's me. Lily."

He let out a sigh. She could picture him perfectly, leaned against the door frame to his kitchen, his hair barely brushing the top of the doorway.

"Lily, I'm glad you called. I'd really like to talk to you."

"Listen, I don't know why you're calling me all of a sudden-"

"I just want to talk," he interrupted. "That's all."

She stepped outside onto the patio beside the pool and dropped into a padded lounge chair.

"Why?"

"Because. I just...I want to know how you're doing."

"Are you kidding? You tell me to leave you alone, so I do. And I don't hear from you for months, and then one day it's suddenly 'Hi, Lily. How ya doing?' Like we're back in middle school or something."

"I'm sorry."

"Don't be. I don't need your apology. I'm doing just fine if you really want to know. So I'll be hanging up now."

"Wait. Don't go yet."

She rubbed her temple with her free hand, her head suddenly throbbing. Why was he doing this now?

"What do you want?"

"Look, I know I said some harsh things that night at my house, and I'm really sorry. If you want to hang up and never speak to me again, that's fine. I deserve it. But I just want a chance to talk to you and explain some things. That's all."

"Fine. Go ahead. Explain away."

"Well, I'd rather talk to you in person."

"I don't think that's a good idea." Her head pounded even harder.

"Come on," he pleaded. "Why don't you come by Mom's for dinner tonight? She's making spaghetti...with the homemade meatballs."

A grin slipped through her lips before she realized it.

"That's not fair. You can't use Mary's spaghetti to manipulate me."

His chuckle drifted over the line, and it made her pause. He had laughed. And it reminded her of the peaceful babble of the stream that snaked through the neighborhood where they'd grown up. The same stream they'd played and fished in during another lifetime.

"I uh-" She stumbled to find her words. She couldn't go backward. Those two kids were gone. "I can't, Jackson. It's just not a good idea."

"Lil..." He paused, and she almost gave in. Almost.

"I'm sorry. I have to go."

"Lily, please hear me out."

"Goodbye, Jackson."

She tapped the end button and put the phone down on the swing beside her. She dropped her head into her hands and massaged her temples. That was the last thing she'd needed today.

Later that afternoon, Lily settled into her aunt's leather recliner and scrolled through the text messages on her phone, one from her mom—just checking in—and three from Jackson. Nothing yet from Alex.

She deleted the three from Jackson without even reading them then turned on the television so she could think of something else. She flipped through a hundred channels of nothing interesting before heading into the kitchen to dig around the pantry for a snack.

Her phone vibrated and popped, letting her know of an incoming text. Jackson again.

Lil, pls let me explain. If not at mom's, then somewhere else. Name it. Pls.

She had to admit she was surprised by his persistence. Maybe it wouldn't hurt to hear him out. Then at least she could put her questions to rest and move on.

She hit reply.

Fine. But no dinner. I'll drop by Mary's around 8.

Jackson widened the blinds with his fingers and checked the street in both directions. No sign of her yet. He checked his watch. Ten after eight. Maybe she'd changed her mind. He checked his phone for any missed calls or messages, but there were none.

He couldn't blame her. In fact he'd expected resistance from her. This was the same girl who had once stopped talking to him in eighth grade for five months straight with no explanation whatsoever. To this day, he still had no idea what had pushed her away back then, no idea what had changed when she'd started talking to him again. And he'd learned not to bring it up.

But this was different. He knew exactly what had pushed her away, and it was entirely his fault.

"You okay?" His mom stepped beside him and wiped her hands on a dish towel tucked into her apron.

"Hanging in there." He forced a smile.

"I'm sure you're a bit nervous, but I'm glad you're doing this. I've prayed for both of you so much lately."

He glanced at her sideways, but had to look away from the hope in her eyes. It was hard enough to think about how much heartache she'd already endured, not to mention how deeply he'd hurt Lily as well. Maybe this had been a bad idea.

Lily's blue Civic pulled over to the side of the street in front of his house, and his stomach plummeted.

"She's here," he said.

His mom gave him a pat on the shoulder as he headed for the front door.

"Tell her we've got plenty of spaghetti left if she's hungry."

"Sure." He reached for the doorknob.

"And Jackson..." She smiled when he looked over at her. "Be patient. And listen to her."

He nodded and closed the door behind him. As he walked down the front steps, he noticed Lily was still sitting in her car, hands on the steering wheel, engine still running. His first instinct was to go pull her out of the car, but he forced himself to stop on the walkway several feet away and wait until she was ready.

She glanced at him and cut the engine; then she pushed herself out of the car and slammed the door. She crossed her arms and leaned back against the car, and the sight of her nearly sucked the breath out of him.

Something was different.

"Well, I'm here." She cut her eyes at him, but then she dropped her gaze to the grass below.

"I was beginning to think you'd changed your mind."

"I did."

"Then why are you here?"

She shrugged. "Changed it back."

Her cold demeanor was like taking a hose to his confidence, which was already shaky. He had no idea where to even begin. He knew what he wanted to say, what he needed to do, but how to get her moving was the question.

A warm breeze lifted her hair off her shoulders, and he caught a glint of hope—she was still wearing his necklace. Maybe he had a chance, if he could just find the right way to reconnect.

"Want to go for a walk?" he asked.

"What? Why?"

He glanced around. "It's a nice evening."

"So?"

"Come on. I need to stretch my knee a little."

She sighed loudly, but pushed away from the car and joined him on the sidewalk.

"Fine. But make it quick."

She took off down the sidewalk with a determined stride, and he grinned to himself as he sped up to match it. Some things were still the same. She was as stubborn now as the day he'd met her.

An image of a pig-tailed stick of a girl flashed in his mind, face smudged with dirt and tears, a defiant stride moving her down the street. How many times had she run away from home that first year they'd moved here? Seven maybe. He couldn't remember. He'd never understood it until last fall—until he himself had wanted to run away.

They reached the end of the street and turned down the dirt path that led into the wooded section of the neighborhood. Squirrels and birds rustled in the long shadows of the trees, and the breeze tickled the leaves above them. Disturbing the serenity seemed wrong somehow, but this might be his only chance to salvage their relationship.

"I know it's asking a lot," he said, "but I was hoping you might find a way to forgive me."

She shoved her hands in the pockets of her shorts, but said nothing.

"If you can't, I'll understand. I treated you like...well-"

"Like I didn't have a right to mourn him," she finished, kicking a rock ahead of them. "And then like I didn't have a right to want to be happy again."

Jackson sighed. He wanted to reach out to her, to pull her close and erase the past, but the chasm separating them was wider than he'd realized.

"I was drowning at that point, Lily. I can't justify my behavior, but please try to understand. I needed some time to figure everything out."

"I never once denied you the time or space you might need."

"I know. You did everything right. It was me."

"Why are we here?" She stopped walking and threw her hands up. "What is it you want?"

The path snaked around the corner, but Jackson stopped at a small break in the trees. It had been a long time since they'd ventured down toward the stream together, but he was hoping for some backup from a place filled with good memories.

"You remember when we first met?" he asked.

She folded her arms over her chest. "Yeah. So?"

"You were running away." She shrugged but said nothing. He'd have to keep prodding. "You followed me down to the stream, remember?"

"So?"

"I taught you how to fish that day." He grinned, remembering the horror on her face as she'd scolded him for killing innocent crickets.

"What's your point? Did you bring me down here to have some sweet little trip down memory lane? That doesn't fix anything."

He sighed and rubbed the back of his neck. "I know. I know I can't fix things. I was just hoping..."

"Hoping for what?"

"Just hoping you'd walk with me. That we could talk, maybe find a way to make things right again." He gestured toward the small opening in the trees. "Just a little further?"

She shook her head and stepped backward. "No. I'm not going down there. I know what you're trying to do, and it won't work."

"I'm not trying anything. I just want to talk."

She bit her lower lip and took another step away before turning back down the path. This was proving more difficult than he'd imagined. He was just going to have to try harder.

"Lily," he called as he jogged to catch up with her.

She walked even faster, but his legs were longer than hers, and he easily matched her pace.

"Come on, wait a minute." He grabbed her arm, but she jerked it away.

"It's your turn to leave *me* alone," she said.

"No."

She stopped and finally looked at him—really looked at him—and for the first time he noticed the dampness around her eyes. It was like running into a thorn bush he had no idea was there, and it hit him that once again he was being selfish. He'd been so focused on getting her to see that he still needed her, to see that he was sorry and that he would never hurt her again— to see *him*—that he had failed to see her. And in that, he *was* hurting her again.

"Okay," she said, her voice cracking. "I forgive you."

He exhaled in relief and started to smile.

"Now, please," she continued. "Will you leave me alone?"

Leave her alone. How ironic that his own words would come back to punch him in the gut. And he deserved it. But he was finally climbing out of the miry pit he'd been drowning in, and he wasn't about to slide back down.

"I just want to be your friend," he said.

She laughed, but there was no joy in it. "My friend? Are you kidding?"

"No. Why would I be kidding?"

"Because you can't possibly be serious."

"We've been friends since we were kids. It shouldn't be that big of a stretch."

She threw her arms in the air and let out a groan.

"There is no possible way that we can still be friends, Jackson. How in the world is that supposed to work? I get to come over and have dinner like old times? Maybe we can hang out at the movies, or even better," she threw an arm toward the stream, "we can go ride bikes down at the creek and go fishing! It will be just like we're kids again!"

"Don't be sarcastic," he said as she huffed and kicked at the dirt. "You know that's not going to help. I just want to try, that's all."

Twilight was fast approaching and her eyes had gone dark with the setting sun, but he thought for a moment he saw a glimmer of hope in them. He reached out and ruffled her hair, and she pushed his hand away.

"You know I hate that." The corner of her mouth tipped.

"I know."

He did it again.

"Stop."

She ducked her head to the side, but he reached for her with the other arm. This time she swung her hand up and blocked him.

"Look, Carter. I don't want to have to beat you down to get you to leave me alone."

"Oh please. I could take you down with my pinky."

She chuckled and pushed her hair back behind her ear, but a small strand still stuck out where he had mussed it. He fought the urge to straighten it for her.

"I don't know about this." She shook her head, and the hint of her smile disappeared as quickly as it had come.

"I know I screwed up. And there's no apology that can make up for that. But I'll do whatever it takes, for as long as it takes to be worthy of your friendship again."

She dropped her head and backed away. The breeze had died, and the stillness in the air made him aware of every nerve on his skin. Even the birds and crickets had gone silent as if they were anxious for her answer.

When she finally looked up at him, her face now streaked with the tears she'd been fighting, it was all he could do to keep himself from pulling her into him. She lifted her finger and shoved it at him.

"You think you can drag me down here and make a bunch of empty promises and say some nice crap to make everything right? Now? After I spent months trying to figure out what I'd done wrong?"

"I'm sorry-"

"I don't care if you're sorry! You can drop dead for all I care!" Her chest heaved, and she swiped at her tears.

It felt like the pain in his chest would split him open.

"I tried that already." He paused and focused on keeping it together. "But not anymore. From now on, I'm choosing to live."

Brunswick, GA

Alex ran his hand along the black vinyl seat of his motorcycle and then across the fuel tank as he gave it a final inspection. The dent in the front fender wasn't even noticeable thanks to the mechanic's hard work over at the shop. Adrian had taken one heck of a swing with that bat.

He stood and stepped back from the bike, looking over at Kyle Blackmon with a forced smile.

"Well, she's all yours."

Across the garage, Kyle furrowed his brow and crossed his arms over his chest.

"You sure about this? You've only had it for what, a little more than a year?"

Alex shrugged. "Something like that." It had been one year, and fourteen days exactly.

"Look, you seem a little attached to it. You want to take some time to think about it?" Kyle checked his watch. "We have to be at the station soon, anyway. I can come back tomorrow."

Alex shook his head. "Nah. I don't need to think about it anymore."

"Okay, if you're sure."

Kyle had that look on his face, the one he hated more than anything, the I-heard-what-happened sympathy look. No telling which version he'd heard. Alex hoped it was the one where he'd gone crazy and tried to kill himself. That at least made him seem more interesting.

He helped Kyle load the bike into the back of his truck then walked to the end of the driveway as it pulled away. Standing at the edge of the yard, he waited until the truck turned the corner. Then he turned to the nearest object he could find—the real estate sign with the cheesy smile of the good-for-nothing agent that hadn't shown the house in weeks—and he kicked it so hard it flew out into the street.

He stood and stared at it for a moment. It would do just as much good laying there as it had sitting up in his yard the past three months. Something had to give. The money from the bike would buy him some time, but it wasn't a long-term solution. He really shouldn't have bought it to begin with. Or better yet, he should have driven it off the Sidney Lanier Bridge. He'd thought about it once.

He turned and walked back toward the house, going in through the garage and into the kitchen. He threw the remains of his take-out into the trash and wiped down the island countertop—the freaking *marble* countertop that he was now stuck trying to sell.

He grabbed a soda from the refrigerator and headed down the hallway, stopping outside the closed bedroom door on the left. He hadn't opened it in over a month, but something about getting rid of the bike made him think he could do it.

He turned the knob and pushed the door open, stepping into the barren room. He stood in its center, drowning in the emptiness, and wondered how everything could have gotten so screwed up.

Birmingham, AL

Back at her aunt's house, Lily pulled the sheets up to her chin and let the cool silk drift over her skin. The first few moments under the covers were normally soothing, but not tonight. She rolled onto her side and punched her pillow under her head to adjust it. The breeze from her box fan across the room rippled over her face pulling strands of hair along with it, and she let out a deep sigh, trying to release the tension still eating away at her.

The nerve of that guy to just pick up a phone after so long and expect to just apologize his way back into her life. And how stupid could she be for even thinking about forgiving him? One moment of weakness. That's all it had taken. One moment of the familiar and she'd almost let him back in.

Friends. He'd lost his mind. How could he expect them to be friends again? It was impossible. Relationships never work when moving backward, and this was definitely backward. If it was so easy for him to just go back, maybe he'd never really loved her as anything more than a friend to begin with. Maybe she'd just loved him so much, she couldn't see that he didn't feel the same way.

Her stomach wrenched, but she pushed the feeling away. No more thinking about Jackson. She reached for a book on her nightstand just as her phone lit up and vibrated. She grabbed it, determined to ignore Jackson's call and turn off the phone if necessary. But it wasn't Jackson. It was a number from Georgia.

Her stomach did a completely different kind of flip. It had to be Alex.

"Hello?"

"Lily?"

Her heart sped up at the sound of his voice. "This is Lily."

"Hey, it's Alex."

"Hey."

A strange silence flooded the line, and she groped for anything to say. Apparently they'd forgotten how to carry on a conversation since their walk on the beach.

"So, how have you been?" he asked. Why hadn't she thought of such a simple question herself?

"I'm good. I'm finishing up a volleyball camp tomorrow. How about you?"

"Not too bad. I just got your message a little while ago. You have no idea how good it was to hear from you."

She smiled to herself, grateful he couldn't see the blush flooding her face.

"It's pretty late over there. What are you up to?"

"Just about to start my shift. I'm working midnights for the rest of the month, so I have to sleep during the day."

"That has to be weird. I don't think I could sleep in broad daylight."

"Yeah, I've contemplated finding a dark cave where I can hang upside down, but you don't find too many along the Georgia coast."

She laughed at the image of Alex wrapped in a dark cloak like a vampire.

"Well, we have some great caves around here if you want."

"Hmm, maybe." He paused. "So when you coming back down here? There's no one left to worship the ground I walk on."

"Oh, I doubt that. I'm sure they came swarming out of the woodwork as soon as I left."

"Well, that's true. But you've spoiled all the fun. None of them resist as well as you did. It's too easy."

"I'm sure you'll manage."

She tried to ignore the pinch in her chest. His arrogance, feigned or not, left her wondering who he truly was.

"Seriously, when can I see you again?" His voice sobered as if he'd read her thoughts.

"I don't know. I have camps every week for the rest of July, and I have to report for preseason the first week in August."

She stopped before she asked him to come see her; that would just sound desperate. Besides, hadn't they already had this conversation?

"Well, maybe we can work something out."

Her heart fluttered and she threw up a silent prayer. "I'll check my schedule. I might have a few days somewhere."

"That would be great. But listen, I have to get going. I have a meeting in a few minutes. I'll call you again tomorrow, okay?"

"Really? Okay."

"Don't sound so surprised. I thought you were starting to buy my whole honorable act."

"I'm starting to wonder which Alex is real. The thoughtful one, or the arrogant one."

"Which one will get to see you sooner?"

"I don't know yet. Maybe the one that wants to see me bad enough to jump on his bike and get up here."

"So that's how it is, huh?" he said. "I guess we'll have to discuss it and get back to you."

She shook her head and sighed. His intentions were good, but it was pointless to get her hopes up.

"I have to run," he said. "Talk to you tomorrow?"

"Definitely. Good night."

She placed the phone back in its stand and snuggled under the covers again. Then she closed her eyes and tried to recreate their walk on the beach, her hand in his, the waves rolling gently toward their toes.

God, I know a relationship with Alex is crazy, but if I could just see him again, just one more time, I promise I'll never ask again. Just once more.

July 13

Birmingham, Alabama

The bell at the top of the door jingled as it closed behind her, and Lily glanced around the small deli for Jackson. He was seated in the back booth, and he sat up straighter as their eyes met. Her insides knotted when he smiled at her, and she almost turned around to flee. But if she was going to move on, she had to face him, and she had to get him to understand. Friendship was impossible.

She pushed up her chin and weaved her way through several empty tables to the booth by the window. He watched her the entire time. She hated the expectation on his face, his large blue eyes, the faint smile on his lips. Where had all this persistent hope been a few months ago? She slid into the booth and dropped her backpack beside her.

"Let's make this quick. I have to be back at the gym in thirty minutes."

"Sure. I won't keep you." He glanced behind her. "You want a bite to eat?"

"No. I'm not hungry." Her stomach growled in protest.

"You sure? It's on me."

"What are you trying to do here?"

She folded her hands on the table and leaned toward him. He tugged his worn ball cap down a bit and shrugged.

"I thought I was having lunch."

"Don't do that. You know what I mean. Why are you pursuing this? I told you the other night, I'm not interested in being friends with you."

"I heard you." He leaned forward onto his forearms. "I just don't believe you."

Heat flooded her face. "Excuse me?"

"I don't believe you. We spent what, seven years as friends before we started dating? And I know what we meant to each other back then. You said so yourself."

"When?"

"The first night I kissed you." He inched forward, even as she leaned back and pushed down the stirring in her chest. "You said it was hard to imagine your life without me."

"I don't remember that." She forced away the sudden images from their past. "But it doesn't matter what I said back then. What I'm saying now is that this won't work."

"Why not?"

She looked out the window, barely registering the cars moving by in a blur. What else could she say? He just wouldn't get the message.

"Lil, please." He reached for her hand, lifting her fingers from the table and folding them into his. "Just give it a chance."

She looked down at her hand, felt the warmth flowing through it. Then she looked up at him, into those eyes that had anchored her for so many years, and she knew she'd lost the battle.

Chapter Nine

Birmingham, Alabama

Lily dropped her duffel bag in her bedroom and darted into the bathroom to turn on the shower. She was running late, as usual, but it had been hard to force herself out of bed that morning and go for a three-mile run. She must have hit the snooze button at least four times.

She glanced at her reflection in the large mirror over the double sinks. Maybe it was ridiculous to shower before doing yard work, but she refused to be seen looking so ragged and sweaty, even if it was just Jackson and his mom.

She reached behind the curtain to test the water, adjusted the temperature, and then pulled off her shirt and tossed it into the hamper. She heard the ringtone of her phone in the bedroom and ran to grab it before it went to voicemail.

"Hello?"

"Hey, Beautiful," Alex said.

Her stomach did its usual flip, and she smiled to herself.

"Wow, what a nice surprise! I thought you had training all day."

"I do, but I got some good news, and I couldn't wait to tell you."

"Let me guess. You made detective without even having to take the test."

He laughed. "No. I wish. But it's just as good. I was asked to join the SWAT team."

"Alex, that's great! Congratulations."

"Well, I still have to go through some evaluations, but I got it in the bag, I'm sure. The Sergeant said my shooting scores have been the best in the department the last six months."

Lily glanced down at her watch. "That's awesome, really. I'm so proud of you."

"Thanks. I have to run in a minute. Can I give you a call later?"

"Uh, sure. I have some stuff going on, but I'll call you back if I miss your call."

"Stuff, huh? What kind of stuff?"

"Just some errands." She paused and tried to shake off the awkward sound her voice had taken on. "And Jackson's mom needs some help around her house, so I agreed to stop by later."

There was a definite span of silence on the other end. Maybe she shouldn't have said anything. Their conversations had been going so well the past few days. She'd hate to ruin it. He cleared his throat.

"Jackson again. I thought you two were history."

"Well, in one sense we are. I mean, we're not back together or anything. He just thinks we can stay friends."

"And what do you think?"

"Honestly, I don't know. I'm not sure it's a good idea."

"Well, it's been my experience that you should go with your instincts when it comes to people. If your gut is telling you it won't work, then there's probably a reason for that."

"You're probably right. I just have a hard time saying no, especially when Mary needs help. I was more at home there than my own house most of the time."

"And he knows that."

Something in her bristled at the fatherly tone in his voice.

"Look, the shower's running, and I have to get going soon. Can we talk later?"

"Sure."

"Okay, well, I hope your training goes well today."

"Thanks." His voice had gone cool. It sounded strange, and she wasn't quite sure what to make of it.

"Congratulations again. I'm glad you called to tell me."

"Hey," he said, this time a little warmer. "You know I didn't mean anything by what I said about Jackson."

"I know."

"I just don't want to see the guy hurt you again, that's all."

She couldn't help but smile. "That's very sweet of you, but I'm sure I'll be fine."

"Whoah, whoah, whoah! Don't *ever* do that again."

"What?"

"Call me sweet. You'll ruin my reputation."

"Yeah, but maybe it needs ruining. It might improve."

"Hmm, we'll see. Talk to you later."

Lily reached toward the back of a rose bush and cupped a spent bloom in her fingers. Its wilted, wrinkled petals were covered with black spots. She carefully traced back down the stem to find a junction of leaves, but there wasn't much left to work with. Mary must not have even touched the rose bushes since last summer.

She did her best to find a node facing outward, and made a quick cut just above it. Then she checked the rest of the pitiful plant. There had only been one decent bloom on the whole thing, and it would fade soon. But maybe things would turn around now. With all the dead blooms gone, the plants would summon the strength to make new ones.

"Come on, girls," she muttered. "Time to quit moping around and get busy growing."

On the other side of the house, she heard the motor on the weed eater cut off followed by heavy footfalls loping up the front steps. She crawled around to the back of the next bush and continued working before she heard the same heavy footfalls coming down the back porch steps this time. A few seconds later, Jackson appeared on the other side of the bush with two tall glasses of tea.

"You ready for a break?" He held one out to her.

"Sure." She crawled back out, stood up, and took the glass from his hand. "Thanks."

He tapped his glass to hers and smiled, and then he took a long swig. Lily tipped her glass back and did the same. She sputtered and coughed.

"Did you make this?"

"Yep."

"Holy cow. How much sugar did you put in there?"

He looked down into the bottom of his glass and shrugged.

"I don't know. I just poured till it looked about the same as Mom puts in there. Why? Is it bad?"

"It's like drinking tea-flavored kool-aid." She handed the glass back to him.

He grinned and set the glasses on the bottom step of the deck.

"Sorry about that. Guess I don't quite have Mom's touch with the sweet tea."

"You can say that again." She smiled up at him before turning back to the rose bushes.

"Hey, at least I tried. It's the effort that counts, right?"

"Sure. Keep telling yourself that."

He nodded toward the bushes. "Want some help?"

"I thought you were edging the sidewalk."

"Already done."

She sighed and looked away. She was happy to help Mary out, but even after a couple of lunches and a few decent phone conversations, being around Jackson was strained. She'd hoped to do most of her work around the flower beds alone.

"Do you even remember how to do the deadheading?" she asked.

"Of course."

"You were always off shooting baskets. You never paid any attention to this stuff."

"Sure I did. Just cause I didn't like it didn't mean I wasn't listening. Mom would have killed me if I'd hurt one of her babies."

Lily wiped the sweat from her brow with the back of her arm and looked over the bushes she'd already pruned.

"They look pretty bad. How long has it been since she's worked on them?"

Jackson fidgeted with his hands and looked away. "Not sure, really. A long time."

"I'm not sure what I can do here. I've never seen them like this."

He jerked his gaze back to hers. "Well maybe she's had a few things on her mind lately besides some stupid flowers."

She stood frozen in place, completely taken off guard.

"I...I didn't mean anything."

"I know. I know. I'm sorry." He shook his head. "I'm just worried about her."

"She seems better."

"She is. It's a huge step that she's even going through the office and packing Dad's things up." He pulled a pair of gloves from his back pocket and slid them over his hands. "Now, what can I do to help? From the looks of things, we don't have much longer to get this done."

As he pointed into the western sky, thunder rumbled low in the distance. What had been a beautiful day only a little while ago was quickly turning dark. Lily pointed at the bags of fresh mulch sitting beside the deck.

"I've only got one bush to go. Then we can spread the mulch and be done with these."

He walked a few steps over to the mulch, grabbing a bag and throwing it over his shoulder. He carried it to the end of the bed Lily had already weeded and dumped it out. As he began spreading it, Lily searched the last bush for any decent-looking nodes that might be encouraged to branch out.

"So how was Gatlinburg this year?" he asked.

She slid her fingers beneath a branch and made a quick cut.

"We didn't go."

"What? No family vacation this summer?"

"No, we took a vacation, just not to Gatlinburg."

He walked over to the mulch and grabbed another bag. "Where did you go?"

Her stomach twisted. "St. Simons Island."

"Never heard of it."

"It's on the Georgia coast. Not too far south from Savannah."

"Oh." He crawled closer to her, spreading more mulch under the bushes. "Did you have a good time?"

"Uh, sure. It was nice. The house we rented was right on the beach."

"You hate the beach."

He sat back on his heels and grinned. She shrugged and focused on some weeds she'd missed.

"It was okay. Kara and Rachel kept me entertained."

He laughed and went back to pushing mulch. "I bet they were all over that. How many adoring worshippers were trailing along behind them by the time you all left?"

"The usual I guess."

"Any left overs for you?"

"I'm not sure what you mean."

He paused, and she tried to concentrate on the branch in front of her.

"Is something wrong?" he asked.

She placed the shears on the branch and focused on a steady, even voice.

"Of course not. Why do you ask?"

"Well, for one thing, you're about to cut off a perfectly good flower."

She jerked the shears away and stared at the beautiful red rose she was about to murder.

"Uh, thanks. Wow, how did I miss that?"

She could feel his eyes on her now, and her stomach knotted even tighter. She had to get out of there before he asked more questions, so she pushed herself up and tugged her gloves off.

"The weather looks like it's going to get rough. Maybe we should go ahead and get everything put away."

She walked around the flower bed picking up tools and dropping them into the metal bucket by the steps. With the clanging of each tool, the silence from Jackson grew more and more unnerving. Finally, she grabbed the bucket and headed for the shed.

She carried the bucket to the back, dropped it next to the fishing poles along with her hat and gloves, and then she turned to leave. But Jackson was standing in the door of the shed. He leaned against the frame and crossed his arms.

"What's going on with you?" he asked.

"Nothing, I just don't want to get caught in a storm."

"It's still a good hour away."

"Well, it can take a while to get things cleaned up."

"Really? Looks like you did it in under thirty seconds."

She rolled her eyes and pushed her way past him. "What's your point?"

"Did you meet someone?"

The question stopped her as if he'd lassoed her, but she couldn't face him. She forced her feet forward until she reached the stairs, focusing on finding her keys. She was sure she'd dropped them on the last step.

"Lily?"

"What?"

She heard his footsteps coming closer. Her gaze darted across the steps and around the grass below them. What had she done with her keys?

"Why can't you look at me?"

He was right behind her now. She settled her nerves and turned around.

"I can look at you just fine. I just need to find my keys."

"It's a simple question." He brushed off his hands and tugged on his cap. "Did you meet someone?"

Her stomach was still knotting, but she was sick of all this. She'd tried to tell him they couldn't be friends.

"I guess you could say that."

"Well, it sounds like you had a good time." He pulled his gloves off and tossed them through the open door of the shed.

She crossed her arms and steeled herself for the argument coming.

"I did have a good time."

"Did he kiss you?"

Her face went hot, and she groped for any response. Nothing came.

"Well, uh..."

He shook his head. "Never mind."

He walked over to the basketball goal at the end of the driveway. Picking up the ball lying nearby, he dribbled it against the cement then took a shot that never even hit the rim. It bounced and rolled until it finally came to rest in the grass on the other side of the pavement. He rubbed the back of his neck for a moment before turning to face her.

"You remember the first time you beat me out here?" he asked.

She hesitated. Where was he going with this?

"It was the only time I ever beat you." She recalled the look of shock then anger that had washed over his face that day. He'd just made the Varsity team as a freshman, and his ego had been ripe for the blow. "You were pissed."

He opened his mouth to speak, but then he stopped and looked away. Thunder rumbled again, but he didn't seem to notice. He walked over to where the ball had come to rest and picked it up, dribbling and shooting again. This time it managed to hit the backboard, but still no rim.

"Are you okay?" she asked. "What's going on?"

He grabbed the ball again and looked over at her, angling his head.

"I learned something that day you beat me. Dad pulled me aside and chewed me out for yelling at you."

"I never knew that."

"Yeah, I know. You took off after I threw my temper tantrum."

"Now that, I remember."

"Anyway, Dad said, 'Son, if you get lazy and take your gifts for granted, you'll lose every time.'"

"Well, I never beat you again. You must have learned your lesson."

He bounced the ball, spun it for a second, and then looked up at the goal.

"Apparently, I didn't."

This time he made the shot, and the net swished as the ball passed through. String music, his dad used to call it. He had taught them both so much more than basketball. She wished he was here now. Maybe things wouldn't have gotten so messed up.

He picked up the ball again and continued shooting. She stepped under the basket and rebounded, passing the ball back to him each time. He moved around the perimeter of the court in a quiet rhythm, sinking each shot like he hadn't missed a day of practice. It was a beautiful sight to see him in his element again, eyes focused on the goal. There was no trace of a limp.

"I see you haven't lost your touch," she said.

He drained another shot and held his hands out for the pass.

"Yeah, well, I've lost a few other things though." He dropped the ball before she could ask what he meant. "Rain's coming. I'm heading in. I'll talk to you later, okay?"

She watched him walk across the yard and jog up the steps of the back deck. He disappeared into the house without another glance back. She waited a moment before finding her keys and phone on the deck; then she walked around the house to the front.

When she reached her car, she took one last glance at the house she had practically grown up in. She'd let go of her dreams of a life with Jackson a long time ago. Maybe now he would finally see what she had known for months. Love couldn't conquer all.

July 23
Brunswick, Georgia

Alex pushed open the garage door and stepped into the kitchen, tossing his keys onto the empty counter beside him. He glanced down at his watch. Still a few hours before he had to be at work. He walked over to the refrigerator and stared at the plate of crumbs that had been his dinner the night before. Take out again. He grabbed the last two beers from the shelf and made a mental note to go to the grocery store tomorrow.

He went to the living room and had to spend several minutes searching for the remote inside the sofa cushions before he found it. Then he set one beer on the lighthouse coaster on the end table and popped the top of the other. He fell into the sofa and searched the channels for the Braves game. Not that he cared this year, but the sound of baseball in the house made it seem less empty.

He pulled his phone off his belt to give the Chinese restaurant a call when he noticed a text he'd obviously missed a couple of hours earlier.

Got your messages and would be happy to meet on the 9th. Your place or mine?

He grimaced and clenched his teeth as he hit reply.

Silverman's office. 10 am sharp.

He set the phone down and sighed. Surely this nightmare would end soon. He took a long swig of his beer and stared blankly at the game. His phone vibrated, so he grabbed it and checked the number. He was relieved to see Lily's name and the picture she'd sent him pop onto the screen.

"Hey there," he said. He muted the television.

"Hey! Guess what?"

"What?"

"No, you have to guess."

He sighed and pinched his nose. "I don't like playing guessing games. Just tell me."

"Are you okay?" she asked.

"I'm fine. Just a long day."

"You want to talk about it?"

"Not really."

His phone buzzed with another text.

"Okay, well, then do you want to hear my great news? Maybe it will make your day better."

"Unless you're going to tell me you're standing outside my door in a bikini, I don't think there's much that could make it better."

"Well, I might have the next best thing."

He chugged another gulp of his beer. "What do you mean?"

"I'm coming down to see you again!"

He laughed. "Yeah, when? In about a hundred years when you're done with school and volleyball and-"

"No. I'm coming in one week."

"What?" He bolted upright. His heart lurched for a moment, and he jumped up from the couch. He headed into the kitchen to look at the calendar on the wall.

"Wait, what date is that?" he asked.

"Um, the fourth through the seventh of August, I think. We're coming down on Monday and staying through Thursday."

He looked over the calendar and breathed a sigh of relief. If she were staying just two days longer things could get ugly. But that didn't matter. All that mattered was that he was going to see her again after all.

"Wait a minute," he said. "Who is *we*?"

"Oh yeah, I almost forgot. My teammates Alison and Emily are coming with me. We're going to make a little vacation out of it."

"Oh," he said, unable to hide his disappointment. "I was hoping to get you all to myself."

"We'll have plenty of time to ourselves. That's why I invited *two* of them. They'll hang out on their own some so we can be alone."

Perfect.

"But don't get any ideas," she said. "I meant what I said about staying a virgin until I'm married."

"Oh but you haven't been fully tempted by the irresistible Alex Walker," he said. "You just got a taste."

She laughed, but he didn't miss the nervous edge to it.

"Alex, seriously, I hope you'll respect how I feel. I need to take things slow, and not just physically. I'm not ready to get in over my head. The past couple of weeks have been great, and I've loved getting to know you better, but still-"

"Hey, I get it. You've made it perfectly clear where you stand, and I respect that. I was just kidding around."

He let out a long breath and returned to the sofa. He'd have to keep himself in check with her. The last thing he wanted was to scare her off. If she really knew him, really knew everything he'd done, would she even speak to him? His conscience whispered doubt in his ear. He should just leave her alone. She deserved better.

He downed the rest of his beer and shut the voice out of his head. He needed her right now. Even just talking to her helped. He was tired of all the meaningless things he'd been chasing after. He needed some faith, some positive direction. She was so good for him, so grounded and sure of who she was. He could make this work. He just needed some time.

"I promise you can trust me," he said. "I won't do anything you don't *want* to do."

"I can't wait to see you," she said.

Birmingham, Alabama

Jackson knocked on the door a second time, but still there was no answer at Rebecca's house. It had been a while since he'd been there, but he was sure this was the right place. Maybe Lily wasn't here.

He should have called first, but with the way he'd left things the other day, he wasn't sure she'd want to talk to him. But he had to try. Their conversation had shaken him, and he'd realized how close he was to losing her.

He stepped off the front porch and shielded his face from the sun as he glanced around the neighborhood. He still had a couple of hours before he had to be at work. Maybe he could wait here. She was probably out running.

He walked around the side of the house to check the pool just in case. As he flipped the latch up on the gate, he heard a splash and paused. He'd hate to sneak up on Rebecca and surprise her. Who knew if she'd even recognize him?

He inched around the corner and saw Lily gliding toward the edge of the pool. He froze, watching as she flipped her legs over and pushed off the side, pumping her arms and legs in perfect rhythm. He had no idea how long he stood there, mesmerized as she flew through the water with the same grace and power she had on the volleyball court.

He finally walked over to the chairs lining the deck and sat down in the corner near the sliding glass doors. She didn't even notice him. He leaned forward and propped his chin on his fists, continuing to watch her as his chest tightened with every stroke she took.

He'd hoped to take things slowly, to rekindle their friendship before even thinking of anything more. But it wasn't working as well as he'd hoped. Maybe he should just tell her everything and hope for the best, but that thought still terrified him. She was still hurt and angry.

She finally stood in the shallow end and rested her hands on top of her head as she caught her breath. Then she ducked her head back under the water one final time. She walked up the steps of the pool and swung her hair over her shoulder, straining the water out.

He wondered if she knew he was there, because if she was trying to torture him, it was completely effective. She had always been fit, but it was obvious she'd been working hard over the past several months. He cleared his throat and she jumped.

"Oh my lord!" she said. "Are you trying to scare me to death?"

He smiled as he walked over to her and handed her the towel from the back of a nearby chair. She snatched it out of his hand and wrapped it around her waist. He tried not to notice the drops of water glistening on her skin.

"Sorry. I didn't want to disturb your workout. Besides, I was enjoying the view."

She rolled her eyes and tried to hide the small grin that escaped.

"What are you doing here?"

"Just wanted to come by and talk for a little while. I know I didn't handle things well the other day, and I don't want to mess up our friendship."

"Look, maybe this isn't a good idea. It's just too hard."

"No, no. Come on. We can do this."

"Really?"

"Of course," he said. "I can handle being your friend. I promise. Go ahead and try me."

"What do you mean?"

"Tell me more about this guy you met."

He couldn't believe he'd just said that. Of all the things he wanted to talk about, some guy who had kissed her was last on the list.

"No way," she said. "You can't handle that."

"Sure I can. Come on. Was he a good kisser? Better than me?" It was like an alien had taken over his mouth.

"I'm not even going there with you."

She shook her head as she walked over to the lounge chairs beneath the awning. He followed and stood in front of her, frustrated by his desire to know what happened, and the nausea he felt coming on.

"Why can't you tell me?" he asked. "I'm just another friend."

"You're hardly just a friend. That's the problem with all of this."

"Look, seriously. How far did things go with this guy?"

"Why do you want to know that? You're just making things harder."

"And you're avoiding the question."

She rubbed her temple and sighed. "I don't think it's any of your business. I just did what you told me to do."

"I did not tell you to go jump a total stranger the moment you met him."

"Excuse me?" She stood and shoved a finger at him. "You don't know anything about it."

"Because you won't answer a simple question!"

His heart was racing with all the images flying through his head. This was not how he'd pictured this conversation.

"Fine," she said, glaring at him. "You want to know what happened? I'll tell you. He kissed me and it was incredible. We took long walks on the beach and he ran his hands all over my skin and I loved it! Is that what you want to hear?"

He turned away from her and kicked a beach ball clear across the pool. His stomach twisted, and he fought back the taste of vomit. How could this have happened? He'd turned his back for a minute, and like that she'd moved on.

He was an idiot.

He took another moment to steady his emotions, and when he turned back around she was seated in the chair again, her arms folded over her chest like armor. He'd completely screwed this up.

"I'm sorry," he said. "This is my fault. I was a jerk. I really don't care what happened on your vacation. It's none of my business, just like you said."

"If you didn't care you wouldn't have reacted the way you did. Besides, it's not going to get any easier. How are you going to react when I actually start dating someone?"

"Not a problem." His stomach lurched in protest.

She laughed, though it wasn't exactly pleasant.

"You barely got that out of your mouth, liar. And you know, I don't think I would be comfortable with you dating someone either. It's just weird."

He dragged a chair over and sat in front her where she'd have to look at him.

"Come on, Lil. People break up and stay friends every day. I still have a little time to deal with all of this. It's not like you're dating someone now. Just give me a chance to get used to the idea."

She glanced at him then, but only for a second. Still, it was long enough to catch the guilt. She hadn't told him everything.

"Lily?"

"This is exactly why we can't stay friends. I feel nauseous just thinking about talking to you about someone else."

"Who are you talking about?"

"Alex."

His mouth went dry. "Alex? Who's Alex? The guy from your vacation? That has to be what, five or six hours from here? How could you be dating him?"

"I'm not really *dating* him. We've been talking on the phone a lot, though. And I'm going back down there for a couple of days."

"*What?*" He jumped up and started pacing the deck. "You can't be serious. Do you know anything about this guy? He could be a murderer or a rapist!"

He faced her, and she was staring at him like he had suddenly grown a horn out of his head.

"Could you just calm down for a minute?" she said.

"You can't go down there by yourself. It's not safe. Is this guy even a Christian?"

"Ugh. You sound just like my dad."

"I can't believe he would be okay with this. Does he know you're going?"

"Yes, but that doesn't matter. I'm not a kid. I can take care of myself. Besides, Emily and Alison are going with me."

His heart thudded in his ears. She was going back down there. To see *him.* It wasn't just a fling she'd had on vacation.

She was getting involved with someone else. Now there was no way he could sit back and take things slow. He had to tell her.

"Lily, listen to me. Don't go down there."

"Just stop."

"No. Just hear me out. I was trying to take this slow, to be your friend first."

"First? What are you talking about?"

"I thought that if we could be friends, you would start to trust me again. That I could show you I've changed, and we could be happy again. I had no idea you were getting involved with someone else."

She let out a slow deliberate laugh then pushed herself up from the chair. Her eyes bored into him with utter contempt.

"This isn't about us. It's about you. You just can't stand the thought that I could be happy with someone else."

He dropped his head and swore under his breath. He could crack himself wide open and she wouldn't believe a word of it. She'd made up her mind, and there would be no changing it. He stood up from his chair and took his keys off the end table near the door.

"I know I can't stop you from doing this," he said. "But I think you're making a huge mistake."

"I think you should go."

"Don't."

"I said go!"

There was nothing left to do but walk away, so he did, slamming the gate behind him. If she wanted to throw everything away for some stupid fling, he couldn't care less. Alex could have her, and good luck to him.

He climbed into his car and slammed the door, trying to force the air in and out of his lungs. *I don't need her. I don't need her.* If he just kept saying it over and over, maybe he could start to believe it.

Chapter Ten

Lily stepped out of her car and smiled as the familiar salty air hit her lungs. She'd never believed it would happen, but she'd actually made it back to St. Simons.

"Wow, Lily, this place is amazing!" Emily said.

She stood from the passenger side and stretched her arms. She twisted her torso back and forth then walked around to the back of the car and stepped up onto the sidewalk. Alison groaned from the back seat.

"Remind me never to ride in the back of your car for more than an hour."

She pushed her arms and legs through the small space between the passenger seat and the doorframe like a granddaddy long leg spider squeezing out of a crack. She unfolded her body into a long stretch and rubbed her back.

"Sorry about that," Lily said. "You should have just told Em to take the back. She's the runt around here."

Alison smiled, her face the picture of pure sunshine Lily had come to love over the years. The wind whipped Alison's hair into a blonde tornado around her face, and she reached up to push it behind her ears.

"Ah, I didn't really mind that much," she said. "She'd have just driven us crazy with complaining for five and half hours."

"True."

Lily glanced around at the hotel Alex had arranged for them. He'd said it was nice, but this was much more than she'd expected. The majestic palm trees surrounded the pool and tennis courts, and the grass looked as though every blade had been hand cut at just the perfect length. She was afraid to even step on it. The grounds and buildings looked like they belonged in a Spanish palace rather than a hotel.

"How much did you say we're paying a night?" Alison asked.

"Who's ready to hit the beach?" Emily clapped her hands and rubbed them together, her wide smile beaming.

Lily popped the trunk of the car open. "There's plenty of time for the beach. Let's get checked in."

She walked around to the back and leaned into the trunk to pull out her bag, but the sudden screech of a siren sent her head flying into the roof of the trunk.

"What the heck?" she mumbled. She stood up and rubbed the pulsing pain in her head.

A police car pulled in front of hers, and Alex stepped out of the passenger side. They smiled at each other for a moment before closing the gap between them like two magnets suddenly flipped over. He threw his arms around her and rocked her back and forth, mumbling in her ear.

"You have no idea how good it is to see you."

She savored his embrace, soaked in the familiar smell of salt and sweet that reminded her of their last night together. Had time really passed since then?

"I missed you too."

She managed to pull away from him long enough to remember her friends.

"Oh, yeah. This is my roommate, Emily Sanchez." She pointed behind her at Emily, whose dark skin was already glistening in the heat. She waved and ducked into the trunk to retrieve her suitcase.

"And that's Alison James."

He nodded his head toward her, and she smiled in return.

"So you both play volleyball with Lily?"

"Yep." Alison walked around the front of the car and stuck out her hand. "We've heard a lot about you. It's nice to finally meet."

"Definitely." He let go of Lily and took Alison's hand. "I hope you like the hotel. I know it's a bit extravagant, but a buddy of mine does security here and owed me a favor."

Emily stuck her head around the side of the car.

"Seriously? Did you save his life or something?"

"No," he said. "It wasn't that glamorous. I just dropped a ticket for his wife."

Lily frowned. "Forgive her. She's enthralled with law enforcement."

"Really?" Alex's eyebrows shot up.

"Yes! I want to be an FBI agent." Emily slung her bag over her shoulder and joined the rest of them.

"Well, maybe we can swap stories sometime," he said. He glanced over his shoulder at the other officer waiting in the car.

"Where's Steve?" Lily asked.

"He's off today. I'm sure Chloe has him swamped in wedding stuff. But I should get going. I'll be done around five. What do you ladies want to do this evening?"

Lily fixed her gaze on Emily, hoping her message was clear. Emily grinned at Alison before answering.

"I think Ali and I will just hang around the hotel tonight. This place is awesome. You guys go out and have a good time." She winked at Lily.

Alex shrugged. "Okay. I'll come pick you up when I get off around five." He leaned over and planted a kiss on Lily's forehead. "See you later."

She watched him climb back into the car and ride away, her stomach still flipping and fluttering. Just a couple of more hours and they would be together again. She'd probably go nuts waiting. Emily stepped beside Lily and watched the patrol car turn out of the parking lot.

"You did *not* do that boy justice when you described him. No wonder you drove so far to see him again."

Lily grinned and turned back toward her car, picking her bag out of the trunk.

"Come on, let's get checked in."

Alex leaned across the checkerboard table cloth with a mischievous twinkle in his eye, like he knew the most wonderful secret he was dying to share, sending Lily's insides into a frenzy again. She'd barely eaten half a slice of pizza, had hardly registered whether she even liked it or not, and had no idea if it was hunger or excitement that was keeping her stomach in knots.

"So what do you want to do next?" he asked.

Freeze time. Drown in your eyes. Kiss you from head to toe.

God, she was turning into a romantic sap. She grinned and reached across the table for his hand.

"It's your town. Why don't you choose?"

He smiled back at her, and she wondered if everyone in the restaurant could see the glow around them. It seemed so bright and warm. How could anyone miss it? She glanced around, convinced the world was watching in envy of their real-life fairy tale. The clatter of the kitchen mixed with love songs drifting from the jukebox and circled throughout the couples and families sharing in her moment. It was perfect.

"Come on." Alex slid to the end of the booth. "I have an idea."

"Where are we going?"

"You'll see."

She followed him out of the door, never dropping his hand. He opened the passenger door to his black SUV and gestured for her to climb inside. She waited for him to come around the car and join her then reached for his hand again, her skin aching to touch his.

"I can't believe you got rid of your motorcycle," she said. "You're seriously putting your bad boy image in jeopardy."

He laughed and kissed her knuckles as he turned around to back the car out.

"Maybe that's the point."

As he turned out of the parking lot and drove back under the interstate, she wondered where they were heading. Jackson's voice suddenly popped into her head. *You don't even know this guy.* She had no idea where they were, or even how to get back to the island, much less her hotel. He could drive her off into a secluded area and do anything he wanted. Her pulse quickened at the thought, but she pushed it aside. Leave it to Jackson to try to ruin her evening from over four hundred miles away.

"Are you having a good time?" Alex asked.

She looked over at him and felt her nerves relax a bit. This was Alex. *Her* Alex. He'd never hurt her.

"I'm having a great time." She squeezed his hand. "But where are we going?"

"Over there." He pointed ahead of them to the docks that lined the highway. "It's where most of the shrimp boats come and go on the intracoastal waterway. It's not as nice as the beach, but it has its own charm."

He pulled into a parking lot along the water and they climbed out. The smell of rotten eggs assaulted her, and she scrunched her nose as she joined Alex on the sidewalk.

"What is that smell?"

"Oh yeah. The paper mill is nearby. Sorry about that. After living here for a while you barely notice it. Does it bother you?"

"Nah, the breeze seems to be dissipating it." She let out a giggle. "You really know how to pick a romantic spot for a date, Walker."

"Hey, don't knock it yet. You might change your mind. There's more to living on the coast than just the beach."

"Yeah, apparently there are wonderful aromas to enjoy as well."

He tugged her down another sidewalk leading away from the water and toward a white-washed pavilion and bell tower. They rounded the front of the building and climbed the three steps leading up to a gazebo attached to the pavilion. Alex sat down on a bench and pulled her down beside him, wrapping his arm over her shoulder.

The sun hung low in the sky, casting a long shadow over the gazebo and the park behind them. A huge ship, old and important looking, sat in the water nearby like it was waiting for someone to admire it. She tried to take in her surroundings and to listen as Alex described the scenes before them. With his arm around her and the warmth of his body so close, she could barely focus on what he was saying as he pointed toward the water.

"And every spring they have a parade with a statue of some lady whose real name I can't remember, but I called her the Fat Lady when I was a kid for some reason. Then they bless the fleet of shrimp boats."

She looked up at him and grinned, not sure what in the world he'd been talking about, but mesmerized none the less. He leaned down and kissed her, his lips tugging at her sensibility.

"Am I boring you?"

She pushed her fingers through his hair and pulled his lips back in sync with hers, not wanting to be separated from them for even a minute more. He pulled her hips closer, folding her into his arms, stirring up desire and heat. Then his hand skimmed up her arm and tickled her throat, bringing chills in its wake.

"Changed your mind yet?" he whispered in her ear.

"Hmm? About what?"

She could barely form words, much less concentrate on his. All she registered was the tingle in her skin as his fingers drifted down the nape of her neck.

"This," he mumbled, covering her mouth with his.

His hand floated further down, and her brain began to register what was happening, but her body refused to cooperate. *Just another moment,* she thought. *Just a little more.* His hand slipped under her shirt and around her waist, testing gently.

Just a little more.

As his hand wandered to her bra strap and pushed it off her shoulder, her resolve faltered. He glided his hand over her skin, and she savored the sweet shiver that passed through them both. Then just as quickly her senses returned and she pulled away.

"Wait. We need to slow down."

"Lily."

Just her name on his breath made her wish she'd never stopped him, and if he kept looking at her like that—like his eyes were swallowing her whole—she wouldn't be able to stop him again. Willing herself to move, she slid further away and pulled her bra strap back in place.

"You are definitely going to be trouble." She couldn't help a small grin. "And no, I haven't changed my mind."

He let out a long, slow breath and sat up straight again. "Too bad. That was just getting interesting."

"I guess you'll just have to be patient."

He chuckled softly. "I guess so."

She looked away and tried to collect her scattered thoughts. She was going to have to get control of herself around him. He was so good at pushing her limits. Then another thought occurred to her.

"So is this where you bring all the women you date?"

"Uh, no. I usually take them home."

"Theirs or yours?"

He laughed and leaned back, spreading his arms along the railing behind him.

"Theirs mostly."

Maybe she shouldn't ask these questions. She had a feeling she wouldn't like the answers, but how else was she going to get to know him? Maybe he made every girl feel this way. Maybe he was much more experienced with women than she'd wanted to think about.

"And what do you do once you get them there?" Her stomach cringed as soon as the words left her.

He shrugged. "I don't know. Whatever happens just happens. I don't usually have an agenda."

"Do you sleep with women on the first date?"

He studied her for a moment, the smile fading from his face. Then he leaned forward and rested his elbows on his knees.

"Is this a test? Because if it is, I'm probably going to fail."

"It's not a test. I just want to know you better, to know how you treat women. I think that's fair."

He worked his jaw before he sat up straight again and looked her in the eye.

"Alright then. I have slept with a woman on the first date, sometimes the only date, sometimes without there even being a date. How's that?"

She blinked. He had said he wasn't a virgin, and she was half expecting that he had slept with multiple women, but he'd also said he was a Christian. She was stunned, not just by his sleeping habits, but also by the anger that colored his confession.

Doubts and questions began swirling through her. How could he be a Christian and have been so cavalier about sex? How had she let herself get involved with someone with such opposite values from her own? And how was she going to keep her values in tact with temptation caressing and coaxing her every time they touched?

Will power. And lots and lots of prayer.

"Look," she said. "I'm not judging you. Whatever you did in the past with other girls is your business. But when you're with me—here, now—this *is* my business. And honestly, you scare me."

"What? Now you're scared of me?"

"I didn't mean it that way. I just meant that this is all very unnerving for me. I don't do this."

"Do what exactly?"

Warmth crept up her neck and cheeks. "Move this fast. I mean, you know. Things were getting pretty heated there for a minute."

His mouth tipped. "I know. And unless I'm completely clueless, you seemed to be enjoying it." He slid closer and reached for her hand. "Come on. You have nothing to worry about." Tugging on her hand, he tucked her under his arm again and kissed the top of her head. "We won't do anything you don't want to do."

But that wasn't the problem. It was what she *did* want to do that scared her.

"Are you uncomfortable with anything we've done so far?" he asked.

"No."

"Then relax, Lily. You can trust me."

She looked up at him and studied his face. She wanted to trust him. She *would* trust him. And when he pulled her into another kiss, she let go of her doubts and let her body savor every moment.

August 5

St. Simons Island

Lily stopped her bike just behind Alex and jumped off. She pulled her water bottle out of the cup holder and gulped down half of it. The sun was intense, beating down on her skin. She glanced over at Emily and Alison as they popped the kickstands out on their bikes and guzzled their water as well. Alison's cheeks were like two ripe tomatoes anchoring her mouth, but Emily barely showed any signs of exertion, just a halo of dark, damp curls framing her face and glistening brown skin.

"Well, this is it." Alex gestured toward the open marsh land in front of them. He pulled the bottom of his t-shirt up and wiped the sweat off his face. Lily noted the muscles flex in his abs and grinned at him.

"Not too bad," she mumbled.

He winked at her and returned the grin, sending butterflies around her rib cage again. Emily walked over next to Lily and let out a huff.

"So what's the big deal? I thought this place was famous. There's nothing here."

"Well, not now," Alex said. "But there was a pretty major battle here for control of Georgia. Who knows, maybe you'd be speaking Spanish if it had turned out differently."

"I *do* speak Spanish."

Alex laughed and shrugged. "Well, then maybe the rest of us would be as enlightened as yourself."

"So what happened here?" Lily stepped over next to Alex and took his hand.

He pointed out toward the sea of grass, and as he described the battle between the British and Spanish soldiers, she pictured all the young men in their tattered uniforms slumped over in the muddy water. How did anyone face down an enemy with a gun pointed at them?

She squeezed Alex's hand. "Have you ever had to shoot anyone?"

Emily jumped in front of him, her eyes bright with excitement.

"Wow, that would be so cool. Have you?"

He laughed and folded his arms over his chest. "You'd probably love riding around in the squad car."

"Could I?" Emily's eyebrows shot up.

Lily tried to hide her irritation at Emily's constant interference all day. She had begged for stories, bombarded Alex with questions, and had not stopped talking about all the real-life crime books she had read.

"I don't think we'll be here long enough for all that," Lily said.

"Maybe next time," Alex said.

Lily had to practically shade her eyes from Emily's smile. They had obviously lost the connection they'd shared the day before because all of Lily's signals were going unnoticed. She looked over at Alison, who just shrugged and smiled. She seemed to be saying exactly what Lily was thinking. *What can you do? You have to love her.*

"So, have you ever shot at anyone?" Lily asked, trying to regain his attention.

"Yeah, once."

"When?" Emily asked. "You have to tell us everything."

Lily flipped her a glare, but Emily was hanging on every word out of Alex's mouth, and she suspected he was enjoying it as much as Emily.

"A couple of guys robbed a restaurant and shot the owner over here on the island one night, so we blocked off the causeway. Pretty dumb when there's only one way on and off the island."

"Anyway, we started searching all the cars, and I saw one approaching that looked suspicious. It fit the description we had, and the guys inside were wearing camo, just like the suspects."

"I yelled at another officer closer to the car to pull them aside, but just as he started to, the driver gunned the car and tried to run him over."

"Wow!" Emily gasped. "What did you do?"

Alex stepped away and re-enacted his movements, pulling an imaginary gun from his hip.

"I pulled my gun and took three shots at the front windshield before I had to jump out of the way."

"He tried to run you over too?" Emily asked.

"Yeah, but several other officers started shooting, and we blew out the tires. The driver jumped out of the car, and we chased him down on foot."

"Oh man. I can't wait to be a cop."

Lily rolled her eyes. "I thought you wanted to be an FBI agent."

"I do," Emily said. "But I want to be a local cop first so I can get some experience."

"That's the way to do it, really." Alex said. "I'd like to be a fed one day myself, but right now, being a cop is a blast."

Lily pushed down the urge to snatch Alex away and glanced down at her watch, hoping it was time to head back to the hotel.

"We should probably get back to the room and get ready if we want to make the movie," Lily said.

Alison stepped forward with her phone flipped open. "How about a picture before we go?"

"Sure!" Emily threw her arm over Lily's shoulder.

Alex stepped sideways and out of the shot, but Lily waved her hand at him.

"Come on, get in."

He shook his head. "No thanks. I don't do pictures."

"What?"

"Nah, it's just a bad idea. You post something on Facebook or the web, and suddenly everybody knows your business. Not my style."

"Okay." Lily shrugged. "Well, then Ali get in the picture and let Alex take it."

Alison handed him her phone and slid under Lily's arm. They smiled while Alex snapped the photo, and then they all headed for their bikes. Lily breathed a sigh of relief. No more competing with Emily.

As she stepped out of the hotel shower, Lily heard a shriek from the other side of the door. She wrapped the towel around her hair and threw her clothes on as quickly as she could. When she opened the door, her mouth dropped open. Alex had Emily pinned face down to one of the hotel beds, her dark waves spilling out around them. Alex's face was flushed, and he laughed as Emily struggled to free herself.

"Do you give up?" he asked.

"Never!" Emily shouted, though the comforter muffled her voice. "I'm going to figure a way out of this, and then I'm going to kick your butt!"

Emily squirmed back and forth as Lily tried to figure out what was going on. Alex finally released her and deftly avoided the swing she took at him. He grinned in triumph then shot past Lily into the bathroom and slammed the door behind him.

"Hey, I wasn't finished," she said. After a moment she heard the shower running. She'd have to put on her make up when he got out.

Emily pushed her hair back into place and stomped over to the door, yelling at it like the door had pinned her down.

"I could have gotten out of it!"

Lily looked over at Alison sitting in the corner by the table and raised an eyebrow. Alison glanced up from the magazine she was reading and shrugged her shoulders.

"Hey, don't look at me. I told her he would win."

"Win what?" Lily asked.

Emily huffed and stretched out across the nearest bed.

"I could have gotten out of it if he had given me more time."

Alison flipped the page of her magazine. "He was talking about how to get out of different positions if someone attacks you. Em said she could get out of anything."

"I can!" Emily looked at Lily as though she should realize this. "I've taken Karate for two semesters now. He cheated."

"Anyway," Alison continued. "Alex started demonstrating some holds, and it just seemed to escalate into a brawl from there."

Lily tried to push down the jealousy bubbling up her chest.

"Well, I'm glad to see you two are getting along so well. You certainly have a lot in common."

Emily pushed up onto her elbows and smiled. "Lil, he's really great. I'm so excited for you. I don't know how you control yourself around him. He's so gorgeous."

Lily cleared her throat, trying to suppress the heat in her cheeks. But Emily knew her too well, and her eyes widened. Lily tried to head her off before she said anything more.

"Em, no. It's not like that."

"Not like what? You don't have to be embarrassed for my sake. I say jump on him."

Alison jerked her gaze up from her magazine. "Emily Sanchez!"

"Yes, Mother?"

"Don't call me that."

"Then lighten up. This is Lily we're talking about. She's almost as uptight as you are. I'm sure you have nothing to worry about." Emily looked back over at Lily and flashed a broad smile. "Or does she?"

Lily shook her head hoping Emily would drop it. Alison would never let her hear the end of it if she knew half of what she'd already done.

"It's none of your business."

Emily grinned, but Alison pursed her face into that look Lily knew too well. Here it comes, she thought. Alison put down her magazine and moved to the bed.

"How much do you really know about Alex?" she asked.

Lily crossed her arms over her chest and shifted her weight. What was with everyone? How else was she going to get to know him if she didn't spend time with him? Besides, Alison had never even kissed a guy, so of course it was easy to sit back and tell everyone else what they should do.

"I know him as well as I could know anyone in a few weeks."

"Is he pressuring you?"

"No, Ali. He's a nice guy."

"I know he's a nice guy, but he's still a guy. I just want you to be careful."

"I'm being careful. Trust me. There's nothing to be concerned about."

Just then, Alex swung the door open and stepped out of the bathroom. He had on a pair of jeans and a black polo shirt that hugged his muscles, and his wet hair glistened like the igneous rocks Lily had studied last spring in Geology.

He grinned at the three of them, apparently enjoying the gawking. Definitely nothing to worry about.

Chapter Eleven

August 6
St. Simons Island

Lily pushed her plate away and leaned back in the wrought iron chair outside a café in the village. A low rumble echoed from the clouds looming over the ocean. They were heavy, full of water, just waiting to ruin the perfect afternoon. In front of her, tourists and locals bustled by with loaded down bags and boxes as if they knew danger was approaching. She hoped the rain held off, or rolled on out to sea. She hated rain.

The thought suddenly reminded her of Jackson's mom tending the rose bushes, her gloved hands working the soil, picking out weeds, clipping off the dead bulbs. She could hear Mary's voice as if she were right in front of her.

"Rain makes the flowers grow even more beautiful," she had said one day as she taught Lily how to care for the roses. "Sometimes it's the unpleasant things of life that make the good parts stand out."

It hadn't made much sense then, but maybe Mary was right. Strange that she had popped into Lily's thoughts now. She felt a tug on her heart, an uneasiness that she had learned over the years to heed. She said a silent prayer for Mary, for whatever reason she could not quite grasp.

Alex's laugh brought her out of her thoughts, and he glanced at her curiously as he set down his tea.

"You okay over there? You looked like you faded out on us for a minute."

She looked over at Emily and Alison who had the same curious look, but she shrugged and smiled.

"Sorry. I was just watching the clouds. Looks like it might rain."

He glanced behind him. "Yeah. I think you're right. Maybe we shouldn't go fishing today."

"No way." Lily sat up straighter.

Alison laughed and placed her soda on the table. "Good luck with that one. I doubt you could stop Lil from going fishing if a hurricane was coming."

"Really?" Alex said. "I had no idea you liked it that much."

"Are you kidding?" Emily added. "I'm surprised she's not majoring in it."

"Trust me, if it was an option, I would," Lily said.

Alex laid down his fork and leaned toward her. "How did I not know this about you?"

Lily glanced over at Emily and Alison, willing them to stay quiet.

"Well, I don't go as often as I used to. I guess it just hasn't come up." Emily's eyes met hers, and Lily was thankful for the understanding that passed between them.

She could tell Alex didn't exactly buy it, but as he was about to open his mouth, someone called his name. Lily looked over his shoulder as he turned around, and walking toward them was a slender red-head holding several bags in her hands. Her stomach wrenched for a moment. Not another beautiful woman panting over him.

"Chloe." He pushed his chair back and stood up.

Relief washed over her. It was just his sister. He took a few steps toward her, meeting her a few feet away from their table.

"What are you doing here?" Alex asked, almost mumbling.

Chloe leaned sideways and looked around him toward the table, but her sunglasses hid her eyes. She smiled up at Alex.

"I was just doing some shopping. Why don't you introduce me to your friends?"

Lily couldn't see his face, but she noticed his body stiffen as he lowered his voice and mumbled something she couldn't here.

Chloe's smile broadened, and she pushed her sunglasses on top of her head. They had the same hazel eyes, even the crinkles on the sides. She pushed Alex aside and stepped around him.

"Oh Alex, really. Don't be rude." She pulled a spare chair up to the table between Alison and Emily and looked back up at him with wide eyes. "Well?"

Alex sighed as he returned to his seat beside Lily. He gestured toward her first.

"Chloe, this is Lily Brennon and her friends Emily and Alison." He gave Lily a smile, but she could tell he was uncomfortable. "This is my sister, Chloe."

Lily extended her hand. "Hi. It's nice to finally meet you."

Chloe stared at her as if she were trying to determine whether Lily was real or imaginary, sending a flush of embarrassment through her.

Chloe finally offered her hand. "Same here."

Lily looked over to Alex again, and this time there was no mistaking the tension in his body. He cleared his throat.

"Lily and her family came down from Alabama on vacation a few weeks ago." She waited for him to explain further, but he barely paused before changing the subject. "So what are you doing here?"

Chloe narrowed her eyes, but before she could answer, the waitress interrupted to take her order.

"I'm not staying," she said, waving her off. Once the waitress scurried away, she turned back to Lily. "So you've been here for several weeks?"

"Oh no. We only stayed a week. I came back down for a few days with my friends."

Chloe paused and pressed her lips into a thin pink line, a flicker of dawning on her face. She took a quick glance at Alex.

"Well," she said. "Saint Simons must have made quite an impression on you. That's an awfully long drive."

The chill in Chloe's voice made her pause. Surely this was not the same woman Steve had spoken so highly of.

"Yes," Lily said. "I really enjoyed it." She glanced over at Emily and Alison, but they looked just as surprised as she felt.

"So how long are you staying this time?" Chloe asked.

"Only a couple of days. We have to be back at school next week for pre-season."

"Pre-season?"

"Yeah. We play volleyball at Samford University."

Chloe smiled, but nothing about it seemed warm.

"How nice."

Alex folded his hands together on the table, and Lily noticed his knuckles go white.

"So, what are you doing here?"

Chloe finally looked at him, and she leaned back in her chair with a smile.

"Like I said, I was doing some shopping and I happened to notice you. Is it a problem? Did I interrupt something?"

Alex just stared at her, so Lily spoke up.

"I'm glad you came over. Alex and Steve both have spoken very highly of you, and I've been hoping to meet you."

A curious look flashed over Chloe's face. "You've met Steve too? Funny. Neither of them mentioned you before."

Now Lily was certain of Chloe's reaction to her, but she had no idea why. She looked over at her friends, but Emily was glaring at Chloe like she was getting ready to pounce on her.

"Lil," Alison said. "Don't move."

"What?" Lily stared at Alison's ashen face.

Emily's eyes widened as well. "Do you have your Epipen?"

"No, why?"

Alison reached her hand slowly toward her. "Just stay still. There's a bee flying around your head."

"What's going on?" Alex asked.

"Don't move!" Emily pointed at him, and he froze.

Lily tried to stay still while Alison carefully waved the bee away, but she'd rather have slapped them both. As soon as it took off, Alison grabbed her hand and pulled her away from the table. Lily nearly stumbled over the chairs as Alex jumped up at the same time.

"What is going on?" Chloe asked, standing as well.

Emily began gathering drinks. "We need to go sit inside. Lily's allergic to bee venom."

"Deathly allergic," Alison added. She tugged Lily toward the front door. "Let's just sit inside."

Lily pulled away and stood her ground. "Excuse me, but I am a grown woman. Please don't tug me around like a toddler. It was one stupid bee. I'm fine. Let's just sit back down."

Alex frowned. "If you're that allergic, maybe it's best."

Chloe stooped over and grabbed her bags. "Well, this has all been very exciting, but I have a lot of errands to finish up."

Alison frowned at Lily. "Come on, Lil. It's not worth the risk, especially without your Epi." She nodded toward Chloe. "It was nice to meet you."

Lily sighed and followed Alison toward the door. She waved at Chloe as she went in.

"Nice meeting you. Good luck with the wedding."

Chloe didn't even acknowledge her. How rude. She watched Alex grab one of Chloe's bags. He met Lily's gaze and smiled a silent apology.

"I'll be right back," he said.

Lily walked into the café with her friends wondering what she could have possibly done to make Chloe dislike her so much.

Alex looked both ways before he stepped off the curb and followed Chloe into the street. He was tempted to fling her into the oncoming traffic, but he restrained himself until they reached her car.

"What is wrong with you?" he growled.

She unlocked her car and slung her packages to the passenger side.

"Me? What's wrong with *you*?"

"Don't even start with me, Chloe."

"How old is she?"

"It's none of your-"

"Does she know anything about you?"

Alex's blood boiled, rippling and rolling with fury.

"I'm only going to say this once," he began, "so listen carefully. You have no say in what I do with my life. I know that somewhere in that thick head of yours you think you're doing what's best." He took a deep breath and steeled himself to the anger in her eyes. "But I swear to God, Chloe, if you don't back off, we have nothing more to talk about. Ever."

She blinked, and her stony demeanor began to crumble.

"I just want you to be happy, and to do the right thing."

"That's just it. I am doing the right thing. You just can't see it."

She dropped into the car and swung her legs under the steering wheel. When she looked up at him again, she was already rebuilding her wall.

"Chasing after some kid who has no idea what she's getting into is certainly not right. And neither is abandoning your responsibilities."

He let out a long sigh and dropped his head. She would never understand. Life was well-defined for Chloe, with edges that ran straight and narrow toward perfection.

"Listen," he said. "After Monday, everything will be fine. You'll see."

She shook her head. "After Monday, you'll have made the biggest mistake of your life."

He placed his hands above the open door and squeezed the frame with all his frustration. He pulled his head up and glanced at the café where Lily was waiting with her friends, and his eyes caught something familiar. It was gone before he could pinpoint what had caught his attention, but something was off.

Chloe reached past him for the door handle, and he backed away.

"Alex, I know you've been through a lot over the last year, and I know you don't want to listen to me. But it's not too late to make this right."

She pulled the door closed and cranked the car, pulling out slowly into traffic. He watched her drive away then looked back toward the café across the street. He still couldn't figure out what he'd seen, though something in him told him he already knew. But it couldn't have been her.

He spotted Lily and her friends through the window getting settled at a table inside. For a brief moment, he considered what Lily would think of him if she knew the truth. In so many ways, she was like Chloe, with her clearly defined boundaries of right and wrong. Maybe she wouldn't understand either.

He shoved the doubts back to the corner from where they'd crept. Lily was good and kind, and he couldn't just walk away from her. No, he'd take care of everything once and for all on Monday. Then maybe he could convince her, and himself, that he wasn't a liar.

"You're such a liar," Lily said and swatted Alex's chest.

She lifted her head from his shoulder and rested on her elbow, her feet mingling with his as they hung out of the back of his SUV.

"Hey, watch the violence." He rubbed his chest. "I *am* an officer of the law, you know." He furrowed his brow, but he couldn't hide the laughter in his eyes. He reached around her shoulder and tucked her under his arm again.

"You expect me to believe that you caught a twenty-four pound bass?"

"I did!" he insisted. "My dad and I used to fish all the time when I was a kid. We even won a couple of tournaments."

"That's a load of crap. If you'd caught a twenty-four pound bass, you'd be the world record holder, and last time I checked, it was still George Perry, who happens to have held onto that record for nearly eighty years."

He shook his head and laughed. "You're too smart for your own good."

Lily couldn't help but smile. The day had been perfect, and the evening was following suit. Alex had parked in a grove of oak trees lining the waterway between the island and the mainland, and she'd almost convinced herself they could stay there forever, pretending the rest of the world didn't even exist. Looking toward the sun dipping below the causeway in the distance, she tried to focus on anything but the fact that it was their last night together.

"Did you have a good time today?" He squeezed her shoulders and kissed the top of her head.

"Yes. That was so nice of your friend to let us fish off his dock. How many people owe you favors?"

"Enough to help me impress you a little. But I'm running out fast."

She ran her hand under his shirt and across his abs, wishing she could stay another day. But then again, she'd just wind up right back here, wishing for another.

"I can't believe I have to leave tomorrow," she said. "It seems like I just got here."

"I know." He reached behind him and folded his pillow under his head. "Is there anything I can say to get you to stay?"

She lifted her head again and looked at him. "I really wish I could. You have no idea."

"I think I do." He pulled her face toward his.

Kissing him had become an addiction. How was she supposed to return to her life as if everything was normal? As he pulled her tighter and the heat between them began to grow, an urgent need to hold onto him threatened to overwhelm her. She didn't even know when she would see him again. He pulled her on top of him, exploring her mouth, her neck, her shoulders.

Don't stop.

She had no idea if she'd thought it, or said it, but she was aware of it all the same. When he pushed her shirt up, the same voice echoed in her head that had wanted more every time he touched her. But this time, it was Alex who pushed her away.

"Lily," he said as he wrapped his hands on the side of her face. "Let's do this."

At the sight of the intensity in his eyes, a wave of heat rushed through her. But somehow, a small voice broke through.

Stop.

"I can't." She pushed herself the rest of the way up. She swung her leg off of him and scooted to the back of the car, pulling her shirt back down and feeling like a complete loser. She let the breeze wash over her, wishing it would wash away her foolishness. How many times had she led him on, only to slam on the brakes? He slid over and sat beside her on the edge of the car.

"Hang on a second. I think you misunderstood what I meant." He chuckled quietly. "At least, I hope that was a misunderstanding."

"What do you mean?"

He looked out over the water and sighed. "Well, I meant that I want to do this." He gestured his hand between them. "You and me. Us." He glanced at her, and she could see his apprehension. "I know it may seem crazy since we live so far apart. But I think we could make it work. What do you think?"

Relief and embarrassment flushed her cheeks, and she couldn't stop the nervous giggle that jumped out of her.

"I thought-"

"Yeah, I know what you thought." He said with a grin.

"You really want to be with me?" she asked. "I have no idea when I can see you again. Wouldn't you rather be with someone you could actually take out on a Friday night?"

"No. Just you."

His answer, so simple and somber, caught her off guard. She hadn't let herself even consider the possibility of a real commitment between them.

"You're absolutely sure?" she asked.

"*I'm* sure." He tapped his fingers to his chest. "Seems like it's you who's uncertain."

She looked out over the water and wondered how to answer. They were so different. Enjoying some time together was one thing, but committing to something more?

"I just don't want you to have to sit around being bored because of me."

"Are you sure that's it? There isn't another reason?"

"Like what?"

Alex looked at her in silence for a moment. Then he lifted the chain from around her neck.

"Like Jackson maybe?"

Instinctively she reached for the necklace and tucked it back inside her shirt.

"No, of course not." Her stomach knotted. "He and I are through. Have been for a long time."

"Then why keep his necklace on?"

"It's not *his* necklace." She pushed her way out of the car and paced in front of him. "You don't understand. The necklace was just a promise to pray for each other. It was never about our romantic feelings. I've had it on since I was nine."

She stopped pacing and watched him mull over her words. What if he asked her to take it off? It was just a necklace, wasn't it? But even as the thought came, in some deep corner of her heart, she knew it was much more than a necklace, and she was sure Alex knew that too.

Alex reached his hand out toward Lily. "Come here," he said.

He'd wondered all evening how she would react if he brought up the necklace. He wouldn't have even mentioned it if she hadn't seemed so hesitant just now. And her nervous pacing only confirmed what he'd already suspected. He had no intention of competing for anyone, even her.

She took his hand and let him pull her back down beside him, and he wondered what he should say next. He shouldn't have even brought it up. It was all he could do to keep from grabbing the stupid thing and throwing it into the water. If she clung to a necklace so fiercely, maybe she was still clinging to Jackson as well.

"I know you've had it for a long time, but you're not a scared little nine-year-old without a Christmas gift anymore. And you're certainly not his girlfriend. You don't need a necklace to remind you to pray for someone. It seems like there's more to it than you want to admit."

She dropped her head, but then she reached behind her neck and unfastened the chain.

"You're right. It's time to let go and grow up."

He watched her fold the necklace and slide it into her pocket, relieved that it was gone. A small doubt still lingered and rattled around in his brain, but he refused to give it a foothold.

"So can I take that as a yes? You want to give this thing a try?"

"*Thing?*" Her lips spread into a smile. "Yeah, we can give this *thing* a try."

He grabbed her knee and gave it a squeeze, loving the squeal that escaped her. She tried to slip away, but he pushed her further into the back of the car, tickling her unmercifully. As she squirmed and laughed, he felt a rush of adrenaline pumping through him, and he finally pinned her arms above her head.

Her body fit perfectly beneath his, and it was all he could do to control himself, especially when he knew she wanted him. He could feel it. He had no idea why she fought it, but he was certain of the battle within her.

He slipped his hand under her shirt, sliding it up while he kissed the skin peeking out at him. Her breathing deepened, and he pushed the limit just a little more, relishing her gasp.

"Alex..."

He brought his face up to hers and pressed their mouths together, quieting any protest.

"Trust me," he said between kisses.

Then he returned his attention to her stomach, and gradually, he worked his way past the latest boundary.

Chloe knew a love-sick puppy when she saw one. That pitiful little college girl had been practically drooling on the table earlier. Though she could hardly blame her. No doubt Alex hadn't told her anything.

She pulled her hair back into a ponytail and began scrubbing the makeup off her face. Too bad she couldn't just scrub the stupidity off of Alex. She hated fighting with him, but he insisted on making one wrong choice after another lately.

She rinsed her face and dried it in a towel. Then she walked into her kitchen and grabbed the phone. She'd tried as hard as she could to back off, but the thought of him making such a huge mistake would keep her up all night unless she did something about it. There had to be a way to make him listen to reason.

She checked her watch and dialed the number. Of course, it went straight to voicemail.

"Hey, Adrian. It's Chloe. Listen, I know you want to do things your own way, but I just thought I'd let you know that you're about to screw up everything. Call me when you get this."

Chapter Twelve

"You need any help in here?"

Lily looked up as Kara popped her head into the open bedroom door at her dad's.

"Yeah, that would be great," she answered. "I left everything to the last minute, as usual."

Kara grinned and stepped over a laundry basket full of clothes and sat Indian style in the center of the room, the eye of the hurricane.

"What do you want me to do?"

Lily glanced around, not sure where to start. Clothes, books, CD's and shoes had overrun her room, and she felt ready to surrender. She hated this part of going back to school. The fact that she hadn't been able to concentrate on much of anything since returning from Saint Simons didn't help much either. Her emotions moved like liquid inside of her, flowing from depression to elation with the smallest tilt. She wanted desperately to think of anything but how much she missed Alex.

"You could start packing up my clothes over there." Lily pointed toward the overflowing laundry basket. "I have some dresses hanging in the closet that I need too."

"Don't you keep anything at your mom's anymore?" Kara asked.

"She was going to be in Nashville most of the summer for work, and I didn't want to have to go there for anything. Didn't really want to run into Jackson."

"I can understand that."

Kara pulled the basket toward her and began pulling items out one at a time, folding and separating them. She worked quickly and methodically while Lily focused on organizing her notebooks and school supplies. It was nice to have some help. Maybe she would actually be able to finish it all tonight.

"Lily, what is this?" Kara asked. She had moved into the closet, and Lily could hear the shuffling of papers.

Kara crawled out of the closet carrying a shoebox in her hand. She placed it on the floor as she sat back on her heels. Then she pulled out a stack of notes Lily practically knew by heart.

"Nothing." She reached for the box and slid it in front of her.

"These are all from Jackson."

"So?"

"So why are you keeping them?" Kara narrowed her eyes and looked at Lily like she'd been hiding a bomb in her closet.

"I don't know exactly. I'm just not ready to throw it away."

Kara rolled her eyes. "You're finally moving on with your life. Alex is great, and you guys are really happy. Now is the perfect time to get rid of all this."

Lily looked down at the collection of notes, cards, movie stubs, and trinkets she had been holding onto for more years than she knew. Every bit of paper held some piece of her past that fit together like the patches of a quilt. How could she just discard them? She pushed the papers around and found the necklace she had placed in there last night, rubbing her fingers over the inscription. She had taken it off. That would have to be enough for now.

"I'm just not ready yet."

She put the letters back that Kara had removed and replaced the top. Then she slid the box under her bed and all the way to the wall. Maybe one day she'd be able to enjoy those memories without the pain that still sliced through them.

"Whatever." Kara dismissed the notion with the wave of her hand and went back to packing.

On the television stand beside her, Lily's cell phone lit up and vibrated. She hoped it was Alex calling for one last goodnight, but it was Matthew's name on the screen instead.

"Lily? Hey. It's Matt. You got a minute?"

"That depends," she said. "Is this about Jackson?"

"Uh, well-"

"I knew it. Matt, please. Stay out of it."

"No, you don't understand." The uneven crack in his voice made her pause.

"What's going on?" she asked.

"It's Aunt Mary. She was in an accident a couple of days ago."

Lily gasped. "Oh no. Is she okay?"

"She has a broken leg, some cuts and bruises. The worst is the head injury, but they don't know how bad it is because she hasn't woken up."

Lily imagined Jackson sitting by his mother's hospital bed, terrified of losing another parent, and her heart ached for him.

"How's Jackson?"

"I don't know. He hasn't said much. I'm worried about him. He won't leave her side." Matt paused, and she knew what he was about to ask. "Could you come down here? Maybe talk to him a little."

"Not a good idea-"

"Come on, Lily. He needs you. We're all he has right now. Just me, and you."

She took a deep breath and tried to set aside the panic rising inside of her. How could she even consider saying no? She loved Mary as much as her own parents, and no matter what she had been through with Jackson, he was still her friend.

"I'll be there in an hour."

Birmingham, Alabama

In the rush to grab a few things and get out the door, Lily had forgotten she needed a shower. As she stood outside the hospital room arguing with her resolve to go in, she came up with one excuse after another to leave, and smelling bad seemed like the best one so far.

Come on, she scolded herself. *It's just Jackson. Just. Jackson.*

She turned the knob and slowly pushed the heavy door open. He sat on a stool next to Mary, his long form folded over the side of her bed as he held her hand. In the instant she saw him, she recognized the tired slump in his shoulders, the same defeated posture she'd faced for months after his dad had died.

Not again, Lord.

The door squeaked as she pushed it open, and he raised his head. He met her gaze with confusion, and then understanding dawned. He turned toward the corner behind him where Matt sat leaning forward, his hands folded together. A look passed between the cousins that Lily couldn't quite read, but she didn't need any further clues to know that he wasn't happy to see her.

"I'm going to get some coffee." Jackson stood and pushed his hair away from his eyes, then walked by without even looking at her, allowing the door to slam behind him.

She turned to Matthew, ready to lay into him.

"He didn't know I was coming, did he?"

He shook his head, but showed no signs of remorse.

"Jeez, Matt. How could you do that to me? To him? He's dealing with enough right now."

"I did what I had to. He needs you, whether he realizes it or not."

She let out a slow breath, pushing down her building anger. She had to focus on dealing with the situation rather than her irritation. She walked over and touched Mary's hand, careful to avoid the IV needle. Her face was badly bruised, and her head was wrapped in bandages. As much as it terrified her to see Mary so banged up, it must have ripped a hole right through Jackson.

"What happened?" she asked.

"Not sure exactly." Matthew frowned. "A truck ran a red light. Caught her on the driver's side."

"What can I do?"

He pushed himself up from the chair and rubbed the back of his neck. His face was tired and seemed to sag despite his effort at a smile.

"Just talk to her. I'll go talk to Jackson."

"What do I say?"

"Doesn't matter. Just talk. The doctor said it was good for her."

Matthew crossed the room and left Lily alone with her fear and doubt. She closed her eyes and tried to calm her racing thoughts. What could she say? Would Mary hear? Maybe she wouldn't even want Lily there. She opened her eyes and rubbed her thumb back and forth across the top of Mary's hand.

"Hey...Mary. It's me...Lily. I'm not sure what I should say, but I want you know how much I love you."

She paused and looked out the window at the blackness beyond. Her eyes ached and burned.

"God, sometimes you really don't make much sense."

Just down the hall, Jackson kicked the coffee machine for refusing to cooperate. Was it too much to ask for a simple cup of coffee? Hadn't he been through enough? He leaned his head against the colorful plastic machine and wished for once something in his life worked out the way it was supposed to—even if it was just a machine pouring bitterness into a cup. He muttered a curse and shook it one last time.

"There ya go. Take it out on a helpless vending machine."

Jackson turned to the voice behind him and found Matthew leaning against the wall, his arms crossed over his chest. He almost looked amused. He needed a good body slam right here in the middle of the hall. But that would have to wait. Instead he walked into the small waiting room across the hall and dropped into a chair. Matthew followed him and took the seat beside his.

"I told you *not* to call her," Jackson said.

"Well, following directions has never been my strong suit."

He met Matt's gaze with disdain. "This isn't funny. I don't want her here."

"She loves Aunt Mary too. She's practically been family since we were all kids. She deserves to know."

If he had to hear about Lily being *practically family* one more time, he was sure he'd lose it. She'd made it perfectly clear that those days were over. Just seeing her walk through the door had felt like a sucker punch.

"Look," Jackson said. "I know your heart's in the right place, but I can't deal with Lily and Mom at the same time."

"Well as I remember it, that was your problem last spring with Lily, and look how well that turned out for you. Don't blow it again. She just wants to help."

"There's nothing she can do." Jackson sat back and leaned his head against the wall. His eyelids felt like lead, and he let them close for a moment. "There's nothing any of us can do but wait."

"She can be here for you. You two need each other, whether you know it or not."

That was almost humorous. Matt had obviously forgotten where she'd just spent the past week. He opened his eyes and lifted his head.

"It's pretty clear she's doing just fine without me."

"You don't know that. Just talk to her, okay?" Matt gave him a pat on the back. "Just talk to her, man."

Jackson stared at their reflection in the window across the room. This from a guy who couldn't manage to have a relationship that lasted more than a couple of months, let alone a love that lasted for the better part of his life. Matt had no idea what he was asking. How could he possibly understand the price he'd have to pay to reach out to Lily?

Jackson shifted forward and rested his elbows on his knees, dropping his head into his hands.

"She's made it clear that she wants nothing more to do with me."

"Then why is she here?"

The question sank into his heart, resurrecting hope he had been trying to bury—hope he wasn't sure he could bear.

Jackson pushed open the door to his mom's room and found Lily bent over her, quietly praying. It was a sight that was both reassuring and painful, a reminder of what he had already lost, and what he still stood to lose. She looked up as the door closed, and he forced himself to speak before he lost his nerve.

"Thank you for coming down here."

She fumbled with her hands and looked back at his mom. "It was no problem. I wanted to come. She means the world to me."

He turned his gaze out the window beside him. Only a few cars remained in the parking lot below, and it looked as empty as he felt inside.

"She loves you too. It would mean a lot to her knowing you're here."

He heard her move out of her chair, felt her come up beside him as if there were a tension-filled rope connecting them. His hand tingled with expectation, hoping she would take it. But she folded her arms over her chest.

"What about you?" she asked. "You didn't exactly look happy to see me when I came in."

"Sorry about that. I just wasn't expecting you. That's all." He glanced over at her, hoping he sounded convincing.

"You sure? If you want me to go-"

"No," he said quickly. "You just got here. Stay. Visit for a little while. The doctors said that talking to her might help."

"Matt mentioned that, but I couldn't think of anything to say."

Despite his swirling emotions, the humor of her statement didn't escape him.

"Come on. You? With nothing to say? That had to be a first."

She let out a laugh that was more of a sob, and it seemed to release some of the tension. She rubbed her eyes with her palms.

"So how are you holding up?" she asked.

He hated that question. It seemed like the only thing people had been able to ask him for almost a year. Oh sure, everyone meant well, but what was he supposed to say? Should he open up the dam of fear and anger? He'd figured out quickly that most people just wanted to hear that he was okay—just an optimistic answer that let them off the hook as soon as possible. But not Lily. She'd been ready and willing to take on the brunt of his emotions, if only he'd been able to share them with her.

"I'm okay." He looked over at his mom and tried to push down the guilt and fear rising again. "I'm not the one lying in a coma."

"No, you're not. And you can't beat yourself up thinking it should be you-"

"But it should. She's absolutely the last person who should be suffering. Why does God keep doing this to my family?"

She reached for him, and her hand on his arm was like a soft blanket, soothing and warm. But it was gone too soon. She hugged her chest and rubbed her arms.

"I wish I had answers. I know this is hard."

She looked at him for a moment, her eyes assessing him with an intimacy he had never shared with anyone else. How could he have wasted so much of the past year pushing away the very person he'd needed the most? Now, she was right in front of him, dangling what he'd lost like a mirage in a desert. It was pointless to even try to reach out for the illusion.

"You need to get some rest," she said. "You want me to drive you home?"

"I'm not leaving her. What if she wakes up?"

"Matt will call you."

"I shouldn't." Just the thought of his mom lying there alone made his throat tighten.

"Come on. Mary would freak out if she woke up and saw you looking so pathetic. I'll drive you to your mom's and you can sleep for a few hours. Then I'll bring you right back."

"All right," he said, still unsure. "But I can drive myself."

"Don't be silly. You're exhausted. Just let me help."

"Fine. I don't have the strength to argue with you. But it's pointless. I won't be able to sleep anyway."

August 9

Birmingham, Alabama

Lily awoke on Mary's sofa with Jackson's head cutting off circulation to her lower extremities and her bladder about to explode. So much for his not being able to sleep. She gently slid out from under him and shook her legs to wake them up. Then she stretched out the ache in her back as she headed for the bathroom down the hall.

When she returned, the couch was empty, so she wandered into the kitchen. Jackson straightened after retrieving a pan from under the cabinet, his hair shooting out in all directions. He still wore his t-shirt and gym shorts from the night before, but she noticed for the first time how his shoulders filled out the sleeves. He'd been working out again. If not for the dark circles under his eyes, he might have looked like the boy she'd always known.

"You hungry?" he asked.

"Sure. But you don't have to make anything. I can go to my mom's."

"Nah, you might as well stay now. Bacon and toast okay?"

"Sure."

He set the pan on the burner then dug through the refrigerator until he found the bacon. Watching him peel apart the slices and place them onto the pan, she marveled at how simple routines from their past had become so complicated with emotions. How many mornings had she come over for bacon and toast? It had to have been thousands. Part of her ached for the security of their history. It still felt like home. Only now, it was mixed with so much heartache.

"You must have been pretty uncomfortable on the couch last night." He turned and leaned back against the counter, crossing his arms over his chest. "Sorry about that."

"No problem. I'm just glad you got some rest."

"You didn't have to stay all night."

He had been groggy when she'd helped him onto the couch. He'd obviously forgotten asking her to stay, and she was content to leave it that way.

"I wanted to make sure you were all right."

He started to speak, but gritted his teeth and turned away. He stood in silence, turning the bacon over and placing some bread in the toaster. When he placed his hand back on the stove, he jumped back and swore under his breath.

"Are you okay?" She stood and walked over to him.

"Just a little burn. No big deal." She reached for his hand, but he pulled it away as soon as she touched him. "I'm fine. Really."

She reached for the faucet. "Well, put it under some cold water for a few minutes. That should help."

As he soaked his fingers, he leaned his head against the cabinet and slumped his shoulders.

"I'm such an idiot."

"You're not an idiot," she said, rubbing his back. "You're just a little distracted."

She stepped over to the stove and removed the bacon from the pan. Then she placed a couple of pieces on the toast and brought the plate over to him.

"Thanks," he said. "But I'm not hungry. You go ahead."

"You're not going to eat?"

"I can't." He leaned back and reached for a napkin, wiping his hand dry. "Thanks. It actually does feel better now."

"You need to eat."

He met her gaze, and his eyes blazed with a sudden intensity.

"Lily, I don't need you to mother me. It's the absolute last thing on Earth I need right now."

Surprised by his sudden anger, she started to bolt. But before she could move, he reached out and gripped her elbow, pulling her closer instead.

"I'm sorry. I'm so sorry. I didn't mean anything by that. I'm just scared."

Scared. She couldn't remember him ever admitting to fear. Not once. It made her pause, and her heart softened.

"I know this is hard for you. But God's taking care of your mom. She's going to be okay."

He leaned his head down until his forehead rested on hers, so close she could sense the tremble in his chest.

"Lil," he whispered. "I miss you."

Her chest tightened, and it felt like her throat might close up.

"I miss you too."

She wanted to step back—she needed space to breathe—but her legs wouldn't move. As his hands held her cheeks, she felt the memory of his lips brushing hers as if it were real. Maybe it was. Maybe she wanted it to be real. If she just concentrated on his hand caressing her hair, her cheek, her neck, maybe she could go home again.

The sudden ring of the phone jolted them apart, and he stared at her as if waking from a dream. The second ring seemed to register, and he walked over to the doorway and took the receiver off the hook.

"Hello?"

He glanced at her, his eyes still glazed as though he didn't remember where he was. She felt like her own head needed a good shake. Had he just kissed her, or had she imagined it? Either way, she needed to get out of there. Her heart thudded so loud in her ears, she could barely think straight.

"Thanks, Matt." He hung up the phone and turned around with a huge smile. "She's awake."

The ride back to the hospital had been tense. They'd ridden in silence—Jackson staring out the passenger window, Lily staring at the road ahead. Now, as they approached Mary's room, Lily reached out and touched his arm, jerking it back as soon as he turned to her.

"I think I should head home now." She clasped her hands and began massaging her palms.

"Why? She'd want to see you."

The hope in his eyes only confirmed that she needed to get out of there.

"You should spend some time with her. I'll just be in the way."

He reached for the door handle. "Come on. Don't be ridiculous. She'll be hurt if she knows you were here and didn't come in."

She hated to disappoint Mary, and she especially hated thinking that her feelings would be hurt. Still, she couldn't get rid of the overwhelming desire to flee.

Jackson pushed the door open and beckoned her in, and her feet stumbled forward. Mary's face, still badly bruised, lit up with a pained smile. She reached her arms out as Jackson leaned down and embraced her.

Lily hung back, still tempted to slip out the door unnoticed. But Mary's gaze found hers, and she waved Lily closer.

"Come in, come in."

Lily leaned down and gave her a light hug, afraid of hurting her. She felt Mary's ribs, and her throat tightened.

"How are you feeling?"

Mary held onto Jackson with one hand, and she grasped Lily's with the other.

"I'm okay. Tired. Hungry. But I'm okay."

Lily glanced up at Jackson. His face was strained, but he smiled down at his mom.

"Is there anything I can get you?"

"Maybe some water."

He dropped her hand and turned to the tray beside her bed, pouring a glass of water. He handed it to her, and she took a small sip. Her hands seemed frail and wrinkled, like Lily's grandmother's. Around the IV, blood pooled beneath the surface, making a quarter-sized bruise. Lily gently squeezed the hand that still grasped hers.

"I really should get going. I'm glad you're okay."

Mary's blue eyes widened as she looked up. "Don't rush off. It's so good to see you again. Stay and visit."

Lily looked from Mary's pleading eyes to Jackson's and felt like the most horrible person in the world. Staying would be the right thing to do. But everything had changed. Everything.

She let go of Mary's hand and stepped toward the door, guilt and shame rushing through her.

"I'm sorry. I just...I need to get going. I still have so much to do before school starts."

Mary's expression fell, but she smiled again. "I'll see you soon, okay?"

"Okay." She slipped over to the door and pulled it open. "I hope you feel better soon."

Lily slipped through the door and tried not to race for the elevator. She punched the down arrow and paced in front of the doors, chewing her thumbnail. The bell dinged, and when the doors opened she jumped inside. She pushed the button for the parking garage, and then jammed her thumb into the button to close the doors.

When the doors opened to the garage, she took a deep breath and felt some of the tension leave her. But as she crossed the parking lot, she heard her name from somewhere behind her. She turned as Jackson jogged out of the stairwell beside the elevators, and the tension returned.

"Hey, wait up," he called.

She took the last few yards to her car as quickly as she could, but he had reached her by the time she opened her door. He put his hand on it, and she finally stopped and looked at him.

"Wait, can we talk a minute?" he asked.

She closed her eyes and hoped for strength. "About what?"

"Us. This morning. We almost-"

"Nothing happened." She forced herself to look at him, to make sure he got the message.

He wrinkled his brow, a crooked grin playing on his mouth. Not the mouth. She looked at his eyes instead, but the way he looked at her—as if he knew something she didn't—unnerved her for reasons that made no sense.

"Something definitely happened," he said. "You said you miss me."

"So?"

"Come on, Lil. If I've learned anything in recent history it's that I have to seize moments when they come around, and I'm trying to seize here. Give me a break."

"I think you got the wrong idea."

"No, I got the right idea. You're just trying to pretend it didn't happen. Why?"

"Nothing happened," she repeated. She tried to keep her composure, but he stepped a little closer, speeding her pulse. "Jackson, don't."

"You miss me."

"I miss our friendship. That's all. And whatever you think happened was all in your head. I was just trying to be a good friend. Please don't make me regret it."

He paused and looked down at her. She could practically see the questions flying through his head as he weighed her words against his hope. He leaned back against her car and crossed his arms, studying her. She felt like the frog she had once pinned down and dissected in high school Biology—utterly exposed.

"You're lying," he said.

"No I'm not."

"Yes you are. Your eyes. They do this fluttering thing when you lie."

"Don't be ridiculous." She'd never been more aware of trying *not* to flutter her eyes.

He smiled as though he had just solved one of the world's great mysteries.

"You still love me."

She couldn't believe his arrogance. She had wanted to avoid hurting him, but obviously he needed a stronger dose of rejection.

"My love for you was never in question, and as I recall, it wasn't good enough. You tossed it aside like it was a burden. So it isn't yours anymore."

"What is that supposed to mean?"

"I'm moving on with my life. You should too."

He nodded his head and looked away, but not before she saw the flicker of anger in his eyes.

"Is this the part where you tell me you're moving on with Alex?"

"We're done talking."

She reached for her door, but he slid in front of her and blocked her from reaching it. She stepped back and tried not to think about punching him in the mouth.

"I guess you had a nice little trip down there. Is he your boyfriend now?"

She steeled herself and forced her eyes to meet his.

"Yes."

He tried to hide it, but she saw the word slap him in the face.

"So how long did you wait before you let him grope all over you? You know he just wants to get-"

"Shut up!" She shoved him away from her door and pulled it open.

"I'm sorry-" He reached for her, but she pulled away and slid behind the wheel of her car.

"I came here to try to be your friend," she said as she shoved the key into the ignition. "Your gratitude overwhelms me."

She slammed the door before he could say anything else. Then she backed out of the parking space, almost hoping she'd run him over. As she slammed her foot into the gas pedal, she glanced into her rearview mirror and saw him standing right where she had left him.

Well, good riddance. He could miss her for eternity for all she cared. She had Alex. Finally she had found someone she could trust.

Chapter Thirteen

Brunswick, Georgia

"Where are you? You were supposed to meet me at the lawyer's office two hours ago. This is getting ridiculous! Call me."

Alex jammed his phone back onto his belt and pounded his fist into the kitchen counter. He should have known she'd do this. It had to be the fifth time in the past ten months she had ducked out on him. He racked his brain for the number at the newspaper office, but he couldn't remember the last four digits, and the harder he tried, the angrier he got.

He paced his kitchen in a frenzy, reciting numbers out loud hoping some combination would be familiar.

"Seven, eight, three, four. Seven, eight, four, three."

He stopped and took a deep breath.

"Eight, seven, four, three."

That was it.

He grabbed his phone again and dialed the number. After several rings, voicemail again. He swore under his breath. Then he repeated his message for the third time, though by now he began to realize the futility in leaving them. He hung up and immediately dialed Chloe's number. Maybe she would at least have some answers.

"Where is she?" he demanded as soon as she picked up.

"Excuse me? Don't you even bother with hello anymore?"

The coolness in her voice only infuriated him further.

"Hello. Have you heard from Adrian?"

"I have no idea what you're talking about."

"Yes you do," he spat through clenched teeth. "I'm sick of the games. If you know where she is, just tell me. I know you two talk all the time."

She sighed, and immediately he knew what was coming.

"You're handling this all wrong."

"Chloe, I swear to God, I don't need a lecture from you right now. Just tell me where she is."

"I think she said something about an assignment overseas or something. Let me guess. She didn't bother to tell you? I told you this was not-"

He hung up and slammed the phone onto the counter. He'd heard enough. And he had waited for her to come to him too many times. It was time to take action himself. He hated being manipulated, but there was obviously no other way to resolve the matter. And as soon as he got to a computer at the station today, he would book a flight to New York, and give her exactly what she had wanted all along.

August 11
Samford University
Birmingham, Alabama

Jackson looked down at his watch for what had to be the hundredth time since he'd climbed out of his car and leaned against the hood of Lily's. He only had another twenty minutes before he had to be at work. If she didn't come out of her dorm soon, he'd have to come up with another plan.

The parking lot was basically empty, except for a few cars outside a couple of the dorms where the athletes lived. This section of campus was tucked away in a wooded area, and the dorms formed a quaint red-bricked neighborhood. Jackson remembered how excited Lily had been to get into these dorms as a sophomore, how they'd played like little kids two winters ago when a freak storm had frozen the roads and dumped a foot of snow across the South. That seemed like a lifetime ago.

A door slammed shut a few feet away, and Lily walked down the front steps of her dorm. He pushed away from her car and took a deep breath to settle the adrenaline racing through him. This couldn't be any harder than preparing for a basketball game. He just needed to focus on the game plan. But when their eyes met, she visibly stiffened. Not a good sign. She adjusted her backpack and shook her head as she walked toward him.

"I don't have time for this right now, Jackson. Go home."

He'd expected resistance, and finally hearing it actually solidified his resolve.

"I just need a minute."

She stopped in front of him and shifted her weight to one hip. Her eyes still blazed with the same anger he'd seen just before she'd driven away from the hospital.

"I only have thirty minutes to get to the training room and get treatment before practice. This is going to have to wait. Or better yet, let's just postpone it indefinitely."

"I know you're upset-"

"I don't want to hear anything you have to say."

She started for her car, but he stepped in front of her and blocked her path.

"Please, just listen for a minute."

"Now I *am* going to be late since I have to *walk* there."

She turned and stomped away from him toward the bridge that led to the main campus.

"Come on Lil. Quit being so stubborn and let me drive you to the gym. You can't tell me extra sprints are worth avoiding me."

She stopped and turned around, obviously weighing her options. When she finally walked toward his car, he breathed a sigh of relief. That was half the battle right there. Now the real fight was on.

"Fine." She reached his car and swung the door open. "Just make it quick."

As he climbed in beside her, she slammed the door closed.

"Hey," he said. "Take it easy. She's about to fall apart as it is."

"Everything eventually falls apart."

She crossed her arms and stared out of the window while he tried to figure out what to make of her attitude. He hated it when she was like this—completely fenced off and impenetrable. But then again, he'd been the same way not so long ago. She was only acting this way because he'd hurt her. She looked at him and frowned.

"Well, are you driving me or not?"

He cranked the car and headed out of the parking lot, turning onto the road that circled the main campus. It was a fairly short drive over to the gym, but it might be enough time to at least get her attention and turn things around.

"I want to apologize," he said.

"Done. Apology accepted. Now you can leave me alone."

He sucked in a breath and said a quick prayer. *Lord, give me patience.*

"Why are you so angry with me?" he asked. "It can't be because of one stupid remark I let slip."

She stared out of the window like she was desperate to jump out and run.

"Can you speed it up a bit? I do need to get there today. I swear, you drive like a grandmother with an infant tied to the roof."

"That's a new one. How long you been saving that one up?"

Not even a hint of a smile. He was running out of time. He pulled into the parking lot of the gym and shut off the engine. Before he could say another word, she jumped out and started walking toward the back entrance. He ran to catch up with her, finally overtaking her at the bottom of the hill leading around the back of the gymnasium.

"Wait, Lily."

He reached for her arm, but she pulled it away and kept walking.

"You asked for a minute. You got it. I accepted your apology. Now we're done. For good this time."

"No, we're not. Now stop and listen to me."

She reached for the door handle that led to the training room, and panic surged through him—like she might disappear forever if she went inside.

"Lily, I love you. Please! Just listen to me for a minute."

She stopped and faced him, honey-streaked strands of hair whipping across her cheeks as though they were as angry as she was.

"How dare you say that to me now. You don't know if you love me, remember? You're just jealous. You can't stand that I could actually be happy with someone else."

He had to admit she was right, at least about being jealous. She had been his for so long. How could anyone else know that the only way to make her giggle was to breathe in just the right spot behind her ear? Would any other man even care how she got the scar over her right eye that had gradually receded into her hairline? No, she was his from the beginning, and no one was going to change that.

"You're right. I am jealous. I get sick to my stomach just thinking about some other guy touching you. But I do love you. Don't make this about Alex. There's no way you could choose him over what we have."

"What we *have*? Are you serious?" She thrust her hand into his chest and knocked him back a step. "If what we *had*, Jackson, was so great, then why was it so easy for you to let it go?"

He regained his composure and moved closer, leaning down until he made eye contact.

"Believe me, absolutely nothing about the last few months of my life has been easy. I never wanted to let go, I just didn't have the strength to hang on!"

She shook her head and stepped away from him, obviously fighting tears. She was still angry, but he could see tiny cracks forming in her wall—the same cracks he had seen the other morning in his mom's kitchen. She would have kissed him. He was sure of that. But she'd denied even getting close.

Then suddenly it all made sense.

"I was right," he said.

"What?"

"That's why you're so mad. I was right, and you know it."

"I don't know what you're talking about."

He moved closer to her, but she retreated again.

"You still love me," he said.

"No-"

"Yes, you do. It's the only thing that makes sense."

She straightened to her full height and met his gaze like she was staring down an opponent.

"I don't love you."

Her eyelids fluttered, and he had to force back a smile.

"I don't believe you."

"I don't care if you believe me or not. We're through, Jackson. With everything. We can't even be friends."

He moved closer again, and this time when she backed away, the brick wall stopped her. Instead of stepping any closer though, he stopped and studied her. He had one chance left to get through to her.

"Prove it," he said.

"What? You're not making any sense."

"Prove to me that you don't love me, and I promise I'll leave you alone."

He tipped her chin until she looked up, her gaze full of the same emotions swirling around in his head. She put her hands on his chest to push him away, but there was no strength in them.

"*Prove* it?" she asked. "How?"

"Kiss me."

Her eyes widened. "No."

"It's the only way to get rid of me. If you don't love me, it won't mean anything."

"You're crazy."

He leaned in closer, keeping his lips barely an inch from hers.

"Lily, just kiss me."

He felt the tension between them drawing him into her, and hope rose like a wave inside of him. If he could just kiss her, she would remember—she would have to see. He reached for her face, cupping her cheek in his hand. But the dampness of her skin stopped him cold, just a breath away from what he wanted. Then a voice as clear as his own echoed in his head.

Don't do this.

He felt her hands shaking on his chest, saw the same pain in her eyes that had been there that night at his house—the night he had let her walk away. His heart sank. Sure, she might kiss him. She might even still love him. But trying to take it from her would just hurt her again.

"I'm so sorry." He wiped the tears from her face. "I shouldn't have said that. You don't have to prove anything. That's what I'm supposed to do. And it's about time I did it."

"Now what are you talking about?" She sniffled and pushed some strands of hair off her cheek.

His stomach wretched as he realized what he was about to say, and he nearly doubled over. But it was time to stop hurting her, and start loving her.

"I'm the one that has something to prove. I do love you, and more than anything in the world, I want you to be happy. Part of me wants to grab you and shake you until you see what a mistake it is to give up on us."

He paused as his words sank in. Had she felt the same way about him when he was wallowing in his own misery?

"I can't make you give me a second chance," he continued. "And I promise I won't try to force it anymore. If you need time and space, you have it. I'll leave you alone."

He touched his lips to her forehead then backed up, needing to put more space between them. Every inch of his being still ached to finish that kiss. He needed to get out of there before he changed his mind.

"I'll always love you," he said. "Always. If you ever need me, or want to talk, call me. I'll be here for you."

Then he turned and walked up the hill as fast as he could. His head throbbed and his stomach swam with nausea. He had just let her go again. How could he have done that? Hadn't he come here to do anything to hold onto her?

When he reached his car, he pulled open the door and took one last glance at the back of the gym. She was gone.

Lily scrubbed her hair with the towel one last time and tossed it over the top of the shower curtain. She stepped in front of the mirror on the medicine cabinet, running a comb through her hair then paused for a moment. Her eyes were still a bit red, but the shower had helped to wash away the remnants of her frustrations from the long afternoon.

Stepping out of the bathroom, she crossed the small dorm room she shared with Emily and sat down at her desk, thankful for the quiet. The team had all gone to dinner after practice, but Lily had complained of a headache and headed back to the dorms. She'd noticed the look from Emily and knew she'd have to explain better later on, but for now it was enough to have the room to herself.

They'd spent the better part of the morning figuring out how to arrange the furniture. Not that there was much to arrange—a couple of desks, two beds, a couple of waist-high chest of drawers. But with two workouts and a three-hour practice all in the first day back, there hadn't been much time to unpack her things, and the room still felt empty.

She debated on unpacking her clothes, but her body was already beginning to ache, so she opened her laptop instead. She opened a web browser and checked her email. It was mostly junk, with several notifications from Facebook, but one of them was a complete surprise. Chloe Walker had sent her a friend request?

She was sure Chloe had disliked her, but maybe she'd been wrong. Maybe she'd just been having a bad day. She started to click on the link to her Facebook account, but her phone rang on the desk beside her, and she grabbed it.

"Hello?"

"Hey beautiful." Alex's voice still made her stomach take a quick dip.

"Hey, how's your day going?"

"Can't complain. How about you? How was your first day of practice?"

"Okay."

She grimaced as she thought of her terrible performance that afternoon. She'd been a step behind in every drill.

"Just okay?"

"Guess I'm a bit rusty. It wasn't my best practice, and Coach laid into me a bit, but I'm sure tomorrow will be better."

"I'm sure it will. Besides, if volleyball doesn't work out you can just move down here and hang out with me every day."

She laughed and shook her head. "Nah, you'd just get sick of me. Toss me aside with all the others."

"Please," he said, lowering his voice. "I could never toss you aside."

Her cheeks flushed as she smiled to herself, and she suddenly missed him so much it ached.

"So practice didn't go well," he continued, "but how about the rest of your day? You getting settled in?"

She cleared her throat and wondered whether she should mention Jackson's visit. But if the roles were reversed, she had to admit she'd want to know.

"The rest of the day was okay too." She paused. "Jackson dropped by, but that turned out to be nothing."

"What do you mean he dropped by?"

"When I went out to my car, he was outside waiting. He just wanted to talk. I told him to leave me alone, and he said he would."

"I don't like that he thinks he can just show up whenever he wants. Doesn't he know about us?"

"Of course. That's why I told him to leave me alone from now on."

"I thought things were over between you two."

"They are!"

"Then why is he always around? First it's his mom, and now he's just showing up at your dorm. Are you sure you're over him?"

Her chest heaved, and she leaned her head into her other hand.

"Alex, listen to me. It's over. I'm over him. We tried to be friends, but it didn't work out. He's gone for good now. Can we please not talk about him anymore, and just move on?"

He sighed and mumbled more to himself than to her. "This is crazy." Then louder. "Is this crazy?"

"What do you mean?"

"You and me. I've barely spent any time with you, and you're all I can think about."

She smiled and felt the building tension evaporate.

"It's definitely crazy. When am I ever going to see you again?"

"Soon. I promise."

They sat in silence for a moment, and Lily imagined his arms around her. She could still smell the salty air, still feel the heat off his skin. She shook her head, pushing away the daydream.

"Hey, your sister sent me a friend request on Facebook. Maybe she doesn't hate me after all."

"What does that mean?"

"You know, on Facebook. She sent me a friend request."

"I don't use Facebook. And I didn't know Chloe did." He paused, and the silence grew uncomfortable. "Maybe that's not such a good idea."

"What's not a good idea?" she asked.

"You and Chloe being friends. She's a little..."

"What?" He didn't answer. "Come on, Alex. What's the deal with you and Chloe?"

"Look, there's no deal. We just don't see eye to eye on things, and we haven't been getting along lately."

"So you don't think I should be friends with her?"

"I'm not saying that." He forced out a hard breath. "Look, do whatever you want. I just don't know if it's a good idea. That's all."

She looked at the email again, an uneasy feeling working its way through her. She hadn't imagined Chloe's cold demeanor toward her, or the tension between the two of them that day at the cafe. She was beginning to think their disagreement had something to do with her, but she couldn't imagine why. And if Chloe didn't want Alex seeing her, why would she reach out to be her friend?

August 13

Birmingham, Alabama

It wasn't until a couple of nights later when Lily had a chance to go through her email again, and as she cleaned out her inbox, she noticed the friend request from Chloe again. This time she clicked on the link, and it took her to her friend page where she confirmed the request.

She clicked on Chloe's page, but there wasn't much there— several friends and a few photos. She scrolled down the friends list, wondering if she'd see anyone she knew, though that seemed impossible. Alex had been pretty tight-lipped about his family, but maybe Chloe would lead her to more information.

None of the names rang a bell, but a couple had the last name of Walker, and she wondered if they were related. Maybe his mother was on Facebook, or some cousins. Had he even mentioned he had cousins?

She went to the first name and tried the page, but everything was blocked. So she went back to Chloe's page, and there she noticed something interesting. The first name on Chloe's friend list had been an Adrian Walker, and though she couldn't see the page, Adrian also had a fan page, and Chloe had recently subscribed.

Lily clicked on it, and the page loaded with the beautiful picture of a blonde woman seated on the edge of a desk, her long slender legs crossed at the ankle. She smiled at the camera, her high cheek bones and pale skin giving her an almost haunted look. In fact, as Lily looked closer, something about her eyes seemed hollow, as if only her mouth were smiling while the rest of her was miserable.

Lily looked over the page. She was a journalist in New York, and there was a link to an article. Lily followed it, curious now about the haunted woman whose last name was Walker and how she might be linked to Alex.

She picked up the phone and decided to try his cell. No answer, so she left him a message.

"Hey, I know you said it might not be a good idea, but I accepted Chloe's friend request. I thought it might be interesting to see if you had any cousins or relatives out there, and I ran across an Adrian Walker, a journalist in New York. Just curious about her. Call me when you get a break."

She hung up the phone and scanned through the article profiling the newest hire at the paper, Adrian Walker from Brunswick, Georgia. There had to be a connection to Alex.

She read through a short description of Adrian's accomplishments and her freelance pieces that had been published around the country, including a major article on women in the work place. She'd almost reached the end when her phone rang. It was Alex.

"Hey," she said.

"What are you doing?" The abrupt tone in his voice caught her off guard.

"Just sitting at my computer. Why? What are you doing?"

"Look, uh, we probably need to talk." His voice sounded strange, almost panicked.

"Alex, what's wrong?"

"Just, stop what you're doing and let me talk to you for a minute."

She looked back at the computer screen, and a vague sense of dread started working through her.

"Are you getting freaked out because I'm asking about your family?"

"No, it's not that. I'm not freaked out. I just need you to hear me out."

She looked at the last paragraph of the article, and Alex's name practically jumped off the screen at her. She had to back up and read it again. She'd read it wrong somehow.

"Lily, I have to tell you something, and it's not easy to explain."

"You're married."

Her eyes swam, and it felt like she might fall out of her chair for a second.

"Not...exactly. Just listen to me."

"Wait." She dropped her free hand to her knee to support herself. She suddenly felt nauseous. "You're not married? What, are you divorced?"

The line was silent, and she wanted to reach through it and grab him by the throat.

"Alex! Are you married or not?"

"Technically, yes," he said. "I am still married. But we've been separated for nearly a year."

The room tilted, and the walls swayed around her. Somewhere in her head he spun sentences around and around, but nothing made sense. All she could hear was his voice crushing the bud of trust that had been growing between them.

"Lily? Are you still there?"

"I can't do this. We can't see each other anymore."

"Why?"

"Because you're *married!*"

"No, listen. When I go there and she signs the papers-"

"It doesn't matter. You lied to me." She heard her own voice like it was coming from somewhere else, raspy and defeated. No amount of talking to him was going to change anything, and all she wanted to do was find a dark hole to crawl inside and hide.

"I didn't lie to you," he said. "I just kept thinking it would be over soon and it wouldn't matter. Then she kept stalling, and I wasn't sure how to tell you, or when the right time would be."

"A thousand times before now would have been better! I can't believe you've been hiding this. You know how important my faith is to me, Alex. How could you make me commit adultery?"

"*What?* Adultery? You haven't committed adultery. Don't be ridiculous."

"Ridiculous? You're calling my beliefs, my faith, ridiculous?"

"No, I-"

"I'll tell you what's ridiculous. What's ridiculous is that you would expect me to just smile and say it's okay that you're still married, and that it doesn't matter that you never told me."

"I'm not really married-"

"Yes you are!"

Her face grew hot, and she couldn't sit still any longer. She jumped up and paced the room. If only he was there so she could strangle him!

"Alex, I believe marriage is sacred. It's a promise to love each other forever. I can't be your girlfriend while I wait for you to get divorced from your wife, and still be true to my faith. It's adultery in God's eyes."

"I don't know about God's eyes. I do know that my marriage is over, whether you choose to stay with me or not. You're not breaking it up. Believe it or not, I think marriage is sacred just as much as you do-"

"Then why aren't you doing everything you can to save it?"

"What makes you think I haven't?"

She paused and tried to gain control of the shaking inside of her. She didn't know him at all.

"Let's just calm down and talk about this reasonably," he said. "You're hurt and angry, and you have every right to be. I should have said something sooner."

"Why did you wait so long to tell me?"

He sighed, but said nothing. Her body had run out of steam, so she sat back down on the bed. Could this really be happening?

"Look," he said. "At first, I didn't say anything because I barely knew you. I had no idea where things were going with us. And I really hate talking about it."

"You should have told me before I came back down there."

"I couldn't. I wanted to see you, and I didn't want to mess everything up. She was supposed to sign the papers the Monday after you left, and I thought I could talk to you about it then. But she never showed, and now everything is all screwed up."

"What do you want from me?"

She dropped her head into her hand, massaging her temples. This was exhausting. None of it really mattered anymore anyway.

"You know," he said, his voice softening. "I was drowning till I met you. I thought what I wanted wasn't possible, wasn't real. I thought I'd never give another thought to marriage. But all I can do since you came down here is think about a life with you."

Her eyes ached, and her throat knotted. How could he have found another dagger to drive into her? What a fool she was. She'd been dreaming of a future with someone who had already committed to sharing his life with someone else. No matter what either of them wanted, she couldn't be a mistress, not even for a short time. She laid her head down and buried it in her pillow, yearning for him and hating him at the same time.

"I need to go," she said. "I can't talk to you right now. You don't get it. I can't do this."

"Don't hang up yet, Lily."

"I have to go. Please don't call me again."

"Lily wait-"

She ended the call and crumpled into a heap on her bed, gripping the terrible ache in her chest.

Not again, God. Please, not again.

She pulled the pillow over her ears as the phone began to ring. He could call until the end of eternity for all she cared. She was through with Alex Walker.

Chapter Fourteen

Alex dialed Lily's cell again, but after four rings it went to voicemail. He pushed his phone back into the clip on his belt and slammed his hands down on the handlebars of his bike. Beside him, Steve took a sip of water and watched him with an infuriating look of sympathy.

"No answer?"

Alex pulled his leg over the bike then stood next to it for a moment, gripping the seat and a handlebar with all his might.

"Don't you dare say I told you so."

"Hey man, I wouldn't do that." Steve shook his head. "But you had to know she'd find out sooner or later."

Alex shoved the bike away from him into the bushes beside the convenience store where they'd stopped. Across the lot, a small group of thug wannabe's grew quiet and looked over at him before scattering like roaches. Alex shook his head as he paced back and forth beside the store.

"I knew Chloe wouldn't be able to stay out of my life. She has to stick her freaking nose into everything!"

"Don't start berating Chloe, man. You've made your fair share of bad choices."

"So you think what she did is okay?"

"I'm not saying that-"

"I should have been able to tell her in my own time, in my own way. Chloe had no right!"

"You don't even know if she did anything. Sounds like Lily found out on her own."

Alex stopped pacing and stared at Steve. He always saw the best in everyone, a trait that was normally lovable, but right now it was maddening.

"You've got to be kidding. This is Chloe we're talking about. She knew exactly what she was doing." He bent over and grabbed his bike from the bushes. "Come on. We're going to pay her a little visit."

Steve put his hands up. "Hey, I'm staying out of this one. The last thing I need right now is drama. I've barely gotten my things moved into the apartment. I'm not killing my marriage before it even gets started."

"Well thanks for the support. You know, you were a much better friend than you are a brother-in-law."

Alex knew instantly he shouldn't have said that. Knew it wasn't true. And the hurt that flashed in Steve's eyes only confirmed it.

"Look," Alex said. "I'm sorry. I know you're in a tough spot. I just can't keep forgiving Chloe because somewhere in that thick head of hers she thinks she's doing what's best for me."

Steve sighed and leaned onto the handlebars of his bike.

"Maybe it would be a good idea to wait. Talk to her after you've calmed down."

"No. I'm talking to her right now. You can drive me over there in the patrol car, or you can follow me on my bike."

"I don't want to have to pull rank. You can't just take off for Chloe's while we're on duty. We stay together."

"Then we better load up the bikes on the patrol car."

Alex stopped on the sidewalk outside Chloe's apartment and dialed Lily's phone again, but it went straight to voicemail. He was going to kill Chloe. He marched up the stairs to her door and pounded on it. Then he glanced back down at Steve hiding in the patrol car. Coward. Turning back to the door, he pounded it again and rested his hands on the door frame. She finally swung the door open, and Alex raised his head.

"I guess you're happy now."

She crossed her arms over her chest and swung her weight over to one hip. "What did you do now?"

"What did *I* do? That's rich. The queen of meddling in my life has finally succeeded in ruining the best thing I had going. Are you proud of yourself?" He pushed past her and then swung around to face her. "It isn't enough for you to lecture me constantly, to look at me like I'm a monster. You have to actually destroy the one good thing I have in my life!"

She took a step toward him and pointed her finger at him. "You destroyed the good things in your life, Alex. Not me. You could have worked things out. You could have stayed together."

He almost had to laugh at the absurdity.

"You think you know so much. You think your precious best friend is so innocent, and I'm the horrible bastard abandoning her! You don't know anything, Chloe!" He brushed past her again and stopped just outside the open door. "Stay out of my life from now on. Don't talk to me, don't talk to Lily. As far as I'm concerned, you don't exist."

He slammed the door as she stood open-mouthed in the living room. Then he jogged down the stairs to the patrol car below. He pulled out his phone again as he climbed into the passenger side.

August 15

Birmingham, Alabama

Lily threw her practice jersey in the laundry basket and slammed her locker shut. It echoed through the small locker room. She glanced over at Emily who raised an eyebrow as she adjusted the ice on her shoulder.

"Bad day?" Emily asked.

Lily shoved a bag of ice under her t-shirt and secured it against her lower back.

"Don't ask."

"You better tighten up soon. Coach is starting to notice."

"I know!"

She slipped her feet into her sandals and tried to settle her gnawing stomach. Emily stuck her head out of the door and glanced down the hall before letting it close again. At least she was respecting Lily's wish to keep her situation quiet for the time being.

"Have you called him yet?" she asked.

"No."

"How many messages has he left on your phone?"

"A lot." She'd erased them all, the texts too.

"Seems like he really cares about you."

Lily grabbed her keys off the bench and started for the door.

"Maybe. But I can't talk to him right now."

As they made their way down the hall toward the side entrance of the gym, Emily shook her head.

"I don't see what the big deal is. So he's getting a divorce. It's not like he's been happily married with kids and keeping you on the side."

"It doesn't matter. He lied to me. And he put me in a position that compromises my beliefs. I committed adultery."

She could have sworn Emily chuckled at her. "Don't be so melodramatic, Lil. It's not adultery if you don't know you're doing it. Besides, you didn't even sleep with him."

Lily held her tongue. They were so completely different. It was one of the reasons she had liked Emily so much. She never held anything back, just stormed ahead with her feelings and thoughts, thoughts that were never seasoned with any amount of faith. Emily didn't even believe there was a God. Although Lily adored her, she could never take her advice on such a matter.

She pushed open the double door to the outside and shielded her eyes from the sun. Whistles off to her right signaled the end of football practice, and she looked over to the stadium just as the players were huddling in the center of the field. At least she'd have time to eat lunch before they overran the cafeteria like a herd of elephants.

As she topped the slope of the sidewalk and stepped into the parking lot, she caught a glimpse of movement near her car. Alex pushed away from leaning against it and began walking toward her. She stopped and shielded her eyes once more. Maybe they were playing tricks on her, but she knew that stride from any distance.

"Oh no," she said.

"What?" Emily turned her head to see what Lily was looking at.

"He's here."

"Who?"

"Alex. He's coming this way."

Emily looked again, shielding her eyes as well. "You're right. That's definitely him. I can understand your dilemma. Married or not, he's gorgeous. He could throw me in handcuffs anytime."

Lily slapped her shoulder. "Hey, you're not helping."

She would have scolded her further, but Alex was within ear shot now. She'd have to face him, ready or not.

"Lily?" he called out.

She glanced at Emily. "I'll meet you back at the room."

Emily grinned. "Good luck."

Lily turned back toward Alex and steeled herself as he drew closer. It was hard enough trying to make sense of the right thing to do without having to face her overwhelming attraction to him.

"What are you doing here, Alex?"

He stopped just in front of her, and he started to reach out, but he paused and swept his hair away from his forehead instead.

"I don't know. I just needed to see you. You won't return any of my calls."

"I can't deal with this right now. I have to concentrate on practice and my training. Coach has already said something about my lack of focus. I'm not screwing up my senior year."

"Just hear me out. That's all I'm asking."

"It won't change anything. You're still married."

He paced in front of her, letting out a deep sigh. "Why do you have to be so rigid? Everything isn't always black and white, right and wrong. Sometimes things just get messed up beyond repair, even when we've done everything we can."

She watched him pace, saw the frustration and pain in his face. This was hurting her too. Didn't he know that?

"I understand that relationships get messed up beyond repair. But marriage isn't just any relationship. It should be a commitment to stick together through everything. *Everything.*"

"You can't stick with someone who refuses to stick with you. Believe me, I've tried."

"God can heal anything."

He glanced up to the sky, seemed to mouth a prayer, or maybe a curse. Then he looked back at her and frowned.

"Don't do this. Don't shut me out."

Her eyes burned, and her head swam with shame for the desire swelling inside of her. She wanted to let go of her conscience, let go of this unrelenting need to be perfect. She reached for his arm and ran her hand over his skin. Immediately he pulled her to him and wrapped his arms around her, and just like that her already shaky resolve crumbled. He cradled her head and mumbled in her ear.

"Did you ever consider that maybe God means for us to be together? That maybe he *is* healing me?" He pulled back and tipped her chin. "He's giving me a second chance."

"I don't know about this."

"Shh." He rested his cheek on her head. "Don't worry. We'll work everything out. It's all going to be all right. I promise."

Alex took a bite of his sandwich and glanced around the cafeteria. It was mostly empty, but the girls at the table near the entrance—he assumed they were Lily's teammates—darted glances at them now and then. He must have sprouted another head recently. They looked at him like he was an alien.

"So, how long can you stay?" Lily asked from across the table they'd found in the back.

She still looked shaken. Doubt clouded her eyes, and she hadn't even touched her food.

"I have to leave in a couple of hours. I left when my shift was over at eight this morning, and I have to be back by ten to start tonight's shift."

Her eyes widened, and she looked him over more closely.

"You haven't slept? Why didn't you take a vacation day?"

"I didn't have time to wait around for approval. I just made up my mind to come here and left."

He took a sip of his coke. Caffeine was good.

"Alex, you shouldn't have done that. You could fall asleep on the road."

"I'll be fine. I've been through worse."

He watched her pick at her pasta with a fork, her thoughts obviously still racing with all that he'd told her. How long would it take before she started asking questions? How honest would he have to be?

"Are you okay?" he asked.

She looked up from her plate and dropped her fork. "Yeah, just not very hungry."

"Do you, uh, want to talk about anything?"

"I don't know. I do, but, then again I don't."

"I'll tell you anything you want to know. Just ask."

Somewhere in his head he knew that was a lie. But maybe she wouldn't ask too much yet. She hesitated, leaned back in her chair and folded her arms over her chest like protection.

"How long have you been married?"

"Two and half years. Nearly three now, I guess."

She leaned forward and picked at her pasta again, this time took a bite. She folded her arms on the table, her eyes floating around the room. She wasn't looking at him. Not a good sign. She practically winced as she finally met his gaze.

"How do you know for sure it's over?"

The heaviness building in his chest felt all too familiar. It was why he hated talking about his loss. It made him weak, pathetic. How could she be attracted to someone she pitied?

"I just know." Honesty was one thing. Digging up the dead was another.

"She changed," he continued. "Her work became everything to her, to the point she preferred a job offer in New York rather than marriage with me."

"That's why you have to go to New York." She wrinkled her brow and shook her head. "But if she wanted to leave, why is the divorce taking so long?"

"At first she wanted me to go with her. She thought if she took the job and fought hard enough, I'd eventually agree and move there too. When that didn't happen, things turned nasty. At one point she claimed I'd abused her."

"What?"

"Yeah, it's been a nightmare. I could just wait a couple of more months and the divorce would be final anyway. Under Georgia law she abandoned the marriage when she moved. I thought I could wait, but..."

"But what?"

"Look, I know we've joked around about my bad boy image, but it's not really a joke. I've made some bad decisions, and I thought I'd never let myself get attached to anyone again. Not like that anyway. But, with you, everything's different."

She reached across the table and covered his hands with her own.

"Different how?"

He thought of all the other women, some of them just a blur. They'd been a moment's reprieve, a band aid over the gaping hole. But not Lily. She'd awakened something in him he thought was dead.

"Better," he said. "I can be better."

Chapter Fifteen

Alex stood in front of the apartment door and gathered his nerves, preparing for a confrontation. He shook off the remnants of the rain from his hair, and then he reached out his fist and knocked three times. At least he knew for certain she was here. The guard in the lobby had confirmed that. Of course, he'd also had to flash his badge to get up here, so the guard might have already alerted her that he was coming. If she tried to duck out again he might just lose it.

Just when his frustration began to mount, Adrian swung the door open. The first thing he noticed was the satisfied grin that spread over her face. It nearly made him sick. He tried to appear unaffected as she stretched her arm up the door frame and rested the other on her hip. She'd dyed her hair blond, and she'd lost weight since he'd seen her back in March, too much weight.

A black cocktail dress hugged her slim waist and dipped dangerously between her breasts. Her eyes flickered with amusement, a cold green he could swear had once been a soft brown. But then, so many things had changed it was hard to keep track.

"Well, hey there, stranger." She ran a glance up his body until her gaze returned to his. "I knew you'd show up here sooner or later."

"You didn't leave me much choice."

Her grin was her only response. God, he hated playing into her manipulations, but it was the only way to finally be free of this nightmare.

"Look, can we just get this over with?"

"My house is your house." She pushed the door open wider. "Come on in."

He followed her through the foyer into a modest-sized living room, apparently decorated professionally. What struck him was the complete absence of color. Everything in the room was white or silver and oddly immaculate.

"I thought you hated white furniture."

She glanced back at him and lifted an eyebrow. "I never said that."

"You said it was arrogant to flaunt it if you were rich enough or anal enough to keep white furniture clean. It was why you didn't want to rent that house on Reynolds Street."

"No, I just didn't want to be scared to walk out the door to my car."

"So you moved to New York instead?"

"Are you really here to argue with me about white furniture?"

He willed his mouth shut. He didn't need to get distracted by petty arguments. It was exactly what she wanted.

"No, let's just get on with it."

She gestured to the sofa. "Would you like to sit in here, or do you want to get a drink and sit in the kitchen?"

"I don't care."

"Well, you look like you could use a beer. Follow me."

She led him into the kitchen where he took a seat at the glass-topped breakfast table. Again, he noted the stark white floor and counter tops. The whole place was blinding. She'd never been messy, but she hated cleaning. It would take a full-time maid to keep her apartment this spotless.

"You, uh, have a nice place here," he said.

She pulled a beer out of the refrigerator and walked over to the table. She slid the bottle to him.

"Thanks."

"You must be doing well for yourself."

"I am. You ever read the column?"

"No. I don't get the Times in Brunswick."

"Ah, well. I've been freelancing as well. Gives me a chance to travel and see all the places I've always wanted."

"That's nice." Trying to figure out a way to carefully move into a discussion about the divorce papers, he glanced down at the bottle in his hand. "Killian's?"

"It's your favorite."

"I thought you hated it."

"I do."

She grinned as realization sank into him. How had she known he was coming? He shook off the thought. It didn't matter now. All he cared about was getting out of there with signed papers as soon as possible. Adrian rested her chin in her hand and smiled.

"So what brings you all the way to New York City? Did you miss me?"

"You know why I'm here."

"I do?"

"You never show up in Brunswick when you're supposed to. I figured this was the only way to hold you down in one place long enough to get those papers signed."

She walked her fingers across the top of the table toward his hand.

"Hmm, hold me down. Now that sounds like fun."

Her touch on his skin made it prickle. Pulling his hand out from under hers, he popped the top off his beer and took a long gulp. He couldn't afford to get caught up in her game, or lose his temper.

"Can we just get this over with? Don't you think it's time?"

She leaned back in her chair, narrowing her eyes. "Don't you even have time for pleasantries, for old time's sake?"

"Come on, Adrian. It's over between us, and you know it. Don't make this more difficult than it has to be. You don't really want to be married to me anymore. All of these games are just a way for you to enjoy making me suffer."

"Fine." She pushed away from the table and straightened her dress. "I'll have to go look around the office for the papers. I can't remember what I did with them." She walked toward the doorway and glanced back at him as she left. "You might as well come help since you're in such a hurry."

He finished off the last of his beer and followed her down the hallway, trying to ignore the deliberate swing in her hips. Passing through the bedroom, he stepped into a small office that must have been a walk-in closet at one time. A mahogany desk was situated at the back with neatly stacked folders and an open day timer on top. Her computer monitor flashed various headlines across it as a screensaver. He guessed they were ones she'd written.

"Why don't you start there." She pointed to a file cabinet to his left.

She dipped down behind her desk and shuffled through some papers, while he turned to the cabinet. He had to close the door to pull the drawers open, making the room seem even smaller, and his skin crawled with the sensation of being trapped. He pulled on the top drawer. It didn't budge.

"It's locked."

She fished out a set of keys from her briefcase. Instead of tossing them to him, she walked over to the cabinet and reached across him for the lock. She grinned as her arm brushed across his chest, and he tried to step back. Feeling the wall at his back, the hair on his neck stood to attention. This wasn't good.

She turned the key, but left it dangling in the lock as she faced him. The familiar aroma of lavender and mint surrounded them. He'd loved the scent that trailed behind her—at least, he used to. Now it sent a shiver up his spine.

"You're shaking," she said, sliding her hands up his chest. "You scared of me?"

He grabbed her wrists and pushed them back toward her.

"No. And it's more of a repulsive shudder."

She dropped her chin and batted her eyes, a look that had made him weak in a different lifetime.

"Come on, Alex. Haven't you missed me even a little bit?"

"No. Not lately."

She pushed her hands back to his chest and up around the back of his neck, tickling the ends of his hair. As hard he fought it, he couldn't help the heat stirring within, especially with the view just below his line of sight. After weeks of fighting through his temptations with Lily, his resolve was faltering.

Lily.

The thought of her sent a strange mix of guilt and desire through him, and before he could sort out reason from the sensations coursing through him, Adrian pounced. When her lips crushed his, instinct took over, and he pulled her into him like a starving animal diving into a meal. He felt his feet moving, pushing her away and gripping her tight at the same time.

He had no idea how they wound up on the bed, didn't care. He just reacted, felt the freight train of adrenaline rush through him and explode. He pushed her arms over her head and dug his hands into hers. He needed to stop. He knew it as sure as he knew he couldn't.

God, help me stop.

He pulled his mouth away from hers, forced himself to take a breath. As the reality of what was happening began to register, a new surge of anger flowed through him. He was an idiot. A hormonal idiot.

"Don't stop," she said, her chest heaving.

"I can't do this. Not anymore."

"Sure you can. It's been months." She leaned up and kissed his neck then ran her hands up his back. When had he lost his shirt?

"Adrian, don't."

"Don't what?" she breathed into his ear. "I can't seduce my own husband? You know you want me."

She pulled his hips into hers, and it nearly undid him. He did want her, he couldn't deny it. But the memory of the last time he'd given into her sobered him quickly. He pushed away from her and off the bed.

"I'm not doing this."

He readied himself for the fight he knew was coming, but she laughed instead.

"Well, well. The great Alex Walker is turning down sex. This is new." She slithered off the bed, straightening her dress and hair. "You must have it bad for your little girlfriend."

He tried to catch the look of shock he was sure passed across his face before she could notice, but it was too late. How did she know? She smirked as she walked past him and back into the office.

"What's her name again? Daisy or Sunflower or something?"

"I see you've been talking to Chloe." He reached for his shirt crumpled on the floor and pulled it over his head. "You shouldn't believe everything you hear."

"Oh please, Alex. You really think I care about who you're screwing around with? Although, I do think it's sad you had to resort to chasing after jailbait."

He gritted his teeth and bit back a retort. Stepping into the office doorway, he watched her push some papers around on her desk for a moment.

"Adrian, what did I *ever* do to you to make you hate me so much?"

She glanced up at him, but he couldn't read her. Was it sadness, or just indifference?

"You were there. I don't think it's necessary to rehash everything."

He walked over to the desk and leaned toward her, resting his fists on top.

"I tried everything I could think of. I really did."

"Except coming with me."

He shook his head. The same old conversation.

"You had no right to take that job without even talking to me, without even considering-"

"No *right*?" She stood and leaned toward him, shooting daggers with her eyes. "I was nothing down at that little Podunk town paper. This was the chance of a lifetime. It was my dream."

"And now you have it. Was it worth losing everything else?"

She pulled back and stared at him for a moment, her face showing no emotion.

"I'd already lost everything else. It was all I had left."

Pain shot through him like an arrow, one he was sure she'd aimed at him.

"You still had me. And we could have tried again. The doctor said-"

"I don't care about what the doctor said. And it doesn't matter anymore." She folded her arms over her chest. "I never wanted it anyway."

There was no way she could mean that. He remembered the glow in her face at the sound of the fluttering heartbeat, her excitement the first time he could feel movement in her belly. How could a woman so warm with the joy of impending motherhood have turned so hard and uncaring? Tragedy changed a person. He knew that. But shouldn't he still be able to recognize some part of her?

She bent over, pulling on the bottom drawer of her desk.

"Oh, here they are. Silly me. I put them in the junk drawer." She pulled out a stack of papers and flung them onto the desk then reached for a pen. "You're sure you want me to sign these?"

He picked them up and flipped through them to make sure they were the right papers, and then he tossed them back to her.

"Sign 'em."

With her pen in hand, she slowly turned the pages, pretending to read through them. He held his tongue as long as he could, but he felt like his head would explode at any minute.

"What are you doing? They've been the same papers for the past ten months!"

She ignored him and continued to read through each page. When she finally reached the end, he snatched them up and double checked the signatures to make sure she hadn't missed any.

"Thank you," he said.

Adrian pushed the mouse on her computer and kept her eyes on the monitor as it came to life.

"Well, you got what you came for. I trust you can show yourself out. I have some work to do."

He turned to go, but before he made it out of the bedroom, she called out to him again.

"Alex, wait. I have something that belongs to you." She met him at the office doorway with a box wrapped in duct tape.

"What is this?" he asked.

"Just some of your junk I still had."

Getting out of there seemed more important than going through the box, so he took it and left. As he closed the door behind him, a sense of relief washed over him. Finally, after over a year of shattering heartache and guilt, maybe he could get on with his life—a life without the torment of Adrian hanging over him.

Alex wrapped a towel around his waist and stepped out of the bathroom, thankful the shower had washed away the foulness lingering on him from his encounter with Adrian. He'd almost gone too far, and it would have killed any chance he still had with Lily. Thank God he'd come to his senses, and that it was the last time he would have to endure her hatred.

He looked around the hotel room for the remote to the television, but spotted the box in the chair instead. He debated opening it. No telling what was in there. It was probably best to leave it until later, but the cop in him wouldn't let it go. He walked over to it and pulled the tape away, pushing the sides back.

He shuffled through a mound of ripped and gnarled pictures—some from when they were in high school, others from the wedding and their life together. His letters to her from when he'd been stationed overseas briefly were torn and scattered through the box like confetti. It didn't surprise him in the least, and he was about to take it out to the garbage when one particular photo sucked the air out of his lungs. It was the only one still intact, and it was her last and most effective blow.

He pulled out the ultrasound photo, the one from her five month check-up, his favorite. The baby's face was turned toward the camera, tiny legs crossed Indian style. They had laughed so hard that day as the doctor tried to maneuver the camera to see the baby's gender. It had twisted and rolled all over the place, but they finally caught a quick look.

He would have had a son.

"Evan."

He rubbed his finger over the face and sat down on the edge of the bed. He closed his eyes, trying to force out the images now roaming through him like a ravenous lion. Adrian crying hysterically. Evan lying lifeless in his arms. The doctor confirming that the cord had strangled him. Only one quiet lullaby before saying goodbye.

The memories sent him to his knees, broke him again and again, and he shook with anguished sobs.

August 24

Birmingham, Alabama

Lily's stomach churned and twisted as she stared into the refrigerator. Just the thought of food made her ill. She wished Alex would call already. Waiting was agony. What if Adrian had refused to sign the papers again?

Guilt washed over her, mixing with the anxiousness already unsettling her stomach. How could she call herself a Christian while she basically cheered on the end of a marriage? This was still so confusing. She couldn't even talk to anyone about it, especially not anyone from church. She'd tried approaching her Sunday school teacher earlier that morning after class, but she couldn't force the words out. The truth was, she knew in her heart right from wrong, and nothing could change that.

Her phone rang in her room, so she closed the refrigerator and left the community living area they shared with Alison. At least she was out to lunch with others from church. Avoiding the topic of Alex all week had been hard, but she'd managed to keep the situation to herself. Well, mostly. Emily sat sideways on her bed with her back against the wall, and she lifted an eyebrow as Lily passed her on the way to the phone.

"Hello?"

"Hey," Alex said.

In that one simple word she heard a thousand. He was exhausted, beat down. It made her fear double.

"You're back. How did it go?"

"She signed them. It's over. Now I just have to get them over to my lawyer tomorrow."

She sighed in relief, but she couldn't help but wonder why he seemed so melancholy. She thought he'd be glad, but maybe now he regretted it.

"Are you okay?"

"Let's just say I hope to never see her horrible face again."

"What happened?"

He paused, and she listened to his ragged breathing. Never had she heard him so shaken. She'd give anything to be able to wrap an arm around him now.

"Ah, God Lily. I don't know if I can talk about this."

"Maybe it'll help."

More silence followed, and she searched for something to say that might comfort him. But she had no idea what was causing it. So she did the only thing that came to mind.

"Lord, please be with Alex right now. Whatever hurts, whatever you're doing in his life, let him know that you're there, and give him your peace."

She sat in silence on her bed and glanced over at Emily. She just stared at the book before her, pretending not to notice. Maybe praying for him would make him feel awkward and push him away, but she couldn't think of anything else.

"Thanks," he said. She could swear she heard a sniffle. "I really needed that."

"Alex, what happened?"

"I didn't tell you everything. I didn't think I could talk about it. But maybe..." He cleared his throat. "Maybe you can help me make sense of it."

"Of course. I can try."

He took a deep breath before continuing. "Adrian got pregnant about a year after we got married."

Her stomach lurched. Now there was a child involved? It seemed like there would be no end to the blows to her gut. But she waited and decided to hear him out.

"I was so excited," he continued. "She was too. I found us this house right away, and I even fixed up the nursery. Everything was perfect. The baby was perfect, her pregnancy was perfect. And I was getting out of the Marines so we wouldn't have to worry about moving all the time."

"Sounds like you were really happy."

"We were. But in the last month, everything changed so fast, I still don't really know what happened. One minute Adrian's panicking because she hasn't felt the baby move in hours, the next minute some doctor's telling me she can't find a heartbeat."

"Oh Alex. Don't tell me-"

"She had to deliver the baby knowing he was already dead."

Lily covered her mouth and glanced over at Emily. She shook off her concerned expression.

Alex cleared his throat again. "It was a boy. Seven pounds exactly. We named him Evan. He was so beautiful. I only got to hold him once, but I remember thinking that he looked like he was sleeping, and if I could just shake him a little bit..."

A tear slipped down Lily's cheek. "I can't even imagine the pain you went through. I think I'd want to die right there with him."

"I did. I prayed so hard that God would somehow take me instead. Or just take me with him. But I saw how broken Adrian was, and I knew she'd need me. I thought we'd have each other and that we'd get through it together."

Lily waited in silence for him to continue, or for some words of comfort to come to mind. How could she possibly offer anything that might help?

"I can't believe I knew you for so long and never really *knew* you. I thought of you as this carefree, laid back guy who liked to cut up all the time. I actually thought you were arrogant and insensitive the first time I met you. Turns out you're actually one of the strongest people I know. And you're going to be an incredible father someday."

"Thank you. That means a lot to me." He paused and cleared his throat again. "Can I ask you something?"

"Of course."

"Do you think he's in heaven?"

She hesitated, knowing that sometimes her beliefs were not easy for people who had lost loved ones.

"What do you think?" she asked.

"I don't know sometimes, and that scares me. I heard a preacher say once that all children go to heaven if they die before some kind of age of accountability, but that sounds strange to me. How can there be some set age where we finally become accountable for our actions. Doesn't the Bible say we're all born sinners?"

"Yes."

"So if Evan was a sinner, and he never accepted Christ, doesn't that mean he isn't in heaven?"

She thought back on conversations with her dad about the infant baptisms in their church, and the explanation given by the pastor. She felt so inadequate to answer his question, but she had to try.

"I can't give you an exact answer. I wish I could. The Bible doesn't say what happens in cases like Evan's. But I do know this. When God made a promise to his people, it was for them *and* their children. He makes it clear that our children are part of his family and that he loves them. And my dad always said that if he could trust God with his own salvation, he could certainly trust God with his children's. If your faith is in Him, then I think you have every reason to have faith that Evan is with Him."

"Thank you, Lily." She could feel the relief in his voice, almost see him smile. "That was more reassuring than anything anyone else has said to me, including the priests and pastors who've tried to answer my questions. And it's not because you said what I wanted to hear, but because I think God just spoke to me through you. Maybe he hasn't forgotten about me after all."

Chapter Sixteen

Lily hit a hard shot at Emily, and the ball sailed off her arms toward the stands. As Emily jogged after the ball, Lily glanced around at the students filing in, and a swarm of butterflies took flight in her stomach. The first home game of the season always did this to her, but she was more anxious than usual, and she wasn't sure why. She needed to get those first few points out of the way. Then she'd settle into her zone. But for now, she'd have to keep her nerves under control.

Emily returned and tossed the ball at her, and they continued to warm up, hitting the ball harder and harder at each other, until Lily had to dive after an errant hit. She missed, and the ball rolled toward the opposite corner of the gym. She jumped up and jogged after it, still trying to shake the feeling that something was off.

She grew more and more uncomfortable as the warm ups continued, and as she waited in line to enter a drill, she looked around again at the crowd. The basketball players had taken up their usual spot in the bleachers and were already cheering obnoxiously loud. Several football players would join them as soon as their own practice was over. The sound system blared out an upbeat rhythm that should have intensified her focus, but something wasn't right.

She tapped Alison standing in front of her. "Hey, did we forget to do something?"

Alison glanced over her shoulder and shouted back. "What do you mean?"

"I don't know. Something seems off, like we forgot something."

Alison looked at her like she'd said she was running off to join the circus.

"Like what?"

"I don't know. I can't put my finger on it."

Alison shrugged and stepped onto the court. As she passed a hit from Coach, Lily took another look around. What was she looking for? She looked up into the balcony, then behind her at the entrance. Nothing. Then she glanced over at the double doors leading out into the hallway and down to the locker rooms, and suddenly it hit her.

That was his spot. Before nearly every home match, Jackson had stood in that very corner, smiling at her as she warmed up, finally taking a seat behind the bench. It had always steadied her nerves and made her smile in return. But now the corner stood empty, and it seemed so strange and sad. For a moment, she felt the familiar sensation of heaviness in her chest.

She jogged over to a group of balls behind her and gathered them up, staring again at the gaping emptiness of the corner. It shouldn't matter anymore. She probably just missed having someone at her game, not Jackson in particular. If Alex lived close by, he'd be the one smiling at her. She dropped the balls into the basket and returned to the line waiting to enter another drill. That was all it was. She just missed Alex. She missed *Alex.*

"So did you win?"

Lily slipped out of her towel and rung the water out of her hair with one hand while holding the phone to her ear with the other. She was pushed for time, so she tried to talk to Alex and change at the same time.

"Yes, we slaughtered them," she said.

"Great! How about you? Did you play well?"

"Yeah, I guess so. I got a few kills, some blocks, a couple of aces."

"I have no idea what you just said, but it sounded good."

She couldn't help but laugh. "Maybe one day you can actually come to a game and learn a little bit."

"Yeah. I still feel bad about not making it to Atlanta last weekend."

"Forget it. You had to work. I understand. I'm pretty busy myself. School is going to kick my butt this semester."

"Do you have any games closer to me?"

"Hang on." She dropped the phone onto her bed, slipped her shirt over her head, and grabbed her schedule off her desk.

"How far are you from Charleston?"

"A couple of hours. When are you playing there?"

"October fourth. I think that's a Saturday. Are you work-ing?"

"Actually, I'm not. I'll be off every Saturday from now on... since I made detective."

"That's great! Congratulations!" She pulled her jeans the rest of the way up and grabbed her powder from the medicine cabinet. "Detective Walker. I like it!"

"My first case is a string of burglaries over on Sea Island. The guys have gotten out of there with nearly a quarter of a million dollars so far."

"Wow. Sounds like fun."

"I know. I'm going over Monday to start interviewing people."

She applied some lip gloss and took a final glance in the mirror. That was good enough.

"Listen, I want to hear all about it, but I have to run right now. Can I call you later?"

"Where are you going? It's after ten thirty there."

She paused at the fatherly tone in his voice. "There's a bonfire for the football game tomorrow. And one of the basketball players is having a party at his apartment afterward."

"And you're going?"

"Yes. Why? Does that bother you?"

He said nothing at first, and an uneasy feeling moved through her.

"I guess I didn't figure you for the partying type. You're such a straight arrow all the time."

She relaxed and walked over to the bed where she slipped her sandals on.

"I don't really party. I just hang out a little and mostly make sure my friends get home safe. It's no big deal."

"If you say so.

September 30

New York

Adrian Walker had never been one to give up easily, and this was no time to start. She'd signed the papers. There'd really been no way out of it. But she wasn't about to just fade into the darkness while Alex rode off into the sunset with his sweet little princess.

She tapped her fingernails on her desk in her cramped little closet and looked over the email account she'd set up a few months back that captured and stored all of Alex's texts. Stupid klutz. Anyone so easily duped had no business being a police officer, let alone a freaking detective. She clicked on a group of messages from the week before and reread them.

> *Lily Brennon: morning! hope u have a great day! <3*
> *Alex Walker:* Thx. call me after ur 1st class. Miss u!
> *Lily Brennon: k. miss u2!*
> *Alex Walker: working out w/ steve. would rather b w/u.*
> *Lily Brennon: at dinner. will call u in a min. bad day*
> *Alex Walker: why?*
> *Lily Brennon: C on my quiz. bad prac. Hav 2 run mile @ 6am.*

She clicked on more texts, most of them the same boring, mushy crap. It was pointless to read them. What did that pampered princess know about having a bad day? Just as she was about to logout of the account, a new message appeared. She opened it and read the line from Lily to Alex.

Lily Brennon: 4 days! Can't wait to see u in Charleston!

Adrian read it again. Stupid, wretched little girl. He should have dumped her by now. He'd never stuck with any of the others this long.

She picked up her cell and dialed Chloe's number. As it rang, she wondered what was in Charleston. She brought up a new browser window and typed the first few letters of Samford. It auto-filled from her previous searches, and she tapped enter.

"What do you want?" Chloe said.

"Hey, so what's the deal? You said this chick would be gone soon."

She scrolled through the website until she found the volleyball schedule. They were playing in Charleston on Saturday.

"I thought she would be. Thought for sure she'd dump him once she found out about you."

"Well, I guess she doesn't care anything about stealing someone's husband."

Chloe sighed, but said nothing. Her support had been waning lately, and she was becoming downright annoying.

"Is he going to Charleston on Saturday?" Adrian asked.

"Look, I've told you everything I know. Several times in fact. Alex isn't talking to me anymore, so I don't know anything."

"Well, if you find out anything-"

Chloe huffed. "Like I said, I don't know anything."

"Fine. Sorry to have bothered you."

"If you wanted to hang onto him so much, why did you sign the papers?"

Adrian took a sip of her coffee and placed it back on its coaster. She was tired of talking to Chloe. She had nothing useful anymore.

"Look, I'm sorry to have taken up your time. I'll let you get back to work."

She hung up the phone and reread the message again. More texts had appeared while she was talking to Chloe, and she opened the message.

Alex Walker: Can't wait to hold u again. Call me 2nite. Tough day. Need prayer.
Lily Brennon: Thought it might be. Prayed 4 Evan in chapel. Adrian 2.

Adrian's stomach churned. How dare she? And how dare Alex tell some college kid about her life? She supposed Little Miss Perfect pitied her. Probably thought she was some pathetic loser. No telling what Alex had told her.

Prayers. She better save her prayers for herself.

So they were meeting in Charleston. She tapped her fingernails again. Who did she know in Charleston?

October 4

Charleston, South Carolina

"Well, this wasn't as bad as I was expecting." Alex leaned across the corner of the table and took Lily's hand.

Her mouth spread into a wide smile. He loved how strands of her hair curled around her face after she'd been sweating, like a golden halo.

"What do you mean?" she asked.

He nodded at the rest of her teammates lining both sides of the table. He'd laughed when he joined them at the restaurant and noticed the only seat left was at the head of the table—where they could spy on him no doubt—but it had definitely made him uncomfortable.

"They've been keeping a watchful eye on me, but at least I've gotten to talk to you."

She followed his gaze. "Yes, they've behaved remarkably well. But I knew they'd like you." She looked back at him and squeezed his hand. "But everyone always likes you, don't they?"

"You mean the way you did? I seem to remember being called a complete jerk."

She laughed and looked away for a moment, her eyes dancing in the soft light. He wished he could get her alone, make her giggle and hold her close. It was completely unfair to have to share her with the people who got to see her every day.

"Maybe I just caught you on a bad night." She shrugged her shoulders and pushed her plate away. "My opinion of you did improve considerably over the next couple of days."

He leaned in closer, lowering his voice to nearly a whisper. "It was when I kissed your hand, wasn't it? That's when I had you."

"What?"

"The night you apologized for being so mean. I kissed your hand and-"

"Yes, I remember. And you apologized and admitted that you were indeed a jerk."

Her eyes sparked with the hint of indignation that had entertained him so much the first week they'd met.

"Yeah, well I had to say something to get things turned around in my favor."

Her eyes widened.

"Oh, don't worry," he said. "You should feel proud. You held out longer than any other woman ever has."

She slapped his shoulder and crossed her arms over her chest, but she couldn't quite suppress her laughter.

"Okay, I take back every nice thing I ever said about you, Walker. You're a pig."

Just then the waitress returned with the bill and credit card for her coach, so the team gathered their things to leave. As they stood, Lily tugged on Alex's hand.

"Coach said we're going to walk around the city for a bit, see the sights and stuff. You want to come?"

"Sure."

They followed the crowd of girls out the door, hanging back just a bit. He almost laughed out loud when a few of the younger girls kept glancing back at them.

"What is their fascination with me?"

"Oh, that. They were all asking a bunch of questions about you on the bus, and Em indulged a little. She has them convinced you're some kind of super government agent."

He had to admit he liked the sound of that. He threw his arm over Lily's shoulder and pulled her closer, looking around downtown Charleston. It was beautiful, but he'd seen it all before. There were so many live oaks draped with Spanish moss around Saint Simons and the surrounding areas, it had lost its mystique for him. He'd much rather be back at the hotel alone with her.

He leaned down and nuzzled her ear. "So when can I get you all to myself?"

She shuddered and smiled. "That tickles." She tried to pull away, but he held her tighter.

"Come with me." He pulled her to the side and between a couple of shops.

"Alex!" Lily glanced over her shoulder. "Coach is right over-"

He pressed her against the brick wall behind her and covered her mouth with his, finally tasting what he'd been wanting for weeks. Without hesitation she responded, wrapping her fingers around his head. His blood warmed and rushed through him, demanding more.

He reached for her shirt and pushed his hand underneath, the feel of her bare skin only driving him further. He moved to her neck, tasted the salt that still lingered.

"God, I can't wait to get back to the room and get you alone," he said.

She pushed him back and looked down the alley toward the street. "I can't. Coach will kill me. She'll kill me now if she sees me."

"Why does she care? You're a grown woman."

"With responsibilities. I'm a team captain, and I can't be sneaking off into alleys and hotel rooms to make out with my boyfriend while we're at a play date. Coach makes a big deal about us representing our school."

"Okay fine. I get it."

He backed away a step. The last thing he wanted was to get her in trouble, but what was the harm in stealing a few moments together?

"Don't you ever get tired of trying to be perfect?"

"What's that supposed to mean?"

He saw her anger flash and knew he was pushing buttons better left alone, but his own frustration sent words out of his mouth before he could stop them.

"You always have to follow the rules, and do what everyone else thinks is right all the time. When do you ever just relax and enjoy yourself? You can't be perfect all the time."

"I'm not trying to be perfect. I just want to make the right decisions."

"And who decides what's right?"

She crossed her arms and narrowed her eyes at him, opening her mouth to speak, but nothing came out. She looked back down the alley, and he followed her gaze. Something, a movement out of place, caught his attention momentarily.

"Did you see that?" he asked.

"What?" She huffed and crossed her arms.

"I thought I saw something." Or had it been someone? It had happened too fast.

"I didn't see anything."

He turned his attention back to Lily as she started to make her way back toward the street.

"Look, I'm sorry. I didn't mean to upset you. I just want to spend some time with you."

They stepped out of the alley and continued down the street. At least they hadn't lost sight of her team. The stream of volleyball players had stretched out into smaller groups moving slowly down the sidewalk. It wouldn't take long to catch up. He reached for Lily's hand, her silence filling him with regret. He should have just held his tongue.

Finally, she stopped and faced him with the stiff posture he recognized from their first encounters.

"You know, you may not understand why I make the decisions I do. But please don't act like there's something wrong with me just because I have principles. It's who I am, and it's not going to change."

"I know. I'm not asking you to."

"Yes you are-"

"No, don't misunderstand me." He tipped her chin and forced her eyes to meet his. "I think you're incredible exactly the way you are. I just want you to enjoy yourself sometimes, to let loose and smile." He brushed her lips with his. "It's such a beautiful smile."

When her face finally broke into a grin, he relaxed a bit. He hadn't lost his touch. But he wondered how she managed to keep her principles intact. Every time he kissed her, he could literally feel her struggle to maintain control, and he suspected she was closer to giving in than she realized. And what then? If she ever faltered, just once, would he be able to stop himself?

October 6

Birmingham, Alabama

"Hey ladies!" Lily jerked her head up at the sound of Coach Hampton's voice. She had stuck her head around the corner of the locker room door. "Great job this weekend in Charleston, and great practice today. I've decided to give you the weekend off, so we'll practice at five thirty Friday morning then we'll pick back up on Monday with the regular schedule." She pushed her eyebrows together and pointed a finger at them. "Just don't make me regret it."

When she disappeared again, a few of the girls groaned about a five thirty practice. So much for partying on Thursday night at the clubs. Lily suspected that was the true motivation behind

Coach's announcement, not a weekend off. She was notorious for sniffing out party plans during the season.

Lily tossed her sweaty clothes into the hamper then pushed her ice pack under her shirt and tucked it next to her lower back. As she headed out the door, Emily caught her elbow.

"Hey, you have any plans for this weekend?"

"Uh, no. I haven't had time to think about it yet. Why?"

Emily grinned and Lily knew immediately she was plotting something.

"Chris has been begging to get together ever since he started grad school in Atlanta. I was thinking we could take a little road trip."

Lily continued down the hall and pushed open the double doors leading outside. There had to be a polite way to decline. As much as she enjoyed spending time with her, being Emily's third wheel for the weekend was not appealing.

"I would, Em. But I'll probably go see the family for the weekend. I don't really have the money to go to Atlanta."

Emily looped her arm through Lily's and rolled her eyes.

"I'm not talking about Atlanta. I'm talking about picking Chris up in Atlanta on our way somewhere else." She grinned. "Somewhere warm, near the beach. Like Saint Simons Island maybe?"

Chapter Seventeen

Lily's excitement had been brewing all week, and when she finally pulled into the parking lot of the hotel Alex had arranged for them, her stomach was in knots. To make matters worse, she hadn't been able to eat all day, so the knots were rolling and groaning with hunger. It was a nauseating combination.

She pulled her car into the parking place beside Alex's SUV and jumped out, practically leaping into his arms. As she lost herself in his kiss, her nerves finally settled.

"Excuse me?" Emily said from behind her. Lily pulled her face away long enough to catch the knowing gleam in Emily's eyes. "Why don't you two get a room?"

Alex smiled at Lily and took her hand. "I think I can accommodate you." He pulled her toward the sidewalk.

"Wait," Lily said. "Don't you want to meet Chris, and go get some dinner?"

"Not really." He tugged her up the stairs like a kid desperate to show off his new toys. When they reached the landing, he leaned over the rail and tossed a small envelope down to Emily. "You and Lily are in room 224. We'll give you a call when we're ready to go eat."

Emily smiled and waved. "Have fun."

Lily barely had time to wave back before he pulled her to a door where he slid the card into the lock.

"Alex, I really am hungry."

He pushed open the door, and before it even closed he had pulled her body into his. He slid a hand under her shirt, his touch sending an exhilarating rush of desire through her.

"I'm hungry too," he mumbled into her ear.

His mouth covered hers as he slid both hands up her torso. Then in one rapid motion he lifted her shirt over her head, followed by his own. His skin was warm as it grazed hers while his lips explored her neck. A tidal wave of sensations tickled her skin, rolling through her stomach, before finally bursting up through her chest.

He turned her around and walked her to the bed. As he laid her down, she raked her hands through his hair, drinking in more, despite the warning beginning to sound in her mind. It was a distant buzz of an insect compared to the thunderous pounding of her blood racing through her.

"Alex...we should...slow down..."

He pushed away more of her clothing, and as he tasted her skin, she gasped.

"Alex."

More alarms sounded as he started working at his own clothes.

"Alex, wait."

He looked up at her, pushing her hair back away from her face. His eyes bore into hers, the twinkle of mischief now replaced with hunger.

"Lily, I want to be with you. Let me show you."

He ran a hand along the nape of her neck then down her chest and ribs. She could barely breathe, let alone think straight. Somehow, she managed to find her voice, and she cupped his face in her hands.

"We have to slow down. I can't-"

He covered her mouth with his and slid his hand back up to her chest, obliterating the rational thoughts she had started to form. *God, help me,* she prayed. And suddenly her mind cleared. She pulled Alex's face back and forced him to meet her gaze.

"Alex, please listen. Slow down. Please."

He finally paused, but a darkness clouded his eyes she didn't recognize, and he pushed himself off the bed without a word. He turned in a quick circle as he looked at the floor, rubbing the back of his neck. Then he picked up his shirt and pulled it over his head. Without even looking at her, he headed to the sliding glass doors and stepped out onto the balcony.

She lay on the bed wondering what had just happened. She'd come too close to losing it that time. Something was going to have to give, and she suspected that was the same conclusion he had just reached.

She stood and pulled her clothing back on straight. Outside, he leaned onto the wrought iron railing, staring out over the marsh at the horizon as it burned a deep golden orange with the setting sun. She stepped out onto the balcony with him and cleared her throat, but he didn't turn around. She moved beside him and leaned her back against the rail.

"What's wrong?"

He turned to face her, but took a deliberate step back and leaned on the opposite rail.

"I can't keep doing this."

She reached for his arm. "I know. I'm sorry-"

"Don't." He pushed her arm away, shaking his head. "It's hard enough to stop myself once. I feel like a complete idiot."

"I'm sorry-"

"Stop apologizing. I'm not blaming you."

He looked away and folded his arms over his chest. *Here it comes,* she thought.

"Maybe I'm just not the man you're supposed to be with."

Fire shot through her eyes. "Don't say that. This is my fault. I keep sending you mixed signals. It's hard for me too."

"Then why do you fight it so hard?"

"Sometimes, I don't know! Part of me does want to be with you too. But when I'm thinking clearly, I know waiting is the right thing to do. Sex is meant to bring two people so close they become one, and I know if we gave in now it would tear us apart."

He turned and grasped the rail in front of him, his shoulders sagging in defeat.

"Maybe it's just not meant to be. Have you thought about that?"

Her tears threatened to break their dam, and she stepped away from him. She had to get out of there. She walked back into the room and headed for the front door, sucking her breath in as the ache in her chest tightened. As she reached for the door, Alex caught her arm from behind.

"Where are you going?"

She couldn't turn around, couldn't look at his eyes. "Home. I can't-" She had to breathe. "Please let me go."

"No. Look at me." He turned her around, but she kept her eyes on the ground. "Why are you crying?"

"Are you kidding me? You're breaking up with me. What am I supposed to do?"

He pulled her into his chest and wrapped his arms around her, and her tears flowed freely.

"Shh, don't cry. Please. I wasn't breaking up with you. I'm sorry." He held her even tighter, rocking her gently back and forth until her tears subsided. Then he tilted her head up to meet his gaze. "I swear. I wasn't trying to break up with you. I just get so frustrated sometimes. Don't you get it?"

"Get what?" she sniffled. She wiped away the dampness from her face with her palm.

"I'm so in love with you, it's making me crazy. I want to be with you so much I can't stand it, and I'm afraid of doing something to screw it all up. I don't want to hurt you."

"You're in love with me?" A new sensation fluttered through her, and he smiled at her.

"Isn't it obvious? I've been a complete dope for months now."

"Then why did you say we weren't meant to be together?"

He let go of her and ran a hand though his hair. "Because I'm confused. I know I love you, and that I want to be with you. I want our bodies to become one, just like you talked about. I don't see things the same way you do—I don't think it *would* tear us apart. We're just so different, and I don't know how to be the man you want me to be."

"What do you mean? I want you to be yourself."

"No you don't. I don't want to stop anymore. I want to be with you for good. As far as I'm concerned, you are what I want for the rest of my life. And making love to you could not be more right for me. It's what people do when they're in love, Lily. It's natural. I just don't see anything wrong with it."

"Then why isn't it worth waiting for? Can't you wait just a little while longer?"

Alex pressed his forehead against hers and ran a finger down her cheek.

"I can do my best for you, baby. I promise I'll do my best."

October 11

Birmingham, Alabama

Jackson drove up in front of his mother's house and shut off the engine. He stepped out and looked around, noting her white sedan in the driveway. A small silver car was parked just on the other side that he didn't recognize. Maybe she had a friend over and that was why she hadn't answered her phone.

He walked up the front walkway and jogged up the steps, trying to push down his anxious thoughts. As he opened the door, he called out to her, but there was no answer. He turned to his right and walked down the hallway, checking all the rooms. Then he went back through the living room and into the kitchen, hoping she just hadn't heard him. But the kitchen was empty as well.

Now his heart pounded in his ears as all kinds of images flashed through his mind. What if she'd fallen, and she was lying unconscious, unable to call out for help?

He swung open the back door, felt a blast of cool fall air and caught the faint whiff of smoke from a grill somewhere. His eyes canvased the backyard, the shed, the shaded area in the back where she often retreated.

Nothing.

Then he heard it. Off the porch to his right came the soft sound of scraping, and all he could think about was her lying below, scraping at the ground to get up.

He ran down the back steps, leaping over the last three, and rounded the porch. There on the ground was his mother, kneeling between the rose bushes and scraping at weeds with a trowel, her right ankle still covered with a large walking boot.

"Mom! What are you doing?"

She turned and looked over her shoulder before returning to the dirt.

"Just cleaning some weeds out. What are you doing here, honey? I thought you had to work this afternoon?"

Jackson let out a long breath and wiped the sweat from his forehead.

"You scared the crap out of me. I've been calling for over an hour. Where's your phone?"

"Inside somewhere, I reckon."

"You need to keep it with you."

"Why? I never have before. What are you so worked up about?"

It was maddening how she kept on weeding the roses as if everything were perfectly fine. He knelt down beside her.

"Here, let me finish this. You shouldn't be out here working like this."

She slapped his hands away. "I'm not a helpless old lady. I can pull a few weeds."

He looked at her closely. Her cheeks were flushed pink, and a couple of beads of sweat had escaped from under her straw hat, streaking down her temple. She did look a little tired, but he had to admit, there was a light in her eyes. She looked more alive than he'd seen her in almost a year.

He smiled and shook his head. "You are definitely not an old lady. But maybe you could let me help a little...for old time's sake?"

She continued digging, but he saw the grin on her lips. "Well that's fine as long as you don't go killing anything. Go get the shears and we'll get these dead bulbs out of here."

He went to the shed and returned with the shears, working quietly beside her as she guided him through the deadheading. Her gentle voice reminded him to feel along the stem for nodes facing outward, to cut just above them so the new shoot would be forced out. She smiled and laughed with him, teaching him lessons from a time in his life he'd almost forgotten.

When they'd finished and he'd cleaned up the area, he handed her the cane leaning against the house, and they headed up the back stairs. He positioned himself behind her, cringing as she took each step, but he didn't dare say anything.

As they entered the kitchen, she removed her hat and gloves and hung them on the wall. Then she grabbed two glasses out of the cabinet. "Sweet tea?" she asked.

"That sounds great. Why don't you let me get it?"

She lowered her chin. "Sit down."

She poured the drinks and took some leftovers out of the fridge, unwrapping them and dipping them onto a plate.

"You hungry?" she asked.

"You don't have to go to any trouble for me," he said. "I'm not really that hungry."

She gave him a sharp glance and pointed a finger at him. "Don't hand me that. You're too thin. You need to eat. Especially if you're going to start playing ball again."

"Speaking of which, that's why I came over here. Coach Martin let something slip yesterday at practice I don't think he was supposed to. Did you have anything to do with him helping me get that tryout in Atlanta?"

She didn't turn around, just kept fumbling with pots on the stove. "I don't know what you mean."

"Yes you do. I don't care, Mom. Just tell me what you did."

She turned and faced him, clearly indignant. "I just called him to see what he could do. He always took such good care of you at UAB. He said he would think about it and make some calls. That's all."

"I see." He watched her return to her cooking, pondering this new information. It was embarrassing enough trying to keep pace with college players who were in top shape, but to have his mom calling the coach? That was humiliating.

"What about Mr. Clayton?" he asked.

She turned the burner on the stove down then took a seat at the table across from him. "The agent? What about him?"

"Did you call him too?"

"I wouldn't call that sleazy, good-for-nothing...Wait. Did he call you?"

He studied her face, unsure if her concern was genuine, but his mom had never been one to lie.

"So you *didn't* call him?" he asked.

"No. Why?"

"He called me yesterday and wanted to know if I was playing anywhere."

She slammed her hand on the table and furrowed her brow. "He's got a lot of nerve calling after the way he treated you last spring. What did he say you were?"

"Washed up."

"Exactly. I hope you told him where he can stick it."

Jackson couldn't help but laugh. It was so unlike her to hold a grudge, and seeing her angry was almost comical.

"No, I didn't tell him to stick it. He said he may be able to get me a tryout for a team in Italy."

"Italy!" Her voice rose to a squeal, and her eyes widened in horror. "That's so far away."

"Yeah, it is. But it might be a way for me to work my way into pro ball back here in the states."

She looked at him for a moment, and he could swear she was fighting back tears. Then she covered his hand with hers.

"What do you really want?" she asked.

He could ponder that for a lifetime and still never come to a conclusion. What he wanted wasn't possible anymore, but maybe he could still chase down the remnants of his dreams.

"I want to keep practicing with team down at UAB, and I want to give the training camp in Atlanta a try. Overseas ball? I don't know. I'm not sure anymore. My heart just doesn't seem to be in anything right now."

"You still miss her."

His throat constricted just thinking about her. No amount of praying had brought Lily back. So he had accepted that God meant for him to lose her, on top of everything else. He leaned forward and rested his elbows on the table, rubbing the ache out of his eyes.

"I do miss her. But there's nothing I can do. I have to get on with my life."

"Maybe-"

"No more maybe's, Mom. Lily and I weren't meant to be. It's time to move on."

Jackson closed the door behind him and jogged down his mom's front steps. Out of some distant habit, he glanced down the road toward Lily's house, half expecting to see her strolling across the lawns with her fishing pole in one hand and a cooler in the other. How long would it take to forget, or at the very least separate his memories from the sadness that came with them?

He walked to his car and unlocked the door. He started to climb inside, but he noticed the same silver car from before still sitting on the other side of his mom's driveway. This time he took a closer look, and he could see that someone was in the driver's seat.

He'd never seen it before, so he made his way over to the car to get a closer look. After all, it had to have been there for over an hour now. A woman was seated behind the wheel, and she typed furiously on a small laptop computer. He bent down and tapped on the driver's window, causing her to jump and send the laptop sideways into the center console. The woman snatched it back to her lap and closed the lid before rolling her window down.

"Hi. Just wanted to make sure everything was all right. You need any help or anything?" Jackson took a quick glance around the inside of the car. Nothing seemed unusual.

"Uh, no, I'm fine." The woman smiled up at him, her blond hair lifting just off her shoulders as a breeze swept through the window.

"Well, I noticed you've been out here for a while, and I didn't recognize the car. You can't be too safe these days."

"That's true. No need to worry, though. I'm perfectly harmless."

"Are you from around here?"

Her mouth stiffened into a tight line, and her bright green eyes narrowed slightly. Maybe he was being overly nosy, but with his dad gone, he had to look out for his mom, even if it meant ticking off a perfectly nice young woman.

She placed her laptop in the passenger seat and pulled her purse into her lap.

"Would you prefer to see some identification?"

"No, no. I'm sorry. I didn't mean to be rude."

"I'm sure you didn't." She relaxed again and returned her purse to the seat. "Actually, the truth is, I'm thinking about buying a house not far from here, and the realtor said my daughter would be zoned for the elementary school right down the street. I just wanted to get a better sense of what the surrounding areas were like in case she has to walk some mornings." She winked and gave him a crooked grin. "You can't be too safe these days."

He returned her smile and had to laugh. "Very true."

"Do you know much about it?"

"Sure. I went to school there. Then I worked at the after school program a couple of years in high school. And I played ball on the playground most of my life."

"So then this is a safe neighborhood?"

"Definitely. I don't think you have anything to worry about."

Chapter Eighteen

As he turned off the ignition and sat completely still behind the wheel, Lily wondered what was going through Alex's mind. Maybe this was a bad idea. She wasn't even sure why she'd asked him to bring her here. But she'd wondered too long about the things he'd kept hidden from her, and she needed to see them for herself. She reached over and covered his hand with hers.

"You okay?"

He looked at her and smiled, though it seemed forced.

"Sure. Why do you ask?"

"You seem a little quiet. Are you uncomfortable bringing me here?"

"Nah, I'm fine. You ready to go in?"

She nodded and they climbed out of his car. As she came around the front, she couldn't see very far past the driveway and small yard except to make out a bird bath near the walkway and a For Sale sign near the road. The houses were spread out so far, she couldn't even see the next one over through the trees. It was nothing like the cramped little neighborhood she'd lived in with her mom where there were barely a few feet separating her house from her neighbor's.

She took Alex's hand as they walked along the stones leading toward the front porch.

"It's quiet out here."

He nodded. "Hmm. Yeah, I guess it is."

They climbed the steps onto the porch, and as he slid the key in the door, she took in the view with a strange sense of walking through a dream. She'd tried to imagine his house, tried to picture how he lived, but she hadn't been prepared for the emptiness of it.

A small wind chime twisted in the breeze, and the gentle ding of the notes drew her eyes to the corner of the porch. Two rocking chairs sat on either side of a small glass-topped table, and she wondered if he'd shared evenings out here with Adrian. Had they laughed together? Had he kissed her or shared a cup of coffee with her in the morning? Maybe they'd sat there after dinner, his hand on her belly, feeling the baby move.

She suddenly felt sick.

Alex pushed open the front door and gestured for her to go in. But her feet wouldn't budge. She couldn't shake the feeling that she shouldn't be here.

He gave her a curious look. "You want to go in?"

"Yeah."

She forced her feet forward through the door and into a small foyer. The light from the chandelier cast a golden hue that spilled into the living room just beyond where the hardwood ended. She glanced around the foyer for any signs of his former life—pictures, artwork, books—anything that might fill in the blanks. But the walls were bare, and there was no sign of any life whatsoever, not even a small table or a coat rack. It was just...empty.

She walked forward to the edge of the light where the foyer opened into the living room. To her left stretched a dark hallway, and to her right was the kitchen. Alex flipped the light switch behind her, and the room brightened, but the emptiness remained. How had he lived like this for so long?

"Well, this is it." He walked around the sofa and stood before her with his arms outstretched. "It's not much."

She wasn't sure what to say. Part of her ached for him, sensing this place was filled with sorrow. It had to be like living with ghosts.

She forced a smile. "It's a pretty house. I like it."

"You do?"

"Yeah. Not too big. Not too small. I can't believe you haven't been able to sell it."

He shrugged. "I don't know what else I can do about it. The realtor said to pack away all the personal stuff, which wasn't much anyway. I try to keep it clean, but beyond that, I just don't know what else to do."

She walked around behind the recliner and toward the opening to the kitchen.

"Mind if I look around?"

"Make yourself at home." He followed behind her into the kitchen. "Can I get you something to drink? I wasn't expecting company, so it's not much, but I have some soda."

"Sure."

She caught a glimpse of the refrigerator as he opened it. Not surprisingly, it was pretty bare as well. The counters were a beautiful marble that glinted with the light occasionally, and the tiled floor matched their pattern. It was beautiful, but like everything else, cold and hollow. The only personal item around was a calendar hanging on the wall with a picture of a farm on it.

"Here you go." He handed her the soda and leaned back against the counter.

"Thanks."

She opened it and took a gulp then put it down beside him. She reached out and ran her hand along his arm, feeling the tension in his body.

"I'm sorry," she said. "I shouldn't have asked you to bring me here."

"Why? I don't mind."

"I can see how uncomfortable this is for you, and honestly, it feels a little weird to me too." She took his hand. "You want to go somewhere else?"

He sighed and squeezed her hand. "Actually, no. I like having you here. It adds a little life to the place. Maybe you can give me some ideas to spruce it up a bit."

She grinned and shook her head. "That's definitely not my area of expertise. My idea of sprucing it up would be putting a sand volleyball court in the back yard."

"I like that idea. Would you come play in your bikini if I did?"

"Absolutely."

He pulled her face to his, and the heat of his kiss warmed everything around her. For a brief moment, she forgot about where she was and just felt the excitement he stirred inside of her.

"Hey," he mumbled in her ear. "There's more to see." He kissed her neck. "If you want."

She let him lead her back through the living room and down the hallway. As she passed a closed door on her left, her curiosity got the better of her.

"Hey, what's in here?" she asked.

He stopped and faced her, his lips fading into a frown. "Ah, that would have been, uh, you know...Evan's room."

"Oh." She dropped her gaze to the floor. "I'm sorry."

"Don't be. You want to go in?"

"No, no." She shook her head.

"It's okay. There's nothing in there." He pushed the door open and stepped halfway inside. "See?"

She glanced through the doorway into the room, which was indeed empty. The only clue as to its intended use was the wallpaper border of trains and cars around the top of the walls. She shouldn't have asked about it. She remembered the first time she'd gone in Jackson's house after his dad died, the way his absence hung over every room, every piece of furniture, even every word they'd spoken. Maybe that was why this room was bare.

"I don't know how you live here like this," she said.

"Like what?"

"With all the memories. I've seen other people I know go through things, and I just don't know how you do it. I can't imagine."

He stepped back into the hallway and pulled the door closed again.

"Well, it hasn't been easy. But you have to figure out a way to keep going." He gave her a small smile and kissed her. "In fact, I'd like to show you something."

She followed him down the hallway to an open door at the end. As he stepped inside, he flipped a switch, and a lamp beside the bed lit up the room. She walked through the doorway and immediately felt a difference.

In here at least, there seemed to be evidence of life—an empty glass on the table, a dresser with change spilled across the top and a photo of Alex, Chloe, and an older woman who had to be his mom. A large plush blanket with the Marine Corps emblem on it lay crumbled at the foot of the bed, and the sheets were strewn in all different directions. She walked to the end of the bed, taking in the room she'd been trying to imagine him in each night as they'd talked on the phone.

Alex pulled open the drawer of the bedside table and pulled out a small square of paper. Then he sat on the edge of the bed and motioned for her to join him.

"I hope it's okay to share this with you." He gave her the paper, which she realized was an ultrasound photo. "He was, uh, about four months here."

It took her a minute, but she could make out the lines enough to see the face.

"I don't exactly know what to look for. Can you show me?"

She glanced up into his eyes and saw the moisture there, but he smiled and pointed at the photo, drawing with his finger as he talked.

"This is his face here. And right there is his arm. His legs are right there. He kept crossing them every time we tried to see if he was a boy or girl, like he knew we were looking."

He chuckled a little, and Lily smiled back at him, relieved he seemed to be enjoying his memories.

"Thank you for sharing this with me," she said. "I wish...I wish I could say something or do something..."

He held the photo in his hand for a moment before placing it on the night stand. Then he took her hand.

"You don't have to say or do anything. Honestly, just being with you has made me realize that I don't have to stay trapped in the past. You've helped me see what's possible, that being happy and loving again isn't betraying his memory."

She rubbed his hand with her thumb, thinking of her own struggles to leave the past behind.

"I love you, Alex."

His face broke into a smile, and he cupped her cheeks in his hands as he kissed her.

"I love you, too."

He rolled her onto the bed, tucking her body beneath his, and this time when he touched her, the connection felt so complete, so right, every other thought fell away. There were no alarms in her head, no thoughts of right or wrong, just the fire building between them that spread to every inch of her body.

"Lily?" he murmured. "Do you want me stop?"

She knew what to say, but she couldn't form the words. His hands on her skin were the only sensations that made sense. He kissed her throat, moving down her body slowly, taking every last drop of her resolve with him.

"Don't stop," she breathed.

Birmingham, Alabama

Adrian took one final look around the neighboring yards, making sure no one had seen her, before she closed the back door. Then she flipped the small flashlight around the room—apparently the kitchen. Probably nothing interesting in her

She moved through the doorway into the living room, and to her left a tiny ancient television reflected the light back at her from across the room. An old sofa sat against the wall by the kitchen doorway, and it saturated the air with a musty smell that could only come from years of improper cleaning, if any at all.

Directly across from her was a small wooden desk with a few books and a black chair. She walked over and ran her gloved finger along the top. Didn't anyone around here believe in dusting? She moved a few papers around, but nothing struck her as interesting.

She glanced around the small open space to her right that probably should have been a dining room, if anyone had cared to try to fit a tiny table in the space. There was only a pitiful excuse for a chandelier hanging too low.

She turned and went between the sofa and television into a miniscule hallway—if you could even call it that. It was basically walled-in space separating the two bedrooms and the bathroom. She glanced to her right. That had to be Little Miss Perfect's room.

She walked around the double bed in the center of the room, looking over photos on the dresser. Nothing but boring faces and sickly smiles. A trophy case stood in the corner, all three shelves stocked full of plaques and trophies from at least twelve years prior. Bet they made Miss Perfect feel good about herself when she was praying.

She picked up a shorter one in the front—Most valuable Player of something or other—and she turned the golden girl on the top until she faced backward. Then she returned the trophy to its shelf.

She turned and looked at the bed, not exactly sure what she was looking for. Something had to be in here that would give her some insight, some weakness or secret. Everyone had secrets if you dug around long enough.

She shined the flashlight across the bed at the vanity, and it seemed more promising. She walked back around the bed to get a closer look. There were pictures stuck to the mirror of various insignificant faces, but one in particular jumped out at her. A guy in a basketball jersey draped an arm over Little Miss Perfect in her volleyball uniform, and something about him seemed familiar. She lifted it off the mirror and studied it more closely.

Then it hit her. That was the guy from earlier that day, the overzealous idiot who made her drop her laptop. Interesting. She turned to the bed and night table behind her, dropping to her knees to look under the bed. Nothing there. But under the night table she found a photo album and a yearbook.

She pulled them out and thumbed through them slowly, a smile spreading over her face. Now this was promising. Miss Perfect did have a weakness—a handsome one. And it would hit Alex right where it hurt.

She'd have to find out his name and dig up some more information, but she knew what direction to go now. She pulled out the portable scanner from her satchel and ran several photos through it, concentrating on the ones that were likely the most intimate.

It figured Miss Perfect would have Mr. Jock at her side. Weren't they just the most perfect couple? And from the looks of things, they'd been that way for a long time. Maybe, if she played this right, she could make all three of them get what they deserved.

She put the scanner back and returned the album and year-book. But as she pushed the books back under the table, a small card fell onto the floor. She picked it up to shove it back in, but the emblem on the front caught her attention.

It was a circle divided into four sections, with the letters of the word *love* inscribed. She looked more closely and realized it read, "True Love Waits."

Surely Miss Perfect wasn't actually *that* perfect.

She flipped the card over and read the vow on the back, chuckling to herself. So the perfect princess was waiting for her prince charming to marry her sorry ass before she soiled herself. That had to be killing Alex. No wonder he'd been so uptight in New York. Even better.

She tucked the card away again and stood, satisfied with what she'd found. She'd need some more information, a few names maybe, and she'd have to get a little dirty, but this new development would fit nicely with what she'd already set in motion. Then she could just sit back and watch all three of them suffer.

Brunswick, Georgia

The magnitude of what she'd done didn't hit Lily until she was lying in the quiet darkness of Alex's bedroom, his heavy breathing signaling he was finally asleep. But when it hit, her world spun completely off its axel.

Oh God. Oh God. Panic surged through her. *Oh God. I'm not a virgin. What did I do?*

She tried to remember the exact moment she had let her virginity slip through her fingers, but it was a blur. She wanted desperately to take it back, to somehow erase what she'd done, but it was over. She had made love to Alex, and the happiness he'd shared with her afterward only sickened her more.

She closed her eyes and hoped it was a dream—a nightmare—but her stomach continued to lurch and roll. How could she have let this happen? She'd been so sure of herself, of everything she believed in. She had set herself out as an example to other girls, convincing them to wait for their husbands. How could she look any of those girls in the eye ever again?

She wanted desperately to pray, to beg God to take the shame away, to promise she would never do it again, but there was nothing she could say, no way to make it right again. She turned her face into the pillow and sobbed as quietly as she could. How could she promise God anything? She was liar.

Chapter Nineteen

October 16

Birmingham, Alabama

Lily stared at the Abstract Algebra notes she'd copied from a classmate, trying to make sense of what seemed like a foreign language. She could barely focus on how to add and subtract, much less theorems and corollaries about fields and rings.

She closed her book and shoved it off her bed. It landed with a thud, and from her bed across the room, Emily glanced up at her.

"You okay?"

"I'm going to fail my mid-terms." Lily leaned back against the wall and put her palms to her eyes.

"You're not going to fail. You say that every semester, and you always do fine."

"Not this time. I don't get this. I mean I *really* don't get it. I've failed the last two tests, and the only reason I still have a *C* in the class is because the professor takes pity on me when I

come to him crying every week when I can't do the homework!"
She pushed herself off the bed and started pacing. "Em, I'm really going to fail. And not just this class. I'm drowning, and I
don't know what to do."

Emily set her own books aside. "Hey, it's going to be all right.
You just need to get some help. Is there someone you can study
with?"

The desire to flee swelled inside of her, and she tried to take
a deep breath. She sat back down on her bed, dropped her head
into her hands, and rocked back and forth. She felt the pressure
on her bed shift as Emily moved beside her.

"Lil, is there something else going on?"

She wanted to pour out all of the guilt and shame that had
been building the past five days, but words attached painful reality to her feelings. Saying them out loud was as good as plastering them to a billboard.

She looked up at Emily. "Nothing else is going on.

Emily dropped her chin. "Really? You're sure?"

"Yes, I'm sure. Nothing's wrong. At least, nothing I can't
deal with on my own."

"Okay, well, if you need to talk, I'm here."

"Thanks, but I'm fine."

"Obviously. I've never seen you happier. I'm sure your eyes
are so red because of the tears of joy."

"I don't want to talk about it."

"All you had to say." Emily raised a hand in defense and
stood. "I felt the same way when I lost it."

Lily jerked her head up and watched Emily walk toward the
bathroom.

"What are you talking about?"

Emily turned around, crossing her arms over her chest. She let out a sigh and seemed to think for a moment before she spoke. That was something new. When had Emily Sanchez ever filtered her words?

"You slept with Alex, didn't you?"

Lily swallowed hard. "I...I don't know how to talk about it."

"What's the big deal? You love him don't you?"

"The big deal? I was waiting until I got married. You knew that."

"Yeah, but I never understood it."

"I wanted to be able to say that the only man I had ever been with was my husband."

"Who would you say it to?"

"What? I don't know. No one. It's just a figure of speech."

Emily shrugged. "Maybe, maybe not. Maybe you wanted other people to look up to you. Maybe you want to be better than everyone else."

Lily couldn't believe what she was hearing. Sure, they'd always seen things differently, even argued from time to time. But Emily had never said something so hurtful before.

"Do you really think that about me?"

"No, of course not. Purely hypothetical. But, you could still say the only man you've been with is your husband. Just marry Alex."

"How can you be so flippant about this? I compromised a principle that was very important to me. What kind of Christian am I if I just throw away my beliefs, even if it's for someone I love?"

Emily softened. "I know you feel bad. I didn't mean to sound callous." She rejoined Lily on her bed, chewing on her lip for a minute before continuing. "Aren't you always the one telling me that God forgives anything? I don't get it. If you really believe that, then why are you taking this so hard?"

Her words struck Lily in the heart. God did forgive; she knew that. But it didn't take away her shame. All she wanted was to go back and make things right again, to erase what she'd done. But that was impossible now, and she had no idea how to deal with it.

"Have you talked to Alex about it?" Emily asked.

"I've tried, but I don't really know how. I'm afraid he'll think I regret it."

"Did I miss something? You do regret it."

"I know, but I don't want him to feel bad."

Emily smiled and shook her head. "Well, you can't really hide it. You're way too easy to read. He probably already knows something is wrong. Everyone else does."

"What do you mean?"

"Coach asked me if something's going on with you. Alison too. You've been a bit off in practice this week, and holing up in your room hasn't helped."

Great. So everyone, including Coach, knew something was up. Between her performance dropping off and her grades slipping, she was in danger of landing in some real trouble.

"What did you tell them?" Lily asked.

"That I didn't know."

"Thanks."

"Sure. What are roomies for?"

A prickly silence fell over them, like a wool blanket that made your whole body itch. Did Emily look at her differently now? How long before other people figured it out?

Brunswick, Georgia

From the moment she answered the phone, Alex could tell Lily was building up to something, and he didn't need three guesses to figure out where she was going. She hadn't been herself since the last night they'd spent together. She'd practically slunk out of his house the next day.

He propped his feet on the coffee table and popped the top of another Killian's.

"I've been thinking about our last night together," she said. "I wanted to talk to you about it."

"Sure. I'm all ears. Spill it."

The phone was so quiet he could practically hear the crickets outside her window. Then she cleared her throat.

"I, uh, I don't feel right about what happened last weekend." She paused, but he waited. "I mean, I loved being with you. But my beliefs haven't changed. What I did was wrong, and I hate feeling that way about us."

He was speechless. There was no pleasing her. Hadn't he asked her, not once, but several times if she wanted him to stop?

"Alex?"

"Yeah?"

"Well?"

"Well, what?"

She cleared her throat again. "Aren't you going to say anything?"

"I don't know what you want me to say."

"I'm sorry. I know-"

"I've tried to love you the only way I know how, and it isn't good enough. I really don't think I'm the man you want to be with."

"That's not true-"

"Yes it is. You want someone who believes the same things you do. Someone who'll stand up to your measuring stick and not fall short. That's not me. You don't want me."

"Yes I do."

Her voice was small and it cracked, and he pictured her face with tears streaming down her cheeks. Then he forced it back where it came from. He didn't need that image right now. It weakened him. This back and forth crap had to stop.

"I can't change who I am," he said. "I can't change the fact that I want to make love to you when we're together. Lily, nothing has ever felt so right. I loved being that close to you, and that you shared your first time with me. It was so perfect."

"This was a huge step for me, one I don't think I was ready to take. I can't change who I am any more than you can. Waiting until I was married was so important to me."

"So you regret it. Great. Now I feel like I forced myself on you."

"No. I don't feel that way."

"But *I* do!" He took a deep breath, forced his voice to stay even. "You wish it had never happened. So that makes me a complete jerk."

"I just wish we had waited."

Did she think that made him feel better? Her trying to protect his ego only made the bruise larger.

"So now what?" he asked.

"I don't know. Can't we just decide it won't happen again?"

He had to stifle a laugh. One, it wasn't funny. Two, she was so naïve it made his chest ache.

"That's just not possible."

"Why not?"

"Lily, I think you're being a little unrealistic here. We've been heading toward this for a while now. It didn't just happen. And the feelings that landed us here haven't gone away. We're still going to be tempted, and once you do something once, it gets even harder to stop. Trust me."

"I just want to go back to the way things were," she said.

"We can't. You can't move backward. We'll just end up right back here again."

"Alex, I don't want to have sex again."

He set the beer down and rubbed his head. It throbbed with the anger he was trying to suppress. She wanted the impossible, and apparently so did he.

"Then I don't know how we can keep seeing each other."

He heard her breath catch and felt the blow to his own chest. He couldn't believe he'd just said that. What was he thinking? What was she thinking right now? Probably that he was an arrogant jerk who'd slept with her and was dumping her for not wanting more.

That was smooth, Walker. Smooth.

"I'm sorry," he said. "I didn't mean that."

She sniffled, and the image he had blocked out minutes earlier invaded him again.

"Why are you so frustrated?" she asked.

Because you make me weak.

"I don't know," he said. "I know I shouldn't be. I'm sorry." He sounded like an idiot. What kind of man let a woman make him so crazy? "Look, I just want you to be happy. If you don't want me to even touch you, I promise I won't."

"So you don't want to break up with me?"

"Of course not. I'm sorry. I didn't mean that."

She let out a long breath, and a small amount of relief broke through.

"It's okay. Let's just forget all this even happened. Please?"

"Whatever you want, Lily. Whatever you want."

October 23

Birmingham, Alabama

She should have thought this out better. When Emily suggested they go out and have some fun at a local club, Lily had thought it was a perfect chance to drown out her conscious for a night. Had she known it would bring on such a headache, she might have at least taken some ibuprophen beforehand. Too late now. She chugged down her soda instead, hoping the caffeine would alleviate the throbbing.

From the table she and Emily had grabbed, she watched a hundred some odd people dancing in a space probably meant for half that. With so many sweaty bodies rubbing up against each other, she understood why only drunk people seemed to enjoy it. Top it off with strobe lights and the smoke choking her lungs, and she wondered again why she had thought this would help.

Maybe she should've stayed in her room. Alex had wanted to watch old movies on television together while they talked on the phone, but things hadn't been the same between them lately. He was trying too hard to make her happy, and she was trying too hard to forget.

He'd already called twice since she'd gotten to the club, and she couldn't bring herself to answer. She looked down at her phone again. He'd sent a text message.

You ok?

"Still brooding about Alex?" Emily said from beside her. She was already drenched with sweat from dancing and a few dark curls were plastered to her forehead.

Lily shrugged. "Trying not to."

"Forget about him tonight. He's not here. Just relax and have a good time. You need it."

Lily shook her head then rubbed her temples. "I don't think this was such a good idea. My head is killing me."

"You need something stronger." Emily gave her a knowing grin. "Why don't you let me liven that drink up a bit?"

"No way."

At times like this, it'd be easier just to take a few drinks to relax, and Emily had been more than eager to help her out. She'd never let herself even taste the stuff, though she couldn't remember why. Maybe it had all been part of the same pledge to avoid temptation. How long till she blew that one too?

"Come on, Lil. Let's dance. Let loose a bit."

"Fine." She threw up her hands in surrender. Anything to direct her thoughts away from her guilt, even flat out embarrassment.

She followed Emily out onto the dance floor and darted her gaze over the swarm of people moving around her. Just copy what they were doing—that seemed simple enough. She moved awkwardly at first, conscious of every limb. But she soon realized no one was even paying attention to her, and she closed her eyes to focus on the music. It gradually started to feel good. She let go of her fear, just let the music move through her, let the anxiety slip down her arms, waist, hips and then around her ankles. Complete surrender.

It was a brief reprieve, but it was worth it. When she finally took a break and returned to the table with Emily, the relief was palpable. She needed more of that.

Her phone buzzed in her back pocket. Another text.

Starting to worry. You ok?

Emily leaned across the table and grabbed the phone. "No more brooding!"

"Em, come on. I need to tell him I'm alright or he'll just keep calling and texting."

Emily turned the phone off and shoved it in her pocket. "It'll be fine. Just have a good time!"

Lily rolled her eyes and caught a glimpse of a familiar face come through the entrance.

"What's T.J. doing here?" she asked.

"Oh, I uh, forgot to mention it, but I invited him and a couple of guys to meet us down here. Hope that's okay."

"T.J.? I thought you two broke up months ago."

Emily gave her a sheepish smile. "We did. But we've been talking the past week or so, and you know..."

"What about Chris? The whole weekend trip to see him? What was that about?"

"I don't know. It was just fun." Emily shrugged, smiling as she waved to the guys.

Lily turned and watched T.J. and some of the other basketball players from school moving through the crowd, their heads at least six inches above everyone else in the room. No way you could lose them in a crowd, especially T.J. With his sun-streaked hair and easy-going gait, you'd think he grew up on a surf board in California rather than the mountains of Tennessee. He waved back and flashed the dimpled smile that had caused a good deal of drama among her friends throughout their Freshman year.

"You don't mind, do you?" Emily asked again, as if it mattered.

"Why would I?" She stood and gave T.J. a hug as the guys reached the table.

"Hey, Lil!" He squeezed her tight, forcing the air out of her lungs. "What are you doing hanging out with us heathens?"

Good lord. Did everyone think she was so judgmental? She stepped out from under his arm and smiled at Emily.

"Just trying to have a little fun."

She started to suggest they head toward the dance floor again, when she noticed a new face. He was standing off to the side talking with another basketball player, scanning the club like he'd never seen it before.

"Who's the new guy?" she asked T.J.

"Who? Oh! That's Shane something-or-other. He just transferred from junior college in Ohio. I don't know too much about him yet."

Lily looked him over again, and this time he noticed. He smiled. It was nice. He wasn't good-looking in an obvious way, but the smile was genuine. She walked over to him and stuck out her hand.

"Hi. I'm Lily Brennon."

"Shane Harper." He shook her hand.

"I hear you just transferred. Where you from?"

"A little town outside Midlothian, Texas. How about you?"

"Oh, I'm from around here."

"You play a sport?"

"Yeah, I'm on the volleyball team."

"That figures."

"Oh really, why's that?"

He smiled again, almost apologetic. "Well, the tall girls with the awesome legs usually play volleyball."

"Nice. That was pretty smooth. You got any more?"

He threw his head back and laughed. "Nah, that's the best I got." He looked over her shoulder, and Lily followed his gaze. Emily and T.J. were already entwined on the dance floor.

"You want to dance?" he asked.

"Sure."

Alex would probably disapprove, but she wanted to feel the music lift the weight of her conscience again, so she followed him out onto the floor. Thankfully, he didn't get too close, like he sensed her need for space. Still, it was nice to have someone to laugh with, and as the night wore on, the lights and people blurred like a painting in the rain, the colors washing together and taking her convicting thoughts with them.

October 24

Birmingham, Alabama

"Here's your phone."

Lily glanced up from her Abstract Algebra notes as Emily took a seat across from her in the campus food court and slid her phone across the table.

"Thanks." She barely glanced at it as she shoved away her notes and leaned back in her chair.

Emily winced. "How did your test go?"

"Terrible, I'm sure."

"At least it's over."

Lily leaned forward and grabbed her phone, turning it on to check the time. As the screen came to life, several chimes sounded in a row.

"Lots of messages," Emily said, taking a bite of a French fry. "Three guesses who they're from, and the first two don't count."

Lily scrolled through the messages, noting the frustration that colored Alex's texts. She'd been so focused on her test this morning, she hadn't thought to respond to his messages from the night before. Her stomach knotted knowing he'd be upset with her.

"I should call him," she said.

Emily shrugged and continued eating. Lily grabbed her things and shoved them into her backpack. She told Emily she'd catch up with her later then headed out through the student center toward the Math and Science building.

She pulled out her phone to call Alex, but noticed she still had one more notification, an email to her student account. She opened her email application and glanced through it. She clicked through the junk mail, the last one from the Baptist Student Union.

Be careful whom you play with. I'm always watching.

~God

She stopped walking and read the email again. What an odd message, and she'd never even been to a meeting at a Baptist Student Union. It had to be some kind of joke or mistake. She wondered if anyone else had gotten one.

She deleted it, and then she dialed Alex's cell. Her stomach tightened again.

Chapter Twenty

October 28

Brunswick, Georgia

Alex walked up to the window of the ramshackle building that served the best hot dogs in town and ordered his usual two chili cheese dogs. Then he made his way over to the wooden table in the shade where Steve awaited him, already half-way through his sandwich. He took a seat and grabbed a French fry from Steve's plate.

"What's up?"

Steve smirked at the swiped fry. "Thanks for meeting me. How you been?"

"Pretty good. I'm working on a burglary over at the mall."

"I heard you solved the Sea Island case. Nice job. How much did those guys get away with? Something like a quarter of a million, right?"

"Yeah."

Steve grinned. "Not too shabby for your first case."

"Just the beginning, my friend."

Steve looked around, so Alex followed his gaze. Three women were seated at another wooden table behind him, just beside the hot dog shack. But otherwise, the place was deserted. The only sounds were the few cars driving past and the frogs down at the creek behind the parking lot. As a cool breeze lifted the Spanish moss from the branches nearby, Alex took a closer look at Steve.

"Everything okay with you?" he asked.

Steve folded his arms across the table, looking desperate to say something. But he looked very uncomfortable about it.

"Maybe you should give Chloe a call soon."

So that's what this was all about. Alex had figured as much, but he'd hoped to have a relaxing lunch with his friend without getting into sore topics. He had no idea what to say.

"Maybe," he offered.

"She misses you."

Alex cleared his throat. "Is that why you wanted to meet for lunch? To plead her case?"

Steve sighed and looked around again. "Well, no, actually. I need to talk to you about something else."

"Sure, what's going on?" Alex grinned. "You miss me? Maybe I can talk to the Chief, and we'll see about making you a detective."

Steve shook his head. "Alex, I'm serious. I need to tell you about something, but it could get me in trouble...you too."

He had never seen his friend so concerned. He looked worried. And Steve never worried.

"What's going on?" he asked.

Steve leaned forward and lowered his voice. "You know Hoffman?"

"Of course."

"He told me something the other day...something he shouldn't be telling me, but he knows we're friends, and it's probably nothing, but still...You need to keep this to yourself."

Alex's nerves tightened. He didn't like the connections forming in his mind. Hoffman, Internal Affairs, privileged information—none of it sounded good.

"Just tell me what's going on," Alex said.

"Hoffman says they got an anonymous tip from the department website—some female claiming that you sexually harassed her during an interview."

"What?"

Steve raised a hand as if to calm him. "Don't get upset. They know it wasn't real. At least Hoffman says they're not going to open a case on it."

"I don't understand." Alex racked his brain trying to remember when he'd interviewed a female. No one came to mind.

"They were able to come up with an IP address, and it came back to an Andrew Carter in Alabama." Steve paused as the words sank in.

"Alabama? But..."

"Look, I don't know all the details. But what I do know is that whoever was assigned to check out the story decided it was most likely untrue. But you know how these things go. It's in your file, and if anything suspicious ever happens..."

"Yeah, I know. But none of this makes sense. I don't think I've even interviewed a female. I mean, there were some maids working in the Sea Island houses that I talked to, but none of them alone."

Steve folded his arms over his chest, looking cautious. "I hate to point out the obvious, but you and I both know only one person from Alabama."

"It couldn't be her. Lily wouldn't do something like that."

"Is everything okay with you two?" Steve raised an eyebrow.

"Yes. Definitely."

"Do you know anyone named Andrew Carter?"

"No, but I'm going to find out. Did Hoffman give you the IP address?"

"Hey, man. I don't think that's a good idea."

Alex pressed his fist down onto the table and tried to stay calm. "I have a right to know who this person is. They're messing with my career here."

Steve sighed and looked around again, like he was expecting uniformed officers to come around the corner and arrest him at any moment.

"Just promise me you'll keep your cool."

"Of course I will. You know me."

After everyone else had cleared out for the day, Alex sat at his desk still chewing on what Steve had told him. He couldn't just search out information on someone when they weren't really connected to any of his cases, but he had to know who made that tip. He wouldn't be able to use the department's databases or search software, but maybe he could still get what he needed.

He started with a simple search through White Pages, and found four listings for an Andrew Carter in Birmingham, Alabama. He glanced through the addresses, none looking familiar. Then he read through the list of associated people for each one. And right away he saw it.

At first, he couldn't believe it. He leaned back in his chair, looking at the names again. It had to be him. But what was he trying to accomplish?

He sat up straight again and went back to the computer, pulling up the CLEAR website and logging in. It might not be exactly legal, he wasn't sure. But he had to find out exactly who he was dealing with before he went charging in.

Just as he typed in the name, his personal phone vibrated on his belt. He pulled it out and glanced at it—a text from a number he didn't recognize. Actually, he realized, it wasn't a text. It was a picture.

He did a reverse search of the number, and this time wasn't surprised at the information. This guy had some nerve. First coming after his job, and now what?

He opened the picture, and at first he couldn't make out what he was seeing. Then, slowly, the image cleared. His blood raced through his head, and he threw the phone against the wall.

"You're going out to another club?" Alex leaned back against the couch and stared at the ceiling, trying not to shatter his phone's guts again. This was getting ridiculous. Something wasn't right here.

"It's just a Halloween party downtown," Lily said. "I've been going since I was in high school."

"To clubs?"

"Well not that part. But the clubs are the most fun. Why does it bother you when I go out with my friends?"

"I don't care if you go out with your friends. It's that you're going to places that aren't safe. Why can't you go out to a movie or something?"

"Stop giving me a hard time. I've been really stressed. Midterms are finally over, and I just want to go out and enjoy myself a little."

"Like you did last week?"

"What is that supposed to mean?"

He sat up straight again. Maybe he was wrong.

"Did you go to the club last week with a guy?"

"What? No! Why would you think that?"

He reached up and massaged his forehead. If she would just tell him the truth, he could deal with it. But not lies.

"So you did not go out dancing with a guy last week?"

"Alex, you're acting strange. Where is this coming from?"

She was avoiding the question. It had to be true then.

"I just want you to be careful. You never know anything about the people you meet in those places."

"I don't hang out with strangers. Trust me, I only stick with the people I know."

So she knew him. Someone from school maybe. It could have been Jackson for all he knew. That would explain everything.

"Lily, are you sure you want to be with me?"

"Yes. Why are you asking all these questions?"

"I'm just concerned about you." He looked down at the picture he'd printed out at work after reassembling his phone, unable to erase the image and all its implications from his mind. It was a little dark, but the couple in the center of the photo was clear enough. They were dancing together, laughing like they shared a secret. It sent a wave of fury through his core.

Who was that dancing with Lily?

October 31

Birmingham, Alabama

"You've been sitting there for nearly an hour," Emily yelled at her over the pulsating music. "When are you coming out here?"

Lily looked over the dance floor, packed full of people enjoying themselves. At least, they appeared to be enjoying themselves. How many others were drowning their consciences with her? She should have worn a costume—like that girl by the bar dressed as a witch, with hideous moles all over her face. Then at least her outside would match the ugliness of her inside.

"Hello! Earth to Lily!" Emily stood in front of their table with her hands on her hips. She had come as Cat Woman. It was so cliché. And so Emily.

"I just need to warm up to the music for a bit. You know that."

Emily rolled her eyes. "Whatever. You want anything to drink? I'm heading over there."

"A coke."

A smirk slipped across Emily's lips, and Lily pointed a finger at her.

"No funny business tonight, Em. Straight coke."

"Okay." Emily threw her hands up. Then she turned and weaved her way into the crowd.

Lily's head vibrated in time with the beat, and her throat ached from the smoke. This was a bad idea. She needed to be in her dorm room right now buried in her Bible and begging God for forgiveness. She was just making things worse. But she felt like she had as a kid when she'd crashed her bike into a ditch full of thorn bushes. She could see the pit coming, and that her path was headed straight for it. But she'd frozen, and fell tumbling into the prickly shrubs.

She was sick of feeling like this, sick of arguing with Alex, sick of herself. She was ruining everything. He wouldn't even return her phone calls today. He was probably sick of her too.

Suddenly a large hand slapped her on the back, rocketing her breath out of her lungs.

"Lil! Whatcha doing over here by yourself?"

T.J. fell into the seat next to her and slid his drink onto the table. His eyes were already getting red, and his cheeks were flushed and damp with sweat. His smile spread from one adorable dimple to the other. He was a happy drunk.

She couldn't help but smile back. She leaned toward him to avoid more yelling than necessary.

"Just waiting for you to come sweep me out onto the dance floor."

"Awww. I'd love to, but Em's wearing me out!"

"I can see that."

She let her gaze wander around the club again while T.J. slumped further in his seat. She watched the couples on the dance floor and tried not to notice the ones groping each other. Some people had no regard for others' gag reflexes.

Finally Emily came back with their drinks and took a seat beside T.J. as she slid Lily's across the table. But before Lily could even take a sip, T.J. elbowed her in the ribs, nearly knocking it out of her hands.

"Hey, isn't that your boy Jackson over there?"

She turned to see where he was looking, and felt her stomach lurch into her chest. It was him alright, weaving through the crowd near the back of the club. She watched him walk across the room, his movements so familiar they struck her like blows to the gut. What was he doing here?

Then she noticed the blond walking behind him, her hands tucked into the back pockets of his jeans, and it wasn't just any blond. It was Addison Thomas. She'd know that relentlessly perky ponytail anywhere. With her long neck and angled chin, she reminded Lily of a praying mantis.

Jackson's eyes locked on Lily's, and he gave her a slight nod. She averted her gaze to Emily.

"Are they coming over here?"

"I think so," she said.

She glanced toward the back again. Sure enough. He and Addison were headed for their table, though Addison looked less than enthused. Jackson never took his eyes off Lily.

"Hi," he said when they finally reached the table.

"Hi." Her voice barely squeaked out.

They stared at each other for an excruciating minute before T.J.'s voice boomed through the tension.

"Hey, J-man! Pull up a seat."

Jackson looked at Lily like he was waiting for her approval, and she forced a smile. Then he pulled up two chairs and sat down.

"This is Addison," he said to no one in particular. He gave Lily a pointed look. "You remember Addy, I'm sure."

There was a hint of triumph in Addison's emerald eyes. It had taken six years, but she'd finally landed a date with Jackson. She snaked her arm through his and gave Lily the slightest smile. How subtle.

"Yes, Addison. Of course I remember. How are you?"

"Great. I'm finishing up my degree in December, then it's on to medical school."

"Well, good luck with that."

Lily turned her attention back to the dance floor, ready to escape as soon as possible. She was about to stand when she heard T.J.'s question.

"I thought I heard you might be playing in Atlanta?"

Jackson glanced at Lily before answering.

"Uh, yeah. I tried out for the Vision a couple of months ago and got invited back. I head over there in a few days as a matter of fact."

"That's great," T.J. continued. "Man, you had it rough last year. I didn't think you'd make it back."

Jackson shrugged and moved his arm away from Addison's.

"I had my doubts. But things seem to be going well for now. It's just the ABA, but it's a start." He peeked over at Lily again. "I may even try my hand at some ball overseas."

"That's sweet!" T.J. gave him a high five then chugged down another long gulp of his beer.

"Overseas?" Lily asked, leaning forward in her chair. "When did this happen?"

"A few weeks ago. It's not for sure yet, and probably not until next summer. But Clayton said he could get me a tryout in Italy."

Italy? The Italy on the other side of the ocean? Last year he'd balked at the idea of playing in another country. It was too far from home—and her. Besides, he was terrified of flying. He'd pass out before he made it onto the plane.

Addison slid a delicate hand up Jackson's arm and gave his shoulder a pat.

"He'll be back home with a professional team in no time."

And a professional salary. Surely Jackson hadn't forgotten what a snake she was.

"So what are you going to do?" Lily asked. "Hop an ocean liner to get you there and back?"

He shook his head and chuckled. "That's a dilemma I'll have to seriously consider."

Addison wrinkled her brow. Served her right. Did she think she could compete with twelve years of friendship and love? But the thought sacked Lily in the gut. Why on Earth would she be competing for Jackson? He was free to see whomever he wanted.

But *Addison Thomas*?

"Well," Lily managed, "I'm glad to hear you're playing again. That's really great."

T.J. slapped his empty bottle onto the table and sighed. "Yep. Me too, J-Man. You deserve it." He pushed himself up from the table. "I'm getting a refill. Anybody else need anything?"

Emily stood. "I think I'll join you."

They walked toward the bar, T.J. swerving through the crowd like someone kept tilting the room on him. She might have laughed if she didn't feel like she'd swallowed a tangle of hot wires. Jackson leaned over and said something in Addison's ear. She glanced at Lily, let out a huff, and then took off toward the bar.

He didn't even give Addison a second glance as she left. He just leaned back in his chair and watched Lily. It made her squirm. Did she look different?

"So...Italy, huh?" she asked.

He laced his fingers on top of the table and leaned forward, his clear-blue eyes intense.

"We need to talk."

"About what?" She couldn't even look him in the eyes.

"Are you okay? I mean, is everything all right?"

"Sure. Why?"

He started to answer, but then seemed to rethink it, and he leaned back in the chair again. He stretched out his legs and crossed his arms over his chest.

"The volleyball team's doing well. I saw the article in this week's paper."

Her brain struggled to shift gears. Something wasn't right. There were unspoken accusations in his eyes.

"Uh, yes. I guess so."

"Sounds like Saturday's game is a big one."

"It is. If we win, and keep Georgia Southern's score low enough, we'll win the western side of the conference."

"And host the tournament, I read."

"Yeah. Everyone's pretty excited."

He began to bounce his knee up and down. "Okay. I'm just going to ask you about this. Just humor me if it sounds weird."

She nodded.

"Has anything strange happened lately?"

"Like what?"

"Like odd phone calls or texts, something like that."

She started to say no, but then she remembered all the hang-ups, and the email.

"There was an email that seemed strange."

He stiffened, and his eyes widened. "Do you still have it?"

She pulled back, dread growing inside of her. "It didn't even make sense. Probably just a prank."

"Maybe not. What did it say?"

"I don't remember exactly. I deleted it. Something about being careful who you play with."

"Did you recognize the sender address?"

"No. But I think it was fake."

He leaned his forehead down into his hand and rubbed it. Then he glanced back up at her.

"Can we go for a walk?"

She scanned the club for her friends, hoping for an escape somehow. Nothing about this felt right, and it had nothing to do with her guilt.

"Uh, well-"

"Come on. It's too loud in here. I just need to talk to you for a minute."

"Okay."

She stood and followed him through all the people as they shifted and moved like schools of fish. She tried to stay right behind him, but she was definitely *not* putting her hands in his pockets.

Once outside, the fresh air bathed her lungs with relief. But he didn't even seem to notice. He strode down the sidewalk like he was on a mission, and they ended up in the parking lot a couple of blocks down. He began pacing in front of her as she watched him.

"I'm worried about you," he said. "Something's wrong. I feel it."

"Why are you acting like this?"

He stopped and faced her, a frown creasing the edges of his mouth.

"I got something in the mail," he said.

"What do you mean you got *something*?"

"Pictures. And a note written on one of them."

"What kind of pictures?"

He reached inside his jacket and pulled out several photos bound by a rubber band.

"See for yourself."

She slid the rubber band off and took a look at the first photo—the one from Jackson's senior prom. He and Lily were nestled close in a horse-drawn carriage. She recognized it from the yearbook. The next photo was one of Lily dancing with Shane at Jasmine's the previous week. The angle of the photo made it look like they were much closer than they'd actually been. Who would be this creepy?

The last photo was the one that sent her stomach rolling. She was with Alex in the alley in Charleston, and they were kissing, his hand pushing her shirt up much higher than she'd remembered.

"Turn it over," Jackson said.

She flipped the photo over and read the note on the back, her skin crawling as she read.

Your little flower isn't so innocent anymore.

The world tilted beneath her feet. Who would do this? She had to get out of there. She had go back to her dorm.

"Lily?"

She looked up at him, her questions and fear reflected in his eyes. She tried to stammer out an explanation.

"I don't, I don't know what this is." She took a step back. "I have to go."

She ran back into the club, the rhythmic noise even more sickening. Her head throbbed and swam. Where was the table? She needed her keys. Where were Emily and T.J.? She searched for only a moment before giving up. She'd just call them later and tell them she'd left.

She finally found her table just as Jackson caught up to her again. He grabbed her elbow and spun her around.

"Talk to me, Lily. What's going on?"

"I don't know!" she yelled over the music.

"Is something going on between you and Alex?"

"What do you mean?" Her stomach swam again, and her throat ached. She wanted to claw at it, but she reached for the coke still on the table instead. It was mostly water now, but who cared? She gulped half of it down before an unfamiliar taste assaulted her.

She slammed the glass down. Emily!

"Lily!" Jackson shouted, still gripping her elbow. "The photos came from Brunswick."

"What?"

He let go of her and stepped back just as T.J. rejoined them.

"Hey! J-Man. You look like you need a drink. Here, take this." T.J. handed off his beer bottle, but Jackson didn't even look at him. He just set it on the table and looked at Lily.

"Are you okay?" Jackson yelled. He seemed to be getting farther away.

"I'm just confused. Who would do this?"

He leaned down and looked her over more closely. Her lungs constricted and her stomach continued to swim.

"Come on, Lil. Who else do you know that lives in Brunswick?"

No, it couldn't be Alex. The thought sent another wave of nausea through her, but this time her knees buckled. She put her hand on the table to steady herself, trying desperately to breathe.

"No-"

She tried to tell him it wasn't Alex, but her tongue was cotton in her mouth. She sucked in more air, but it only hissed and trickled into her lungs. Her chest tightened even more, like an outside force was squeezing every drop of oxygen out.

"Lily?" He reached out for her and steadied her. Then realization struck them both at the same time. "Where's your Epipen?" He gripped her shoulders, holding her up as more nausea rolled through her body.

She shook her head, unable to speak anymore. She grabbed his arm, fear spreading with her nausea. Suddenly there were two Jacksons.

Air. Breathe.

As her knees finally gave way, Jackson caught her in his arms. The last thing she heard was his voice drifting up through a tunnel. "T.J. get the door! Now! And call 911!"

Lily wheezed and her body shook as Jackson pushed his way out of the front door of the club, cradling her like a baby. Fear was about to split him wide open. He took a deep breath and focused on what he needed to do until the ambulance arrived.

Lay her down flat. Keep her still. Elevate her feet.

T.J. paced the sidewalk, giving their location to the 911 operator. Then he closed his cell phone and turned to Jackson.

"They're on their way. What do we do now?"

"I got to lay her down." Jackson hurried over to the edge of the sidewalk closest to the building. He leaned back against the wall and slid down until he was sitting. T.J. helped him stretch her out. "Get her feet up!"

T.J. knocked over a nearby trash can and slid it across the sidewalk, nearly tumbling over himself in the process. Jackson lifted her feet and rested them on top. She exhaled, but it sounded more like the slow leak of a punctured tire. Her cheeks and throat looked swollen, and her eyes kept opening and closing. Where was her EpiPen? He dug into her pockets. Nothing, but he did find her keys.

"T.J., where's her car?"

"I don't know."

He tossed the keys at T.J. "Go to the parking lot and find her car. Look for her EpiPen. You know what it looks like?"

"Yeah." He sprinted away.

"Check the glove compartment!"

He leaned over and stroked the hair away from her face.

"Lily. Lily. Can you hear me?"

Her mouth opened, but there was no sound. She started to move, but he pressed his hand to her abdomen.

"Don't move. An ambulance is coming. Just lay still. I've got you. I won't let anything happen to you."

A scratchy noise came from her throat. She moved her lips again. His heart pounded in his ears, followed by the distant sound of sirens. Finally. If she could just hold on a little longer.

A small crowd was gathering around them, but Jackson kept his eyes on Lily. He stroked her hair and held her hand, mumbling prayers under his breath.

Her breathing grew more shallow, and her lips began to turn blue. The ambulance finally turned the corner.

"Come on Lil. Breathe."

She sucked in another shaky gulp of air, and then stopped all together—like her throat had sealed shut. He forced her mouth open wider and covered it with his own, pushing in a breath, hoping to force it through. Nothing happened.

"I got it!" T.J. yelled as he pushed through the crowd.

Jackson swiped the EpiPen from his hand and plunged it into her thigh. An EMT knelt beside him.

"What's going on?" he asked.

"Anaphylaxis. She's not breathing."

The EMT took over at CPR as Jackson pulled the EpiPen out. He watched her chest, waiting. The epinephrine was supposed to work immediately, but moments seemed like hours. Finally, she gasped and coughed. She inhaled a precious mouthful of oxygen, and he fell back against the wall. He closed his eyes and dropped his head into his hands.

"Thank you, God," he mumbled.

Chapter Twenty-One

October 31

Birmingham, Alabama

Jackson was sick of hospitals. Literally. Just being in the room with Lily's shallow breathing brought back every nightmare he'd experienced at this very place, and his stomach was swimming with nausea. Her eyes fluttered for a second, and she let out a low groan.

"Lily?" He pushed her hair away from her forehead, hoping his touch might bring her back. "Come on, Lil."

Her eyes finally opened, but they seemed to look right through him. She took another shaky breath and coughed.

"Jackson?"

He couldn't understand why she was still so out of it. She should have been alert and back to normal by now.

"How are you feeling?" he asked.

"Strange. My throat hurts."

He reached for a cup of water on the table nearby and helped her raise her head for a few sips. Then she dropped her head back onto her pillow.

"What happened?" she asked.

"You had an allergic reaction to something. Do you remember getting stung?"

"No."

"What were you drinking?"

"Usual. Coke." She coughed again, but then her eyes widened. "It tasted funny."

"What do you mean?"

"I thought Emily had spiked it. She always jokes about it. But I don't think-"

"Hang on a second."

He walked over to the door and stuck his head out, catching T.J.'s eye down the hall.

"Hey, where's Emily?"

T.J. walked toward him, his steps more even now.

"Bathroom. She'll be right back. Lily awake yet?"

Jackson stepped back and let T.J. in the room. He grinned at her.

"You all right Lil?"

She nodded her head, but her eyes were still glossy and hollow. She blinked slowly, like she might fall asleep again.

"Ugh," she moaned. "I think I'm going to be sick."

That was T.J.'s cue. He slipped back into the hallway, and Jackson came back to her side.

"You need the bucket?"

"I don't know." She rolled her head from side to side, and the color completely drained from her face. "I just want to sleep." Her eyes closed, and she didn't open them again.

He reached for her hand and strummed the back with his thumb, remembering the first time they'd realized she was allergic to bees. They'd been fishing down at the creek the summer before his eighth grade year. He'd never forgotten the look of terror on her face, or the panic that raced through him when she began struggling to breathe. He'd had to carry her the last block to his house then call 911. He'd known that day, in those moments of caring for her, that they belonged to each other in some forever kind of way. Maybe he'd been too young to fully understand it, but he had loved her. He still loved her.

God, he always would.

Emily pushed open the door and peeked inside. She was still in her Cat Woman outfit, and her mascara was smeared around the edges.

"T.J. said she was awake."

He motioned her into the room. "She was for a few minutes. But now..."

"She doesn't look good." She walked to the other side of the bed.

"She said her drink tasted funny, like there was something in it. Did you spike it?"

"No, no way. I mean, I know I joke around with her but I would never really do it." She paused as realization hit them both. "But that means..."

"Someone else did."

"Are you sure? Maybe it was something else. Maybe she's allergic to something new."

Jackson's stomach tightened again. He didn't want to believe someone could have intentionally put something harmful in Lily's drink, but it was beginning to look like a strong possibility. He pushed himself up from the chair he'd pulled beside her bed.

"I need to take care of something. Can you stay with her for a little while?"

"Sure," she said.

He squeezed Lily's hand again before releasing it, and then he headed out the door with his cell phone. Maybe the police would be able to figure out what was going on.

November 1

Birmingham, Alabama

"Do you remember being at the club?"

As her dad paced beside her bed, Lily tried to answer his questions, but everything seemed to be floating up to the surface through a fog.

"What were you doing there?" He threw his hands up and finally collapsed into a chair.

"Just hanging out with Em and T.J. for Halloween. How did I end up here?"

He leaned forward and rested his elbows on his knees.

"I hate when you go to those places, Lily. This is exactly what I'm always afraid of. Why don't you ever listen to me?"

"Dad, what are you talking about? What happened?"

"We think someone may have put bee venom in your drink last night. Apparently you can buy the stuff in a bottle."

"Wait a minute. *Bee venom?* Are you sure?"

"The doctor found antibodies in your blood. It's the only explanation. You went into shock. If it hadn't been for Jackson and T.J...." He shook his head and turned to the window.

Jackson. She'd been with Jackson. The fuzziness lifted briefly, and she remembered talking to him at the club, the music pounding in her ears, and Addison slinking away from their table. He had been upset. They got up and walked out. He showed her the pictures.

The pictures.

"Dad-"

"Lily, you have got to be more careful!" The fear in his eyes sank into her, igniting her own. "You can't just leave your drink lying around. You could have died! And you know you're supposed to keep your Epipen on you at all times." He shook his head. "You shouldn't even be in places like that!"

A knock on the door startled her, and she looked over to see Alex pushing his head through the door.

"Okay if I come in?"

"Alex! What are you doing here?" Her heart leapt, and she nearly jumped out of the bed.

He came through the door and gave her dad a nod. Her dad stood and reached for Alex's outstretched hand.

"Mr. Brennon. I don't think we've officially met. I'm Alex Walker."

"Nice to finally meet you."

"I wish it were under better circumstances." Alex moved beside Lily and leaned over to kiss her on the forehead. He gave her a tight smile. "You okay?"

"Yeah, I'm fine. How did you know I was here?"

"I called your room this morning, and Emily told me what happened." He lowered his chin as if to scold her. "Your dad's right, you know. You don't need to be in those places."

"Can we get into that later, please? I'm still pretty confused about everything. I just want to figure out what happened."

He looked over at her dad. "What do you know so far?"

"Nothing definitive. She said her drink tasted funny, and the doctor said there were antibodies in her blood, so it had to be bee venom. Apparently you can buy it in droplets."

"Have you talked to the police?"

"The police?" Lily's nerves sparked to life.

Alex looked at her like she was crazy. "Bee venom doesn't just happen to get in your drink by accident. Someone did this to hurt you. Someone who knows you."

Her dad crossed his arms over his chest. "The police don't have much to go on. All they know is that she had an allergic reaction. In fact, I got the distinct feeling the cop I spoke to had better things to do."

"Maybe I should talk to him," Alex said.

"Would you? I'd really appreciate it." Her dad dug into his wallet. "Here's his card."

Alex took it and shoved it into his own wallet. "Look, I'll go see what I can find out. I'll make some calls and be back in a little bit."

"You're leaving?" Lily asked. "You just got here."

He leaned down and kissed her lightly across the lips.

"I won't be gone long. I want to take care of this while your dad is here with you. Then I promise, we'll get everything figured out. I won't let anyone hurt you."

He straightened and nodded once again to her dad. He headed for the door, but as he reached it, Jackson pushed it open, and they almost collided. Lily's breath caught in her throat.

"Excuse me," Jackson offered as he stepped to the side. Then he took another look at Alex, studied him from head to toe.

Alex returned the stare before finally sticking out his hand.

"Hi. Alex Walker. And you are?"

Jackson's eyes narrowed, and his back stiffened. He slowly took Alex's hand and gave it a firm shake.

"Jackson Carter."

They stared at each other for what seemed like eternity before Lily cleared her throat. Alex broke the silence first.

"Well, excuse me. I need to get going." He glanced back at Lily again, and she saw an unfamiliar coldness in his eyes. "I'll be right back."

When he left the room, she finally exhaled. Jackson stepped closer to the bed, his brow furrowed into a scowl. He looked over at her dad and practically growled.

"What is he doing here? For all we know, he's the reason-"

"Now, Jackson." Her dad raised his hands. "We don't know anything for certain yet."

"What are you talking about?" she asked. "What do you mean we don't know anything yet?"

"I told your dad about the pictures." Jackson leaned over and rested his hands at the foot of her bed. "And that they came from Brunswick."

"You think this had something to do with those pictures?"

"I think someone's trying to send us a message. And you could have been hurt, or worse. I already told the police what I know, but a lot of good that did."

She sat up and her head swam. For a second she thought she might fall out of the bed. She reached for the small metallic rail beside her for balance. This had to be a mistake somehow. Who would want to hurt her? Why?

"Is the doctor sure it was bee venom? Maybe I'm allergic to something else. Maybe I developed a new allergy. Maybe it wasn't in my drink. There's got to be an explanation."

"There is," Jackson said. He gripped the foot of her bed so tight his knuckles were white. "Someone wants to hurt you."

"But who?!"

"Alex!"

"That's not possible!"

Her dad stepped forward and shot Jackson a warning glance. "Hey, let's calm down. We're all confused and upset."

"I'm not confused." Though Jackson had regained control, fury still lurked in his voice. "And I'm not going to let him get away with this."

"Let's not jump to conclusions," her dad said. "You've told the police everything you know. And I think Lily's right. I'm sure Alex didn't do this, and it sounds like he might be able to help. We just have to let the police do their job."

Jackson pushed away from the bed and threw his hands in the air. "He's one of them! You can't trust him."

"Stop it!" Lily's whole body trembled. "You're not helping. It's not Alex."

"The pictures came from Brunswick."

"That doesn't prove anything!"

"It proves he's involved. Even if he didn't send them himself, he's connected to all this somehow."

He paused while his words sank in. Then he pointed toward the door and raised his voice again.

"And how did he get here so fast? Brunswick is more than six hours from here. He had to have already been here following you around."

"No-"

"He saw us talking and he got jealous. So he put something in your drink."

"Just stop!"

She couldn't take any more of this. It was impossible. Alex loved her.

"Jackson," her dad said. "I understand how you feel, believe me. I'm frustrated too. But upsetting her isn't a good idea right now. Let's just take a walk."

"I'm not leaving her alone. If he comes back-"

"Just step outside with me for a minute, son."

Her dad placed a hand on Jackson's shoulder and led him toward the door. Though their voices were lowered, she could still hear pieces of the conversation.

"...she's okay now...let her get some rest..."

Jackson's exhale seemed to fill her entire room.

"Okay. But please let me know if I can do anything."

Then he stepped around the corner of the doorway and walked over to her bed, leaning down till their eyes were level.

"I'll check on you later. Please, promise me you'll be careful."

She gave him a nod, and held his gaze for a moment longer. So many conflicting emotions swirled around inside of her. She wanted to reach out for him, like he held some part of her that was still true and safe. The instinct was so familiar, and yet it completely surprised her. In that gaze, for just a few moments, she was a kid again, and he was the boy she had given her heart to.

As Lily got out of her dad's car, Alex pulled into the parking space next to her and climbed out, slamming his door shut. His conversation with the police still had him agitated. She'd been surprised he hadn't been able to do more, but her dad had been right. The police just simply had nothing to go on.

She wasn't convinced there was anything more to be worried about anyway. She couldn't believe anyone would seriously want to hurt her. She couldn't even think of anyone that could be angry with her.

"I still think you should come home until this gets sorted out," her dad said as he came around the back of his car and joined them.

"He's right, you know." Alex darted his eyes toward a guy jogging by on the sidewalk.

Lily longed for an escape. She'd give anything to be able to practice today, but Coach had said no.

"I can't go home. I have classes, and a huge game tomorrow night."

Alex rolled his eyes. "You can't be serious. Your life is more important than a stupid volleyball game."

She jerked her eyes up to his, shocked he would say something so callous. Didn't he understand her at all? She crossed her arms over her chest, determined to stand her ground.

"Nothing is going to happen."

"Something already did."

Her dad pat Alex on the shoulder, and she could see him stiffen.

"Look, Alex. I think she's all right as long as she stays on campus." Then he shifted his gaze to Lily. "You promise you'll stay on campus until we figure this out?"

"Yes. I'll stay here."

Her dad pulled her in for a hug and kissed the top of her head.

"Call me if you find out anything or need anything at all. I'll see you at the game tomorrow."

He shook Alex's hand again, and Lily could have sworn she saw a hint of a smile in the corner of her dad's lips.

"Looks like you have your hands full. Good luck with that."

She watched him drive away then turned her glare on Alex.

"What?" he asked.

"*Stupid* volleyball game?"

"I'm sorry. I didn't mean-"

"This game is important, Alex. And not just to me. There are other people depending on me."

He reached out and pulled her waist toward him, his scent filling her head.

"I get that. I do. I just don't want you getting hurt again."

"I'll be fine. You'll see."

Her anger softened and she reached her hands behind his neck. He wrapped his arms around her waist and kissed her gently, but it did nothing to sooth the doubt and fear still roaming through her. A shiver sent goose bumps up her arms.

"You cold?" he asked.

"Just a little. I'll be fine." She tilted her head toward the bridge heading over to the main campus. "You want to get a bite to eat? I'm starving."

"Sure."

She took his hand, and they started down the sidewalk toward the bridge. A blast of wind picked up several leaves from the wooded area beside them and sent a colorful mini-tornado across the parking lot. From above, birds chattered back and forth, occasionally swooping down to sit on nearby bushes. Alex walked in silence, still brooding.

"What are you thinking about so hard?" she asked.

He let out a long slow breath, and still he didn't look at her.

"Just trying to figure out what's really going on."

"What do you mean?"

He stopped as they reached the old chapel and faced her, his lips pressed into a frown. It had been so long since she'd seen the carefree twinkle in his eye. He hadn't cracked a joke in weeks. He looked tired, drained—the same way she felt.

"Why were you with Jackson last night?"

"I wasn't *with* Jackson. I was with Emily and some friends-"

"This guy T.J.?"

"Yes."

"Another basketball player."

"Yeah. Why does it matter? I was there with some friends, and Jackson came over to talk to me about the pictures he got in the mail."

He crossed his arms over his chest. "Did you see the photos?"

"Yeah. Why are you questioning me like I'm a criminal or something?"

He ran his hand through his hair and shifted his weight from side to side.

"This isn't easy for me. I just want to figure out what's going on. Asking questions is what I do."

"I get that. But I'm not a suspect. I'm your girlfriend-"

"Are you?"

The question blindsided her, and she took a step back. This was the last thing she needed right now. She started to speak but he cut her off.

"It seems like you're trying awfully hard to shut me out lately. You haven't been yourself. Going out to clubs, dancing with strange men-"

"Strange men?"

"I got a picture too."

She froze again. Not more pictures.

"It was of you and some guy dancing it up at one of these clubs." His eyes burned with more accusations, but he stopped short of saying them.

"You got a picture of me? In the mail?"

"No, on my phone. Now I want to know what's going on, Lily."

So did she.

"I don't know what's going on any more than you do. I have no idea who would do this."

He exhaled again. "I'm not talking about that. I want to know what's going on with *you.* Something just doesn't feel right here. It's like your drifting away from me."

"Nothing is going on with me. I'm fine."

"Then why are you hanging around with Jackson again?"

She threw her head back and groaned. "I told you, we ran into each other at the club. It wasn't planned."

"Maybe not by you, but he certainly planned it. I don't trust the guy. He's probably the one that tampered with your drink."

"You have got to be kidding!" She almost had to laugh at the absurdity. "There's no way Jackson's involved in this. He got pictures too, remember."

She continued down the sidewalk. Alex caught up to her and matched her stride.

"Did he have the envelope?"

"No. But that doesn't mean anything."

"He could have taken those pictures, and then pretended like he got them in the mail. Wasn't one of them from your high school yearbook?"

She stopped again. "How did you know that?"

"The officer I talked to this morning told me."

"Wait, do the police think Jackson did this?" No answer. "Did you tell them that he did?"

"Listen, Lily. I don't think you really know what that guy is capable of."

Her heart raced with her growing anger, nearly spilling words she knew she'd regret. She took a deep breath and tried to stay calm.

"So you think he followed us to Charleston? That he took pictures of me, of us? There's no way he could have done that. Besides, Jackson would never hurt me."

"Why? Because he still loves you?"

"I don't want to talk about this anymore. Just forget about Jackson. He isn't the one doing this."

"You still love him too, don't you?"

She saw the pain behind his eyes and wanted to explain, but her anger and fear still clouded everything. The truth was so complicated.

"Yes, I do love Jackson, but not the way you're making it sound." He started to speak, but she cut him off. "Let me finish this. I want to be absolutely clear. Jackson has been my best friend since we were kids. I can't just suddenly stop caring about him."

He looked away for a moment, and she thought he might actually walk off. He took a few steps toward the library, but then he turned back.

"I don't want to argue with you, Lily. I wish you'd just trust me. Jackson is bad news. I know you think he would never hurt you, but he already did. You spent the better part of this year hurting because of him, and now he's taken things too far because he can't let go. Don't let this guy back into your life."

A raindrop hit her cheek, and she looked up at the clouds moving in. Perfect. They were probably about to get soaked.

"We better get over to the student center before the sky opens up."

He looked up as well, and nodded in agreement. Then they finished their trek in silence. By the time they reached the side door of the student center, the sprinkles were steadily dampening everything. Alex held the door for her as she scooted past him.

He followed her inside, and he looked at the surroundings like he was assessing the risk. She wished he'd just relax. Her nerves were getting raw.

"You hungry?" she asked. "The food court is just over there." She pointed into a large open area to her left.

He looked over at the eating area, but turned to the campus post office behind him instead.

"You got a box here?"

"Yeah, why?"

"Which one?"

Her stomach dropped. She hadn't even thought about checking her mail box.

"This one."

She showed him and turned the combination before stepping away like a bomb might explode when the door opened. She stood behind him, agonizing while he sifted through the mail. Then he turned around with a single envelope in his hand. It was small, and the address on the front was written in block letters. He held it on the corners as he turned it over in his hand.

"It's got your name and box number on it. Nothing else. No stamp or anything."

He walked over to the window where a lanky guy in jeans two sizes too big stood behind the counter.

"Excuse me," Alex said. "What's your name?"

"Harold." The young man pushed several strands of his long, black hair behind his ear. He looked a little shaky, especially when Alex whipped out his badge and slid it across the counter.

"Can you answer a question for me?"

Harold nodded, his eyes wide.

"How do letters with no stamps get delivered?"

"Oh, well if you bring it to the window it doesn't need a stamp. We just put it in the mailbox. Do you need me to deliver something?"

"Ah, no. But does this look familiar to you?"

Harold leaned over and studied the envelope then looked back at Alex.

"No, sir. Sorry."

"Thanks anyway." He turned back to Lily, his brow furrowing. So much for returning to normal.

"Should we open it?"

"Might as well."

He took out his pocket knife and slid it slowly along the edge of the envelope. He still held onto the sides as he pulled the slip of paper out. Before he even unfolded it, Lily saw the dark block letters, and her stomach knotted. Then he used the knife to lift the top open.

Dear Sweet Lily,

Your hero saved you last night, but don't worry. You will reap what you've sown. You may have fooled everyone else into thinking you are good and pure, but I know the truth. You will get a hypocrite's just reward.

-God

She shuddered with the ripple of fear that went through her. This person—whoever it was—seemed to know her very thoughts.

"We can't just dismiss this as a bad joke anymore," Alex said.

"So what do we do?"

"We take this to the police and hope they'll take it seriously now. Whoever put the bee venom in your drink has been here. Today."

Chapter Twenty-Two

November 2

Birmingham, Alabama

When the whistle blew, the referee signaled a time out and Lily jogged over to the end of the bench to grab a cup of water. This was it, and this was exactly where she wanted to be—the ball in her hand as she served the final point of the match. GSU could try to ice her with a time out, but it wouldn't matter. She never missed her serve on game point.

A few feet away, the rest of the team huddled around Coach Hampton as she laid out the strategy for the final play. Music blared over the sound system, and the basketball team had started stomping the bleachers, led by T.J. of course. Coach Hampton patted Emily on the back, a hearty blow that shook her ponytail.

"Let's get Em a good set outside," she boomed, "and she's going to put it down the line."

That shot had been working all night, but Lily had no intentions of the play ever getting that far. She reached her hand into the middle of the huddle and yelled with the rest of the team. Then she caught the ball from the line judge as she trotted back to serve.

She bounced the ball three times, pulled it up in front of her, and surveyed the court. The crowd in the stands went crazy, chanting and stomping coming from the basketball team to her right. Then they fell silent when the referee blew the whistle and signaled for the serve.

She eyed the left back corner, pictured the serve landing there, and then tossed the ball out in front of her. She took a broad approach, put everything she had into one last jump, and then snapped her arm through the ball. As soon as she connected, she knew it was an ace, and the ball streaked into the left back corner. No one even touched it.

Her entire team jumped into the air and came together in the middle of the court, their arms raised in celebration. Lily ran to the center and joined them, slapping hands and hugging her teammates. The crowd cheered, and she relished the exhilaration flowing through her. She could take on anything right now. Anything.

She looked over to the stands behind the bench. Alex stood with her dad and Kara, all of them clapping and smiling. This was the way it should be. Everyone happy. Everyone confident. No doubts. No fears.

She wasn't going to let stupid emails and pictures frighten her anymore.

As she walked through the heavy double doors onto the court, Lily looked around for her family and Alex. The crowd had thinned down significantly while she was changing in the locker room. Only a few family members and friends still hung around the stands. She looked to her left and found her dad, Kara, and Alex standing behind the score table.

"Nice serve!" Kara said, giving Lily a high five when she reached them.

"You played great, honey." Her dad threw an arm over her shoulders and gave her a big squeeze. "I'm so proud of you."

"Thanks." She looked toward Alex, who returned her smile. She could tell it was a bit forced, but he pulled it off nicely. "I'm glad you guys could come."

"Wouldn't miss it." Her dad managed to hold his smile for only a moment before his face sobered. "How are you doing? Have you heard anything else from the police?"

"Nope. Nothing. I'm sure it was just a bad joke that went too far. Nothing to worry about."

He glanced skeptically at Alex. "What do you think?"

Alex met Lily's gaze. She hoped he'd get her silent message. She didn't want her dad any more worried than he was already. Alex looked back at her dad and frowned.

"I'm not sure it was just a bad joke. But I promise I'm not going to let anything happen to her. I should be hearing something from the detective I spoke to today soon. He mentioned an idea he was checking out."

Her dad scrunched his forehead, his eyebrows forming a single line of concern.

"Maybe you should come home tonight-"

"Dad, stop. I'm fine. I want to stay here. Nothing else is going to happen." He didn't look convinced. "Please, just go back home and get some rest. I'll be fine."

He finally relented. "Okay. Just promise me you'll be careful."

"I will."

He hugged her again, and then Kara hugged her as well. She waved goodbye as they headed out the side door. She let out a sigh of relief and turned back toward Alex, but the look on his face almost forced the air back in. His eyes were practically shooting bullets over her shoulder, in the direction her dad and Kara had just gone.

"That guy's got some nerve," he mumbled.

Lily followed his gaze up to the balcony. Standing in the shadow of the bleachers was Jackson. His face was partially obscured by his baseball cap, but she was sure it was him. Before she could react, he turned and walked out the balcony door to the stairway.

"Stay here," Alex said. He trotted across the gym and flung open the double doors leading out to the front lobby.

She couldn't just stand there and let those two go at each other, so she took off after him. As she entered the lobby, she saw Alex follow Jackson out the front doors and heard him call Jackson's name. Jackson kept walking like he didn't hear him, and the doors closed behind them.

Through the glass Lily saw Jackson finally turn around on the front walkway, throwing his arms out. His mouth formed the word "what" as he faced Alex. She pushed the door open just as Alex raised his voice.

"What do you think you're doing?"

She rushed down the steps to get between them, but she stopped when Jackson looked at her. He raised his palm to her, telling her to stay back.

"Excuse me?" Jackson said.

"I said, 'What do you think you're doing here?'" Alex clenched his teeth and practically growled, his whole body stiff.

Jackson stepped forward and stiffened as well. "Making sure Lily's okay."

"Are you stalking her or something?"

"What?"

"How come you keep showing up everywhere?" Alex inched closer. "Why don't you just leave her alone?"

Lily's heart raced. Jackson might have a good four inches on Alex, but he certainly didn't have the training. Had Jackson ever even been in a fight? Alex would surely hurt him, but Jackson wasn't backing down. In fact he looked ready to spring at any moment.

"If Lily doesn't want me around, she can tell me so herself," Jackson said.

She stepped toward them, hoping she could diffuse the situation.

"Guys, please. Both of you need to calm down."

Alex turned his head toward her, but kept his eyes focused on Jackson.

"I thought I told you to wait inside."

"I just don't want to see you get into a fight. You're both overreacting."

Jackson glanced at her again. "Can I just talk to you for a few minutes?"

"Man, you really don't get it do you?" Alex snapped. "She doesn't want to be with you. Get over it and move on already!"

"Why don't you let her speak for herself?"

They glared at each other, hatred shooting arrows between them. She had to think of something.

"Look," Alex said, "I know Lily thinks you're a real nice fellow and all, but I'm not buying this whole nice-guy routine. I know what you did, and you better believe the police already know too."

"What I did? What are you talking about?"

"The anonymous tip? That was a nice touch. By the way, the next time you try to sabotage someone's career, make sure you're intelligent enough to pull it off. You didn't even bother to mask your freaking IP address!"

"Yeah, the detective you sent to my house this afternoon mentioned something about that. I'll tell you the same thing I told him. I never sent anything. And you can search every computer I own, which is none by the way. But why would you bother with checking out simple little things like facts?"

Lily stepped between them to get their attention. "Wait a minute. What's going on?"

Alex finally faced her. "I've been trying to tell you, Jackson isn't who you think he is. He sent a message through the website at the police department claiming he was a female I'd interviewed, and that I had sexually harassed her."

"What?" Lily turned to Jackson, hoping there was some kind of mistake.

"Internal affairs had to check it out," Alex said from behind her. "And the IP address on the message came back to him, or rather to his dad. But still-"

"Still," Jackson interrupted. "Still you didn't bother to check out whether I could have sent the message. I don't even own a laptop. And the computer at my dad's has barely been used by my mom since he died last year. So your little story doesn't add up."

Lily took a few steps back now, wondering how things had gotten so messed up. She studied Jackson's face, looking for something that would tell her the truth. So much didn't make sense.

"Jackson?" she asked. "Did you send anything?"

He took two steps toward her, but before he could say anything, Alex blocked his path and shoved him back.

"Don't even think about it."

"Alex!" She grabbed his arm, trying to hold him back.

She cringed and waited for the first punch to come flying from one of them, but Jackson suddenly took a step back and put his hands up.

"I'm not trying to start anything with you. I just want to speak with Lily and make sure she's all right."

He looked at her with the same tired eyes they all seemed to share. Then his expression softened, and he almost grinned. In the flash of that moment, she wanted nothing more than to link her arm through his and head down to the creek for some fishing. How strange.

"I'm sorry," Jackson said. "I didn't mean to upset you."

She couldn't take her eyes away from his. They were so safe, so true. In some strange way, it was like looking into a mirror after nearly forgetting what she looked like. She started to tell him to stay, that she wanted to talk with him and straighten all this confusion out, but Alex cut her off.

"You're really a piece of work aren't you? So kind and concerned. I'd almost believe it myself if I didn't know any better."

"What is your freaking problem?" Jackson said.

Alex stepped forward and this time drove his finger into Jackson's chest.

"You are my freaking problem, and if you so much as breathe wrong, you will pay."

Lily's heart leapt into her throat as Jackson pushed his finger away.

"Keep your hands off me."

"Just stay away from Lily, and stay away from me."

Jackson looked at her once more and this time didn't hold back his smile.

"Listen, Alex. Lily and I have been friends for more than twelve years. You can't change that. And no matter how much you think you love her, you do not own her. And my guess is that the harder you try to control her, the more you're going to see the look that's on her face right now." He raised a finger and pointed at her. "She's terrified of you."

"The only reason she's terrified is because of you. Now get out of here before this gets ugly."

Jackson nodded in Lily's direction. "Do you want me to go?"

She didn't know what she wanted. Maybe she wanted to leave with him. But that thought was too confusing right now.

"Maybe that would be best for now," she said. "I'm fine, really."

"If you need me-"

"She doesn't need you!" Alex said. "Now get out of here!"

Jackson sighed and took one more look at Lily. Then she watched him walk toward the parking lot, his hands shoved in his pockets. He gave her one last glance as he rounded the corner of the gymnasium.

"We need to talk," Alex said from behind her.

"You better believe it." She spun around. "You have no right to tell me who I can talk to. Jackson has been my friend for-"

"Twelve years. Yeah, I caught that part. And I love you with all my heart Lily, but honestly I don't care how long you've been friends with the guy if he's the one threatening you."

She threw her hands in the air and groaned. "I do not want to have this conversation with you again! Jackson would never hurt me! And the way you were talking to him was-"

"What?"

"It was scary Alex."

"So now you're scared of me?"

"No, that's not what I'm saying, but I've never seen you so angry."

"Can you blame me? The guy is obviously following you! He's just magically shown up everywhere you've been lately."

"He was just checking on me to see if I was okay. The last time he saw me I was in the hospital for crying out loud!"

He reached for her hands, but she pulled away. She couldn't face him right now, couldn't separate her anger and fear enough to know what she was supposed to do.

"Look, I'm sorry I upset you." He pulled back and let out a heavy sigh. "I just don't trust him."

"Alex, I don't know who I can trust right now. I just need to be alone for a little while so I can think straight."

"Lily, no. I told you, it's not safe for you be alone until we figure out who's doing this."

"I'll be fine. I just want to go back to my room and be alone for a little while. Give me a break."

He opened his mouth to respond, but then his cell phone interrupted him. He pulled it from his waist and looked at the screen.

"It's Detective Brody. Maybe his lead panned out." He opened the phone and brought it to his ear. "Detective Walker."

He scrunched his brow. Maybe they'd found something, and this nightmare could end soon.

"I don't understand," he said. "What about Lily?" He sighed and rubbed the back of his neck. "Can't you just tell me what you found out?"

He began to pace in front of her, his entire expression hardening.

"I see. Yes, sir. I'd be happy to cooperate. I'll meet you there." He turned off his phone and shoved it into his pocket. "I have to go meet with him. He found something, I'm sure of it. But all he'll say is that he really needs to speak with me." He shook his head. "Something's not right. I'm missing something here."

The breeze had grown cold, and Lily wrapped her arms around her chest.

"Can you take me back to my dorm first?"

"Just promise me you won't go anywhere until I find out who's behind this."

She nodded her head, but she refused to make that promise out loud. There was one trip she needed to make alone, and there was no way she was going to let him keep her from going. She had to figure out once and for all how much Jackson was involved.

Jackson was surprised to hear his doorbell ring. He had hoped she would come, but he didn't actually believe it would happen. In fact, it was probably just Matt at the door. He forgot his key at least once a week.

He tossed his damp towel into the hamper as he left the bathroom and stopped in his bedroom to pull on some jeans. Most of his clothes were already packed for Atlanta, but he managed to find one clean pair.

The shower had settled his anger and his racing heart, though it had taken a while. It was by the grace of God he hadn't come to blows with Alex.

He pulled open his front door to find Lily waiting on the steps, and his heart plunged into his stomach. She stared back at him, her gaze fluttering over his bare chest. The momentary spark of attraction lifted his hope, but he pushed it back down.

"Where's your boyfriend?" he asked.

"At the police station." She glanced around like she was nervous. "The detective wanted to talk to him."

"It's about time."

"Don't start." She bit her lower lip. "Can I come in for a minute?"

"Sure."

He pushed the door open wider and let her through. She stood in the middle of the living room gripping her hands in front of her. She looked so uncomfortable. Of course, it had been nearly a year since she'd been to his house, since he'd blown everything to hell and back. He should never have let her walk out that door.

He was sick of the tension between them, sick of trying to make sense of a life without her. When she looked up at him

again, he reached for her hand and pulled her into him. She
didn't resist, and as her body relaxed into his, she let out a deep
sigh. Wisps of her damp hair tickled his chin. She smelled like
apricots.

Her cheek was cool against the heat of his bare chest, and his
heart pounded against it. Her fingers grazed his back. If he
could just freeze this moment, hold her long enough, maybe they
could get back to each other. He slid his hands up her arms,
found her hair, and touched his lips to her forehead.

Then the moment was gone. She stepped away from him,
pulling his hope with her. She wrapped her arms around her
chest and darted her gaze away from his.

"I'm sorry about earlier," she said.

"You have nothing to be sorry about. He's the jerk."

She frowned. "He means well. He's just worried, that's all."

"I think it's more than that."

"I didn't come here to argue about Alex."

"Why did you come here?"

"I need to know for sure. Did you try to get Alex in trouble at
work?"

"I swear. I didn't send anything. You know I didn't." Doubt
still clouded her expression, but he was sure it wasn't directed at
him.

"I believe you," she said. "It just doesn't make sense. None of
this does."

"You just can't accept that he could be doing this."

She looked up at him in that withering way she always had
when she was tired of fighting. Then she dropped onto the futon
with her head in her hands.

Why wouldn't she just listen to him? Her incessant devotion to this fairy tale relationship was maddening. How could she not see the truth staring right at her? She lifted her eyes to his and patted the futon next to her.

"You seemed pretty anxious to talk to me earlier. What is it?"

His determination to make her see the truth was waning. As much as he wanted to get Alex out of her life, he didn't want to hurt her. And she was bound to be devastated by what he'd found.

He stepped over her feet and joined her, leaning his head back against the worn cushion. He stared at the latest crack threading its way across his ceiling. Thank God he was finally getting out of this dump.

"Do the police know anything more?" he asked.

She shook her head. "I got a note in my mailbox at school-"

"What?" His heart sped up again. "When?"

"Yesterday. Alex took it to a detective to see if they could get fingerprints off it or anything. But he said it was unlikely. Too many people have handled it."

"Are you okay?" He reached over and rubbed her arm.

"I'm not going to let this person scare me anymore. If they want to come after me, let them."

"Lily, no-"

"I mean it, Jackson. I'm sick of feeling helpless."

"You're not alone, you know."

She leaned back against him with a heaviness he recognized, and he fought the urge to wrap his arm around her. She was so close, and her body next to his felt so right, so peaceful.

"Look, this may not be the best time for this," he said. "But I thought you should know what I found out."

"Okay. Shoot."

"It's why I wanted to talk to you. I did some digging around the past couple of days, and I found out something about Alex."

She jolted upright and faced him. "You did what?"

"He's not who he says he is."

"You had no right to do that."

"I just want to protect you. He's lying to you."

"What are you talking about?"

He gripped her hands, preparing for the blow he was about to deliver.

"He's married."

She rolled her eyes, and he could swear she almost laughed.

"Is that what all this was about?"

He couldn't believe it. Not only was she not surprised, but she seemed to think it was funny.

"You don't care that the guy you're dating is married?"

"It's not that I don't care. You just don't know the whole story."

"Wait a minute. You knew?"

"Look, he's not married anymore. He's been divorced for a couple of months now."

Was this the same girl he'd known most of his life? Where was the Lily that refused to compromise her principles, that held onto her faith at all cost?

"I don't believe this," he mumbled. "I thought you believed marriage is sacred."

"I do, it's just that-"

"I don't even know you anymore. What is going on with you? Are you so blinded by your feelings for this guy that you'd just throw away your beliefs?" She stared at him open-mouthed, guilt all over her face. "Do you even pray anymore? Or go to church?"

"No." She looked away, rubbing her thumb against her palm. "I can't. I've tried, but I've messed everything up so badly. There's no way to fix it."

Her hands were shaking now, and despite the risk of pushing her away, he took them in his own.

"Things are never so messed up that you can't fix them. This guy is all wrong for you. Can't you see what he's doing? He's manipulating you and trying to control you. That's not love."

"You don't understand. And it's not like I can talk to you about it."

"You can talk to me about anything."

A tear slipped down her cheek, and it felt like it would rip him open.

"Not this. Not about Alex. Not when I still..."

She stopped and seemed to catch herself before she said anything more. Then she pulled her hands out of his grasp, stood and walked toward the door. God, he wished she would finish that sentence. Did she still love him?

He moved around the coffee table to cut her off, and he leaned down until their eyes met.

"When you still what?"

"I still care about you. I don't want to hurt you anymore. And I thought that if we just stayed away from each other, it would be easier to move on."

"Easier for who? You and Alex?"

"No, for you...and maybe me too."

"You don't get it, do you? I've tried staying away from you. It's not any easier. It hurts more than I can bear every day, especially now, when you may be in real danger and I can't do anything to protect you. Meanwhile, Alex has you convinced he's your knight in shining armor, when he could be the very one behind all of this."

"Uggh!" She sighed and looked up at the ceiling. "You guys are stressing me out with this. Alex is not trying to hurt me."

It was all he could do to control the urge to grab her and shake some sense into her.

"Oh my God, Lily! Wake up! The guy is a control freak. He just wants to keep you on his leash like a little pet. He has you so turned around you're not even holding onto your faith anymore. I bet he's already tried to get you to sleep with him, hasn't he?"

Her face went white and her eyes shot open. He saw the look of complete guilt wash over her, and immediately he wished he hadn't asked. She stammered out a denial, but her eyes fluttered.

His stomach lurched.

"Forget it. I don't want to know."

But his head was already filling with sickening images of Alex's hands on her, touching her, groping her. Heat rushed up his neck and face, and it suddenly felt like his skin was covered with hives. He paced the living room, trying to force the images out.

She couldn't have. She would never do that. Her virginity meant everything to her. It was her gift to her husband—to him.

Everything within him wanted to let it go, to forget he had even thought about it, but he had to know. He had to hear her say it. He stopped pacing and faced her. She looked like she'd seen a ghost.

"Did you?" He couldn't keep his voice from breaking.

She just looked at him, saying nothing. Only her eyes spoke now, and they betrayed her.

"Lily! Tell me the truth. Did you sleep with him?"

When she still didn't answer, anguish took over. He walked over to her and grabbed her shoulders.

"Please. Tell me you did not have sex with him."

"I can't explain it. I'm sorry. I know it was wrong, and I wish I hadn't, but I can't take it back."

Rage shot through him. He wanted to hurt her, just as badly as she was hurting him. He wanted to hate her, to push her out the door and never look at her again.

"You need to leave," he said.

"Jackson, I'm sorry-"

"Please, Lily. Just go. I don't know who you are anymore, and I can't even look at you. I can't believe you would do this. I can't believe you would give everything to this guy when you barely even know him."

Tears poured down her face as she backed toward the door.

"Please don't hate me."

He lifted his gaze to hers. He wanted to take her in his arms and make all of this go away, to somehow go back to that horrible day last spring when he could have just told her he loved her. How could he have been so stupid? But everything was different now. She was different. And there was no going back.

"I could never hate you, Lily. But I can't talk to you right now. I just need some time alone."

She turned and quietly slid out the door, and his heart ripped to shreds all over again. He fell into the recliner and dropped his head into his hands, finally giving into the sobs. It was the final blow. God had finally leveled him. He had taken her away all right, just as he'd always feared, but in a way he'd never imag-ined.

"Why are you punishing me?!" he screamed to the ceiling. "How could this possibly be for your glory?"

He had known that their romantic relationship was probably over. But he couldn't help holding onto a grain of hope that someday she would come back to him. The last couple of months without her had been agony, and he had spent most of it in prayer for her. A lot of good that had done.

He didn't know how long he sat there, fighting tormenting images, but a knock on the door made him jump. Had she come back? Part of him wanted her so badly, and the other wanted to leave her standing out there forever. He waited, and the knock came again, more urgent this time. So he walked over to the door and pulled it open. But it wasn't Lily on the front steps.

It was Alex.

"Look, I know what's going on," Alex began. But before he could finish, Jackson connected a right hook squarely with his jaw.

Chapter Twenty-Three

November 2

Birmingham, Alabama

Lily tried to make out the road ahead of her through her tears, but everything was a blur. The car was driving itself at this point. It didn't matter anyway. The physical pain of a wreck couldn't hurt much worse than the look on Jackson's face. He would never forgive her, and she couldn't blame him.

She turned into the small neighborhood where they had played as children just as a flash of lightening streaked across the sky. She turned right at the elementary school, and another flash illuminated the basketball court, the net barely clinging to the rim by a single strand. A loud crack of thunder followed.

She drove past the school and onto the road that snaked past her house, squeezing the wheel with all her might. It shouldn't matter. She'd let him go, and she'd moved on. But she couldn't shake the image of his face, the disappointment and shame so heavy on her heart reflected in his eyes.

She turned the car into the driveway, though she knew it was empty. She glanced over a few houses and saw the light on at

Mary's, and for a second she longed for the comfort of pouring her heart out. But she'd never be able to tell her everything, and she couldn't bear disappointing Mary as well. No, it was better to be alone.

As she climbed out of her car, large drops of rain plopped on the hood. She jogged to the front steps, getting her key in the lock just as the sky opened up. She pushed open the door and flipped on the living room light.

It looked the same as it had for more than twelve years now—empty table tops, a bare desk with only a few papers scattered across it, not even a dining room table. There was no evidence of this being a home. In many ways it reminded her of Alex's, only without the cloud of despair hanging over it.

It looked the same. But nothing was the same anymore.

She dropped her keys on the glass top of the coffee table and the clatter echoed through the empty house. She turned into the hallway and went to her bedroom, hoping for comfort from something familiar. She flipped the light switch and looked around the room, finding a small amount of comfort that her mom had kept things as she'd left them.

Next to her closet, her trophy case still displayed her favorite accomplishments, but something about it seemed hollow. She walked over and stared at the awards, letting her fingers run over the tiny golden statues till she came to the one she'd treasured most. She picked it up and looked closer.

Somehow it had gotten turned around. How appropriate. She'd gotten herself turned around alright, and now she'd never be able to fix it. She turned the girl on the statue back to the front, wishing it was that easy to fix herself, and then she sank onto her bed.

Her photo album stuck out from under the side table. She picked it up and flipped to the back, right to her favorite photo—Prom night from Jackson's senior year.

They'd gone for a carriage ride around the block, and just as she had climbed out of the carriage, she'd stumbled and Jackson had caught her. Anyone else looking at it might think they were dancing. It looked more like a dip than a save. But it wasn't really the photo that she loved. It was the words he'd said in her ear later that night as they had laughed about it.

I'll always be here to catch you, Lily.

But not anymore. She'd seen to that. She dropped the album on the floor and curled up on her bed. Pulling her pillow under her head, she gave into her sobs.

Alex's head whipped sideways, and the pain that shot through his jaw sent sparks of light through his vision. Before he could even process what had happened, his gut reacted, and he buried his shoulder into Jackson's chest. Their momentum carried them through the doorway, and Jackson went sliding across the hardwood on his back.

"What the hell are you doing?" Alex roared.

Jackson scrambled up from the floor and came at him again. This time Alex was ready, and he side-stepped the blow. Jackson stumbled forward, but regained his balance and turned into another punch that glanced off his temple. Alex stepped back again, crouching with his hands out in front of him.

"Don't do it, man."

Jackson lunged forward again. Alex chopped the sides of his neck, right on the carotid artery, stunning him long enough to grab behind his neck. He put his leg behind Jackson's and took him down to his back with a thud that pushed the air out of his lungs. Alex pushed himself away, and Jackson rolled to his side sputtering out coughs.

"We don't have time for this," Alex said. "Where is Lily?"

Jackson came up on his knees and wheezed. Then he sucked in a breath and finally gathered himself to his feet.

"Don't you dare come in my house and ask me about Lily!"

"I know who spiked her drink! Now where is she?"

"Who was it?" Jackson straightened, and his face went white.

"Just tell me where she is, and I'll take care of it."

He shook his head and came at him again, but this time he simply drove a finger into Alex's chest.

"You're the reason she's in danger in the first place! Why should I help you?"

The words gutted him as if Jackson had driven a sword into him instead. He was right. But there was no time to dwell on it now.

"Look, I know you hate me, but right now, Lily's safety comes first. Anything we need to settle between the two of us can be done after she's safe."

Jackson continued to scowl at him, but he backed away and his body relaxed.

"I don't know where she is," he said. "She was here. But she took off a little while ago."

"When?"

"Not long. Maybe ten minutes or so."

"Where would she go?"

Jackson ran his hand through his hair and shook his head. "I don't know. Have you tried calling her?"

"Of course I've tried calling her! She's not answering her cell." Did the idiot think he was a moron or something? "Where else would she go? Didn't she stay with an aunt or something this summer?"

"I'll start making some calls." Jackson strode over to the coffee table and picked up his phone.

While he dialed, Alex called Chloe. She answered after a couple of rings, and it was all he could do to keep his composure.

"Chloe, do you know anything about where Adrian is right now?"

"No, Alex. I don't. I've already told Steve and that detective in Alabama everything I know."

"When was the last time you talked to her?"

"I'm not sure. Maybe a month ago." She paused. "Alex, she wanted to know if you were going to Charleston."

"How did she know about that?"

"I don't know. Honestly."

"Thanks. I'll call you back if I need anything else."

"Alex?"

"What?"

"I'm so sorry."

He hung up the phone and shoved it in his pocket. He couldn't deal with Chloe right now. He had to find Lily, and Jackson was his best chance. Across the room, Jackson hung up his phone as well.

"She's not at her aunt's," he said. "And she's not back at the dorm. Emily's calling the other girls on the team, and she'll call me back if she hears anything."

"There has to be somewhere else you can think of." Alex sighed and tried not to punch the wall. "Come on, you've been *best friends* for twelve years! Think of something!"

Jackson's face went dark, and Alex thought he might lunge for him again, but he stopped and started dialing another number on his phone.

"Mom, is Lily there?" He waited a second and shook his head at Alex. "Have you heard from her at all?" He paused again, longer this time. "No, just stay inside. I'll be right there."

He hung up the phone and darted out of the room. Alex yelled after him.

"What is it?"

"She's at her mom's house. My mom says her car is in the driveway, but it's pouring, so she can't go over there." Jackson came back into the room with a t-shirt on. "I'll call Lily from your car. Let's go."

A loud crash of thunder startled her awake. Lily sat up and looked around the pitch blackness, confused by her surroundings. Lightening shot a streak of light through the room, illuminating her reflection in the mirror over her vanity. Then the sickening dread in her stomach returned.

She stood and made her way back into the living room, reaching for the light. She didn't remember turning it off. Her hand grazed the switch. Flipped it down. Then up. Nothing. The power must have gone out. Great.

A sliver of light from the kitchen window helped her find the sofa. Then a flash of lightening showed her the coffee table. She grabbed her keys as thunder shook the house. Maybe it was best to head back to her dorm. An eerie sensation crawled through her, and the hair on her arm stood to attention. It was definitely time to get out of here.

She headed for the front door, but stopped when she heard something fall and roll across the back porch. It rumbled for a second before coming to a stop. Turning toward the kitchen she wondered if she should check it out. Probably just something blowing over in the wind. A trash can maybe.

She reached for the door again, but a sudden pounding on the other side sent her reeling backward. She clutched at her chest, her heart pounding in her ears. She scolded herself, remembering that she'd decided to stop acting like such a girl. She stepped over to the window and peered out of the blinds. Through the rain, she could see Alex's pathfinder parked behind her car.

He pounded again, this time calling her name. "I'm coming!" she replied. How did he know she was here? He'd never even been to her mom's house. She pulled open the door, and he practically mowed her down coming inside.

"Why didn't you answer your freaking phone?" he growled. "I've been calling for over half an hour!"

She blinked, trying to get her brain to catch up to his.

"I must have left it in my car."

He picked up the house phone on the end table and pressed a button.

"It's dead. No wonder."

"How did you know how to get here?"

He didn't seem to hear her. He paced around the room and ducked into the kitchen, flipping switches and mumbling to himself. He leaned over and looked out of the kitchen window.

"Lights are on next door."

The light coming through the window lit his face just enough for her to notice the bruises. His jaw looked swollen and his left eye too. In fact, he looked completely disheveled. He moved back into the living room like he was on a mission.

"All right," he said. "We got to get you out of here."

"What happened to you?"

"What?" He looked at her like he'd just realized she was there. Then he rubbed his jaw absently. "Oh, this. Yeah, Jackson packs quite a punch." He went back toward her bedroom, still looking around.

"You fought with Jackson? Oh my word, Alex. Is he okay?"

He stepped back into the living room, his body stiff.

"Yes. *I* am fine. Thanks for asking."

"You're a cop! You could have seriously hurt him."

"He's fine."

She headed toward the door, and he yelled after her.

"Wait for me!"

"Just back off!" She whipped around and pushed her finger into his chest. "I'll make sure he's okay. Just leave me alone."

She opened the front door again, ignoring his protests.

"Lily, listen to me! He's fine! He came here with me!"

She stepped onto the front porch and froze. He was right. Jackson was standing at the other end of the porch, a cell phone pressed to his ear. Her heart sped up as he met her gaze. He was giving her address to someone. Then he pushed his phone into his back pocket and looked at her for just a moment before dropping his gaze.

She lifted her hand toward him to speak just as a loud pop sounded. Heat seared through her chest, and she gasped for air. Jackson ran toward her.

"Lily!"

The world went white around the edges. Another loud pop sounded, and something hit the side of the house. Someone screamed. Jackson caught her just as her knees buckled. She spun in a circle. Or maybe the sky did.

"Get her inside, now!" Alex's voice filled her ear.

Another pop. Glass shattered. Jackson stumbled and nearly dropped her. She saw his face, strained, terrified. She gripped his neck. Tried to focus on breathing, but there was no air in the room. The walls moved like waves. Then the ceiling danced. Alex's face was above hers now, his voice loud and echoing in her head. He pushed down on her chest, called her name. She sputtered and looked for Jackson.

Alex pressed his hand over Lily's chest as Jackson fell onto the floor with his back against the couch, his eyes wide. Blood seeped through Alex's fingers, wet and sticky. Another gunshot rang out and glass spewed across the room.

"Get over here and put pressure on the bleeding," he said.

Jackson crawled along the floor and pulled himself up to his knees. As he leaned over and placed a hand on Lily's chest, Alex saw the blood on the back of his shirt.

"You hit?" he asked.

"I'm fine." Jackson gripped his abdomen with his free hand. "What do we do now?"

"I'm going after her."

Something shattered in the kitchen. The back door crashed against something. Alex jumped up and drew his gun, the wall behind the couch the only thing separating them. Glass crunched.

He slid to the end of the couch where Lily still gasped for air, moaning as her eyes drifted open and closed. He darted across the doorway of the kitchen and pushed his back against the wall. For just a moment, everything went silent except for Lily's labored breathing. Then in a thin slice of light he saw the muzzle of a gun approaching the doorway.

"Drop the gun, Alex." The familiar voice came at him like a punch to the gut. He had hoped he was wrong.

She stepped into the sliver of light, rain glistening on the hood of her coat.

"I can't do that, Adrian. You know I can't."

"Then shoot me." She stopped just before she reached the doorway, still partially hidden in the shadows.

"I don't want to have to do that. Just drop the gun."

"Not until I finish her off."

"Adrian, this is crazy."

"Maybe. I don't care. But she deserves to suffer, and so do you."

She inched toward the doorway. He had a clean shot. His training told him to take it, but he hesitated.

"Don't you think we've all suffered enough? Evan wouldn't want this."

"Don't say that name to me!" She stepped closer. "He never existed! He couldn't want anything!"

Just a little more. If she'd just step into the room a little further, maybe he could grab the gun. In his peripheral, he could see Jackson crouching as he kept pressure on Lily's chest. He just had to keep Adrian's focus on him, and get her to take one more step.

"Adrian, the police already know everything, and they're on their way. Don't make this worse."

Sirens whined in the distance as if to confirm what he'd said. Just one more step. She glanced at the window behind him. She still didn't see Jackson. But she might any second if she took another step forward.

"Just give me the gun," Alex said, trying to keep his voice even. "you won't get hurt."

"Too late. You already took everything from me."

She stepped forward and started to turn toward the sofa. Jackson sprung, knocking her back. The gun went off, sending a bullet through Alex's shoulder. He stumbled, dropped his gun, and landed on his back on the floor. Pain seared down his arm and into his fingers.

He saw a blur of movement, wrestling bodies. His eyes refocused. Lily rolled off the couch, staggering toward Jackson and Adrian as they struggled on the floor.

"Lily, no!"

Alex lunged for his gun just as Adrian kicked Jackson in the gut. He shrieked and curled into a ball. Lily tried to grab onto Adrian, but she shoved Lily away like a doll, sending her crashing into the opposite wall. Lily's eyes went wide. She slid down the wall leaving a smear of red. Alex raised his gun again.

"Adrian!"

Jackson pushed himself up on all fours and began to crawl toward Lily. Adrian raised her pistol and an eerie smile spread across her face.

Alex yelled again. "Don't!"

Jackson threw himself in front of Lily as both guns exploded.

Jackson's weight crushed her against the wall for a second, pushing Lily's breath out of her lungs. The impact ripped at her chest and sent sparks around the edge of her vision. Jackson's momentum rolled them onto the floor, and she wound up underneath him. His body pressed down on hers, blocking any more air. He moved. Groaned. They gasped at nearly the same time.

"Jackson?"

She rolled enough to help him off, trying to gulp down air. She coughed again, and blood splattered from her mouth. She looked around, desperate and dizzy. Alex knelt beside Adrian feeling her neck.

"Alex." Lily's voice came out raspy and distant.

"Lily!"

He was beside her instantly. She pushed herself up on all fours, coughing and sputtering. She looked down at Jackson.

Blood. Everywhere.

Breathe.

Pooling underneath him. She had to stop it.

Breathe.

She looked up at Alex, panic nearly crushing her voice.

"Help him. Please?"

He stood and ran toward the hallway, tugging linens out of the closet. He rushed back and placed some over Jackson's stomach.

"We have to keep pressure on the wounds. Keep him warm."

Lily leaned over him, his eyes wide and glazed over.

"Jackson? Please." She coughed up more blood; the taste was nauseating. "I love you. Hang on, please."

He looked at her, but his eyes were hollow, and he said nothing. Her chest tightened even more, and the room took a serious dip. Alex moved across Jackson and put an arm around her, tugging her away.

"You need to lie back. I'll take care of him."

"No!"

She pushed him away. He groaned and gripped his shoulder. She turned back to Jackson and kept her weight on his abdomen. The towels were soaked. Her hands were sticky and smeared with blood. Everything swam with the crimson liquid. Her stomach dipped, and she thought for a moment she might vomit. The edge of her vision grew darker by the second.

Another set of hands reached for the towels covering Jackson. She started to push them away, but she realized he was helping. When had the paramedics arrived? Her head throbbed, and her chest burned as pain shot across to her shoulder.

Breathe.

Alex wrapped an arm around her and pulled her back. She couldn't keep her grip on Jackson's hand any longer.

Breathe.

Her chest buckled, and she groped to find air. She sensed movement around her, voices, prayers. Some of them even sounded like Mary. But it was fading into darkness, into a murky liquid where everything was numb. She was so tired, and cold. Her eyes closed, and she finally slept.

Lily tried to open her eyes, but she couldn't quite overcome the weight holding them down. Something moved beside her. Hands tucked a warm blanket around her. Her throat ached, and she tried to swallow but couldn't. She managed to lift her eyelids for a moment. A dark figure leaned over her as a warm hand covered her arm.

"I think she's coming around."

"I'll let her family know."

Something blurry to her left moved away. Where was she? She tried to speak, but something was in her mouth, choking her. She couldn't even cough. Her vision began to clear, and now she could see a nurse moving equipment around, checking the numbers. She moved back to Lily's side and offered a wide smile. Her eyes were kind and deep brown.

"Hey there, honey," the nurse said. "Don't try to talk. Just rest."

She pushed a button on the side of the bed and it lifted Lily's head a bit. Then the door opened, and her dad rushed in with the doctor. Her dad leaned over the bed, stroking her hair away from her face.

"Are you okay?" he asked.

She nodded, and her head swam. Something sucked air into her lungs then pushed it out.

"You need to rest right now." He pulled back and took her hand. "Don't worry. Everything will be all right." He looked at the doctor and lowered his voice. "Does this mean she's out of the woods?"

She tried to make out his answer, but all the noises blended together, and her eyes wouldn't stay open. She caught something about a chest tube and blood pressure before her eyes closed again. Somewhere in the distance, frantic beeps came at her out of a tunnel before fading into the blackness.

Chapter Twenty-Four

November 3

Birmingham, Alabama

Alex watched the rise and fall of Lily's chest and tried to block out the relentless questions that plagued him. But one wouldn't be suppressed. One kept his head spinning no matter how hard he tried to reason with it.

How could he have not seen this coming sooner?

He replayed the last moments of Adrian's life in his head over and over—her body turning toward Lily, her arm stretching the gun forward, her finger squeezing the trigger. He went through a thousand scenarios where he could've saved her. But would he have lost Lily instead?

Somewhere inside of him, in that place he buried so deep he could pretend it didn't exist, he knew.

He'd lost Lily anyway.

Her hand twitched in his, and she groaned. Then her eyes shot open and she gasped. He leaped beside her and stroked her hair.

"Where is she?" Lily croaked.

"It's okay. You're safe."

She tried to sit up, but he held her shoulders down as gently as he could. She coughed, and tiny drops of blackened blood spattered the white blanket.

"Jackson...where's Jackson?"

"Lily, baby. Calm down. You're okay."

He pressed the call button for a nurse. Lily shook her head, her eyes wide with terror.

"She was here. I saw her. Jackson...She was shooting..."

Her eyes darted around the room, dazed and wild. Then she reached a hand toward his shoulder, as if to make sure he was real.

"You're hurt." She coughed again and wheezed as she took a breath.

"I'm okay." He'd never been so far from okay, but he had to find a way to soothe her. "We're all okay. Just rest, baby."

A nurse entered the room behind him and went to the other side of the bed. He barely registered her question and mumbled something about Lily being upset. He brushed the hair away from her face and smoothed the worry from her brow.

This was all his fault.

The nurse moved around the room, checking the machines and her chest tube. She asked her if she was alright, and Lily nodded. She reassured him that Lily seemed fine.

He thought about decking the nurse. She wasn't fine. None of them were.

After they were alone again, he helped her sit up a little, and got her a drink of water. Her hands shook as she brought the cup to her mouth. He took it from her and put it away.

"Are you..." she started. "Are you okay?"

"I'm fine. See?" He pulled his arm up a bit, trying not to grimace. "Nothing serious."

"What about Jackson?"

He sat back down beside her bed and took her hand, unsure of what she could handle.

"He'll pull through," he said. "He's strong."

"Pull through? What happened? Where is he?"

He glanced away for a moment, unable to bear the weight of her fear. "I don't know much. He was in surgery most of the night, and he's in ICU now. He's...holding on."

"What about...her?"

His throat closed up, and he saw Adrian again, lying lifeless on the floor, bleeding out from the shot he'd delivered. He shook his head.

Lily closed her eyes and dropped her head against her pillow. A tear slipped out and ran down her cheek. Her chest heaved, and she let out a sob. It ripped him into pieces. He was useless, unable to protect her, unable to comfort her.

"I'm so sorry this happened," he said.

She opened her eyes and swiped at her tears. He handed her a Kleenex from the tray near her bed, and she wiped her nose.

"Do you think they'll let me see Jackson?"

"I don't know, Sweetie. I doubt it."

"Did you see him when they brought him in?"

He nodded as more images he'd been trying to suppress fought their way to the surface—Lily passing out, all the blood, Mary's ashen face as she prayed in the ambulance. Jackson's heart had stopped twice just in the ride to the hospital.

"Was he...?" She balled her hands up in her lap. "I don't know what I'm asking."

"Like I said. He'll pull through. He's a fighter. Don't worry." He stroked her hair again, and her eyes blinked slowly. "Go back to sleep, baby."

She closed her eyes again. He had no idea how long he sat there caressing her hair, wondering what lay ahead. He wanted to believe the worst was over, but he knew better.

Lily awoke to a dark, cold room, and she was covered with several blankets. Slowly, everything took shape as her eyes adjusted. She blinked and rubbed them, feeling the slight pull of the IV in her hand. She reached up and rubbed her aching chest, feeling the tube protruding out. Breathing seemed a little easier at least.

Gently sliding her legs over the side of the bed, she pushed herself into a sitting position. Outside her window, the stars and moon highlighted the rolling hills in the distance, and a few solitary cars made their way along the main street. What time was it? It had to be after midnight.

Her bladder was seriously full, but she cringed at the tiny bowl the nurse had shown her earlier in the day. No way that was happening. Maybe she should call someone to help her to the bathroom, but something deep within her needed to do it on her own.

After giving herself a good pep talk, she tested her shaky legs. The room dipped, and she steadied herself against the bed, waiting for the chair in the corner to come back into focus. Then she stepped into the bathroom, her IV stand in tow. When she finished, she felt better and more confident on her feet, so she opened the door to her room and checked the hallway. It was empty. Maybe she could find Jackson.

She crept down the hall toward the nurses' station, sure that they would send her back to her room with a good scolding. But the desk was vacant, and only a couple of voices drifted from the rooms behind her. She glanced at the clock and saw that it was well after midnight. Maybe they were changing shifts.

She continued to wander down the hallway until she found a directory on the wall, following its direction to the elevators. A middle-aged woman carrying snack cakes got on the elevator with her. She gave Lily and her IV stand a lifted eyebrow, but she said nothing, just kept her focus on the numbers on the panel lighting up one by one.

Lily stepped off the elevator, and after a few minutes of searching, she finally found the Intensive Care wing. The air was thick with the aroma of fear and antiseptic, and it made her pulse quicken. Up ahead on the right was a nursing station. The two women behind the desk spoke quietly. Maybe they smelled the fear too.

She wanted to avoid too much scrutiny, but she had no idea where to find Jackson. The nurses were her only option. When she approached them, they stopped talking and frowned at her. She'd be lucky if they didn't call security. She probably looked like an escaped mental patient.

"Can I help you?" the one on the right said.

She was older, and tiny, maybe not even five feet tall. But there was a sense of authority in her voice, like she was used to ordering people around.

"I, I don't know. I'm looking for someone."

"Where are you supposed to be right now?"

Lily glanced at the other nurse, the same look of concern clouding her eyes. She was young, with a fresh face that had probably never seen a day of makeup. She looked ready to spring to Lily's side and escort her back to where she'd come from.

Lily gulped down air and tried again.

"I was brought in last night with Jackson Carter. He was shot." Her voice cracked. "I just want to know how he's doing."

The nurses' eyes darted at each other before the short one came around the desk and looked up at Lily.

"You really shouldn't be out walking around by yourself."

"Please. I just need to know if he's okay." Tears slid down her cheeks and she wiped them away as quickly as she could.

"I can't give out medical information to anyone but family."

"I...I am family." It was almost true, but the nurse looked doubtful. "I'm his sister."

"I'll see what I can find out for you." She glanced back at her colleague who gave her a slight nod. "Why don't you wait in there?" She pointed to a waiting area down the hall, and Lily made her way to a hard blue chair in the corner.

A country music video played on the television on the opposite wall. She tried to ignore its melancholy tune. Waiting was agony. It seemed like hours passed. She finally dropped her head, closed her eyes and tried to pray, but she couldn't form a single word in her head. Nothing. Just an overwhelming feeling of helplessness. She tried not to cry, but her body shook uncontrollably.

A hand touched her shoulder, and she jumped.

"Lily?" It was Mary. She looked down at her with surprise, then concern. "What are you doing up here, honey? You should be in bed."

She stood and threw her arms around Mary, nearly toppling the coffee in her hand. It was all she could do to stand.

"I'm so sorry. I'm so sorry."

"Shh. It wasn't your fault." Mary held her and let her cry for a minute, hushing her like a baby.

Once Lily finally regained control, Mary encouraged her to sit back down and took the seat next to her. She kept her arm around Lily's shoulders, continuing to reassure her. She couldn't hold back the dam of emotions that had exploded. They poured out of her, and the whole time, Mary soothed her.

"How is he?" Lily asked.

"He's holding on." Mary gave her shoulder another squeeze. "He made it through the first twenty-four hours. That's a good sign."

"How can you be so calm?"

"Oh, I've been far from calm. But after Andrew died, I guess I realized that our lives, and our deaths, are in God's hands. He loves us. Even if I don't understand this, I'm clinging to my faith in Him. It's all I have right now."

"Mary, I've been so foolish. I don't-" The nurse stepped into the waiting room, and Lily hurried to her.

"Is he okay?"

Mary joined her, her face suddenly pale. "Is everything all right with Jackson?"

The nurse raised her hands as if to push back the rush of panic that came at her.

"He's okay, Ms. Carter. This young lady asked how he was doing, and I was going to speak with her for a minute. I assume you two know each other..." She paused and gave a pointed look toward Lily. "Since you are family."

Lily nodded. "How is he? Can I see him?"

"Visiting hours are very strict in the ICU."

"Please." Lily had to restrain herself from grabbing the woman and begging. But she was starting to feel desperate. "I just need to see him for a minute. I have to see him myself."

Mary stepped forward and rested her hand on the nurse's arm.

"Surely a moment or two is all right," she said. "It might do him some good to hear her voice."

The nurse looked from Mary to Lily, and back to Mary again. Just watching her consider the request made Lily's insides feel like they were boiling over. Didn't this woman understand? None of this was real until she could see it for herself. The nurse frowned, her wrinkles deepening around her mouth.

"I could get in trouble. But I suppose a few minutes wouldn't hurt."

Lily fought back the urge to hug her. Instead she turned to Mary and wrapped her arms around her again.

"Thank you."

"You're welcome. Give him a kiss for me."

"I will."

Lily pulled back and shoved away a tear on her cheek. She started to follow the nurse out of the room when Mary called out to her at the door.

"You know, Lily. I don't know everything that happened over the past year, but I know he loves you. I hope you know it too."

Lily had no idea what to say. She nodded her head and gave Mary a sad smile before turning away. As she followed the nurse through a set of heavy double doors, she thought back on her last conversation with Jackson. Maybe he had loved her up until that night, but not now. He had saved her because he was a good man, and instinct had taken over, not because he still loved her.

The nurse stopped outside another door and turned around to face Lily.

"Just a few minutes. I'll come back by after I check some patients down the hall."

Lily nodded. "Thank you."

She pushed the door open and peered inside, terrified of what she saw. Tubes, wires, monitors—all sorts of intimidating machinery surrounded him, measuring every breath, every heartbeat. He was pasty gray, except for the couple of bruises on his face.

She walked closer, tiptoeing like she was afraid she'd wake him. Maybe it was absurd, but something about this place demanded silence, and except for a steady beep from one of the machines, it was eerily quiet. It was as if she'd stepped into a different world, one where she didn't know the rules.

She rolled a stool over to the side of the bed and sat down next to him. His chest rose and fell, slow but steady. At the same time, hers felt like it would burst wide open. It seemed like death was waiting right outside for him, and she was sure that it would take him as soon as she left. She reached for his hand, surprised when he didn't squeeze hers in return.

She dropped her head onto his lap and closed her eyes, letting her tears flow freely. How had they gotten here? Why couldn't they just go back? She'd give anything to be that little girl again, tagging along to the creek or playing basketball to-gether. Nothing had ever really hurt her back then. He'd always protected her, even when she didn't realize it. She couldn't lose him. Not like this. If she could just hold on tight enough for both of them...

"Just hold on," she whispered. "Please. Hold on."

Late February

Six Years Ago

"Lily, hold on!"

Lily turned around at the sound of her name. She looked through the crowd filing out of the gym into the lobby, and stepped aside as a large man in a gold shirt pushed past her. Must have been cheering for the visitors. The ladies in the con-cession stand called for last minute deals on cokes and popcorn, and cheerleaders bounced from one side of the lobby to the oth-er like they'd somehow contributed to the big win.

Then she saw him. Jackson snaked his way through a group of players and lifted his hand in the air to get her attention.

"Hey, hold on a sec!" he yelled across the lobby.

He made it a few more steps before Mr. Whitten stopped him, slapping him on the back and bellowing congratulations.

It was so weird to watch people fawn over him. They didn't even know him, not like she did, and she could not for the life of her figure out what the big deal was. Sure, he was a great ath-lete, and maybe he was good-looking on some level, but he was Jackson. This was the same kid who threw up if you even men-tioned an airplane near him.

He finally fought his way over to the railing where she was waiting.

"Hey, can you give me a ride home?" he asked.

"Seriously? I'd like to get home before midnight. Can't one of your adoring fans give you a ride?"

He chuckled and tousled her hair, pulling a few strands out of her ponytail. She slapped his hand away.

"But I want my *biggest* fan to do it."

"Hmm, then that would probably be one of the cheerleaders over there gawking at you."

She pushed the strands of hair he'd loosened behind her ear as he turned wide-eyed in the direction of the cheerleaders.

"Really? Where?"

"You're such a dork." She slapped his shoulder. "I can't believe all these people haven't figured that out yet."

He winked at her and flashed his crooked grin. "But that's why we get along so well. You know all my secrets, and you still adore me." He took the towel from around his neck and wiped his brow. "Come on, Lil. Give me a ride, or I'll wipe my sweat all over you."

"Okay, fine. But I'm not waiting out here all night. Hurry up."

"Thanks!" He popped her with the towel before sprinting back into the crowd.

"Hey!" she complained as she rubbed her leg.

She watched his head bob up and down until he disappeared down the stairs and into the locker room. Then she turned and leaned against the railing, resting her chin in her hand. She stared at the portraits of past star athletes that lined the wall of the lobby. Jackson would be up there this year. He was a shoo-in for All-State. She wondered if she'd ever make "The Wall."

Suddenly she felt someone move next to her and lean against the rail as well.

"Hi, Lily."

She turned and nearly fell backward with surprise. Why would Addison Thomas be talking to her?

"Uh, hi Addison."

Her blond ponytail was still perfectly in place, even after hours of swinging it in time with her cheers. She looked at Lily as though they were best friends, which could only mean she wanted something.

"So what's the deal with you and Jackson?" Addison asked.

"What do you mean?"

"You two have always been close right?"

"Yeah."

"Only friends?"

"Yeah. Why?"

"Just curious." Addison shrugged and looked around at the dwindling crowd. "Never more than friends. Interesting."

Lily turned around and rested her back against the rail. She didn't need two guesses to figure out where Addison was headed. She'd made her intentions toward Jackson clear for some time now. Of course she would come to Lily. They always did.

"Look, Addison. Jackson and I are just friends. Always have been. He's a free man, so go for it if you want."

Her eyes widened. "What? You think I want to go out with Jackson?"

"That is why you're talking to me, right?" Lily fought the urge to roll her eyes and laugh.

"Of course not! I saw you standing here and just thought I'd come over and say hello."

Lily turned her head away to hide the smile she couldn't force back. It only took another moment before Addison asked the inevitable question.

"But since you mentioned it, maybe you could give me a little advice."

"Advice?"

"You know. What does he like to do? What does he like in a girl?"

Certainly nothing you have to offer, Lily thought.

"I don't know. He likes fishing and sports. That's pretty much it."

"That's all you've got?"

"Well what did you expect? He's not really into cheerleaders anyway."

A flicker of anger crossed Addison's face. She huffed and placed her hands on her hips.

"Well maybe you just don't know him very well. From the way he's been eyeing me for the past few weeks, I'm pretty sure he's into me. Maybe you're just jealous."

"What?!" Lily pushed away from the rail and faced her. "I am not! I just know he wouldn't go out with you, that's all."

Addison flashed a brilliant smile and looked over Lily's shoulder. She turned and saw Jackson walking through the lobby doors.

"I guess we'll find out soon enough." Addison pushed past her and headed straight for Jackson, her ponytail swinging with each step.

She intercepted him before he got to Lily. She couldn't quite make out the conversation, but the body language was clear, and she could hear Addison's voice dripping with syrup. She leaned close to him, resting her hand on his arm, and Lily's cheeks flushed warm.

He should have shoved her away and told her to get lost, but he looked like he was enjoying the attention. He returned Addison's smile and chuckled when she gave his chest a girly shove. He was actually going for the whole routine. Lily's heart sank, but she wasn't sure why. He could date whoever he wanted. Lord knows he'd had plenty of opportunity.

Addison finally removed her claw from him and walked back by Lily, throwing her a triumphant grin. Lily watched her for a moment then turned back to Jackson. He was watching too, but not Addison. He was looking straight at Lily.

She stared at him for a moment, afraid to think about the whole encounter with Addison for too long. Then the strangeness evaporated like it had been sucked out of the room. He smiled and tossed his gym bag over his shoulder as he walked over to her.

"You ready?"

"Yep. Just waiting on you to finish shaking hands and kissing babies."

When they reached her car, he tossed his bag into the back and slid the passenger seat as far back as it would go. It always made her laugh to see his knees practically touching his chin whenever he rode in her tiny car.

"You seem a little quiet," she said as she pulled out of the parking lot.

"Hmm. Well, I do have the weight of the entire basketball world on my mind."

"I'm sure it's a tough life." She could sense his grin without even looking over at him.

"Oh, you couldn't even imagine."

Maybe she wished she could. What would it feel like for every college around to want her to play volleyball? She tried to tell herself she had plenty of time, but realistically she only had one year left. If they didn't recruit her by the end of her junior year, she could pretty much hang it up for Division I ball.

Her stomach started to knot again. Time to think about something else.

"So, I know it's supposed to be a big secret and everything, but are you going to tell me who the big winner is?" she asked.

"What do you mean?"

"Don't play dumb. You know what I mean. What lucky college is going to get the privilege of paying for your education?"

He laughed. "You're as bad as all the rest of them!"

"I am not. But I'm supposed to be your best friend. Surely you can tell me."

"Sorry, but you'll just have to wait like everyone else."

Lily gave up and concentrated on driving until she turned the car into their neighborhood. As she passed the cement basketball court, she had an idea.

"I'll play you for it," she said.

"What?"

She pulled into a parking spot near the court, barely lit by a few flickering street lights.

"I'll play you for it. If I win, you have to tell me where you're going."

"Come on! You haven't beaten me in over a year."

"Then what are you scared of?"

"I'm not scared. I just don't feel like wasting my time. Besides, I'm pretty exhausted."

"Chicken."

He raised an eyebrow then looked over at the court. "All right. But only a short game. We'll play to five."

"Five? That's not a game."

"Like I said. I'm tired. Take it or leave it."

She thought about it for only a moment. It was getting late, and she was pretty tired from her own workout earlier in the afternoon.

"Deal."

They climbed out of the car, and Lily grabbed her basketball from the trunk. She threw it at Jackson's chest, and he caught it with ease. His hands nearly swallowed the ball.

"You're kidding, right?" he asked. "We're not playing with a girl's ball."

"It's all I've got. Take it or leave it." She grinned as she jogged over to the court and began stretching her quad muscles.

He shook his head and rolled his eyes. Then he walked over to the goal and took a jump shot that sailed over the backboard. He put his hands on his hips and sighed.

"I can't believe I agreed to this."

They each took a few warm-up shots, and then Jackson tossed her the ball.

"Ladies first," he said.

"You're such a gentleman."

He shrugged. "I am wonderful."

She dribbled the ball and tried to drive toward the goal, but he cut her off. Her body slammed into his, and she bounced back. He had hardly budged. She pulled back a bit and then switched to her left hand and drove the other side. He cut her off again. She dribbled back to the top of the free throw lane and contemplated her strategy. It was the same routine as always. She dribbled around as long as she could until something opened up, then she'd take a shot.

"We going to be out here all night?" he asked.

"Maybe. If that's what it takes to beat you." He straightened and huffed, and she took advantage of his pause. She dribbled past him and laid the ball off the backboard.

"One to zero."

He caught the ball out of the net and held it while she walked back to the top of the free throw line. He had the strangest look on his face, one she didn't recognize. Almost like he was looking at someone he didn't know. He bounced the ball back to her.

"Tell me again why you quit basketball," he said.

She caught the ball and turned it over in her hands.

"Just didn't love it like volleyball."

"Such a shame." He walked closer to her and spread his arms, preparing to guard her more closely this time. "You're still pretty good."

She started to dribble, taking a step to her right, but he reached behind her with his long arms and slapped the ball away, recovering it before she could get to it. He took two hard dribbles, then two long strides to the basket and laid the ball off the backboard.

"Ones." He caught his own rebound and jogged to the top of the free throw line. He tossed her the ball.

"Check."

She bounced it back, and before she could take another step he threw up a jump shot that barely touched the rim as it went through.

"Two to one."

She caught the ball and held onto it this time. He raised an eyebrow.

"Come on, Brennon. Where's the D?"

She walked over to him and handed him the ball as she crouched into a defensive position. It had been a while since they played, but she hadn't forgotten how cocky he could be. It only motivated her more. But her skills were rusty, and he wasn't a four star recruit for nothing.

Before she could barely blink he'd scored two more baskets, announcing the score with the same enjoyment he'd always had when picking on her.

"I see you have a little bit of energy left," she said.

He held out his hands for the ball. "I'm starving. Let's finish this up."

"There doesn't seem to be much point in my being here." She tossed him the ball.

"You give up?"

"Yes. I'm starving too. Let's just go."

He took a step back in dramatic fashion, his eyes wide.

"What? Lily Brennon is giving up? I don't believe it."

"This is definitely your game." She reached up and tightened her ponytail. "But if I ever get you on a volleyball court, watch out."

He walked over to her, dribbling the ball between his legs. He spun it on top of his finger for a moment then caught it and looked at her curiously.

"Why do you care where I go to college?"

She crossed her arms, more to press back her own confusing feelings than anything else.

"I don't guess it matters. I just wonder, that's all. Things'll be different with you gone."

She could swear he had moved closer, but she hadn't noticed him take a step. He kept his eyes on hers, like he was searching for something in them.

"Different in a bad way?" he asked.

"Well, of course. Who will I go fishing with? And who'll sit by me in church and try to make me laugh? It's hard to imagine life just moving on without you."

He didn't laugh, just kept looking at her, making her skin tingle.

"Lily, do you ever wonder about us?"

"What do you mean?"

"Do you ever wonder if maybe we're supposed to stick together?"

She wasn't sure about his word choice, but something in his question rung true. There was an underlying connection between them that she'd always known was there. And lately she was beginning to wonder what life might be like without him. She had to admit it felt strange, even painful.

"I haven't decided where to go to school yet." He shifted his weight, looking a bit uncomfortable.

"You still have some time to decide."

"I know what I want." He looked down at the ground and rubbed the back of his neck. "I'm just not sure if it's possible yet."

"Are you kidding? Any college in the country would take you."

"That's not what I mean." He looked back into her eyes again, that same searching gaze hitting her in the gut. "I want us to be together."

Her stomach flipped over. "You mean, go to college together? But you're a year ahead of me, and I don't know-"

"No, listen to me."

She stopped, and he stepped even closer this time. She could feel the heat coming off him, and the hair on her arm stood, like it sensed her desire to reach out for him, even before she realized it.

"Why do you think we've been friends for so long?" he asked. "Isn't it obvious that we're meant to be together?"

"I, uh. I don't know. Maybe. I haven't thought about it."

"Me either. Not until I started all this college stuff. And then I realized that no matter what school I went to, I wanted you to be there."

"Me? But we're just friends."

"Come on, Lil. It's always been more than that. And you know it."

She did know. But knowing it in her head and saying it out loud were two very different things. She couldn't risk losing him, not when everything that made sense in her life was wrapped up in him.

"What are you trying to say?" she asked. "You want something more?"

"Don't you?" He reached down and cupped her cheek in his hand.

"I don't know. I don't want to mess up our friendship."

He slid his hand behind her head and touched his forehead to hers.

"I think we already have."

Then he kissed her, and it was like the pieces of her heart fell into place, making their connection even stronger. And in one single moment, she knew with certainty that no matter what lay ahead, no matter where either of them went to college, they would be together for the rest of their lives.

November 4

Present Day

"Lily?"

Movement under her face startled her awake, and she sat up abruptly. She'd been dreaming. Or was it remembering? She could swear she still felt the kiss lingering on her lips and hear him whispering her name. But Jackson still lay motionless in the hospital bed beside her. Then she looked again.

His mouth moved. And his hand had closed around hers. She scooted closer to him.

"Jackson?" His eyes lifted open then closed. She rubbed his hand. "Jackson, please wake up." This time his eyes opened and found her.

"Lily?" His voice was barely a whisper. "You're okay?"

She nodded her head, unable to form words with the huge lump in her throat. He squeezed her hand again, sucking in a shallow breath. He tried to smile, but only the corner of his mouth twitched. Then his eyes blinked slowly. She felt an overwhelming panic surge through her, a desperate need to grab onto him and not let go.

"Jackson, I'm so sorry. For everything."

"No," he whispered again. "Me." She leaned in closer, unable to make out everything he said. "Forgive me."

"You? What's to forgive?" She pushed her tears off her face and shook her head.

"Always, Lil." He paused and his eyes closed. Her heart lurched, but then he opened them again. "Always loved you. Just couldn't say it. Forgive me."

"No," she said as her chest nearly ripped open. "This is all my fault. I should have listened to you. I should have tried. I was just scared. I'm so sorry." She put her hand on his cheek and tried to look into his eyes, but they were fading.

Then his eyes closed completely and every machine in the room suddenly went haywire. She panicked and grabbed his arm, trying to literally pull him back to her. The door flew open behind her and the nurse that had brought her to his room rushed to his side.

"Jackson!" Lily shrieked.

The machines continued to scream as a blur of people rushed into the room. Lily was pushed to the side as a doctor and two other nurses moved quickly around the bed. The rush of fear and nerves in her body sent her head spinning, and she could barely register the commands of the doctor. But when she saw paddles being placed on Jackson's chest, she realized with sudden clarity exactly what was happening.

"Oh God," she whispered. "No. Please. Please don't."

Chapter Twenty-Five

Birmingham, Alabama

Lily sat next to Mary in the waiting room, holding onto her hand like it was a life preserver. Mary's prayers surrounded them, drifted upward in a constant stream, and kept Lily from losing her sanity all together. She could barely form a coherent thought, much less prayers. Her heart raced, and her hands were damp with sweat. A chill swept over her, and she squeezed Mary's hand even harder.

Mary paused and looked over at Lily, her eyes red and swimming in tears. She looked like she had aged years in the span of a couple of hours.

"You should go back to your room and get some rest," Mary said.

Lily shook her head before she finished her sentence.

"You look pale, sweetheart," Mary continued. "It won't do you any good to pass out here in the lobby." She stroked Lily's hair then squeezed her shoulders. "I promise I'll let you know as soon as the doctor tells me something."

"No." Lily's throat ached, and the pain in her chest was almost more than she could bear. "I can't. I have to stay."

Mary didn't press her. She just continued praying under her breath. Lily laid her head on Mary's shoulder and wrapped an arm around her. In some small way it was like holding onto Jackson.

She glanced up at the clock. Nearly thirty minutes since his heart had stopped. Was that bad or good? She had no idea, and as the minutes passed, the searing pain in her chest grew until she thought it would consume her.

When a nurse finally appeared, it was all she could do to keep from running across the waiting room. A doctor followed close behind, and he raised a hand toward Mary to get her attention.

The older gentleman looked like he'd been through the ringer himself, and it seemed like it took an hour for him to amble over to Mary. But finally he spoke with her and set them both at ease.

"We were able to revive him."

Mary looked like she might collapse, and Lily nearly did. Her knees wobbled, and she pulled Mary against her, weeping like a baby in her arms.

November 5

Birmingham, Alabama

Alex knew it shouldn't have surprised him when Lily wasn't in her room. She'd already disappeared for several hours the night before, and it didn't take a genius to figure out where she'd gone. He walked down the hall and found her dad at the nurse's station filling out paperwork.

"Excuse me, Mr. Brennon?"

He turned and smiled. "Alex! I didn't know you were still here. How's your shoulder?"

"Better. I'll be stuck behind a desk for a while, but it should be fine."

"That's good to hear."

"Yes, sir. I was wondering if you could tell me where Lily went."

Mr. Brennon frowned and glanced down the hall.

"She went to see Mary. She should be back by now. I'm trying to get these papers filled out for her release. Would you mind checking on her and reminding her that we need to get going?"

"Sure."

He made his way toward the elevators, and then he punched the button for the fourth floor. The last thing he wanted to do right now was intrude on Lily's time with Mary. He already felt like a third wheel. He should have just waited until she'd left the hospital to see her. But then again, maybe if he saw it with his own eyes, he wouldn't be able to kid himself any longer.

The elevator door slid open, and he followed a sign to the ICU. He found a deserted nurse's station, and a waiting room nearby, but no Lily or Mary. He looked both ways down the hall. Nothing. Then he walked over to a set of double doors to his left and looked though the small window.

Lily stood about halfway down the hall looking into a window as well. Although he couldn't see her face completely, what he did see said everything. She stared into the room with a longing he recognized in his own soul, but one he had never seen in her until now. She could say what she wanted, but her love for Jackson was clear, and it was more than he could bear to watch.

He stepped back into the empty waiting room, his pulse racing. He needed to hit something, but there was nothing around to absorb his frustrations.

He dropped into a chair next to the wall and hung his head. He was sick of being weak. Sick of losing people he loved. If there was a God, he was either ignoring his requests, or God just hated him.

"Alex?"

He glanced up, expecting Lily, but instead it was Mary looking down at him. She looked tired, but better than he'd seen her two nights ago. He stood and extended his hand.

"Hi, Mrs. Carter. How are you doing?"

"I'm okay. But what are you doing out here?"

"Just waiting on Lily. I was going to tell her that her dad's waiting on her, but she looked...well, preoccupied."

Mary studied him for a moment, making his insides squirm. Could she tell how much he envied her son? That some horrible part of him he couldn't control wished Jackson had just died.

"Do you mind if I ask you a strange question?" she asked.

He shook his head. "Not at all."

"Could I pray for you?"

Alex stared at her dumbfounded. Pray for him? Of all the things he needed right now, that wasn't it. Talk to Lily, or ask her son to stay away from her—those were things he needed right now. Even a beer would do more for him at this point.

"Mrs. Carter, I can't tell you not to, but I don't think it would do much good. Besides, Jackson needs your prayers more than I do."

"Everyone needs prayer. And I get the feeling you need quite a bit of it right now. Let me guess, you're wondering if God even cares about you, or even exists for that matter."

"Excuse me?"

"I don't know if Lily told you anything, but Jackson's dad died very suddenly last year, and I really struggled to come to terms with it. I don't think I could have ever imagined that kind of excruciating pain. And it was all God's fault."

Alex met her gaze, expecting a fake smile, a nice little story about how she'd figured everything out, but her eyes held no hint of pretense. In fact, he sensed a deep ache that resonated inside his own heart.

"For a while," she continued, "I thought that maybe God didn't even exist if he could let me hurt so badly. If he loved me, then he should protect me from something so horrible. I even thought maybe I deserved it, that He was punishing me for something."

His chest ached with her words. He wanted to grab onto her and ask if she'd ever found peace. If that peace was water, he would drink a river to be filled with it.

"How did you...?" He wasn't even sure what he wanted to ask. But she knew.

"People will tell you things to try to help. Like, 'God works in mysterious ways' or 'He works everything out for our good and His glory.' None of that ever made me feel better."

He nodded. "I know what you mean."

She reached out and squeezed his elbow, and he realized that she did understand. Maybe he wasn't alone or the only person to doubt.

"You know, you're supposed to be tough," she said. "I get that. I was supposed to be tough too, for Jackson's sake at least. But I couldn't do it. And once I realized Jackson was struggling with the same feelings, I knew I had to get it together. But even then...even after I knew I was crumbling, I couldn't fix it."

Her words were like cannons aimed directly at his walls. She could easily be talking about him and about the life he'd been leading since Evan's death. He couldn't keep living this way, but what else was there? Give in to the pain? Let it crush him until he couldn't function? No, he'd managed somehow to survive, and he'd have to do it again.

"Look, Mrs. Carter, I'm sure you mean well, but I don't have much hope left in God."

"It's okay, you know. It's okay to doubt and ask questions. You don't have to have it all figured out. But when you're down at the bottom of the pit, and you feel like you can't possibly even try to climb out, pray. Ask for wisdom, and He'll show you all you need."

"So that's all I have to do? If I pray, God will just take all of the pain away? I'm not sure I buy that."

"He may not take all your pain away, but He does promise peace. And He really is the only thing that will fill up the hole in your heart. Jesus says He is 'living water.' That whoever drinks of that water will never thirst again."

Alex felt a jolt inside his chest, like his heart leapt. Yet something inside of him refused to hope. She meant well, and he could appreciate that. But it was too late for him. God had already taken everything.

"I can't, Mrs. Carter."

"Not now, but you will. When it's the right time, one day, you'll remember this conversation. You'll feel a sudden urge to pray or open your Bible just to see if maybe it might help. And when it does, there will be nothing else like it in the whole world."

As her dad climbed into his car to wait for her, Lily's stomach turned and her heart sped up. Alex leaned against his car on his good arm, his gaze drifting around the hospital parking lot. He looked tired, beaten down. He had to know she was questioning everything. She just hoped he didn't expect any answers right now.

"You okay?" he asked.

No, she wasn't. "I guess so. You?"

He shrugged. "Same here."

He stared at her like he was waiting for something then looked away when it didn't come. She should say something, but she had no idea what it was.

"Thank you," she managed, "you know, for everything. You saved my life."

He gave her a tight smile. The little wrinkles around his eyes that had made him seem so full of laughter had deepened. Now they just framed the sad emptiness they both shared but couldn't speak.

He looked away again. "No need to thank me. I just did what I had to."

"It was more than that. I know it was hard-"

"You think we could talk about something else?" He pushed himself away from the car and shoved his hand into his pocket.

"Uh, sure. Sorry."

"It's okay. I just don't want to talk about it anymore."

"What do you want to talk about?"

He started to speak, but then he caught the words before they escaped. He tried again, but nothing came out. Funny how she knew exactly what he meant. There were things that needed to be said that seemed to have no words.

"Listen, Alex. A lot has happened over the past couple of days. It might be good to take some time to work through everything. I know I could use some sleep and some down time. I'm sure you could too."

He nodded and pressed his lips together. He wanted to push her—she could see it all over his face. He wanted to know where he stood, and she couldn't blame him. It wasn't fair to hold onto him just because she was scared. But she *was* scared—like a kid who'd seen a monster come out of the closet.

"That sounds like a good idea," he finally said. "I'm heading back to Brunswick to handle some things there. But I'll call you tomorrow."

"Handle things?"

"With Adrian's family. And Chloe."

"Chloe? What did she have to do with this?"

"She's the one who told Adrian about you."

Lily's chest tightened at the mention of Adrian's name. "So she was part of this too?"

"Not really. She didn't know Adrian would go off the deep end, at least that's what she says. But she gave her enough information about you to get her started. Whether she meant harm or not, she's still responsible for her part."

Lily felt sick. She'd known all along that Chloe didn't like her, but to sic Adrian on her like a guard dog was unforgivable.

"This just keeps getting worse by the minute," Lily mumbled.

"I know. I'm sorry. I feel like I brought all my problems into your life and almost..." His voice caught. He looked away again. "Anyway. I'm sorry."

She looked down at the sidewalk and watched an ant carrying a crumb twice its size. How could something that small be so strong when she was so weak? She could barely carry herself, much less anything else.

"I should get going," Alex said, pulling his keys out of his pocket.

"Alright."

He walked over to the driver's door and lifted the handle then looked back at her, hesitating as if he were hoping for something more. She forced her legs to move closer, and she wrapped her arms around him. It was like trying to push the wrong ends of magnets together. He held her only for a moment, and then he climbed into his car.

As he backed out of the parking spot, she thought about how different their last two goodbyes had been, especially this one. There were no smiles, no joyful tears, not even a kiss. Only relief that he was taking the tension with him for the time being.

Chapter Twenty-Six

When Mary threw open the door to her house, she smiled at Lily like she hadn't seen her in years. Lily endured the hug with a grimace, the shot of pain in her chest sending a flash of the gunshot through her mind before she could stop it. Would she ever forget the images of that night, or at least go through a single hour without something reminding her? Mary let go and continued to smile.

"I'm so glad you called this afternoon. I've been wondering how you're doing."

Lily tucked her hands into her pockets, and her fear into the pit of her stomach.

"I'm okay. Getting better."

"Let me take that." Mary closed the door and reached for Lily's jacket. She hung it in the nearby closet then ushered her toward the kitchen.

"Jackson's still sleeping, but you can visit with me until dinner is ready."

Lily followed her through the living room toward the kitchen. This house was as familiar as her own, with almost the exact same layout—even the couch and coffee table. Blood and shattered glass could just as easily fill this room. She shuttered and took a seat at the table while Mary picked up a wooden spoon and stirred a large pot of soup.

She added some spices, stirred again, and then finally took a seat across from Lily. She looked at her the same way everyone did now, with the you-poor-thing expression. It made her insides turn.

"So, how are you holding up?" Mary asked.

"I'm okay. It's a little hard to get back into the swing of the everyday, but I'm taking it one day at a time."

"You know, it may be a good idea to talk to someone about what happened."

Same speech her dad had given her, and Alex for that matter.

"I may. We'll see."

Mary shook her head. "I worry about you kids. You both went through a terrible ordeal and neither of you want to talk about it."

Lily looked down at the table and played with her hands. Then Mary reached over and placed a hand on top of hers.

"You know, it's okay to be scared still. No one expects you to just pick up with life as if nothing happened."

"But I want to." Lily fought to keep her tears at bay. Even now she could hear the back door crashing open, screaming, glass crunching. Talking about the shooting just made it come alive again, and all she wanted was to bury it deep in the earth where it could never be found.

"You have to try to deal with what happened, honey. Something that frightening changes you. If you let your fears decide how you're going to feel and what you're going to do, you'll be miserable."

"You sound like my dad."

"He's a pretty smart guy."

"He wants me to go see my Aunt Catherine in Connecticut. She's a shrink."

"You should go."

"Maybe I will at some point. But I just can't right now."

Mary nodded and rubbed Lily's hands again. Then she walked over to the stove. She stirred the soup and tasted it.

"Hmm, just right. Why don't you go wake up Jackson and see if he's hungry. I'm sure he'll be glad to see you."

Lily's stomach knotted at the thought, but she walked through the living room and into the hallway. She pushed open Jackson's door and took a peek inside. Classical music drifted from the speakers, and the glow in the windows was a warm golden orange from the setting sun. He lay stretched across several pillows, his feet hanging off the end of the bed. It was a much more comforting sight than what she'd seen nearly a week ago.

She walked closer to him, studying the shape of him—the contours of his muscles, the familiar hand dangling over the side, and the tiny scar on his chin from a trip down to the creek one afternoon when they were kids. A warm tingle spread through her, from her stomach and chest out to the ends of her fingers.

She knew.

She'd always known. They belonged to each other, and trying to deny it had cost them so much.

But what now? Tell him? She had no idea how. Maybe they had hurt each other too much. The way he had looked at her that night still haunted her, like she was a stranger. But she clung to the one moment in the hospital when he had opened his eyes.

Always, Lil.

And so she reached for his hand.

Strange images swam around him, filled with muddled screams. Jackson couldn't grab onto any of it. Sometimes the images flew past him, and others were in slow motion—the bullet, his legs moving him forward as though they were weighted down. And just as the bullet struck him in the back, he screamed and shot forward.

"Oh God!" Someone jumped back from his bed and nearly fell over his desk chair.

He swung his legs to the side of the bed and tried to regain control of his breathing while Lily stared at him, her hand over her chest.

"Lily! Jeez!"

"I, I'm sorry."

"Are you trying to give me a heart attack?" He took a long slow breath and held onto the side of the bed as the room dipped.

"That's not funny."

His mom appeared in the doorway. "Jackson?"

He dismissed the panic in her face with a wave of his hand.

"I'm fine, Mom. Just a little startle."

She nodded, though she didn't look entirely convinced, but she disappeared back down the hall. He was grateful she hadn't pressed him. He couldn't take much more of her fussing. He took in a deep breath, and once his pulse began to slow, he took a closer look at Lily. She looked as terrified as he had just felt. What was she even doing here? Maybe the drugs were playing tricks on him. The strange glow in the room was enough evidence for that.

She eased closer and fidgeted with her hands. "I just came by to check on you, and your mom wanted me to stay for dinner. She sent me in here to wake you and see if you were hungry."

"Not really." He pushed himself up from the bed, his head swimming through the fog of painkillers. "But if I don't try to eat she'll be all over me."

He unfolded his body slowly, like old parchment that might crumble. His bones ached, his insides hurt, and now his nausea had returned. He hadn't thought she'd come this soon, hadn't really had a chance to get his thoughts together.

He walked over to the closet and slipped his t-shirt over his head, reaching for another. When he turned around, she was staring wide-eyed at the bandages wrapped tight around his midsection.

"Are you okay?" she asked.

"It's not as bad as it looks. I'm short a kidney, but I hear we keep an extra around for emergencies anyway. Doctor says I should be fine."

She glanced from his bandage to his eyes then looked away.

"You almost...I thought-"

"Hey. I'm okay. Really."

She nodded, but something was off. Or maybe he just didn't know her anymore. He wanted to look away, but it might be the last time he'd see her. He wanted to remember everything about her—her deep blue eyes, the wisps of hair that she tugged at frequently, the way she grinned when he teased her. She was so beautiful she practically glowed.

He pulled the shirt over his head, and Lily sat down in his desk chair. She reached up and twisted her hair around her finger—a sure sign she was preparing to say something difficult. He wasn't sure he could take it right now. His head throbbed.

"Jackson, I uh, I wanted to thank you for what you did."

"No need for that. I'm just glad you're okay."

"Well, still. Thank you. And I wanted to apologize too."

"What for?"

She kept twisting her hair, but dropped her gaze. "That night. When I told you about Alex and me-"

"Lily don't." His gut wrenched again, and he reached for the bookshelf nearby to steady himself. He didn't ever want to think about any part of that night, especially that conversation. She started to speak again, but he couldn't stand it.

"Listen," he said. "I've had a lot of time to think the past few days, and I realize now how stupid I was. I've been living in a fantasy world."

"What do you mean?"

"All of this...trying to rescue you like some ridiculous hero or something. And hoping that somehow you'd magically figure out that you still loved me."

"But Jackson, I-"

"Just let me finish, okay? I wanted so badly just to be with you again, I just couldn't see what was really going on, that you didn't love me that way anymore. But that night, that night you told me-"

"Jackson, please-"

"Lily, just stop. I don't want to know anything else. And I can't even think about what I do know. I just think the best thing for both of us is to go our separate ways. For good this time."

His stomach dove again, and the room swam. He needed to sit back down. He wanted to hold onto her, but he had finally learned his lesson. If he really loved her, he had to let go, completely this time.

"You won't even let me explain?"

He could think of nothing worse at the moment than listening to her talk about her feelings for Alex. And it was obvious the guy loved her. He may be all wrong for her, but who was he to tell her what to do with her own life?

"No, no more explanations. Let's not make this any harder than it already is. I thought I knew you, but I don't. The girl I fell in love with doesn't exist anymore."

He turned to the window, trying to shut out the pain in her eyes. If he looked into those eyes for too long, he'd be right back where he had started. No, this horrible ache in his chest had to end, and he only knew of one way to do it. Cut it out.

"What about that night in the hospital, when I came to your room? You said..." Her voice trailed off and disappeared.

"I don't...I don't remember."

"You said you always loved me."

He dropped his head and steadied himself with the bookshelf. Maybe he had said that. But all he remembered of the hospital was confusing dreams and a sense that he wasn't in his own body—about the same as he was feeling now.

He had always loved her, but what good had it done? She had thrown it all away. He could forgive her for anything, but how could he ever forget? He couldn't keep clinging to a dream. As painful as it was, he had to wake up and face reality.

He turned around to ask her to leave, but the room was empty.

November 14
Birmingham, Alabama

Lily lay on her bed staring at the ceiling, desperation nearly overwhelming her as she waited for Coach Hampton to call her back. If she couldn't play tomorrow, if they didn't win, it was all over. And it was all she had left.

Emily stepped around the corner from their closets and spread her arms. "How do I look?"

Her black dress clung to every curve and left little to the imagination.

Lily shook her head. "Perfect if you're heading down to the clubs. A little much for an athletic banquet."

Emily winked and flashed her smile. "Then it's just right." She turned back toward the mirror and ran her hands down her hips. "You getting dressed? We have to leave soon."

Lily groaned and sat up. She needed to focus on finding a way to overrule the doctor's decision to bench her for the Conference Tournament.

"Coach said she would call me right back. It's been, what, thirty minutes now?"

"I can't believe that sorry excuse for a doctor wouldn't clear you. Didn't you explain the situation? This could be your last game. Ever."

"Yeah. I cried like a toddler. He said my lung wasn't ready for heavy exercise. It could collapse again."

"Wow, that does sound serious. Maybe it's better-"

"Don't you dare." She glared at Emily. "I need at least one person on my side."

"You're right. I'm sorry." She threw her hands in the air. "Screw the lung. Who needs two lungs anyway? One's plenty. I'm behind you all the way."

"That's more like it. Thanks."

"What are friends for? Now get dressed. I'll keep vigil by the phone."

Lily walked over to the closets and stared at the clothes, but everything looked the same—the story of her life right now. It was as if the colors had faded from everything, leaving only shades of gray. What was the point in dressing up? What was the point of the banquet? None of it really mattered anymore.

She reached for a dress, barely registering which one it was. As she pulled her t-shirt over her head, the phone rang. She dropped the dress and sprinted to the phone, nearly tripping over a chair.

"Hello?"

"Hey beautiful," Alex said.

"Oh, hi." She couldn't hide the disappointment in her voice, didn't really make much of an effort.

"What's wrong?"

"I was hoping you were Coach."

"What's going on?"

"She said she'd make a call for me to see if I could play tomorrow."

"Why?"

She paused, surprised by the complete lack of sympathy. Of course, nothing had been what she had hoped lately, especially her relationship with Alex.

"Because I want to play. If we lose, the season's over, and so is my volleyball career."

"You don't think they can win without you?"

"Of course I don't think that. I just want to be in the game. I can make a difference. And if we lose at least I'll know I did everything I could."

Alex sighed. She could hear his impatience, and she wondered for the hundredth time why she hadn't just ended things. For that matter, she wondered why he hadn't. They seemed to be clinging to something that didn't exist anymore, hoping it would somehow reappear.

"Lily, I understand how badly you want to play. But if it's not safe, then you should listen to the doctor. He knows what he's talking about."

"You don't get it," she said. "I need to play. Everything is spinning out of control here, and I need to do something I know I can handle. My lung is fine. My body is fine. Why can't you just support me?"

"Okay, Sweetie. Okay. I just don't want anything to happen to you."

But something already had. How could he not understand that? She didn't need protecting. She needed to feel strong. She needed to fight a battle she could win, instead of fighting ghosts in the dark.

"Look," he continued. "I support whatever you do."

"Really?"

"Really."

She forced out a breath, and some of the tension in her shoulders as well. Maybe she was over-reacting.

"Thanks. I guess I'm a bit stressed out. I didn't mean to take it out on you. I know you just want me to be safe."

"It's okay. I understand."

An awkward silence settled over the phone. There had been lots of those recently. Moments of emptiness they had no idea how to fill. He cleared his throat. She wished he'd just say good-bye.

"Well, while I have you on the phone, I was wondering if you'd like to come down for Thanksgiving."

Her stomach tightened, but it wasn't from excitement. "I don't know. Dad's still trying to get me to go to Catherine's."

"Oh. Well, I thought I would ask anyway. It'd be good to see you again. Especially down here. We could take a walk on the beach, talk, spend some time together." He let out a heavy sigh. "I miss you, Lily."

"I know. I'm sorry. I just don't know yet."

She hoped he wouldn't notice, but she couldn't say in all honesty that she missed him. She did care about him, and some part of her missed the time they'd spent together in the summer. But right now, even talking to him seemed to make her stress level rise. She couldn't explain it, but she was terrified of being alone, yet annoyed by all the people around her who just didn't seem to understand anything. It was maddening.

She let out a sigh and started to explain further, when the call waiting beeped.

"Alex, I need to get the other line. It might be Coach."

"Okay. Call me back later."

"Okay. Bye." She didn't wait for any further response before clicking over. "Hello?"

"Lily? It's Coach Hampton."

Her hope soared for a moment. "What did you find out? Can I play tomorrow?"

"I'm afraid it's not good news."

November 15

Birmingham, Alabama

Lily watched as Emily threw open the door to their room and slung her bag into the bottom of the closet. Lily simply dropped hers in the doorway. She was completely spent, and she hadn't played a single point in the match. As Emily fell onto her bed and buried her face in the pillows, Lily sat on her own and stared at the room around her. It had all ended so quickly, like a semi-truck speeding toward her she was powerless to stop.

They'd lost three straight games in the span of an hour and a half, and she had sat at the end of the bench completely horrified. No amount of begging had worked, and now it was over. She'd never play college volleyball again.

It was like a horrible nightmare that just kept coming and coming, and she couldn't wake up. One thing after another was falling apart. Was this how Jackson had felt last year—completely overwhelmed and defeated? All that was left to do now was flunk out of school.

She dropped her head into her hands and tried to push down the panic rising in her chest like a volcano, but it finally erupted. Jumping up from the bed, she grabbed her pillows and threw them against the wall, followed by her dirty clothes, books, pa-pers—anything she could get her hands on.

She moved through the room in a blur, unable to grasp the fear and anger driving her, so she settled for the physical objects around her. Books thudded, papers fluttered to the ground, and CD cases shattered. And when she could find nothing else to grab hold of, she collapsed on the floor.

She sat there panting, her lungs aching with each breath, and she looked around at the destruction. Finally, something made sense—everything on the outside looked like it felt on the inside, and something about it seemed right.

"Um...so. Feel better now?"

She looked up at Emily staring back down at her like she was a lunatic. Maybe she was.

"Yeah, I think I do."

Emily raised an eyebrow and looked around the room. "Interesting form of therapy. I've been wondering when you would finally explode, but I wasn't quite expecting this."

Lily pushed herself up onto her bed, her heart racing. "I think it's time to go see Aunt Catherine."

Chapter Twenty-Seven

November 21

Avon, Connecticut

Lily set her suitcase down beside the bed and walked over to the window of Catherine's guest bedroom. The valley below spread out in a beautiful patchwork of reds, yellows, and oranges, with a meandering stream that reminded her of home. The children playing in the yards were like tiny characters in a child's dream world, and she was a giant. She wanted to reach out to play with all the little pieces, and then dip her fingers in the stream.

"Lily?" Catherine called from downstairs. "As soon as you get settled, come on down for dinner. It's almost ready."

"Okay. Be there in a minute."

She walked over to the adjacent bathroom to wash up, glancing longingly at the huge Jacuzzi tub. She made a mental note to ask Catherine for some bubble bath. Then she washed her hands and face and headed down the stairs to the kitchen.

Catherine glanced up at her and smiled when she walked through the door. Although her long brown hair was graying around the edges, she looked years younger than fifty-six, and her casual business suit hugged her body perfectly. Lily hoped she looked half as good at that age.

The aroma of lasagna and fresh-baked bread filled the room. She breathed it in, and then looked suspiciously at her aunt.

"No offense, but I don't remember you being much of a cook."

She laughed and pulled a large casserole dish out of the oven, her apron and pot holders looking deceptively domestic.

"None taken, honey. I'm no cook, and I don't pretend to be one. I went down to Harper's Bakery and my friend Malinda's restaurant and stocked up on some delicious goodies for us while you're here. This lasagna is to die for." She pulled a spatula out of a drawer in front of her. "Grab a couple of plates out of the cabinet over there, and let's dig in."

Lily obliged and took the heaping portion Catherine set on her plate. She walked over to the table by the bay windows of the kitchen. It was amazing how Catherine's home seemed so spacious and cozy at the same time. The kitchen was full of aromatic plants that seemed to bring a garden feel right into the room.

"I love your house," Lily said between bites. "It's so quiet and peaceful out here."

"Yes, it's nice." Catherine glanced around as if she was just noticing the kitchen for the first time. "I wish I spent more time here. Seems like the office is my real home, and this is just a little getaway."

She continued to enjoy the lasagna—Catherine had been right about how wonderful it was. She stared out of the windows mostly, taking in the rolling mountains spotted with farmhouses. It had been years since she'd been here, and she barely remembered any of it. Something about it called to her, like she was supposed to be here. She couldn't wait to take a walk along the path around the garden, maybe even hike the rest of the way up the mountain.

Catherine's fork scraping against her plate caught Lily's attention. She was surprised the time had passed so quickly. She stood and walked her plate over to the sink where Catherine was washing hers off.

"Can I help?"

"Nah. I just rinse them off and leave them for the housekeeper. She'll get everything in the morning."

"Seems like you're doing really well here."

Catherine paused and smiled. "I'm very blessed. That's for sure."

"Any regrets?"

"So many I can't count them all. But I don't dwell on them. If I did it would eat me up inside."

"Like it's doing to me."

"Exactly."

Catherine reached for a towel and dried her hands. "Why don't we go into the reading room and talk for a little while?"

She followed Catherine into a snug little room filled with bookshelves, an overstuffed sofa, and a leather recliner. A fire crackled beside them and lit the room with a soft glow. Catherine reached over and turned a dial on the wall, sending the flames a bit higher, immediately warming the room.

"You take the recliner," Catherine said as she handed her a chenille afghan.

Lily sank into the leather heaven and wrapped the afghan around her shoulders. "I could definitely get used to this life. A beautiful home, cozy furniture, someone else to keep it clean."

Catherine chuckled as she pulled another afghan out of the closet. She walked over to the couch across from Lily and tucked her legs under her.

"Oh, honey. Don't even begin to envy what I have. It's not worth the price I've paid for it." She looked at Lily pointedly. "And I'm not talking about money."

Lily nodded. She was vaguely aware of Catherine's past—her leaving home at seventeen, her three marriages and abrupt divorces, and a lifelong rebellion against her conservative upbringing. Lily admired her determination to chase her dreams, but she'd always sensed loneliness in Catherine.

"Still," Lily said, "how could you ever get stressed out living here?"

"Trust me. I manage." Catherine took a sip of her coffee before setting it aside. "So, what's been going on with you lately?" She smiled, a bit too innocently.

"Please. Don't try to pretend like my dad hasn't already called you a hundred times pleading with you to shrink me. I know he's told you everything that happened."

"He loves you so much, you know?"

"I know." She looked down at her hands. They were already shaking.

"And so do I." Catherine watched her closely as Lily rubbed her palm with her thumb. "I know it may be hard to talk about everything, but I hope you feel at ease here. Talking is the best place to begin dealing with everything you're going through."

"I know that in my head. And I do want to make an effort. I'm just not sure where to even start."

"Well, that's what I'm here for." Catherine smiled warmly, placing Lily more at ease. "Let me ask you, sweetheart. How have you been sleeping?"

"Awful. I keep having nightmares, but I can never remember them after I wake up." She shuddered. Nothing specific ever stuck with her, just a vague sense of bullets screeching past her and screams. Then she'd awaken in a deep sweat.

Catherine nodded. "Mmm. What do you think about at night when you're in bed?"

"I try not to think about anything. I read or watch TV until I fall asleep." Lily paused and closed her eyes. "When I lay in bed, in the dark, I can still hear the gun going off. I panic and turn the lights on to make sure no one's there. Then I feel completely stupid for still being so scared. Emily thinks I'm nuts."

"What do you think?"

"I don't know. I hope I'm not losing my mind." She laughed to herself a little.

"What else do you think about, when you're trying to sleep that is?"

"That this is all my fault." Tears began to threaten, but she pushed them back. "A woman is dead because of me."

"Why do you think it was your fault?"

"Because. If I had just-" She sat up and leaned toward Catherine. "This may be silly to ask, but you won't tell anyone what we talk about right?"

"Of course not. You can tell me anything."

"Well, I found out a while back that Alex was still married. He was trying to get a divorce, but she was stalling. And I knew when he told me. I knew I should walk away then, but I didn't. If I had, none of this would've happened. She'd still be alive...And maybe Jackson would still love me."

"It's easy to play the what-if game. But you can't blame yourself for what happened. Alex's ex-wife chose her own path. You're not responsible for the choice she made."

Lily gazed into the fire and contemplated Catherine's words. Maybe she was right. But wasn't she at least partly responsible? She had ignored her conscience, and she had definitely made several wrong decisions. Adrian had made her own choices, but so had she, and her choices had cost her the dearest friend she'd ever known.

Catherine cleared her throat. "Sounds like you have two exceptional men in love with you too. That has to be weighing on your mind as well."

"Not any more. Jackson hates me now. He could barely even look at me."

"Well, then there's still hope."

"Hope? How do you figure that?"

"The greater the love you feel, the more excruciating the pain when it disappoints you. He's hurting so badly because he loves you so much."

"That's not what I'd call hope."

"If he was indifferent, then I might agree. But if he's heartbroken, then he still loves you. If he still loves you, then there's hope."

Lily was doubtful, but she didn't argue any further with Catherine. Maybe he did love her, but that wasn't enough.

"You know," Catherine said, "I don't think that's what you should focus on while you're here. Your life is a mess for a reason, and you need to get to the root of it, not worry about all the problems that have branched out from it."

"You're right."

"You've been consumed with everything that's happened, to you and Jackson, you and Alex, even you and Adrian. But I think you might be missing the big picture."

"Which is?"

"Well, I'm not going to just give you all the answers. Besides, I couldn't, even if I wanted to. You need to find the answers yourself."

Catherine smiled as Lily rolled her eyes and leaned back in the recliner. She knew what Catherine was trying to say, but it held no real meaning yet. Her inability to make the right decision was the root of the problem, but knowing that didn't solve anything.

"I'm terrified of being alone," Lily said, "but I can't stand being around people either. Is that weird?"

"Not really."

"I feel like my whole world has shifted somehow, and I'm on this different planet. But everyone I know is still on the old one, and I don't know how to talk to them anymore. It's like I'm an alien or something."

"I'm sure that can be lonely, and confusing."

Lily pulled the afghan tighter under her chin. The only person in the whole world who could possibly understand, the only person she wanted, would have nothing to do with her anymore.

"You know," Catherine said. "I can understand not wanting to be alone. But maybe that's what God wants for you right now. Maybe He wants your full attention."

Lily could only nod. God definitely had her attention, but what was He going to do with her?

November 23

Avon, Connecticut

Lily sat silently on the quilt she'd spread across the rocks jutting out of the top of the mountain, her Bible opened in her lap to the passage God had brought her to over and over again in the past two days.

"Have mercy on me, O God, according to your steadfast love; According to your abundant mercy blot out my transgressions. Wash me thoroughly from my iniquity, and cleanse me from my sin. Purge me with hyssop, and I shall be clean; wash me and I shall be whiter than snow. Let me hear joy and gladness; let the bones you have broken rejoice. Hide your face from my sins, and blot out my iniquities. Create in me a new heart, O God, and renew a right spirit within me."

She read the verses from Psalm 51 over and over, claiming the words as her own. If King David could be redeemed after adultery and murder, and still be called a man after God's own heart, surely she could be redeemed as well.

She closed her eyes and listened for the small voice in her thoughts that had comforted her so often growing up. She'd let so many things drown it out lately, but not anymore. No more running, no more justifying.

November 25

Avon, Connecticut

The wind whipped around Lily's face, pulling strands of hair across her cheek. Her nose was so cold it burned, but the view was too beautiful to leave just yet. The sun would peek over the neighboring mountain any minute now, and the dew glistened in anticipation. She felt the excitement as well—the joy of beginning a new day with all its possibilities. It would be a long one, but she was looking forward to taking the first steps toward a new direction in her life.

"You ready to head back yet?" Catherine asked as she walked alongside Lily. Her scarf was wrapped tightly under her chin, and she rubbed her hands together.

"I'm sorry," Lily answered. "I know you're cold. Why don't you go on back? I'll be along soon."

"I can wait a few minutes. Besides, I haven't seen the sunrise in a long time. This was a perfect way to end your visit."

They stared out over the mountain, and in a few moments, a glimmer of light flashed at the top. The red horizon faded to orange, and the stars sparkling above them began to grow faint. Lily couldn't help but smile with the hope that had swelled within her over the past few days. God had opened His arms wide and wrapped them solidly around her.

"You seem much more at peace," Catherine said.

"I am. I think I spent more time reading the Bible in the past few days than I have in the entire rest of my life. It was wonderful. Like I was reading a book I had never read before."

Catherine grinned. "I know what you mean. It's amazing how He makes it new over and over again."

"You know, I've been living my whole life in measurements. I was so proud of myself for being such a good girl, and when I failed, it completely crushed me. And He let me fall. He loved me so much, He let me destroy myself, so that He could put me back together. All this time I've been trying to do it myself, and it felt like I was drowning. I just needed a reminder that I can't live my life in my own strength. I have to rely on God."

Catherine blew into her palms. "And what about your relationship with Alex? Or Jackson for that matter."

Lily's heart sank, but it wasn't the overwhelming ache she had felt before. It hadn't been easy to accept, but God's wisdom was perfect, and He had taken Jackson away for a reason.

"You know, if I'm really going to trust God, then I have to believe everything He does is perfect and good, even when I don't understand. It hurts to let go of Jackson, and I hate the thought of hurting Alex, but I have to make the right choice and have faith that God will work things out better than I ever could on my own."

"One of my favorite quotes is from Oswald Chambers," Catherine said. "He says 'To turn your head faith into a personal possession is a fight always, not sometimes.' Living out your faith is a constant battle against your own nature. It isn't easy."

"Well, I know I don't have everything figured out, but I'm heading in the right direction finally. Maybe I won't ever be with Jackson, and I messed up what could have been a great relationship with Alex. But I know somehow that even my failures are a part of God's plan for me." Lily nudged a small rock with her foot and glanced over at Catherine. "And I don't need romance to give meaning to my life. I just need the Lord, and He'll provide for me in His own time."

Lily looked back at the mountain across from her, now unable to look directly at the rising sun. A cold breeze surrounded her again, but she was warm all over with a light burning inside of her. She tugged on Catherine's elbow and tilted her head back toward the house.

"I'm ready now."

They walked along the path near the garden, a rainbow of dried leaves carpeting it. When they reached the front porch, Catherine paused and looked over at Lily with a hint of pride.

"You know, you're years ahead of where I was at your age. It took me a long time to figure out that fighting God's plan is useless—and stupid."

Lily shared in her laughter as they climbed the steps of the front porch.

"Well, maybe He can give us both something new for the future. That is, if you're up for a few changes around here."

"What are you cooking up now? Is this something that's going to get me in trouble with your father?"

Lily grinned and threw an arm over Catherine's shoulder as they headed into the house.

"Absolutely."

November 26

Forsyth, Georgia

As soon as Lily pulled into the parking spot next to Alex's car, her heart sped up and sent a wave of nausea through her. She gripped the steering wheel and breathed in deeply. This might be the most difficult thing she'd ever done.

She forced herself out of the car just as the wind rustled through the surrounding trees and sent a wave of dead leaves drifting down onto the pond at the bottom of the hill. She pulled the hood of her sweatshirt over her head and walked down the hill to where Alex waited, his hands shoved into his pockets while he rocked on his heels. Her heart seemed to thump harder with every step she took, and by the time she reached him, her head had already begun to ache.

"Any trouble with the directions?" he asked.

"No. I came straight to it."

Of course, she didn't mention the twenty minutes she'd spent driving around wondering for the millionth time if this was the right decision. She knew what she needed to say, and that she shouldn't drag it out, but the words seemed stuck in her throat.

"What is this place anyway?" she asked.

"Just a training facility for Georgia law enforcement." He tilted his head toward a rusting Chevy turned up on its side across the pond from them. "That's where I learned the fine art of accident reconstruction. You'd like it. Lots of math involved."

She attempted a smile, though she doubted it was convincing. She needed to move around, work out her nerves.

"You mind walking with me for a bit?" she asked.

He fell into step beside her, and neither of them spoke for a while. He pulled his hands out of his pockets briefly, but he didn't seem to know what to do with them, and he shoved them back inside.

"How was your trip?" he asked.

"Just what I needed."

"That's good to hear."

"Catherine was great. She listened to me, didn't judge me, and she pointed me back to my Bible."

"And did that help?"

"It did. God really opened my eyes to who I had become, and he set me straight on some things."

Alex shook his head. "I've tried a bit of that myself—reading the Bible. I don't really know where to start, though. All of that stuff happened so long ago. I'm not sure it can do me any good right now."

"What have you been reading?"

"I figured I'd just start at the beginning, so I read a little of Genesis."

She tried not to act surprised. Growing up in such a deeply Christian family had led to assumptions she hadn't even realized were there. She'd thought all Christians had the same basic beliefs as her own, that the Bible would be as familiar to them as it was to her. But Alex was different, and she found herself wondering now if he had ever truly been a believer.

"Genesis is great," she said. "There are some really good stories in it. I'm not sure it's where I would recommend you to start, but still, there's plenty that can apply to your life today. Have you read about Joseph yet?"

"Um, maybe. Which one was he?"

"The one whose dad made him the colorful coat. His brothers were jealous of him, and they beat him up and threw him into a well."

"Oh yeah. Didn't they sell him into slavery?"

"Yeah. But then he interpreted a dream for Pharaoh and wound up being the second highest in command in all of Egypt. God used him to reveal a famine that was coming, and Joseph was able to prepare them for it so that everyone had food."

Alex picked up a small stone and skipped it across the water. "See, now that's a good story, but so what? It has nothing to do with me."

She noticed the slump in his posture. He seemed so defeated. She wondered if he had found anyone to talk to. Maybe nightmares haunted him too. She reached over and ran a hand along his back.

"You know, I think that story has a great deal to do with us and everything that's happened. If you keep reading, you'll find out that Joseph's brothers have to come to him for food during the famine, and it's been so long they don't even recognize him."

"So he gets the last laugh."

"Not really. He tests them to see if they've changed, but eventually, he forgives them, and tells them who he is. He brings the whole family to Egypt so they can live in the best land with him."

Alex rubbed the back of his neck and let out a sigh. "He's a better man than I could be in that situation. Still not sure how that applies to us now."

"He forgave them because he realized that even though they meant him harm, God meant their actions for good. Joseph was in exactly the place he was supposed to be when the famine struck, and God used him to save the Egyptians as well as his own family."

Alex looked at her curiously. "And you believe that? That God is sitting up there like a grand puppet master moving us around however he wants to?"

"I might not use those exact words, but in some sense, I guess I do believe that. I know nothing can happen that He doesn't allow, and that nothing surprises Him."

"So you think He meant for my son to die? For Adrian to die?"

She looked away from the pain in his eyes. Maybe she was the wrong person to talk to him about this, especially considering why she had come here in the first place. She said a quick prayer for wisdom.

"I don't want to upset you. You've lost so much lately, and I don't want to make it worse. I just meant that we can take comfort in knowing that God is in control of everything—that their deaths weren't meaningless."

He didn't look convinced. She was completely mucking this up.

"You know," she said. "I was really scared there for a while, even afterward, when it was all over. I was trying so hard to be stronger. But I realize now that Adrian was never in control of what happened to all of us. And neither were you."

He looked over at her again, a flicker of something in his eyes. Pride maybe.

"What's that supposed to mean?"

"You couldn't have stopped her. You were never meant to. What she meant for evil, God has used for my good, and I'm sure he'll do the same for you. You didn't fail."

He shook his head. "You sound so sure. I'm just not there yet. It seems cruel to me. If he's so powerful, and in control of everything, why does he let such terrible things happen to good people? Why Evan? An innocent little baby who had never done a thing."

"I don't know. I don't have all the answers. But I think even our suffering is for our good. If nothing else, it reminds us that this world is not our ultimate destination. Our home is with

Him, and that's where Evan is waiting for you. He's not in pain, and he's not sad. He's rejoicing with the Lord."

Alex turned and looked out over the water like he was suddenly somewhere else. She watched him quietly for a few minutes, studying his features, memorizing him. This was even harder than she'd thought it would be. Doubt blossomed inside of her, tempted her to hold onto him.

Let him go. I'm all you need.

The thought was more like a small voice in her head, and she welcomed its return. It gave her peace. As hard as it would be, it was time to let go.

"Alex?" Her voice came out much more stable than she'd expected. He turned around to face her, and their eyes locked.

"I know why you came here," he said. "I've tried to think of anything I could say to change your mind. But I had to be honest with myself, and I'm not going to beg. So just say what you need to say, okay? Don't drag it out or try to soften it. Just say it."

"I don't want to hurt you."

"Too late."

She winced. "I care about you-"

"Just say it."

"I'm not sure what to say."

"Just say it." He stepped closer, taking her hands in his.

"I've been doing a lot of thinking-"

"Lily, just tell me."

She felt her eyes swell, her chest tighten. Why was she doing this again? Maybe there was a way. Maybe she could keep things with Alex in perspective, not lose sight of her relationship with

God again. If she promised never to sleep with him, never to let herself even be tempted, maybe they could stay together.

I'm all you need.

"Alex, it's time for me to let go. I've made one mistake after another, and I know in my heart that the right thing to do is to walk away."

He dropped her hands and let out a deep sigh. "See. Now that wasn't so bad."

"Yes it was."

"Then why do it? I don't understand. What did I do wrong?"

"Nothing. I did. When I first got the letters in the mail, I thought God was punishing me for sleeping with you."

He shook his head. "I knew it would come down to that. It was one time."

"But it didn't come down to that. I know that I'm forgiven. It's not about the one time. The problem is that you and I view life through completely different lenses, and sooner or later we'll just wind up right back in the same place. It will happen again."

"You don't know that. Listen I know this is important to you. I can wait."

"You knew it was important to me before. That's not the point either."

"Then what is the point?"

"I'm not willing to risk it. I have to focus on rebuilding my relationship with God. It has to be the most important thing to me."

"This is because of Jackson, isn't it? You're still in love with him."

"What? No-"

"I heard you, Lily!" He threw his hands in the air and turned away from her. "You said it, that night when he was shot. You told him you loved him."

Her stomach dipped. "I'm sorry. I know that hurt you. But he isn't the reason. I'm not breaking up with you to be with him."

"Then what is it? I don't understand. You're telling me you're breaking up with me because you need to focus on God? Why can't you do that anyway?"

She tried to settle her racing thoughts, but they were scattering to the wind. Why did he have to bring up Jackson?

"I just can't."

He looked up to the sky and muttered something under his breath. Then he turned his gaze back to her.

"I love you, Lily. I'd never hurt you. You can trust me."

She shook her head, unable to force out any words. Why was he making this so hard? Didn't he know how difficult it already was?

"My trust isn't in you. That was the problem all along. My trust, my strength, is in the Lord."

He threw his hands up. "Okay, fine. Your trust is in the Lord. I get it. So that means I get kicked to the curb."

"Please don't take it that way."

"How else am I supposed to take it? If you don't love me, then say it. Don't use God as an excuse."

"It's not an excuse. It's the truth. I'm trying to get my life back together, and the only way that's going to happen is if I let the Lord put it back together His way."

"Lily, do you know how odd that sounds?"

"Yes! But I don't care. Maybe it doesn't make sense to you, but that's all the more reason why we could never have a future."

"I see. So this all comes down to the fact that I'm not good enough, not Christian enough. And Jackson is."

Lily's head was beginning to streak with pain. She was getting nowhere. He could take everything she said and twist it into something else. He would never see.

"You know I don't mean that. I'm not judging you, Alex."

"Yes you are. And maybe you're right. I'm no saint. I can't quote the Bible or even tell you much about what it says. And I admit I'm not even sure I believe in God anymore." He paused, and his expression seemed to soften. "You're right. You deserve a better man than me."

Without hesitating, she stepped over to him and wrapped her arms around his neck. He held onto her, letting out a deep breath that seemed to come from the depths of his own personal pit. She ached to help him, for him to feel the joy and peace God offered him, even in suffering.

"You're going to be okay," she whispered near his ear. "God brought us together for a reason. Just listen to Him. You have so much to gain. He won't let you down."

Alex tightened his hold, nearly squeezing the air out of her. She felt something pass between them—hope, sorrow, maybe even a little joy.

"I'll never forget you."

"Me neither," she said. "Never."

Chapter Twenty-Eight

"Are there any more questions?" Lily glanced around at the teenage faces that had intimidated her only a few short months ago. Most of them shook their heads. A few began packing up their books.

"Be sure you have the assignment written down, and don't forget to turn it in first thing tomorrow." She gave a pointed glance toward Nathan in the back row as he grinned back at her, his dark hair falling over the mischievous twinkle in his eye.

The bell sounded, and the students shoved their books away and made a dash for the door. Lily sat down on the stool beside the overhead projector, her legs aching from standing for so long. No amount of leg presses or running stadiums had prepared her for being so exhausted from moving around a classroom all day.

"Well Lily, I've been very impressed," Mrs. Blakely called from her desk at the back of the room. "You've really done an excellent job this semester. That was good of you to make Nathan work some problems on the board. You got to keep him on his toes."

"Thanks. I know he can do better. I just don't always know how to get him to try."

"Welcome to high school teaching. But don't worry, you're a natural. I'll be sure to give you a good evaluation when I meet with your supervisor."

"Thank you."

Mrs. Blakely stood and picked up a stack of papers from her desk and added them to the books in her arms. The bundle looked like it might topple her tiny frame. She smiled at Lily, a gentle expression that had always put her at ease, even when she'd been a student in this very room. Strange how so much could change in four years, and yet so much had stayed the same.

"I have to run down to the lounge and make copies of the final exams for next week. Did you need anything before I go?"

"No, thanks. I'm meeting with Mr. Collins for a little while before I leave. He said he'd help me get ready for my interview."

"You nervous?"

"A little." Lily walked to the back of the room and began gathering her things. "I haven't had much of a chance to think about it with graduation coming up next week. Getting everything packed took more out of me than I thought it would."

"I understand. Tom and I moved a lot when we were first married. Packing up a life is hard."

Lily nodded and pushed down the doubt creeping into her thoughts. "Thanks again for letting me have tomorrow off."

Mrs. Blakely walked with Lily to the door, flipping the lights off as they left. "It's no trouble. Although I think the kids will be disappointed to get me back. They usually give student teachers a hard time, but they've really taken a liking to you."

Lily couldn't help but smile. She'd taken a liking to them too. She'd always known she wanted to teach, but it was a relief to be sure it was where she belonged. She loved it, especially watching the light in the students' faces when a difficult concept finally clicked.

As they reached the library, Mrs. Blakely turned and gave Lily a quick hug, balancing her papers precariously in one arm.

"Have a safe flight. You leaving tonight?"

"Yeah. I can't believe it's finally here."

"Well, good luck. It's been a real pleasure. You're a special young lady, and you'll make a wonderful teacher."

"Thank you for everything. I'll email you and let you know if I get the job."

As Mrs. Blakely said goodbye and headed downstairs, Lily turned toward the offices on the other side of the library. On her way through, she waved at the librarian in his glass office hunched over his computer furiously typing. The sight always made her think of a caged monkey at the zoo. He managed a quick wave and pushed up his glasses in one swift motion before returning to the keyboard.

The library was a large room, open on all sides and surrounded by four quads, each assigned to a class, each holding memories of her time here. She could still see her past moving all around her, like ghosts popping up for a visit from time to time. Even now as she neared the waist-high bookshelves separating the library from the walkway, she caught a glimpse of the table in the back corner, and she heard Jackson's hushed voice as he leaned across the table and whispered jokes in her ear.

She'd become accustomed to the intrusion of the images, but they still made her heart speed up a notch. She took a deep breath and forced herself to look away, to concentrate on the office door and what lay on the other side. Soon she could leave all this behind and start building new memories.

Mrs. Sheffield was on the phone at her desk when Lily walked through the door, and she raised a finger to hold Lily in place. Her hair had grayed quite a bit in the past few years, but her smile had stayed warm and inviting, just like the Mrs. Claus character she played each year in the Christmas drama.

She placed the phone on the hook and walked toward Lily, her gait a bit more labored since her knee surgery a couple of months back. She leaned against the counter.

"What can I do for you, Lily?"

"I'm meeting with Mr. Collins today."

"Oh, that's right. The big interview is tomorrow." She placed a hand over Lily's. "I sure wish we could keep you around here. It's been so wonderful to see you grow into such a beautiful young lady." Her smile was infectious. "Looks like we may have a few openings for next year."

"Thank you. I've really enjoyed student teaching here, but I think I'm ready to get out of Alabama for a while."

"Well, Mr. Collins is interviewing someone for the History position right now. You can have a seat over by the window if you want. He should be done soon."

Lily made her way over to the chairs beneath the windows lining the far wall. Taking a seat, she pulled out a book and began to read, but it was difficult to concentrate for some reason.

Her thoughts kept returning to Jackson and the memories they'd created here. Sometimes it was like that. The thoughts of him were stubborn, like a petulant child insisting on having his way.

It didn't help that the smallest thing could trigger a memory, like the huge State Championship trophies—one for basketball and one for volleyball—that still sat side by side in the trophy case in the office. Her junior year, his senior, had been great in so many ways—homecoming King for him, State Championships for them both, scholarship offers, prom. Now it all seemed like a dream, like it had happened to someone else. If it weren't for their pictures hanging together outside the gym, she might wonder if it had actually happened at all.

Now time was measured in how long it had been since she last thought of him. What was she up to now, half a day? Yes, she hadn't thought of him since this morning. Progress.

Down the hall behind Mrs. Sheffield's desk, a door opened and voices drifted toward Lily, a welcome distraction from her memories. Maybe now she could concentrate on preparing for her interview. She stood and walked over to the swinging door that led behind the counter. She waited for Mr. Collins, preparing to thank him for his time today, but the voice she heard stopped her cold. She stared at the corner, waiting for Mr. Collins and his guest. Surely her ears were playing tricks on her.

Suddenly Jackson walked around the corner, headed straight for her, and her stomach flew into her chest. She couldn't move, couldn't even blink. As soon as their eyes met, he froze as well, and Mr. Collins nearly bumped into him.

"Whoa," Mr. Collins said as he changed direction. "Almost ran you over, Jackson." He glanced between the two of them and wrinkled his brow. Jackson towered over him, but then again, a leprechaun might be taller than Mr. Collins.

"Oh, hey Lily! You remember Jackson Carter, don't you? Weren't you two pretty close when you were in school here?"

Lily stared for another long moment before clearing her throat. "Uh, yes sir. We uh, we knew each other."

"Well, it looks like Jackson may be joining our staff as a history teacher and basketball coach next year. Wouldn't it be great if you two were working together?" He gave a meaningful nod in her direction then turned toward Jackson and continued. "Lily did her student teaching with us, and we've been trying to talk her into staying on for the fall. But she seems determined to leave us. Heading off to bigger and better things I suppose."

Mr. Collins paused again, and an awkward silence fell over the room. Jackson never took his eyes off Lily, making her stomach flutter and soar. He'd let his hair grow out, and it swept across his eyebrows like it had when he was in high school. She could swear they'd stepped back in time.

Finally, Jackson looked over at Mr. Collins. He was looking between the two of them like he was expecting something, and it finally registered to her that he had asked a question. But Jackson still looked bewildered.

"Excuse me?" Jackson asked. "I'm sorry. Did you ask me something?"

Mr. Collins grinned. "Yes. I asked if you two had kept in touch after leaving us." Jackson stared back at her again, yet neither of them answered. Mr. Collins seemed to sense the tension, and he cleared his throat.

"Uh, yes sir," Jackson said. "We kept in touch. Though it has been a little while."

Mr. Collins gave Jackson a hearty pat on the back and began guiding him toward the door.

"Well, maybe you can talk her into staying. We're going to need a volleyball coach to take over in the next couple of years. It would be great to have you two back together again."

They moved past Lily and through the swinging door. Jackson shook his head and glanced back at her with a tight smile.

"If I remember correctly, once she makes up her mind, there's no changing it. And I doubt she'd listen to me. If she's determined to move to Brunswick, you won't talk her out of it."

Jackson reached for the large double doors and gave a nod in Lily's direction. Mr. Collins turned to her with a curious glance.

"Brunswick?" he asked. "Is that the town in Connecticut you're moving to? I thought it was Avon?"

All she could do was shake her head. Words seemed like a strange concept at the moment. Jackson let go of the door, and the loud slam made Lily jump. He took a step toward her, oblivious to the shock on Mr. Collins's face.

"Wait a minute. You're moving to Connecticut?"

She nodded.

"When?"

She finally found her voice. "Tonight, actually."

He shifted his weight and ran his hand through his hair, looking from Lily to Mr. Collins, and then back at Lily. He looked completely lost.

"Why Connecticut?"

"Aunt Catherine. She lives there, remember? I just, uh, wanted to start over. I needed a change."

"I thought you were moving to Brunswick." She shook her head, and his confusion began to look more like frustration. His cheeks bulged as he ground his teeth together.

Mr. Collins cleared his throat, catching Jackson's attention. He looked amused by the whole thing.

"Do you two need some time alone?"

"No," Jackson said, gritting his teeth again. "Thank you again Mr. Collins for seeing me today." They shook hands and Jackson once again reached for the door.

"Thank you for coming in," Mr. Collins said. "I'll be in touch soon."

Jackson pushed through the door without another glance toward Lily and let it slam behind him. She stood in shock with Mr. Collins looking at her, his head cocked at an angle, like a dog trying to understand a strange sight.

"Did I miss something?" he asked.

"It's a long story." She let out a slow breath and tried to steady her racing heart. She had no idea what had just happened. He had almost looked angry. But why?

"Maybe you should go talk to him," Mrs. Sheffield offered. "He looked a little upset."

"I don't even know what to say. I don't know why he would be upset that I was moving." She turned toward Mr. Collins. "Do you mind?"

"No, go ahead. You don't need my help. You'll be fine in your interview."

She was already halfway out the door. She called out a thank you just before it closed. Heading toward the front doors of the school, she wondered what in the world she would say, but it didn't matter. She just needed to try.

She looked around the parking lot outside the front of the school for a few minutes, but he was nowhere in sight. Her adrenaline was still rushing, and her chest thundered with each heartbeat. She walked up and down the rows of cars but still came up with nothing. So she headed back inside.

God, please. I'm finally content being on my own. Why are you doing this now?

Tears welled up behind her eyes as she walked back through the building and down the stairs leading to the faculty parking lot out back. She stepped out into the sun and squinted. The rays were warm. Summer would be hotter than usual here. She wondered what summers were like in Connecticut.

The whistles of the soccer coaches blew in rhythm off to her left as players went through drills on the field, and in front of her, the tennis team jogged around the courts. She sniffed back the sob that was threatening and turned the corner to her right.

After months of wanting to talk to him, to just see him one more time, it had finally happened. Yet it didn't give her the closure she had hoped for. Instead her heart ached for him even more.

She finally had her tears pushed back as she rounded the car next to hers, and she pulled her bag off her shoulder to rummage for her keys.

"So what's all this about moving to Connecticut?"

She jumped and dropped her bag, papers and books spilling all over the concrete. Jackson pushed away from her car and grimaced as he knelt down to help pick up the mess. She just watched him in disbelief for a moment.

"You going to help at all?" He looked up at her and squinted with the sun in his eyes.

She cleared her throat and managed to speak. "Uh, yeah. Sorry."

She knelt down and gathered several loose papers, stuffing them into the bag. The breeze picked up a few pages and sent them dancing across the parking lot before she could grab them.

"Oh no," she said and took off after them as they flew away.

Jackson watched her scurry around the nearly deserted lot grasping pages, and he wondered what he was doing. He should have walked out the door and kept going. He was obviously a glutton for punishment. It was like driving by an accident on the side of the road and slowing down to see the gruesome details, even though you didn't want to. Some irresistible force just makes you turn your head.

But he had to know what was going on and why she was moving to Connecticut, of all places. He had expected her to be moving to Brunswick to be with Alex—that at least he could understand. But just up and moving so far away for no reason? Curiosity was killing him.

She finally caught up with the papers and brought them back over to the car just as he stood up with her bag. She shoved the last few pages inside and glanced up at him.

"Sorry about that," she said.

"No, really. It's my fault. I shouldn't have startled you."

She dug out her keys and unlocked the back door; then she flung her back pack into the back seat and closed the door.

"I tried to catch up with you after you left the office," she said. "I looked all over the upper parking deck."

"Really?" he asked. "Yeah, I actually parked back here so I could go in and say hello to Coach Wilson."

"Oh." She shifted her weight under his scrutiny and looked away. "Since when have you been interested in teaching?"

"Since Christmas. I did a lot of praying after I recovered, and I felt like God had made it pretty clear He didn't intend for me to play professional basketball."

"I'm sorry."

"Don't be; I'm not. I have peace about it, and I think I might actually be a good teacher and coach."

"I'm sure you will."

He looked down at her as she rested against the car next to hers. She looked different somehow. More grown up, maybe.

"So what's going on?" he asked. "Why are you moving to Connecticut?"

She shrugged and crossed her arms. "I told you. I need a fresh start, and Aunt Catherine has that old farm house all to herself. It would be perfect."

"Perfect for what?"

"I guess for moving on with my life. Finding some peace. I went there for Thanksgiving because I was having a hard time dealing with everything, and I spent a lot of time praying and reading my Bible, and I talked to Catherine about everything. It really helped."

"So you thought you needed to move there? That seems a bit extreme. What does Alex think about all this?"

She shrugged and looked away. "When I told him, he was pretty upset, but I'm sure he's fine by now. I don't know. I haven't spoken to him since right before Christmas."

"You mean, you broke up with him?"

She nodded, and relief mingled with his confusion. So Alex was history. Thank God. But moving to Connecticut still made no sense.

"So let me get this straight. You went to Connecticut and had some enlightening experience on the mountain with Catherine, and now you want to pack up everything and move there? You know, running away from your problems won't make them any better."

"What do you know about my life?" she huffed. "You haven't even been around. I'm not running away from anything. I just don't want to be reminded every single day of that horrible night, and everything that led up to it. I don't want to be bombarded all the time with memories of us. It's the past, and I want to look to the future."

He sighed and looked toward the sky as mockingbirds argued in the nearby trees. How could this be happening? After months of trying to let go of her and praying for her happiness, and finally finding some sense of direction for a future without her, every ounce of progress he'd made was just wiped away. The sight of her only deepened the ache in his chest, a pain as real as the bullets he'd taken.

"Why is this bothering you so much?" she asked. "I thought this was what you wanted. For us to go our separate ways for good."

"I didn't say that-"

"Those were your exact words!"

"I never wanted that, Lil. Stop twisting everything I say into an attack on you. You can't use me as an excuse for running away. This is about you, not me."

She took a deep breath and closed her eyes for a moment. "Look, I don't want to fight with you. All I wanted was to talk to you and tell you how I really feel. I don't want to waste the last chance I have on arguing about what you did or did not say."

The last chance. The words punched him in the gut.

"If you wanted to talk so badly, why didn't you just call me?" he asked.

"Because I was scared."

"Of what?"

"Of you! Of getting hurt again. You were so angry. And if you'd pushed me away again, it would have killed me."

Jackson threw his hands in the air and groaned. Had she lost her mind? "You've got to be kidding me!" He stepped closer and pointed his finger at her. "*You* pushed *me* away, remember? Being around you was killing *me*. You were in love with Alex. You chose Alex."

"No, I didn't!"

"What? Yes, you did! Would you please start making some sense?"

"I came to your house that night to have dinner with you and your mom, remember? After you came home from the hospital. I was trying to tell you then."

Her voice caught, and she paused, dropped her gaze to the ground. He was still confused.

"Tell me what?" he asked.

She shook her head, refusing to look him in the eye.

"Come on, Lil. I can barely even remember that night. Do you have any idea how much medication I was on? If you were trying to tell me something, I didn't realize it."

"Just forget it. It doesn't matter now anyway. I'm leaving tonight, and we can both move on with our lives."

"Fine. You want to shut me out and run away, go ahead. I can't stop you. But one day you're going to have to face the things that scare you."

Her eyes darted up at him, and he could see the anger flash through them like lightening.

"I can't believe you, of all people, are lecturing me about facing fears! You've been living in fear since your dad died. You're so scared of losing the people you love, you alienate them, and look where it's gotten us. You set all of this in motion when you pushed me away. You are the king of shutting people out. Don't talk to me about facing my fears until you face your own!"

She pushed him aside and flung open her car door, climbing inside before he could say another word. Then she backed out and drove away without even a glance back. Jackson just watched in bewilderment.

The night she'd come to see him was still foggy, and he could barely remember their conversation. He searched his memory, trying to recall her words. Had she tried to tell him she still loved him? He had no idea. All he remembered was her being there and a strong sense that he was supposed to let her go. But now what?

Lily glanced down at her watch and sighed, her nerves still tumbling around in her stomach. She had come to Jackson's house determined to finally tell him everything, but he wasn't home, and she had to leave soon if she was going to make her flight.

Her anger had finally settled down, and she'd realized that, on some level, he was right. But it didn't change anything. He still didn't want her, and she needed to put that part of her life behind her.

She looked down at the letter in her hands one more time.

Dear Jackson,

I've wanted to tell you what was really on my heart for a while, but I've been afraid. I guess fear has been the driving force in my life for a long time. But if there is one thing I have learned over the past year or more, it is that I have to trust in the Lord, especially when I feel weak and afraid. I'm terrified of opening myself up just to get hurt again, but I'm doing it. You were right. I can't move on with my life until I face my fear. So here it is: I love you. I always have. I always will. I realize we're way past apologies, and maybe even forgiveness. I'm sorry for blaming everything on you. I still made choices that landed me right where I am, and I have to live with the consequences. But I am sorry. I understand if you can't forgive me, but I hope that someday the memories of us will make you smile again.

~Lily

"I thank my God every time I remember you."

She rubbed the necklace between her fingers and said another quick prayer. Then she folded the paper and pushed open her car door. She stepped over to the mailbox and shoved the letter inside. It was better this way. She could write it all down and make sure she didn't stumble. And best of all, she wouldn't have to endure his polite rejection. So maybe it wasn't exactly the bravest way to face her fear, but at least she had said it. It was time to move forward. And North.

Jackson pushed open the car door and stepped out from behind the steering wheel. He slammed the door behind him, barely noticing the warm spring afternoon. His mind still stumbled through his conversation with Lily.

"What does she mean I have to face my fears? She's the one running away!"

Matt climbed out of the passenger side and gave him an amused grin over the top of the car. His cheeks were still flushed pink from their basketball game at the Y.

"Maybe she has a point."

"What? You agree with her? So you think I'm a coward too!"

"Hey, I didn't say that. Besides, jumping in front of a bullet isn't exactly the action of a coward."

Jackson huffed and waited for him to explain.

"I just meant that you did shut her out after your dad died, and you have to acknowledge that it hurt her."

Jackson rested his hands on top of the car and sighed. "I did acknowledge that I hurt her. I apologized over and over. She didn't want to have anything to do with me."

"I know you did. But how is she supposed to know you won't do it again?"

"I can't prove anything to her if she doesn't give me the chance." He walked to the end of the driveway and pulled open the mailbox, feeling for the junk inside. "Besides, I don't even know for sure what will happen in the future. How can I promise her anything?"

He shuffled through the papers and envelopes in his hand until he came to one that sent his heart racing. His name, in her handwriting, practically jumped off the envelope at him. He handed Matthew the stack of mail and then slid his thumb under the flap. Staring at the note, he could hardly believe what it said. He had known all along that she still loved him, but she had finally said it. Well, sort of.

"What is it?" Matthew asked. Jackson handed him the letter, and he read over it quickly. "This is great. Does this mean she's not moving?"

"I don't think so. It reads like she's saying goodbye." He shook his head in disbelief. "She's still leaving, so this means nothing."

He walked past Matthew toward the sidewalk leading up to the front steps, and Matthew jogged up beside him.

"You have to stop her."

"When have I ever been able to stop Lily from doing anything?"

"Good point." Matthew's face dropped, but then immediately bounced back. "You stopped her from running away...when you were kids right? You can do it again. Come on. You two have loved each other since you were practically in diapers. If there's no hope for you, then there's not much hope for any of the rest of us."

Jackson stomped up the front steps, wishing Matthew would just let it go.

"I don't even know when her flight is leaving. She's probably already left. Face it. She doesn't want to work things out."

"Yes she does! She just doesn't know it yet!"

"That's ridiculous," Jackson said as he pushed through the front door.

"No, what's ridiculous is letting your best friend, the girl you've supposedly loved for your entire life, make a huge mistake because you're too proud to take a risk. Maybe she was right about you being afraid."

Jackson stopped and turned around. "Maybe. Or maybe I just don't have any fight left in me for all of this. Maybe God wants me to accept losing her and get on with my life."

Matthew's face softened. "Look, when you're lying in bed at night, what's the last thing you think about before you go to sleep? What's the first thing you think about when you wake up?"

Lily. Always Lily.

"When you think about how you want to spend the rest of your life," Matthew continued, "when you picture yourself old and feeble, sitting out on a porch in a dilapidated rocking chair, who's sitting beside you? I know it's not me."

Jackson couldn't help but grin. "You mean you don't want to be roommates forever? You're breaking my heart."

Matthew chuckled and shook his head. "Come on. What do you really want?"

He only needed a second to know the answer.

"Don't you have a friend that works at the airport?"

"We should have thought this through a little more," Jackson said as he turned his car onto the road leading to the airport. "How much time before the plane leaves?"

Mathew glanced down at his watch. "Forty-five minutes. We can still make it."

Jackson punched the gas and merged into the lane heading for the drop off area. "I'll get out and run inside. You park the car."

"Got it."

As he topped the ramp that led up to the second level of the airport, Jackson hit the brakes to avoid the car in front of him, and the tires screeched. He took a deep breath. A wreck was the last thing he needed right now.

He pulled into a spot behind a dark minivan and shifted the car into park. Matthew jumped out at the same time he did.

"Good luck!" he yelled as Jackson took off for the entrance, dodging a few honking cars along the way.

As he entered the airport, the crowd of people in the security line sent a wave of dread through him. He paced back and forth, searching through a sea of faces while trying not to look like a crazy person. Even with four lanes open, the line snaked around into several rows. And Lily wasn't in any of them. He glanced up at the six television screens above him and searched for her flight. Forty minutes. Maybe there was still time.

Without another thought, he jogged over to the Delta terminal. At least that line was short. The only person in front of him was a tiny Asian woman speaking rapidly into her cell phone. Then two spots opened up simultaneously. Thank God.

Jackson rushed up to the young man behind the counter and blurted out a string of incoherent words.

"Excuse me?" The guy looked at him like he was crazy. Jackson stared back at him, unable to put his thoughts together.

Matthew suddenly appeared beside him. "I think he's trying to buy a ticket."

"Okay. Is there something wrong with him?" The man raised an impatient eyebrow.

"I'm sorry," Jackson blurted out. "I'm...I'm fine. I need a ticket to Hartford, Connector."

"What?" Now both eyebrows were up.

"Connecticut." Matthew added. "Do you have any seats left for the flight to Hartford?"

The guy huffed and typed furiously for a moment. "One seat left."

Jackson felt his stomach roll. "I'll take it."

Matthew turned Jackson's shoulders until they faced each other. "Are you sure about this? You do realize you are purchasing an actual plane ticket."

Jackson tried to shrug away the panic rising inside of him. "I'm not getting on. I just need to get through security to get to Lily."

"That will be four hundred and seventy nine dollars."

Jackson turned toward the guy and slid his credit card across the counter. That was a lot of money just to get through security. He took a deep breath. He wasn't actually getting on the plane.

Deep breath.

He signed the receipt and snatched the ticket from the counter, and then he jogged over to the line for the security check with Matthew right behind him.

"Do you know what you're going to say?" Matthew asked.

"No idea."

"Don't you think you should plan it out a little bit?"

"Uh, maybe. I don't know." Jackson shook his hands out and bounced his weight from one leg to the other.

"Maybe this was a bad idea. You look a little pale."

"Don't start being the voice of reason at this stage of the game. I'm getting in there, getting Lily, and getting out. No problem."

"Right." Mathew looked over at the television screens. "Except that the plane is boarding."

"What?" Jackson followed his gaze. Sure enough. The word "boarding" flashed beside the flight to Hartford. And the line in front of him continued to inch forward, like everyone knew how desperately he needed to get through and they were enjoying torturing him.

When he finally reached the front of the line, Matthew gave him a pat on the back.

"I'll wait out here. Hope you get to her. If you're not back in an hour, I'll assume you took off."

That sent another wave of nausea through him, and Jackson actually felt the blood draining from his face. But there was no time to think about it. He darted through the metal detector and set it off, so he was directed back through it again. When it beeped again, he nearly lost it. A female guard pulled him aside and swept over him with a handheld device.

"You're clean," she said. "Now, I need you to take off your shoes."

"You've got to be kidding!"

She widened her eyes and smacked her gum. "Off! Now."

He slipped his shoes off and watched her inspect them. She was obviously enjoying making him squirm. She finally handed them back and he hopped away as he put them back on. With his shoes finally secured, he broke into a jog down the terminal, getting halfway down before he realized he didn't even know what gate the flight was leaving from. What had the guy at the counter said? He couldn't remember, so he found another set of screens.

"A-four," he mumbled and headed back in the direction he'd come from. Of course he'd already passed it.

When he reached the gate, he hurried past the line of people waiting to board, checking each face for Lily. As he neared the front of the line, he spotted her just as she took her ticket stub from the attendant and walked into the boarding ramp.

"Lily!" She didn't hear him. Of course she didn't hear him. God was trying to have a good laugh here.

He turned in a circle and debated his options. Drive to Connecticut? That wouldn't work. Her interview was tomorrow. Call her cell! Why hadn't he thought of that to begin with?

He pulled out his cell phone and dialed her number, praying she hadn't turned it off yet. It went straight to voicemail. He slammed the phone shut and stuffed it back into his pocket. The realization of what he'd have to do made his stomach churn. The last time he'd tried to fly, he was eleven years old, and it had been a complete disaster. He'd ended up puking in the airport bathroom and never even made it to the plane.

But he had to do it. He'd have to get on that plane. Somehow.

He was the very last person to enter the plane, and he had no idea how he even made it down the boarding ramp. Maybe he could find Lily, talk to her, and get off the plane before it took off. Surely they would let a sick passenger off.

He scanned the rows of seats as he walked down the aisle, finally spotting Lily near the back with her forehead against the window. He started to make his way back, but a flight attendant moving toward him with a smile as wide the plane itself pointed behind him.

"I think there's a seat right there, sir."

"Oh, I'm not actually, I mean, I can't fly away. I just want to find Lily and leave."

She wrinkled her brow, but never dropped the smile as she herded him backward.

"Let me just help you to your seat. Do you have any luggage to store?"

"No." He backed up a few paces. "You don't understand. I can't fly."

"Yes, sir. That's what the pilot is for." A few more paces back. She pointed toward the seat. "You need to sit down now so we can get started."

"I want to sit in the back." He forced his legs to stop moving and stood his ground. "There's a seat in the back I want."

She stepped aside and he got his legs moving again. Lily sat in the window seat, staring outside completely unaware of his presence yet. As he neared her seat, his heart thundered in his chest. He had to get a grip. He forced a deep breath in, and it settled him for a moment. Breathe in. Breathe out.

God, give me strength. Give me the words. Settle my fear and help me to trust in you. And please, let her say yes.

Lily watched the men below her finish throwing the last of the luggage into the belly of the plane and wondered again if she was doing the right thing. Connecticut was so far from home and everything she knew. It made her heart race every time she thought about it.

She felt movement beside her and glanced over, expecting to find a stranger taking the seat next to her, but she was shocked to see Jackson.

"What are you doing here?"

"We need to talk." He gripped the armrests, and his knuckles went white.

"You do realize you're on a plane that's about to take off, right?"

"Yes." He took a deep breath and then looked over at her, his eyes wide and filled with excitement. If they'd been anywhere else, she might have thought he was happy.

"Yours doesn't count," he said.

"What?"

"You didn't face your fear. You wrote a letter and scampered away. *I* am facing mine right now. So you have to deal with yours. Tell me to my face. I want to hear you say it."

Her insides twisted and knotted up. She was still unsure of what he was doing here.

"I don't know what to say."

He leaned toward her and lowered his voice. "I know it's scary to want something so bad that you're terrified of losing it. But you can't live your life that way. Just talk to me. Did you mean what you wrote in the letter?"

Tears pricked her eyes and she looked down at the floor.

"Every word."

He picked her chin up until she looked him in the eye.

"Then tell me."

She stared back at him while somewhere in the background a female voice described the proper use of the seat as a flotation device. What was she so afraid of? This was Jackson, her best friend, the man who'd jumped in front of a bullet to save her. And he was here, on a plane, no less. Maybe God had finally brought them back to each other.

"I love you."

His smile widened, and he pulled her into his arms, nearly squeezing the breath out of her.

"Oh my word, Lily Brennon! Was that really so hard?"

"Yes," she mumbled into his shirt. He laughed as they fell back against the seat, her head still resting on his chest. "Did you really just climb onto an airplane to hear me say that?"

"Yes, but that's not all."

"Oh no. There's more?"

"Just this." He slid out of the seat into the aisle, resting on one knee while still holding her hand.

Lily's heart jumped into her throat. "What are you doing?"

"Don't say anything until I finish. I need to get through this before this plane starts moving." She nodded and glanced around. They had already caught the attention of a few passengers nearby, and a couple of older ladies were smiling across the aisle at her.

"This year has been really tough, and I take full responsibility for messing things up. If I had trusted in God and relied on Him, maybe things would have been a lot different. But I also might never have figured out how badly I need you, or how much I really love you, and for that, I'm grateful. God has taught me that He is always God, and you and I never left His hands."

She shook her head and pushed a tear off her cheek. "But I messed up too. How can you forgive me?"

"How can I not? At the end of the day, it's still you and me forever. *Forever.* I'm sure we're not through making mistakes, but you're the only one I ever want to beg forgiveness from. You're the one I want wake up next to every morning. It's your beautiful face I want to see when I look at my children."

He paused, and a huge smile spread across his face.

"So...will you marry me, Lil?"

Her heart nearly leapt out of her chest. "Yes!"

Jackson stood and pulled her into his arms. Then he covered her mouth with his, sending a rush of warmth through her body. It was like coming home after a long, dreadful time away.

It wasn't until a flight attendant walked up to them that she remembered where she was. Lily looked around at all the curious smiles and annoyed grimaces.

"Sorry," she said, unable to suppress her smile.

Jackson waved a hand in the air. "We're getting married!"

A few people applauded, and the flight attendant nearby smiled politely. "That's wonderful, sir. But we really do need for you to take your seat."

They returned to their seats and fastened the seat belts, then shared a nervous grin. Jackson's eyes went wide as the plane began to roll, and the color drained from his face.

"We're moving."

She squeezed his hand. "Yes, and finally it's in the right direction."

About the Author

Jennifer Westall dives into Christian characters to explore her own questions of faith. Inspired by her experiences as a college athlete, *Love's Providence* (2012), a contemporary Christian romance, navigates the minefield of dating and temptation. She's also the author of *Healing Ruby* (2014), the first in the *Healing Ruby* series, which delves into the mysteries of faith healing. She resides in southwest Texas with her husband and two boys, where she homeschools by day and writes by night, thus explaining those pesky bags under her eyes. Readers can connect with her at jenniferhwestall.com or find her on Facebook and Twitter, where they can sign up for email notices of free content, contests, and special discounts only sent out by email.